E.V.T.
CRY
A

ARN

ISBN 0 333 38390 7

First published 1984 by
MACMILLAN LONDON LIMITED
4 Little Essex Street   London   WC2R 3LF
and Basingstoke

Associated companies in Auckland, Delhi, Dublin,
Gaborone, Hamburg, Harare, Hong Kong, Johannesburg,
Kuala Lumpur, Lagos, Manzini, Melbourne,
Mexico City, Nairobi, New York, Singapore and Tokyo

Filmset in Palatino by Filmtype Services Limited,
Scarborough, North Yorkshire.

Printed in Great Britain at The Pitman Press, Bath

This book is dedicated to

CELIA, for her encouragement and understanding.
FRIENDS, new and old,
in Missouri and Texas, for their help.
TEXAS, for its history and inspiration.

My people have never first drawn a bow or fired a gun against the whites. There has been trouble on the line between us, and my young men have danced the war dance. But it was not begun by us. It was you who sent the first soldier and we who sent the second. Two years ago I came upon this road, following the buffalo, that my wives and children might have their cheeks plump and their bodies warm. But the soldiers fired on us, and since that time there has been a noise like that of a thunderstorm, and we have not known which way to go. . . .

Nor have we been made to cry once alone. . . . For camp-fires they lit our lodges. Instead of hunting game they killed my braves, and the warriors of the tribe cut their hair for the dead.

So it was in Texas. . . .

Part of a speech made by Comanche Chief Ten Bears
in 1867

PROLOGUE

IN A COSY WHITEHALL OFFICE in London, an intense, fair-haired young man sat hunched forward on the edge of a hard, leather wing-chair listening carefully to the words of a distinguished, grey-haired man.

At the far end of the room, a fire crackled cheerfully in the fireplace. Behind the older man a large square window framed a sky that threatened the British capital with a snowstorm. It was January 1838, and this was the hub of the Foreign Office. The man talking was John Temple, Viscount Palmerston, Foreign Secretary of Great Britain.

A man of tremendous energy, Lord Palmerston wielded awesome power. A stroke of his pen in this room was enough to spell life or death for tens of thousands of people, and change the course of history for countries far removed from the shores of England. As Foreign Secretary and, later, Prime Minister, Palmerston was to guide the gathering fortunes of Great Britain's expanding empire for much of the next three turbulent decades.

For an hour and a half Lord Palmerston had been detailing the intricate and complex history of Mexico, with particular emphasis on Texas, Mexico's north-eastern province, now claimed by those who lived there to be 'The Independent Republic of Texas'. Its independence from the revolution-torn mother country was an accomplished fact that was hotly disputed by the Mexican government, albeit with words rather than with deeds.

The aristocratic Foreign Secretary glanced at the gold-faced lantern clock on the mantelshelf and frowned.

'I have been talking for too long, Adam, but before you go I wish to make a proposition I think you will find to be of some interest. ....'

The younger man settled back in his chair, the need for concentration now less pressing.

'I am under considerable pressure to recognise the independence of Texas and accept its ambassador. However, I will not be hurried into making a hasty decision. We have friendly relations with Mexico – and are also owed a considerable amount of money by that country. I have no wish to place eventual repayment in jeopardy. Unfortunately, there is a threat of the United States of

America moving in and annexing Texas on the pretext of protecting her many nationals presently resident there. A formal offer of annexation has already been made to America from the new Texan government. Indeed, there are rumours that Texan independence was engineered with this end in view.

'It is vital that Great Britain has a friendly power to the south of the United States of America, whether it be Texas or Mexico. Since gaining independence from Great Britain, the size of America has increased fourfold. Should the United States now gain possession of Texas, she can strangle the Mexican province of California out of existence, and so straddle the continent of America from the Atlantic to the Pacific Ocean.'

Lord Palmerston looked at Adam across the great desk that stood between them.

'Should this happen, our own vast and largely indefensible province of Canada will be at risk, and the United States of America will possess the potential to dominate the world one day.'

Leaning back, the British Foreign Secretary looked grave.

'This is the situation as I see it, Adam. Her Majesty, Queen Victoria, and the British government agree with me and look towards events in Texas with great apprehension.

'We need your help, Adam. Through my friendship with your father I feel I know you well. I grieved when your mother died before you were old enough to know her. I have watched you grow from a baby to a fine young man. You speak Spanish fluently as a result of the years spent with your father on foreign service. This alone is sufficient reason for you to be given special consideration for the mission I have in mind. Add to this your recent experience as a "detective" in Robert Peel's police force and you become the only man for the task I have in mind. I might add that Her Majesty agrees with me.'

Adam inclined his head briefly, his pulse quickening at the Foreign Secretary's mysterious words.

'I am deeply honoured by Her Majesty, and by yourself, for the expression of confidence in me – but just what *is* this "mission"?'

'I want you to go to Texas on behalf of Her Majesty's government. Ostensibly you will be investigating fraudulent land deeds purchased by British nationals. We have received sufficient complaints to justify sending an investigator. You will remain in Texas to deal with any future problems that may occur from time to time.

'In the course of your duties you will no doubt meet many men, Texan and Mexican, who hold the future of Texas in their hands.

I want you to let me know *their* views on the prospect of the country remaining independent. You will also forward your own considered opinions on the course Texas is taking and keep me fully informed of all developments.'

'In other words, you want me to go to Texas as a spy?'

'I much prefer the term "government observer".' Lord Palmerston smiled for the first time that grey afternoon. 'It sounds so much more honourable.'

BOOK ONE

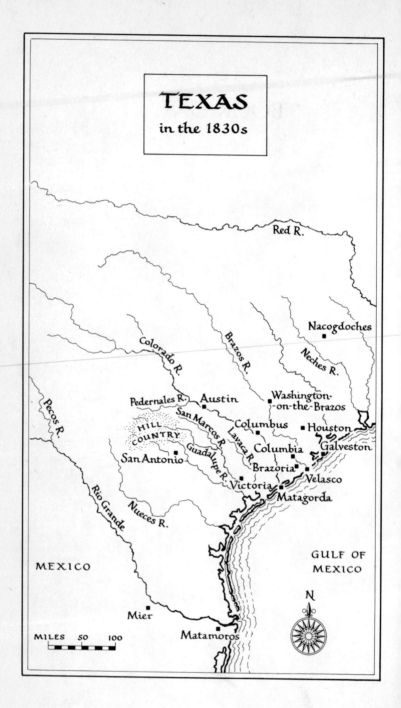

TEXAS
in the 1830s

Red R.

Nacogdoches

Colorado R.

Brazos R.

Neches R.

Pecos R.

Pedernales R.   Austin

San Marcos R.

Washington-
-on-the-Brazos

HILL
COUNTRY

Lavaca R.

Columbus

Guadalupe R.

Columbia

Houston

San Antonio

Brazoria

Galveston

Victoria

Velasco

Nueces R.

Matagorda

Rio Grande

MEXICO

GULF OF
MEXICO

N

Mier

MILES 50 100

Matamoros

CHAPTER ONE

THE decrepit little paddle-steamer *Liberty* wheezed steadily through the sluggish water towards the creaking wooden landing-stage that leaned out from the shore on green-slime pine legs, sunk deep in the brown tidal mud of the Brazos River estuary. On the open bridge of the steamer, the uniformed captain carefully judged the distance between his craft and the landing-stage.

A drinking man, Captain Lelean's face was a network of thin purple veins that disappeared beneath a full black beard. He raised a hand above the bridge in a brief signal, and a Negro slave, waiting expectantly beside the single, rusting funnel, tugged on a slack wire looped about his fingers. The hoarse, strangled sound of a steam-whistle clawed at the air.

Up-river, a flock of mottled ducks beat water with their wings and took off in a loose, banking formation. Closer at hand, a rain-grey heron extended long wings and abandoned the river in graceless flight, head drawn back and stilt-like legs trailing behind.

The single deck of the paddle-steamer was crowded with passengers, all looking shorewards. Their awed, almost reverent, silence was broken by the steam-whistle. Suddenly excited, everyone had something to say. Men and women, with their numerous children, had suffered the restrictions of shipboard life for many weeks – first, in the hold of a transatlantic sailing transport and, more latterly, in the even more cramped confines of the flat-bottomed paddle-steamer.

Captain Lelean's vessel had been designed for river work and the 500-mile sea-voyage from New Orleans had been fraught with danger. When tempers became short the children had suffered the consequences of their parents' anxiety. Now the end of their disciplined ordeal was in sight across a rapidly dwindling expanse of shallow green water, and the shrill-voiced accents of Scotland and Ireland vied with each other in childish excitement.

Not all the passengers viewed the end of the long voyage with uninhibited enthusiasm. For some, relief was tinged with apprehension. The untidy conglomeration of mud-and-roughwood buildings, many of them on stilts, hardly lived up to the description of the 'town' they had expected to find here.

Velasco was not the most prepossessing port in Texas. It was not even the closest port to the immigrants' land-holdings. However, as Captain Lelean had been quick to point out to Adam, the fares of the immigrants had been paid only as far as Velasco. It was doubtful whether the land agent had himself ever come within miles of the shabby little port.

On the bridge of the paddle-steamer, standing behind the captain, Adam Rashleigh echoed the thoughts of those on the deck below: 'Velasco is not the busiest seaport I've ever seen.'

The steam-whistle made another assault on the ears of the defenceless listeners. When the tortured sound died away, Captain Lelean turned bloodshot eyes upon Adam.

'This is Texas, mister. It's been the bare backside of Mexico for so long, I reckon it's forgotten how to be anything else.'

The captain spat noisily and expertly over the side of the bridge into the river. 'Velasco's no better nor no worse than it ought to be.'

The loud-voiced opinion carried to the other three passengers who shared the bridge. They were a Mexican, wearing expensive clothing, who stood with his wife and young son. The boy, of about eight years of age, had a withered left leg. He stood between his parents, leaning on a wooden crutch which was tucked beneath his arm.

Adam suspected that the steamboat captain had toned down his language because of the presence of the woman and the boy, but they had undoubtedly heard Captain Lelean's derisory remarks. For a moment, Adam thought the man would reply. Instead, displaying a dignity that the steamboat captain could never emulate, the Mexican motioned for the others to follow him from the bridge. At the top of the ladder the boy turned, and Adam's wink was rewarded with a smile before the boy's father lifted him to the deck below.

Adam and the Mexican family were the only cabin-class passengers on board the paddle-steamer; but, apart from a stiff, formal bow each morning, the family head had made no attempt to further his acquaintanceship with Adam. His wife seemed even more determined to avoid contact with the others on board, and took all meals in her cabin. Her small son was sometimes seen with the Mexican servant-girl who attended to his needs, but he was rarely allowed out of his mother's sight. Adam inclined his head to the Mexican woman before she, too, passed from view, but she ignored him.

2

'You ever been to this part of the world before?' Captain Lelean had not missed Adam's silent exchange with the Mexican family.

'No, it's the first time I've been on this side of the Atlantic. I'm from England.'

'I wouldn't boast of *that*, if I were you. There ain't a thin louse's difference between an Englishman and a Mexican in this part of the world. An American stands head and shoulders taller, but top of the heap is the Texan. He believes he's just about the biggest man God ever put on the face of this whole goddam earth.'

Edging in towards the landing-stage, the steamer was no more than twenty feet away now. On shore, a wrinkle-faced Indian, wearing rags that might once have been shirt and trousers, waited to catch the mooring-rope. Adam nodded in his direction. 'How high does *he* reach on this social yardstick of yours?'

'An Indian?' The steamboat captain spat over the side once more with casual expertise. 'I was talking about *humans*!'

As the paddle-steamer bumped against the landing-stage, the Indian caught the thrown rope and ran to secure it to a wooden bollard. Captain Lelean rang the telegraph in a signal for his engineer to shut down the engines. They had arrived in Texas.

As Adam turned to make his way to the ladder from the bridge, Captain Lelean called after him: 'I've got another piece of advice for you, son. Texas may be white and free now, but don't stare at a Mexican *señora* for too long, especially if she happens to be the wife of a *hidalgo* – a powerful landowner. You forget that advice and you're likely to wind up spreadeagled in some lonely gully, gelded by the *hidalgo*'s men.'

The steamboat captain grinned, but Adam realised that the words had been intended as a serious warning. This was Texas, an infant republic, spawned in violence and christened in blood. Laws here were enacted by any man strong enough to enforce them. They were personal and flexible – and frequently fatal.

'I'll try to remember. Thanks for the trip. . . .'

Adam's words were drowned by another blast from the throaty steam-whistle. He turned and clattered down the ladder, making his way to the tiny cabin that had been his home for almost a week.

Lifting a large, soft bag, the only piece of luggage he carried with him, Adam felt a thrill of excitement. He was about to begin the greatest adventure of his twenty-two-year-old life.

Adam Rashleigh was not the only one to have his possessions packed and ready. Quick as he was, the steamboat's immigrant passengers were quicker. They had enjoyed none of the scant,

3

but private, comfort of the cabin passengers. Crowded together on deck during the day, they huddled in shivering family groups behind skimpy canvas shelters at night. Now they were eager to leave the pervading smell of unwashed bodies behind and savour the first breath of freedom in this, their promised land.

As the gangway was swung into place, women and the smaller children poured ashore, stumbling awkwardly when they set foot on the landing-stage. They had grown accustomed to the constant rise and fall of deckboards beneath their feet. The boys and younger men, too impatient to fall into single file behind the slower-moving women, scrambled over the side of the boat, casting meagre possessions ahead of them.

Once ashore, men and women clasped each other in an expression of sheer joy. It was coupled with great relief. They had survived the hazards of the sea and finally reached their chosen land. Some of those who had begun the journey with them had been less fortunate. Their bones lay scattered over the mud of the great Atlantic deep.

The happiness of the immigrants was short-lived. Even as the first of the men and boys leaped joyously ashore, a party of men were making their way towards the landing-stage from the huddle of decrepit shanties that formed the town of Velasco. They wore wide-brimmed felt hats of various shades, each sweat-stained and battered with age. Their shirts were, at best, grubby; at worst, torn and filthy. Their trousers were of brown or blue fustian, with here and there a pair of worn leather breeches. All were irrevocably stained on the outside of the thighs where the wearer had wiped greasy, sweating hands. Every man carried a weapon, most being long-barrelled, muzzle-loading percussion muskets.

At first, the celebrating immigrants paid no attention to them. Only when the men advancing from the town spread out to form a line, barring their way to Velasco, did the new arrivals realise all was not well. The chatter ceased suddenly. Women grabbed their children, and the immigrants drew together in an instinctive huddle to face the men from Velasco.

'Who's in charge of your party?'

The accent was frontier American. It was understood by few of the immigrant Scots and Irish, many of whom had difficulty understanding English. The speaker received only blank stares in answer to his question, and a fleeting expression of annoyance crossed his face.

'Did you hear me? Which of you is leader of this party?'

'We have no leader. Each of us is his own man.'

4

Adam recognised the voice of Caleb Ryan, one of the few educated men among the immigrants.

'Then you'll do. Where are you people from?'

'Most of us are from Ireland, the rest from Scotland. We've come to Texas to take up the land that's been bought for us.' As he spoke, Caleb Ryan stepped forward, tugging a rolled-up document from the bundle he carried. 'Here's my land deed. It's in order – and paid for.'

The townsman took the document from him and, without looking at it, retorted: 'Maybe it's in order; then, again, maybe it's not. We'll not know until it's been checked in the Land Registry Office, here in town. But to get there you'll need to pay your Texas landing fee to me, as the senior Texan army officer present.'

Standing on the deck of the steamboat, Adam did not miss the sly grins some of the gunmen on shore gave to each other. He was unaware that Captain Lelean was also nearby until he heard the steamboat captain's derisive snort.

'Senior Texan army officer, be damned! The closest Bo Garrett and his "soldiers" have come to battle is shooting up a saloon in any place where the law ain't strong enough to stop 'em. He's appointed himself officer in charge of militia here in Velasco, and I'll lay a sizeable wager that President Sam Houston knows nothing about it.'

'Nobody said anything about a landing fee when we left Ireland. What's it for?' Caleb Ryan had not seen the exchanged glances, but he instinctively mistrusted the man facing him.

'It's to pay for the war that's been fought and won by Texans to protect the land you say you've bought. It's a small price to pay. Other men have died for *you*, and yours.'

'How much is this "landing fee"?'

'Twenty dollars for every man, woman and child in your party.'

There were shocked gasps from the listening immigrants, and Caleb Ryan's face set in a grim expression.

'We're poor people, mister. We've been sent here by God-fearing landlords who had no work for us, yet weren't prepared to do nothing while women and children starved to death. Many families with up to eight children haven't got twenty dollars between the lot of them.'

Bo Garrett frowned and looked speculatively at the immigrants. 'Well, just so you don't get the wrong idea about us Texans, I'll make it ten dollars for men and women – and half that for each child.'

5

The quick drop in the scale of the landing fee confirmed Caleb Ryan's suspicion that the demand was unofficial.

'You'll get nothing from us. If there's any fighting to be done for our land, we'll do it ourselves. We don't pay others to fight for us. I'll have my land deed back, if you don't mind.'

Caleb Ryan reached out for the deed he had handed to the other man, but Garrett held it out of reach.

'Not so fast. I've told you there's a price to be paid for landing in Texas. If you don't have it, then we'll settle for a few land deeds. This one will do for a start. It's probably worthless, but we'll take that chance – ain't that right lads?'

The grumbling from the line of men at Garrett's back hardly constituted agreement, but he took it as such and said to Caleb Ryan: 'Talk it over among yourselves. Half a dozen land title deeds in lieu of landing fees. When you've decided, bring the deeds to me, in town. Until then my men will stay here to see that no one leaves the landing-stage.'

Bo Garrett turned to walk away. As he did so, Caleb Ryan lunged forward in an attempt to snatch the deed from Garrett's hand. He took no more than a single pace forward when there was the crack of a musket-shot from one of the watching Texans and a musket-ball splintered the flaking bark from a wooden upright, not twelve inches to one side of the Irishman.

Caleb Ryan paused, but only for a moment. Looking steadily at Bo Garrett, he said: 'I've yet to meet the man who'd murder in front of witnesses for ten dollars.'

He took another step towards Garrett. Reassured by his words, a number of the immigrants surged forward to join him. Immediately, there was a succession of sharp reports from the guns held by the men who barred their way to Velasco. Splinters flew up from the rough board planking at the feet of the immigrants as the warning shots struck home.

But not all the musket-balls buried themselves in the wood of the landing-stage. The very last shot struck the broad head of a nail, driven through the crude planking to the heavy timber frame below.

Adam heard the angry singing of the ricochet cut off short, and a boy of about ten years of age fell to the ground. There was a brief, stunned silence from the immigrants. Then a woman wailed as only a bereaved Irish woman can. All the agonised pain of anguished motherhood was captured in the sound.

Immediately, the immigrants began stampeding from the line of armed men, fleeing for the safety of the paddle-steamer. As

6

though this were a signal, the gunmen began firing again, but this time they deliberately fired into the panic-stricken crowd.

Adam sprang over the side of the boat and fought his way through the screaming immigrants. Reaching Bo Garrett, he shouted: 'Stop them! For God's sake, man. Stop your men shooting.'

For a moment it seemed that Garrett would take no notice. Then he bellowed an order, and the line of men lowered their guns.

'Who are you?'

Ignoring the question, Adam stooped over the woman who sat wailing in uncontrollable anguish, the head of her young son resting in her lap. Adam had seen death many times before. He recognised it now, on the still face of the boy, even though the boy's heart continued to pump blood from an ugly wound, low on his chest. Looking behind him, Adam saw two more immigrants lying on the wooden boards of the landing-stage. Both were women and each was wounded in the leg.

Caleb Ryan was one of the few who had not left the landing-stage when the firing began. Now he came to kneel beside the woman and her dying son.

'Fetch a doctor,' he called to Bo Garrett. After a brief hesitation, the self-styled militia commander nodded to one of his men, who scurried away towards the town.

Standing up again, Caleb Ryan spoke to Adam, his words carrying to where Bo Garrett stood. 'The Lord must have great faith in Peggy Dooley to have loaded her with so many burdens since we left Ireland. Her husband died on the boat, no more than three weeks out. Now her only child has been taken from her, murdered by a man who claims to represent the government of this new land.'

'Mr Garrett does not represent Texas. Not its people nor its government.'

The soft-voiced statement was made by the Mexican who, with his family, had been Adam's fellow cabin-passenger on the paddle-steamer from New Orleans.

Since his men had shot Peggy Dooley's son, Bo Garrett had seemed uncertain what to do next. Now, as he looked at the Mexican, his confidence returned.

'Well, now, just look what we've got here, boys. Ain't he the dandiest little greaser you've ever seen?'

Bo Garrett swaggered towards the Mexican and put out a hand to finger the material of his expensive silk-worked coat.

'This is what I call classy – I mean *real* classy. I've known

7

gamblers who'd give a sleeveful of aces to own a coat like this one.'

Looking behind the Mexican, Bo Garrett saw his wife and young son standing uncertainly on the deck of the paddle-steamer. 'I see you've brought your family with you, too. Now, that's real neighbourly. When that General Santa Anna of yours came visiting Texas, he brought an army and a whole lot of grief along with him. You've just brought your family. Because of that I might just let you land. It'll be mighty expensive, of course, but you can afford to pay, can't you, señor. . . . I don't think I caught your name.'

'I am Don Manuel Xavier Tolsa. Yes, I have brought my family with me. We are coming *home*. I was born in Texas. But, like General Santa Anna – who happens to be my brother-in-law – I, too, have an army. They have been expecting me and were summoned by the whistle of the steamboat. If you look around, you will see them, Señor Garrett. You will also observe that they are well armed. Please tell your men not to attempt to reload their weapons, or they will be shot. Order them to drop their guns on the ground and stand back, out of the way. I think this is the doctor coming from Velasco. There are people who have need of his services. Tell your men to drop their weapons, Señor Garrett.'

Don Manuel's words carried both authority and urgency, and most of Bo Garrett's men laid down their guns without waiting for their leader's order.

There was good reason for their haste. Behind them were at least thirty well-armed Mexicans. They sat on their horses impassively, guns trained on Bo Garrett and his dozen or so followers.

'You won't get away with this, Don Tolsa – or whoever you say you are. This land doesn't belong to Mexico anymore. It belongs to us, to Texans. I'm a captain of militia and these are my men. You'll be hunted down and shot before you've travelled a mile from Velasco.'

'I think not, Señor Garrett. You see, I happen to know that your commission is in the *Louisiana* militia. You have never fought for Texas, and you have no authority here. I, on the other hand, *am* a Texan militiaman. A colonel. I and my men fought with President Houston for the freedom of Texas. I am also the *alcalde* – the mayor and chief magistrate – of San Antonio. I am on my way home from the United States of America after undertaking a mission there on behalf of President Houston.'

Don Manuel Tolsa looked unsmilingly at Bo Garrett. 'Am I still the "dandiest little greaser" you've ever seen, Señor Garrett?'

Adam looked at the Mexican with renewed interest. His own passage in *Liberty* had been arranged for him by the British consul in New Orleans. He wondered whether it had been a deliberate attempt to throw him and the influential Mexican together.

Meanwhile, Bo Garrett was doing his best to shrug off the grave error of judgement he had made.

'Hell, we all make mistakes, *alcalde*. I apologise. I can't say more than that, can I? But you're wrong about one thing. I *am* a Texan militia captain. I hold a letter from David Burnet, offering me the rank of captain of militia if I would come to Texas. I came. It wasn't my fault that all the fighting was over before I got here.'

David Burnet had been president of an interim Texan government, prior to Sam Houston's election in 1836, eighteen months before.

'My information is that you were never sworn in by Texan authorities. It does not matter; I have the power to rescind militia commissions. In your case I do that, here and now. In the meantime you will remain in custody in Velasco until arrangements can be made to bring you to trial.'

'Bring me to trial? I've done nothing wrong. Unless it's serving Texas to the best of my ability.'

'Tell that to the woman who grieves for her child, Señor Garrett. I doubt if she will agree with you.' Don Manuel inclined his head to where Peggy Dooley was surrounded by a crowd of immigrant women, all trying in vain to comfort her.

'Will someone tell me what's going on? What's happening?'

The conversation between Don Manuel and Bo Garrett had been carried on in Spanish, and Caleb Ryan was totally bemused as Garrett and his 'militiamen' were ushered off in the direction of Velasco by Don Manuel's men.

Adam gave Caleb Ryan a brief summary of what had been said, and the Irishman looked at Don Manuel gratefully. To Adam, he said; 'Will you thank him for me, on behalf of all of us?'

Adam began to translate the message into Spanish, but Don Manuel waved him to silence. 'I speak and understand English perfectly, young man.'

To Caleb Ryan, Don Manuel said: 'Please convey my sympathy to the woman who has lost her son. If there is anything else I can do to help, please come to see me. My house is no more than a couple of miles up-river from here.'

Turning back to Adam, Don Manuel said: 'You are not with these people? May I ask why you are in Texas? It is unusual to find an Englishman who speaks Spanish as you do. Have you, too, come to seek a new life here?'

'I'm here partly on behalf of these people' – Adam inclined his head in the direction of the immigrants crowded about Peggy Dooley and the two wounded Irish women – ' but mainly because I had nothing to keep me in England.'

Don Manuel Tolsa frowned. 'I can understand a young man's wish to travel, but your business with these people – what is it, exactly?'

Adam pulled a document from his pocket. Attached to it was an impressive seal of office. 'The British government is concerned over the number of fraudulent land deeds being sold to gullible would-be emigrants, those coming to Texas in particular. As I speak Spanish, the Foreign Secretary asked me to come here and look into what is happening.'

Don Manuel looked at Adam sharply. 'You are acquainted with Lord Palmerston?'

'Before my father's death, he and Lord Palmerston were good friends.'

'Ah! I met Lord Palmerston when I travelled in Europe on behalf of the Mexican government. This, of course, was many years ago. He is a very able man. A future prime minister of your country, perhaps?'

'So it's predicted in England. I wouldn't be surprised.'

'You are staying in Velasco?'

'Only until the settlers move on. Right now I would say they need every bit of help they can get.'

'Of course. . . . But such matters can wait until tomorrow. In the meantime you will stay at my house, as my guest. I strongly advise acceptance of my invitation, Señor Rashleigh. Velasco does not provide the traveller with a good example of Texan hospitality. At best you will be given a meal to poison a dog, and find yourself sharing a room with the vermin left behind by a generation of unwashed peasants.'

Adam accepted Don Manuel's offer gratefully. He had no doubt the food and accommodation in Velasco were every bit as bad as the Mexican *alcalde* suggested. More important, it was evident that Don Manuel Tolsa was an influential Texan landowner and an acquaintance of President Houston himself. His friendship would be invaluable to Adam – and to Great Britain. Adam's first report from Velasco would show Lord Palmerston that he had made a good start on the mission that had been given to him.

CHAPTER TWO

DON MANUEL TOLSA's home was everything that the dirty, shabby, waterside town of Velasco was not. Taking advantage of a slight rise on an otherwise featureless but fertile plain, the design was typically Spanish, its whitewashed exterior and walled gardens rich in low, curved archways. There was also a large, cool patio shaded by a wide-spreading oak. The tree was festooned with streamers of Spanish moss and housed quarrelling blackbirds and chattering, disapproving squirrels. From a distance the elegant lines of the house and its surrounding walls were disguised by a fragrant tangle of flowering bushes.

Adam and his host sat on the patio enjoying cold drinks and talking as they waited for Dona Antonia Tolsa and the Tolsas' son, Philippe, to join them for the evening meal.

The conversation ran along mainly impersonal lines, and Adam was made aware of the Mexican view of recent events in Texas. Don Manuel owned three large estates, the largest close to the town of San Antonio. There was also this small estate in Velasco, and another in Mexico itself. In earlier days he had fought alongside his brother-in-law, General Santa Anna, against Spain, in defence of the Republic of Mexico, but Don Tolsa returned to Texas when the brief war was won. Despising the corrupt and tangled politics of successive Mexican governments, Don Manuel had remained aloof from the almost continuous civil war that raged in his homeland.

In Texas, Don Manuel became a great friend of Stephen Austin, the foremost *empresario* in the province. Austin, a gentle, dignified and unpretentious man, had settled American families on the rich land watered by the Brazos and Colorado Rivers, the colony extending a hundred miles inland from Velasco. In so doing, Austin had himself acquired enough land in Texas to make him a landowner second only to Don Manuel.

It was natural that the two men should have common interests but, perhaps, surprising that they should become firm friends. When it became apparent that a break between Texas and Mexico was imminent, both Stephen Austin and Don Manuel worked hard to heal the rift between the mother country and its wayward territory. Stephen Austin suffered a long period in a Mexican gaol and broken health, as a result.

When the rift became war, Stephen Austin was given command of the Texan army. It soon became apparent that, although a brilliant *empresario* and diplomat, Austin was no general. In fact, although Texas had no shortage of men willing to lead an attack, it possessed no strategist, until Sam Houston abandoned his self-imposed exile among the lodges of the Cherokee Indians and put his ebullient genius at the disposal of the people of Texas.

Under Houston's leadership the army of Texas won the war of independence, even though Mexico refused to acknowledge the accomplished fact. At the battle of San Jacinto, Houston first defeated, then captured Mexico's President, the redoubtable General Antonio Lopez de Santa Anna Perez de Lebron.

The fighting qualities of Santa Anna and his soldiers were overshadowed by Santa Anna's savage policy of 'no quarter' at the battle of the Alamo, and his wholesale slaughter of Texan prisoners elsewhere. Santa Anna was returned to Mexico, but his actions had left behind a legacy of anti-Mexican feeling that was inherited by his successors, and also by those Mexicans who, like Don Manuel Tolsa, had put their resources behind Sam Houston and his rag-tag army.

It was evident to Adam that Don Manuel Tolsa was more hurt than angry at the attitude of the English-speaking Texan settlers. He did not expect their gratitude – there was little room for gratitude in the hard frontier way of life – but he had fought as a Texan and he expected to be accepted as one. To men of Houston's stature, Don Manuel *was* a Texan, but there were very few Sam Houstons – and a great many Bo Garretts.

Adam listened with great interest, but said little. He was in Texas to learn all he could on behalf of Lord Palmerston and the British government. He had no intention of taking sides at this early stage.

When Dona Antonia and Philippe came from the house to join the two men, the political talk gave way to a more general conversation. Shortly afterwards a Mexican servant appeared, to announce that the evening meal was ready.

The standard of the meal was impressively high. Had Adam not been able to see armed sentries posted around the house in some strength, and the sparse trees leaning away from the prevailing winds that blew from the Gulf of Mexico, the setting might have been that of a great landowner's villa in Spain.

When Adam commented on the presence of the armed men,

Don Manuel shrugged. 'Unfortunately, such precautions are necessary in Texas. Farther inland many lives have been taken by Indians – the Comanche. They sometimes raid as far as the coast. There are also bandits. Some are Americans who come from the north to take advantage of our troubled times. Others are Mexicans who have changed sides so many times in the revolutions of their own country that they no longer have any allegiance. They fight only for themselves. It is a great sadness to me that the land for which my father died, and for which I myself fought, should be torn apart by the greed of those who claim to be its leaders. It was always my hope that Mexico would follow the example of the United States of America and build a great country, once the ties with Europe were broken.'

'You know America, Señor Rashleigh?'

The change of topic was introduced by Don Manuel's young son, Philippe. It was the first time he had spoken directly to Adam. His voice had the enthusiasm of an eight-year-old and only his eyes showed the pain he so often bore. Philippe's disability was the result of an illness that had left him with a deformed spine and a useless left leg.

'Only New Orleans. I had a few days there before coming on to Texas.'

'Ah, yes, of course. You come here from Europe.' Dona Antonia broke in upon the conversation, her expression one of faint disapproval. 'Do you not think New Orleans is more like France than America?'

'I don't know what to expect of an American town. But, yes, some parts of New Orleans did remind me of France. Of Spain, too, perhaps.'

'You have been to Spain?' Philippe's dark eyes suddenly became alive. Even Dona Antonia was sufficiently interested to forget her disapproval for a moment.

'Yes, I lived there for some years. My father was the British ambassador in Madrid.'

Dona Antonia relaxed visibly. She had strongly disapproved of her husband's invitation to an unknown young Englishman to stay beneath the same roof as their impressionable young son. The Mexican wife and mother did not share her husband's admiration for the English-speaking men who now ruled Texas. Most were men of low birth, who cared little for the protocol and tradition that formed the very foundation of Mexican life. But Adam's father had been the British ambassador in mother Spain. Such a young man would have some breeding.

Don Manuel watched his wife's swiftly softening expression

13

with fond amusement. He had been well aware of her disapproval, and of the reason. He disagreed with both. Philippe was an only child and, because of his crippling disability, he had been coddled more than most boys. He needed to learn more of the world. However, Dona Antonia was fifteen years her husband's junior and usually got her own way with her doting husband.

'Is that where you learned to speak Spanish so well?' Philippe asked eagerly. 'What is Madrid like? Did you see the palaces – and Queen Isabella?'

Don Manuel threw up his arms in mock horror. 'Mexico fought a war to gain its independence from the throne of Spain, yet my son asks after its ruler. We are not even a part of *Mexico* now, Philippe. You do not show such interest when I go to speak with the President of Texas.'

'President Houston is not a *ruler*,' replied Philippe defiantly. 'And the men say Texas will be a province of Mexico once more, before many years have passed—'

'Philippe!' Don Manuel silenced his son quickly. To Adam he said: 'My apologies, Señor Rashleigh. You will forget what my son has said. These are uneasy times in Texas. There are many men who would delight in using Philippe's words against me . . .'

'Of course,' Adam nodded, as Philippe murmured: 'I am sorry Papa.'

The conversation flagged for a few minutes, and then Adam brought smiles to the faces of the Mexican family with an anecdote of his student days at Oxford. Very soon the atmosphere was relaxed once more.

During the course of the meal, Dona Antonia questioned Adam closely about his family background, and Don Manuel had great difficulty in hiding his amusement. Dona Antonia had a number of unmarried nieces, and there were few eligible young men in Texas.

When the meal ended, Dona Antonia announced that she and her son were retiring to bed early and she summoned Maria, Philippe's *niñera* – the nanny who took care of Philippe. But before leaving the room she made it clear that Adam was now deemed to be a fit companion for her son.

'You and Philippe must go riding together tomorrow morning, Señor Rashleigh.' Dona Antonia gave him a rare warm smile. 'He enjoys taking a short ride. The countryside about Velasco is less interesting than San Antonio, but the river is very pleasant at this time of the year. It may be that you will discover Texas has quite as much to offer a young man as the countries of Europe.'

14

The next morning Adam, Philippe and Maria went for their ride, but it was hardly an unobtrusive sally through the surrounding countryside. With them went twenty armed Mexican retainers.

However, released from the inhibiting presence of his parents, Philippe chattered freely and happily as he and Adam rode side by side through the fertile countryside, with Maria riding discreetly a horse's length behind.

As they went, Philippe resumed the questioning that Dona Antonia had begun the night before and drew from him the details of the death of his parents. 'It must be sad to be without any family, Señor Rashleigh.'

'Yes,' said Adam briefly. 'But please drop the 'Señor Rashleigh'. Call me Adam.'

'Thank you ... Adam.' Philippe pronounced the name carefully and precisely.

They chatted easily for a few miles, and then Maria brought her horse alongside them and suggested that Philippe had ridden far enough for one day.

'Of course.' Adam turned his horse. They had ridden in a half-circle that had taken them to the coast beyond Velasco. Their way back would take them close to the town. However, it was not often that Philippe was able to enjoy such freedom from parental control and he was not ready to return.

'Why must we go back? We have not been out very long yet.'

'Long enough, I think, Señor Philippe.' Maria spoke patiently, but firmly.

'Why cannot I be like other boys?' Philippe pouted sulkily. 'In America they do not have a *niñera* with them all the time. The boys there are *free*. I am treated like a bird in a cage. I can see other boys, and they can see me, but I am not permitted to go off and do what *they* do. Even my thoughts do not belong to me until I am locked in my bedroom at night. It is "What are you thinking about, Philippe?", "Philippe, stop frowning", "Go there", "Do this", "Stop *that*". It is so ... tiresome!'

As he was talking, they passed a Mexican boy of about the same age as Philippe. Dark-skinned and almond-eyed, he had a high percentage of Indian blood in his veins. On his back he carried a sleeping baby, its face distorted by close contact with his body. Clinging to his hand was another child, a boy, naked from the waist down. Standing back off the track, the boys stared silently and impassively at the riders as they passed.

'You see that boy? He has more freedom than I.'

15

'He also has two children to take care of and a life of drudgery and too little to eat. Would you wish for that also?'

Philippe struggled with a defiant urge to say 'Yes', but he could not bring himself to tell such a blatant lie. 'No . . . but it would be nice if I could decide *some* things for myself.'

Crossing a narrow wood-planked bridge, no wider than a wagon, spanning one of the many ditches that drained the fields, Adam could see the paddle-steamer *Liberty*, still secured alongside the landing-stage. The small vessel was almost hidden from view by bales of cotton piled high on the landing-stage. Adam counted fifteen wagons on the jetty, or standing on the badly rutted track between landing-stage and town. Some were piled dangerously high with cotton bales, others had been partly unloaded. It should have been the scene of great activity, the landing-stage bustling with toiling slaves and their white overseers, yet there was not a man to be seen, either in the boat or nearby.

While Adam was puzzling about the significance of the strangely deserted scene, he became aware of a sound, as though he were close to a suddenly disturbed hive of bees. It was the hum of hundreds of voices, raised in excitement – and it came from Velasco.

Adam drew in his horse and listened. Then he said to Maria: 'Keep Philippe here until I return. I'm going to find out what's happening in the town.'

Maria acknowledged the order, but Philippe threw up his head and asked rebelliously: 'Do you give orders for me too, now, Adam?'

Before Adam or any of the Mexican escorts could prevent him, Philippe urged his horse forward and was clear of them before they had made a move.

With Maria and the escort close behind him, Adam caught up with Philippe only when his horse was brought to a halt by a large crowd that spilled into the side-streets from the square in the centre of Velasco.

The crowd were all afoot with the exception of two men in the centre of the square. They sat astride saddleless horses in the shade of a gnarled and aged tree, its branches thrown to one side by a long lifetime of conflict with the wind. One man sat staring impassively at the crowd, the other was talking rapidly to the men about him, his face twisted in desperate pleading. The man was so garrulous, it seemed odd to Adam that he was not using his arms to emphasise his words, as most excited men do. Then,

16

as one of the two horses became skittish and turned, Adam saw with a shock that the hands of the man were tied behind his back.

No sooner had he made this observation than two ropes were thrown over a stout branch stretching horizontally above the mounted men. The end of each rope was looped in a running noose, but the full significance of the scene hit Adam only when a noose was slipped over the head of each man. He turned to order the escort to lead Philippe's horse away, when Maria's horrified gasp caused him to look towards the square once more.

One man spun in the air at the end of a taut rope. Even as the other man screamed for mercy, one of the men standing beside him raised a hand and slapped the rump of the horse on which the condemned man was seated.

The horse took no more than half a dozen startled paces forward, but it was far enough. The shrieking man slipped from the horse's back and dangled from the rope. Although his cries were cut off by the strangling rope, his body continued to jerk in obscene protest.

As a great roar of approval rose from the assembled crowd, Adam turned back to Philippe, who watched the scene of horror, all blood drained from his face.

'Get him away from here and take him home.' Adam snapped the order at the leader of the escort. As Maria reached out to take the bridle of Philippe's horse, Adam slipped to the ground and forced his way through the crowd to where the two men dangled at the end of the coarse ropes, the last man to be hanged still twitching.

Caleb Ryan was one of the men in the crowd gathered about the executed men. Avoiding looking at the dangling bodies, Adam spoke to the Irishman. 'What's been happening? Who are these men?'

'Two of Garrett's so-called "militiamen". These two weren't quick enough to steal horses and put distance between themselves and Velasco.'

'I thought Garrett and the others were in custody, awaiting trial for killing Peggy Dooley's son.'

'They *were*.' Caleb Ryan spat his disgust into the dust at his feet. 'But it seems they don't have a gaolhouse in Velasco. Garrett and his men were kept in a feed-barn, at the back of the livery stable. They killed their guards and escaped during the night. That's why there's a hanging this morning. It's nothing to do with Peggy Dooley's boy.'

'They wasted no time bringing them to trial.'

Adam looked closely at the two hanging men for the first time.

17

The terror of the one man was apparent in death as it had been in the last few minutes of his life. Both hanged men were surrounded by an animated crowd, most of them boys. In spite of himself, Adam shuddered. He had seen more than one man hanged outside London's Newgate Prison, but the victims had always been hooded. Looking into the face of a hanged man made the whole affair uncomfortably real.

'That's right; no time was wasted at all. Garrett's men were tried Texan-style. Two men were murdered – these two were caught. It wasn't worth calling in a judge. He'd have found 'em guilty and hung 'em anyway.'

The speaker was a very tall, lean man of about thirty, dressed in the worn buckskin jacket and trousers favoured by many of the men about Velasco. His accent was that of a Tennessee frontiersman. It was so heavy that Adam had to concentrate in order to understand what he was saying. The most striking of the man's features was his eyes. A very pale blue, their lack of colour was accentuated by the dark, leather-tanned skin of his face, half-hidden by a heavy black beard.

Caleb Ryan made the introductions. 'Adam, I want you to meet Eli Varne. He's offered to act as a guide to take us to our new lands.'

'That's not exactly the truth,' corrected Eli Varne, as he grasped Adam's hand. 'I tried to persuade Caleb and his party to give up their mad idea of travelling to the Hill Country. The land they've bought is way out beyond any existing settlement. It's in Indian country – Comanche country – but I doubt whether anyone's bothered to tell Chief Muguera that white settlers are moving in on him.'

'I thought Indians didn't own land in Texas.'

'Depends on who's doing the talking. Listen to a Texan and he'll tell you an Indian's entitled to no more than a hole in the ground – the deeper the better. On the other hand, you'd hear something different from an Indian. He'll say *no one* can own the land. To him, it's the same as the sky. They both belong to God. Indians and white men come and go. The land, like God, stays around. I'm not a religious man, myself, but I kind of like their way of looking at things. This place your friends intend settling is territory the Comanche has been used to roaming at will. Raising cabins and trying to keep him from a place where he's used to going is one certain way of finding trouble.'

'Then why are you taking Caleb and the others there?'

Eli Varne removed the hat from his head and ruffled long, dark hair. 'Damned if I rightly know. One thing's sure – if *I* don't take

18

them, they'll find someone who *will*. I know the country, and I know the Indians – better than any man they're likely to find about here. Without me these sod-busters are likely to die without ever setting foot on their own land. Besides, listening to these folk talk reminds me of the Irish mother I once had.'

Replacing his hat, the Tennesseean added: 'On the other hand, it might be because they've promised me a hundred dollars and a parcel of land to make the trip.'

Adam looked at Caleb sharply. 'Where are you going to raise a hundred dollars? You told Bo Garrett you had no money. It was because of that that Peggy Dooley lost her son, and four other men have died – including these two.' He inclined his head towards the two men still swinging from the tree.

'I was telling the truth. A few of us *are* carrying some money, but it doesn't amount to much. When Garrett and his men were searched, they had nigh on four hundred dollars between them. It was decided to give it to Peggy Dooley. She's agreed to pay for Eli to guide us to where we're going.'

'I'm sorry.' Adam accepted that his accusation had been unjustified. Caleb Ryan was not a devious man. 'When are you setting out?'

Caleb Ryan shook his head despondently. 'I don't know. There should have been wagons here to meet us, loaded with provisions enough to see us to our land and keep us from starving for a few months. They're not here, so we'll need to wait for them . . .'

'If you're dependent on them wagons to get you there, you can forget this promised land of yours,' said Eli Varne, laconically. 'They arrived in Velasco all of six weeks ago. They're still here, parked behind the livery stable – but the goods they were carrying ain't. The provisions found their way into the Mexican stores, right here in town. No doubt the money given to Peggy Dooley is part of what Garrett got for 'em.'

Caleb Ryan could not hide his dismay. 'But . . . we were relying on those stores. We've *got* to have them. Without stores we have no chance of survival . . .'

'Come to the house and speak to my father. He will help you. He helps everyone.'

Adam had not noticed Philippe's arrival. Leaning on the wooden crutch, he had limped through the crowd, Maria and half a dozen anxious escorts pushing their way behind him. The remainder of Don Manuel's men sat their horses nervously at the edge of the crowd.

'I told you to take Señor Philippe home . . .'

19

Philippe Tolsa's chin went up, and for a moment he looked as arrogant as his mother. 'These are Tolsa men. They take orders only from a Tolsa – and so do I, Señor Rashleigh. As for these. . . .' He waved a hand airily in the direction of the gallows tree. 'The sight of two dead criminals does not bother me.'

Despite his bravado, Philippe kept his eyes averted from the two bodies, now being cut down by the men who had earlier hanged them.

Philippe had arrived in time to hear the last part of the conversation and, speaking to Caleb Ryan again, he said imperiously: 'I will tell my father to expect you at the house later today.'

Turning away, the small boy limped back towards the horses. After throwing Adam an apologetic look, Maria followed him, the head of every man in the crowd turning to follow her progress.

'I'd say that young feller's filled with enough pride to bust,' said Eli Varne, his voice full of admiration. 'But you'd best get that *señorita* out of the crowd pretty quickly – though I wish she'd come looking for *me*.'

Maria's progress through the crowd slowed as the men about her began to press closer. Adam said: 'I'll see you at Don Manuel Tolsa's house later, Caleb.' Elbowing aside the ineffectual escorts, he pushed through the crowd after Philippe and Maria.

He was still some distance behind when the thing he feared most began to happen. He had seen the faces of the men crowding about Maria. It mattered nothing to them that she was *niñera* to the crippled son of the *alcalde* of San Antonio. They saw just another Mexican girl – and one foolish enough to risk humiliation at the hands of crude, excited men.

As the men jostled her, one of them, secure in the anonymity of the crowd, put his hand between her legs from behind. Maria's reaction was swift and instinctive. In her hand she carried a short, leather-bound riding-crop. Turning, she lashed out at the nearest leering face. The riding-crop painted an angry red weal from the Texan's mouth to his ear.

The unfortunate man's cry of pain was lost in the whoops of glee from those about him.

'Did you see the *power* in that arm? If she's got the same strength in her legs, *she's* the girl for me.'

'Move over, boys. Let a huntin' dog get a touch of the 'coon.'

The men closed in about Maria, their hands groping, prodding and squeezing. She lashed out indiscriminately, her breath coming in strangled sobs that originated as much from angry

20

frustration as from fear. Then the riding-crop was wrested from her hand and for a moment she disappeared from Adam's sight.

'Up-end her and I'll put a glow on her cheeks with this. . . .'

Adam caught a glimpse of Philippe in the arms of one of the escort, as he battled his way towards Maria. Adam reached her in time for his fist to cut off the Texan's shouted promise. A second blow staggered one of the men holding her arms, but then Adam lost the advantage of surprise. As the men surrounding Maria turned their attention to him, fists and feet struck at him from all sides. One particularly heavy blow to the side of his jaw dropped Adam to his knees. Then above the clamour he heard the sound of a gunshot, and the blows ceased abruptly.

A strong hand gripped Adam by the shoulder and hauled him to his feet. Reloading his gun almost casually as he spoke, Eli Varne said loudly: 'I just burned good powder shooting in the air. I don't like doing that. I won't waste a second shot. You boys better back off if you don't want to be in front of it when it goes off again. Back off . . . you hear?'

He spoke the last words fiercely and all the men except one shuffled backwards, away from him.

'That's better. You were making me a mite nervous. I twitch when I get excited, and I've got a hair-trigger on this gun.'

The men stumbled over each other in their haste to get away, but still one man stood his ground.

'What's all the fuss about, Eli? It's only some Mexican girl. I know you've got a taste for squaws, but Mexican women . . .?'

The silver-bound hickory butt of Eli Varne's long rifle slammed against the speaker's jaw. He staggered backwards until brought up short by the men who had already backed away from Eli. As he did so, a wide-bladed knife fell from the hands he had been hiding behind his back.

'The rest of you carry on moving away, slow and easy – and keep those hands where I can see them. Adam . . . you got the girl?'

'Yes.'

Adam had an arm about Maria and now he led her away, through the ranks of the Irish and Scots immigrants who had moved in to back Eli Varne and Adam. The men stood aside respectfully to allow him through, murmuring sympathetically as Adam steered the pale-faced girl towards Philippe and the voluble but largely ineffectual escort.

'Are you all right?' Adam tightened the arm he had about Maria's shoulders. She nodded, saying nothing. Suddenly, she reached for Adam's hand and gripped his fingers in a bid to stop herself trembling. It was not fright, she told herself fiercely. Even when she had been caught in the midst of the mob, the sweaty, dirty smell of men all about her, their hands pinching, probing and hurting, she had not been frightened. Her reaction had been one of anger and disgust – and frustration because all her attempts to stop them proved weak and useless.

They reached the horses and Adam spoke angrily to Philippe: 'What did you think you were doing, coming into a crowd like that?'

'I . . . I saw you speaking angrily to the man who was on the boat from New Orleans. I thought you were arguing. That there would be trouble. I came to . . . help.'

The thought that an eight-year-old crippled boy had plunged into a crowd because he thought *he* might be in trouble left Adam speechless – but suddenly it seemed that every man in the Mexican escort wanted to talk. Their leader began explaining that he had been prepared to sacrifice his *life* for the son of Don Manuel and his *niñera*. Accompanying his words with dramatic gestures, he insisted that he had been on the point of going into the crowd to go to Maria's assistance, when Eli Varne intervened. All about him the other Mexicans were making similar claims. They, too, had been strategically placed to assist. They were waiting only for the right moment . . .

Adam ignored the men and their noisy attempts to vindicate their lack of action. He lifted Philippe on his horse, then turned to assist Maria.

Looking at Adam, her heavy-lidded eyes opened wide in sudden concern. 'Your face . . . it is bleeding.'

The left side of Adam's face ached. When he put a hand to it his fingers came away streaked with blood.

Maria reached up and turned his face to one side in order to see it better. Her touch was light as she traced the extent of the injury. 'It is not too bad,' she admitted, relief in her voice. 'But the skin is broken and you will have an ugly bruise.'

Looking down at her, Adam's glance went from her face to where her dress had been torn down from the neckline, exposing the half-round of her breast, as far as the nipple. The pale skin was marked by red pinch-marks.

'I think we're both going to be bruised. Thank God – and Eli Varne – it wasn't any worse.'

Philippe spoke little on the way back to the Tolsa house, but more than once Adam glanced at him and smiled, filled with admiration for the courage he had shown in the square.

Adam wondered how much to tell Don Manuel of the

happenings in Valesco. In the end he decided to tell the truth, but playing down the ugly scene involving Maria as much as was possible. Fortunately, neither Don Manuel nor Dona Antonia came from the house to meet them upon their return. Maria was able to slip into the house and go to her room to change, without her appearance being the subject of Dona Antonia's questions.

Unaware of the extent of Maria's rough handling by the Texans, Don Manuel's anger was directed at the men who had lynched two of Garrett's followers without even the pretence of a trial.

'It should not have been allowed to happen,' he repeated for the third time. 'Neither should Garrett and his men have been allowed to escape. It is important for justice and the law to be respected if Texas is to progress as an independent country. Taxes must be collected from the residents of Velasco to pay for a sheriff. The man who drove this mob from the square – who is he? Would he be interested in becoming Velasco's sheriff? I will guarantee his first year's salary myself.'

'Eli Varne? I wouldn't know. He's promised to guide the immigrants to their new colony.'

'I will raise the matter with President Houston when next we meet. I recall him talking of this Eli Varne. They were together in Indian country, I believe. Now, let me send for someone to bathe your face. It is fortunate the blow was not closer to your eye. As for Philippe going into such a crowd before his escort had cleared a way for him . . .! His mother would have something to say about such behaviour, if she knew.' He shrugged. 'But it is no more than any boy of worth would do. If only Philippe were not crippled . . .'

Adam had told Don Manuel that Philippe had followed him into the midst of an over-excited crowd, when he thought him to be in trouble. He had said nothing of Maria being the subject of their crude attentions. Neither did he explain that the newly independent Texans would not have tolerated the servants of a Mexican landowner clearing a path for his young son. Had they tried, it would have provoked a bloody riot. The days of all-powerful Mexican landowners was at an end in the new Texas.

Caleb Ryan came to the house to speak to Don Manuel early that evening. Eli Varne was with him. The Mexican landowner greeted the Tennesseean warmly. 'I owe you my gratitude, Señor Varne. I am told you were able to prevent a regrettable incident from getting out of hand in Velasco today. I am most grateful.'

Perplexed, Eli Varne glanced at Adam. He shook his head almost imperceptibly, and the Tennesseean understood.

'Any thanks are due to Adam, Don Manuel. He saved the *señorita*. I just made sure nobody started any more nonsense.'

Now it was the turn of Don Manuel to appear puzzled. But his son was safe; he had no interest in any young woman who might have been involved.

'I am grateful to you both. Now I am going to ask another favour of you, Señor Varne. . . .'

Don Manuel offered Eli the post he had earlier discussed with Adam. Initially, Eli would come under the direct jurisdiction of Don Manuel, for as long as he remained at Velasco. Don Manuel promised that when he had seen President Houston the post would be made a permanent one.

Eli Varne rubbed his jaw and grimaced. 'It's going to take more than one man to keep any law in Velasco – mainly because no one knows what it's supposed to be. Is it Mexican law, which no one's ever bothered with, or Texan law – which no one's ever heard about?'

'I will authorise you to keep *the peace*, as you see fit. The law is not important for now.'

Slowly, Eli Varne shook his head. 'I'm obliged to you for thinking of me, Don Manuel, but peace officering's not for me. I need to keep on the move. Besides, I'm taking Caleb and his people to their new settlement.'

'It is a pity. Perhaps you will reconsider my offer when you return. Where is this new settlement to be?'

'As far as I can make out, it's up around the headwaters of the Guadalupe River, up in the Hill Country.'

'But that is Comanche country.' Suddenly the whereabouts of the proposed new colony pushed the question of Velasco's law and order to the background.

Eli Varne nodded. 'That's right. Chief Muguera and his people were hunting around there, last I heard. I've tried to put Caleb off, but he won't listen to me. Perhaps you can do better.'

Caleb Ryan had looked uncomfortable when he first entered the expensively furnished room. Now his face set in an expression of Irish stubbornness. 'We're going on. The dream of owning our own land is all we have. There's nothing but starvation for us where we've come from. We've *got* to go on.'

'Even though it might mean death for you and every one of your people?' Don Manuel's words were spoken quietly, but they stilled all sound in the room for long moments.

'Even so.'

The stubbornness was still in Caleb Ryan's expression, but there was something else there, too, now. Adam thought it looked akin to hopelessness.

'I could find work for some of your men. Others could stay hereabouts. ...'

Caleb Ryan shook his head, positive once more. 'No, sir. We've come this far together. We'll go on now.'

'As you wish.'

Don Manuel Tolsa shrugged off his misgivings. He had voiced them. If Caleb Ryan chose to ignore advice, then the consequences must rest with him. In truth, it was to Don Manuel's advantage to have a settlement established in the hills to the north-west of San Antonio. It should serve as a buffer between his own ranch and the Comanche heartland, giving him warning of any large-scale Indian attacks.

'I will provide your party with sufficient supplies and weapons to take you on to your new homes. There will be enough to keep you from starving until you are established. I will also provide oxen for your wagons, and whatever tools are available in Velasco. I will expect you and your settlers to repay me – but I will not press for payment. It will be soon enough when the land is cleared and crops are being harvested.'

Awkwardly, Caleb Ryan began thanking the Mexican landowner for his generosity, but Don Manuel brusquely brushed the thanks aside.

'I do you no favour, my friend. When you are exhausted from battling drought, disease, starvation – and the Indians – you will curse me.'

'All except the Indians are familiar enemies, Don Manuel, and if we leave the Indians alone there's no reason for them to trouble us.'

Don Manuel looked at Caleb Ryan as though he had taken leave of his senses. 'Would you trust a rattlesnake not to strike if you tried to move it from the spot where it lay enjoying the sunshine? I should have more sense than to waste my money and provisions on men who intend inviting the Comanche to kill them and enjoy their women.'

'If they attack us, we'll fight. Indians are human. They can be beaten.'

'Trouble is, nobody's convinced the Comanche of that yet,' commented Eli Varne laconically. 'He happens to believe he's the best damned warrior who ever lived. Few man who've fought the Comanche would argue the point. When a Comanche climbs on a horse you'd swear he changes form. Man and horse become one.'

Don Manuel nodded vigorously. Then, resting a hand upon the shoulder of Eli Varne, he said: 'If words will not stop either of you from heading westwards, let us use them to some good purpose. Come, we will sit outside and you can tell me exactly what you think you will need. . . .'

Adam followed the other men in silence, but his thoughts were racing ahead. Listening to Eli Varne and Caleb Ryan talk to Don Manuel, he had arrived at a sudden and quite illogical decision. He intended travelling with the immigrants on the journey to their new home.

CHAPTER THREE

THE opportunity for Adam to tell the Tolsa family of his decision came that evening, as they sat down to dinner. Don Manuel had been talking of the depredations of the Comanche, only to be reprimanded sharply by Dona Antonia for holding such a conversation in Philippe's presence.

'I am sorry, my dear,' Don Manuel apologised. 'But you know of my feelings towards the Comanche.'

To Adam he explained: 'I have lost two nephews and a niece to them. It happened not far from my sister's home, at Victoria. The boys were killed. My ten-year-old niece was abducted. My sister died of heartbreak, as a result. Her husband still offers prayers that his little girl is also dead. . . .'

Don Manuel caught his wife's angry frown and hurriedly said: 'But the Comanche are a problem only for the settlements. It need concern none of us here, at this moment.'

'It concerns me, Don Manuel. I have decided to travel west with the settlers.'

The surprised silence lasted until Philippe's knife clattered to his plate. 'I thought you would stay and travel to San Antonio with us.' Philippe's disappointment at Adam's sudden decision was evident to everyone.

'I want to see for myself what the settlers suffer on their journey. If this land they've bought is in a dangerous place, I believe my government should stop others from coming here.'

This was the reason Adam had given to himself for wanting to go with Caleb Ryan and his party. The truth was not quite so straightforward, even to himself. Adam *would* inform Lord Palmerston if the land bought for the immigrants was especially dangerous, but Adam also had a desire to see for himself the men who were putting up such a ferocious fight to retain a way of life they had enjoyed for centuries.

To Adam's relief, Don Manuel agreed with him, commenting smugly that a man had to go where his duty lay, and that Philippe would learn this lesson, one day.

'But you *will* come to see us at San Antonio, when you have seen the settlers' land?' Philippe's plea brought a quick response from Dona Antonia.

'Señor Rashleigh will always be a welcome guest in our house, whether at San Antonio or here in Velasco. You will please remember this, Adam.'

Dona Antonia was careful to hide her own disappointment. She had ideas of her own for Adam's future. There was her niece Rosa, for instance. . . . Don Manuel's wife was very concerned for the long-term fortunes of the Tolsa family. She was proud that both she and Don Manuel came from old Spanish families, and that the Tolsa name was one of the most respected in Mexican society. However, Texas was no longer a province of Mexico. It was now an independent republic, with English-speaking men in power. Because Don Manuel had helped in the fight for independence, and because he was a friend of President Houston, there had been few changes in the Tolsa way of life, so far.

But Dona Antonia was a realist. Houston had swept into the presidency as a result of the euphoria that followed upon his decisive victory at San Jacinto. Unfortunately, Houston would be President for only a few more months, and gratitude had a very brief lifespan.

Battle-lines were already being drawn for the election of a new President. With a state of war existing between Texas and Mexico, some of the opposition candidates were already seeking to make political capital from Houston's friendship with those Mexican landowners who had supported him. Others, especially those who had arrived *after* the fighting was over, were even more outspoken in their anti-Mexican stand. They demanded that the large Mexican land-holdings be seized and given to the thousands of immigrants now flocking to Texas from the countries of Europe and North America.

Dona Antonia had observed Adam closely during the time he had been at the Tolsa home. He was a young man of good education and breeding. Other men would look to him for leadership. If such a young man could be persuaded to settle in Texas and become part of the Tolsa family, neither Dona Antonia nor Don Manuel need fear for the future of the Tolsa lands.

Don Manuel confirmed his wife's invitation, adding that when Adam came to San Antonio with a clearer picture of the problems facing Caleb Ryan and his settlers the Mexican landowner would know how best to assist.

Philippe sat through the meal in silence. Later, in the darkness of his room, his pillow felt the tears of a crippled eight-year-old who had found a hero, only to lose him again. Philippe had watched Adam jump ashore from *Liberty* to go to the assistance of the immigrants, and had seen his actions in the square at Velasco. Adam was the type of man Philippe dreamed of being, yet would never be. He would always need to use a crutch in order to get about, and he knew the disability would grow worse with the passing years. To be a hero, a man needed two good legs.

Riding the horse that had been a farewell gift from his generous host, Adam picked his way through the scores of noisy, rowdy immigrant children gathered on the outskirts of Velasco. Shouting, running and pursuing each other in confusing games of 'touch', they exhibited all the symptoms of excitement their parents were trying so hard to hide.

They were about to begin the last leg of their long and hazardous travels. When it came to an end they would be starting a new life – on their own lands. Men and women who had been born to a life of servitude and penury carried with them deeds to more land than was owned by many of their former landlords in Scotland and Ireland.

In truth, the thought of being 'a landowner' blinded many of the settlers of the harsh realities of their proposed new lives. They ignored the blunt fact that they would be making a new beginning with fewer material possessions than they had owned in their native lands. Those who *did* think of it blunted their unease with the oft-repeated homily that all a man needed in Texas was a gun, an axe and a bag of seed. With these, so it was said, a man could feed and clothe his family, build a home, and lay the foundations of a farming future.

There might have been a spark of truth in the trite maxim, had the settlers been American, used to the demands of frontier life. But these were Irish and Scots. One country was in a near-permanent state of rebellion, and to carry a gun was to invite a musket-ball from the first soldier a man met with. Similarly, if a man wandered abroad with an axe in Scotland, he was likely to be presumed to be about to cut down one of the landowner's trees – an offence for which he would be sent in chains to the colonies.

The new settlers had been employed in their native lands by some of the few 'caring' landlords. These men purchased lands in the New World and paid for the workers and their families to sail off to a new life when times became impossibly hard at home. Less responsible employers simply evicted their tenant workers and left them to roam the lanes, begging or stealing the wherewithal to remain alive. Unfortunately, because they *had* been employed by responsible landlords, the new settlers were used to having their lives ordered for them in a land where the weather produced few extremes and there was little to trouble the man who worked hard and kept within the law.

Life in their new country would be very different. Frontier Texas would present them with a harsh and alien environment. They, and those born of them, would come to regard the last lean days in the country that was incapable of supporting them with a bizarre nostalgia that would pass from generation to generation.

These were the people Eli Varne had contracted to guide more than three hundred miles to their new homes. Once there, he would leave them to their own resources – and the attentions of the Comanche.

'You might just as well have let Bo Garrett and his men kill 'em all,' Eli Varne complained to Adam. 'Sure as death, these thickheads will never make a go of it on their own. Most don't even know in which direction they're meant to be heading. Yet all I hear is of the wonderful new life they'll have when they get there. Wonderful new life, hell! I haven't found one who'll stand a chance out on his own in Indian country. Perhaps I'll be able to teach them something along the way, but I doubt it.'

'We'll try together. I'm coming with you.'

Only Eli Varne's eyes revealed his pleasure. 'Can you handle a gun?'

'I'm considered a fair shot.'

This was an understatement. Adam had hunted game with his father and had also received small-arms tuition from military marksmen during his service with Robert Peel's police force. He was an exceptionally fine shot.

'That means there's *two* of us to hunt food and protect these innocents. It should scare the hell out of any Comanche war-party!' Snorting derisively, Eli Varne strode away to remonstrate with a group of immigrants who were stacking sharp-cornered boxes on a wagon already laden with sacks of grain meal.

The conversation about shooting reminded Adam that he possessed no form of weapon. He set off to purchase a personal arsenal at one of the two Mexican owned stores in Velasco's main square. The storekeeper was one of the men who had benefited from Bo Garrett's seizure of the immigrants' provisions and he was at first nervous, believing Adam had come to reclaim the stores still stacked in his storeroom. He was so relieved when Adam stated his business that he brought out all his best guns immediately, in a bid to hasten Adam's departure from the store.

There was a wide selection of weapons, both new and second-hand. As he examined them, Adam heard a woman's voice on the far side of the store. It carried a soft Irish accent. Looking up from the new Patterson Colt five-shot revolver he balanced in his hand, Adam recognised the pale, drawn face of Peggy Dooley.

He had not looked at her closely during the tragic incident which had cost the life of her son on the landing-stage, but he had imagined her to be a woman in her mid-thirties. Now he could see she was much younger, probably no more than twenty-seven. Peggy Dooley must have been a young bride, married off like so many of her impoverished countrywomen in order to relieve a large and hard-pressed family of responsibility for feeding her. She stood by a barred but unglazed window with another immigrant woman, examining a cheap wooden crucifix that dangled from a string of wooden beads.

Acting upon a sudden impulse, Adam crossed the store to the two women. 'I hope you're feeling better now, Mrs Dooley. Will you be travelling on with the others?'

Peggy Dooley's unexpected reaction was to cringe back from him, as though he had aimed a blow at her. Hurriedly, Adam tried to reassure her. 'I was on the boat with you – and on the landing-stage. . . .'

Peggy Dooley looked about her in desperation, her eyes seeking a means of escape. The other woman took her arm and spoke to her quietly, as though comforting a child. 'It's all right, Peggy. It's all right now. Nobody's going to harm you.'

Turning her face up to Adam, Peggy Dooley's companion said: 'I'll thank you not to be reminding Peggy of what happened on the landing-stage – or on the boat. Her mind's not yet ready to face up to any of it.'

The girl spoke with the soft accent of Ireland's far western counties. Of about Adam's own age, she was tall and slim, with long dark-red hair tied at the back of her head. She had deep-grey eyes, and they were hot and angry now as she glared at Adam.

Suddenly, Peggy Dooley shook herself free of the other woman's hand and the hunted expression left her face. 'I remember you now. You tried to stop the shooting. I saw you again when they hung those two killers. Have you caught some more? Are you going to hang them?' Peggy Dooley thrust her face close to Adam's. 'Make them suffer for Michael, mister. Make them suffer.'

The other woman gripped Peggy Dooley's arm once more. 'You must try to forget what's happened, Peggy. You'll need to look to the future now.'

31

'Forget that my son was *murdered*? Is that what you're trying to tell me, Nell Plunkett? Oh, no, I won't be doing that.'

Peggy Dooley's raised voice was shrill, and the other customers in the store stopped what they were doing to listen to her.

'I'm not saying that at all, Peggy. You'll never forget young Michael, but he wouldn't want you to waste the rest of your life in hating. There's a new start ahead for all of us.'

'Stop hating, is it? Those are easy words for you to say, Nell Plunkett. Would you be forgetting so quickly if all you lived for had gone? Would you, now?'

Releasing Peggy Dooley's arm, Nell Plunkett turned away abruptly. Her back was towards Adam, and the only sign of movement was the fists that clenched and flexed spasmodically. He reached out to her hesitantly, but at the first touch of his fingers she stepped away before turning to face him. When she spoke, it was to Peggy Dooley, but the deep grey eyes were on Adam and her words were spoken with a vibrant, carefully controlled passion.

'I lost most of those I loved long before I set out for Texas. You can tell me *nothing* about murder, Peggy Dooley. I was twelve years of age when the soldiers of King George murdered my mother, my father and a brother before my eyes. It happened outside the house my father had built for us in the peat bogs of Dunamas. Yes, twelve years of age I was, but by the time the soldiers had finished with me I was cursing them for not killing me, too. But I didn't die. I lived on. As you'll live on. You talk of hating, Peggy? I'm telling you that you don't know what hatred is. *I* do, but I've not let it destroy me. I've *used* it. At first I used it to keep me alive. Then to fight the soldiers who killed my family. I've not needed it for some time now, but I'd only have to see an English uniform to know it hasn't gone away altogether. That's why I'm here, in Texas. To start a new life, away from so much hate. It's not going to be easy, but I *will* succeed – and so will you.'

The fire inside Nell Plunkett died as suddenly as it had flared into life, and her grey eyes released Adam.

'Come, Peggy. There's nothing here for us. We've just time to look in at the other store before the wagons leave.'

Nell Plunkett walked to the door without another look at Adam. Peggy Dooley followed, but when she reached the doorway she paused for a moment. Looking back at Adam, she stared enigmatically at him for a few moments, then followed Nell Plunkett into the humid heat of Velasco's town square.

Adam purchased three guns from the perspiring Mexican storekeeper. One was the five-shot revolver patented by Samuel Colt and manufactured at his Patterson, New Jersey, factory. Adam was fortunate: the Colt revolver was new to Texas and had not yet become a popular weapon. Within the next few months Texans would be clamouring for the recently produced weapon. Captain Lelean had brought a case of the guns to Velasco in his paddle-steamer.

Adam's other two guns were rifles. The first, a comparatively short-barrelled percussion rifle, had two barrels and, because of its size, would be more manageable when fired from the back of a horse than would a longer-barrelled weapon. The second, longer rifle was not new, but it had been lovingly cared for. Probably at least thirty years old, the stock was inlaid with silver filigree. Manufactured by a skilled gunsmith in Pennsylvania, the gun had been recently fitted with a modern percussion lock.

Adam showed his purchases to Eli Varne, but he was unprepared for the Tennesseean's reaction at seeing the long-barrelled rifle. Taking it in his hands almost reverently, he repeated, over and over again: 'Well, I'm damned. Well, I'll be damned if this ain't downright uncanny.'

Eventually, Eli Varne gathered his wits together and held the gun out towards Adam. 'Do you realise what you've got here?'

'Yes, I've got myself a good gun.'

'Good! Good, you say? You've just bought yourself one of the finest guns in the whole damn world. A Pennsylvania long rifle – and this is the best of 'em all. I should know. Here, take it back.'

Thrusting the rifle into Adam's hands, Eli Varne strode to where his personal belongings were dumped in an untidy heap beside one of the half-loaded wagons. Sliding his own rifle from its saddle holster, he carried it back to Adam and held it up beside the rifle he had just bought. It was identical.

In answer to Adam's bemused question, Eli Varne replied: 'I sold the gun you've bought at the store here in Velasco, not three weeks ago.'

'Why? Why split up such a beautiful pair of guns?'

Eli Varne shrugged. 'A man needs money to live. Besides, it didn't rightly belong to me, exactly.' Avoiding Adam's questioning stare, he went on: 'That gun you've bought was Dan Coutter's. Him and me were partners. We'd been together since the days when we'd skip learning and go fishing, up around Pineville, in Tennessee. Years later we won these guns from a German when we got lucky in a card game in Baton Rouge. Must be all of eight years ago now. The game went on for the best part

33

of a day and a night. By the time it finished, the guns were about all the German had left. He cried like a baby when he lost them, too.'

The Tennesseean pinched the bridge of his nose between finger and thumb as his thoughts spanned the years.

'What happened to your partner?' Adam urged, when Eli Varne had been silent for many moments.

'Uh? Oh, Dan's dead. Killed by Indians.'

'Comanches?'

'Hell, no. We had an understanding with them. These were Apaches, raiding well to the east of their usual hunting-grounds. They took us by surprise. We killed four or five of 'em. Enough to make 'em think twice about a victory dance when they got home, but they took Dan's scalp along with 'em. I didn't think it right they should go home with his gun, though. He was uncommonly proud of that rifle – and I've yet to meet the man who could handle it better.'

Eli Varne walked slowly back to his heap of possessions and returned his own gun to the saddle holster. Straightening up, he said to Adam: 'Dan Coutter was the finest partner a man could wish for. You'll be measured up against him every time you use that gun. It might be better for both of us if you were to return it to the store and choose another weapon.'

Adam looked at the beautiful weapon he held in his hands with considerably more respect than before.

'I'll keep it, Eli. To do anything else now would be defying fate.'

34

CHAPTER FOUR

THE first night's camp made by the trekking settlers was not a happy one. Owing to a late start they had covered no more than five miles by nightfall. The distance fell far short of Eli's target. As a result, they were forced to make camp in a low-lying marshy area, plagued by hordes of viciously stinging mosquitoes and able to gather only enough wood for two fires between them.

The next morning the settlers woke puffy-eyed from insect bites and bad-tempered because they had enjoyed little sleep or hot food. It was a salutary lesson. Overland trekking required disciplined organisation – and an early start.

Late that afternoon the immigrant wagons reached a point in the river opposite the town of Brazoria. Here Eli ordered their second camp. A ferry was in operation across the river and the ferryman, with a keen eye for business, came to the camp to ask their destination. When he saw the swollen mosquito-bitten faces of the unhappy settlers, he tried hard to persuade Eli to cross the river here, craftily suggesting, within hearing of the settlers, that once over the river they could strike inland and leave the insect-infested river behind them.

The suggestion found immediate favour with the immigrants, but Eli said curtly they would continue following the east bank of the river for another day and cross at Bell's Landing. The river was narrower there and the ferry able to carry more wagons on each trip.

Not all the settlers were happy with Eli's decision. They sat about the fires, within the ring of wagons, talking in morose family groups. The children, who had spent most of the day squatting uncomfortably in unsprung, hot, dusty wagons, gathered green wood to throw on the fires. It produced thick, acrid smoke which stung the eyes, but it kept the troublesome mosquitoes at bay.

Later, when the sun had sunk beneath the distant rim of the featureless land, and one or two of the settlers had already lain down to sleep, the sounds of revelry came to them from across the river. Before long the noise grew louder, and now the creaking of the wooden ferry could be heard as it was poled across the sluggish water towards the immigrants' camp. Some of the men about the fires began to grow uneasy and cast frequent glances towards Eli.

The Tennesseean sat smoking a pipe beside the fire he shared with Caleb Ryan's family and Adam, behaving as though he could hear nothing unusual. He did not make a move until voices from the ferry began calling. Standing up almost leisurely, he knocked out his pipe on the heel of a boot, picked up his rifle and set off for the river bank, without saying a word.

After a moment's hesitation, Adam went to where his belongings were heaped about his saddle. Unwrapping the Colt revolver, he stuck it inside the leather belt he wore about his waist and hurried after Eli.

The wagon-train leader stood at the side of the river, the long rifle cradled in his arms. In the dim light of the fading sunset, he nodded appreciation for Adam's support.

'You bring a gun?'

'It's tucked in my belt.'

'Keep it there unless I tell you otherwise – but, if you have to use it, don't miss a shot'.

Adam's stomach contracted in a sudden spasm that combined both excitement and fear. Eli was talking about killing men, yet he had spoken as easily as though discussing the squashing of a bug.

Adam's thoughts were interrupted by a shout from Eli, directed at the men crossing the river.

'That's far enough. State your business from where you are, or I'll cut the ropes and let you drift off downstream.'

The speed at which the revellers quietened down indicated that the men on the ferry were high-spirited rather than drunk.

'There ain't no call for such talk, Eli,' a young man's voice called from the gloom. 'We've come socialising, that's all – and we've brought whisky. Enough for everyone in your wagons.'

'There's women and children in the wagons.' Eli's manner was unbending. 'It's been a hard day for 'em. They want neither your whisky nor your company at this time of night.'

'This ain't late, Eli! 'Sides, from what I hear, your folk have had a bad deal from Bo Garrett and his men. Me and the boys thought we ought to do something to put that right.'

The speaker's enthusiasm was contagious. When Eli hesitated, he pressed home his advantage. 'We reckon we'll show your folks just how sociable Texans can be. Put on a dance for 'em. You can't say "No", Eli. Don't you know what day it is? It's the fourth of July – Independence Day! A day when every red-blooded

36

American should be celebrating, and Texas is as near to being American as makes no difference. Willie Godden's here with his fiddle. We've even brought sarsaparilla and lemonade for the women and kids. There'll be no trouble, Eli. I'll vouch for it. Hec Bowie's a man of his word, you know that.'

'A good shindig would do everyone some good, Eli.' The quiet voice of Caleb Ryan came from the darkness to the rear of the two armed men. Looking over his shoulder, Adam saw the shadowy forms of a number of settlers backing them.

'Is this Bowie to be trusted?'

'Just as long as he's sober and hasn't got a knife in his hand. But he ain't no Colonel Jim, that's for sure.'

Raising his voice, Eli called into the darkness: 'You can come on over, but I'll collect all guns and at the first sign of trouble you'll all be sent packing.'

The men on the ferry set up a yell that scared every frog for half a mile of river bank. The heavy cross-river ropes creaked as the men on the floating platform poled the boat to the bank and the fiddler sawed out a tune that might, or might not, have started life as an Irish jig.

The effect of the music upon the immigrants was astonishing. Their lassitude was forgotten and wood was heaped on the fires within the wagon circle. Those who had already settled down for the night dressed hurriedly, as eager as their more wide-awake countrymen to join the unexpected jamboree.

The men from the ferry shuffled self-consciously into the firelight and handed Eli a whole arsenal of weapons. There were long rifles, muskets and small arms, together with powder-horns, great skinning-knives, and two Indian tomahawks. All were stacked carefully against one of the wagon wheels, in full view of everyone within the wagon circle.

The fiddler had played his 'Irish' jigs all the way from the ferry to the immigrant camp, but the gulf between the Texans from across the river and the new settlers was not bridged until Hec Bowie called for the children to help themselves to sarsaparilla and lemonade from the huge earthenware jars carried from the ferry by grinning, perspiring Texans.

For many of the children it was their first taste of either drink. Others had enjoyed lemonade on only a couple of occasions in their young lives. Their enthusiasm for the rare treat thawed their parents instantly. Minutes later, whisky-jugs were being passed from Texan to settler and men were stamping out one of the fires in the centre of the ring of wagons to clear a space for the dancing.

This would be a special occasion for both immigrants and

resident Texans. Dances were sometimes held in the outlying settlements, but they were usually restricted to a few neighbourhood families who gathered to raise a barn or a new cabin and stayed to celebrate the event afterwards.

In the few small towns scattered about the young republic, men outnumbered women by more than a hundred to one. A dance would have been more in the nature of a stampede. In some saloon 'dances' the only women likely to be present would hold a conversation with a man, at the same time eyeing the saloon doors for fear they might miss the arrival of a customer with more money to spend than the companion of the mercenary moment.

Adam was introduced to Hec Bowie by Eli. The Texan had shoulders like a young bull, and the livid knife-scar bisecting his left cheek branded him as a fighter – an impression confirmed by Eli.

'He's affable enough when he's sober, but he's tolerated more on account of his late kinsman, Jim Bowie, than for himself. He's a bit like Jim was in his younger days, headstrong and finding fighting enjoyable. Jim grew into a fine man. He married the daughter of Juan Veramondi, Governor of Texas under the Mexican government, and finished up owning a lot of Texas land. Jim fell apart when his wife and two kiddies died of cholera, back in '33. Because of that, I don't think he cared a damn about dying when old General Santa Anna massacred him and the rest of the Texan garrison at the Alamo.'

Eli watched Hec Bowie swagger to a family camp-fire and introduce himself with a flamboyant bow to the ladies, before handing a whisky-jug to the eager men.

'I'd like to think Hec was as big a man as Jim, but they weren't cast in the same mould.'

The fireside chosen by Hec Bowie was the one Nell Plunkett shared with her sister Kathie Casey. Kathie's husband and son Dermot, Peggy Dooley, and Caleb Ryan's wife and two young daughters were also here. All around the camp the other Texans were making their own fireside introductions, whisky serving in lieu of a calling-card.

Settling himself on the tailboard of a wagon, little Willie Godden poured half a bellyful of whisky down his throat and began scraping out a toe-tapping musical medley that brought the children of the camp scurrying to secure a place at his feet.

First to step out on the earth dance-floor inside the ring of camp-fires were Hec Bowie and Nell Plunkett. As they passed close to Adam, Nell Plunkett's glance touched on him with a bold and inexplicable challenge.

Adam was still gazing after her in puzzlement when Eli said: 'We'd better grab ourselves one of those whisky-jars while there's still something in it. Caleb's men seem set to spend the night out-drinking the Texans.'

Eli was right. As red-faced, perspiring Texans offered their arms to only mildly protesting immigrant women, the temporarily deserted menfolk readily accepted whisky as a substitute for their company.

The two men made their way to Caleb Ryan's fire. From here Adam watched as Hec Bowie taught his Irish partner some high-stepping American dance. When the whisky-jug was passed to Adam, he raised it to his lips and poured a large quantity down his throat without taking his eyes from the dancers. The next moment he began choking, and concerned settlers rescued the whisky before he spilled any on the floor.

'You all right?' Eli wiped the back of one hand across his lips and thumped Adam on the back with the other.

'That . . . drink . . . What is it?' Adam croaked out the words as he continued to fight for air. He could feel the alcohol burning a path like a lava flow between his throat and stomach.

'What is it? Why, that's best Texan whisky. It'll be gingered up a little, depending on who's making it. If it's a brew from Ed Sawyer, up by Galveston, it might have a live eel or two, and perhaps a dried shark's fin in it somewhere. But that makes it a mite salty, so I don't think *this* is his. It must be Doc Gimble's – the best whisky you'll find in Texas. They say he uses heads and tails of rattlesnakes, three to each barrel, to bring his whisky to perfection. It'll also make you immune to rattlesnake bite – or so they say. I'm not claiming that's the *truth*, but I know some as would swear to it.'

Adam looked at Eli in horror, not certain whether to believe him or not, but the Tennesseean had turned aside to answer a question put to him by one of the Texans. Adam felt disinclined to drink more of the rattlesnake whisky, but by the time the whisky-jug came his way again he was enveloped in such a warm, alcoholic feeling of well-being he decided, snakeheads or not, he would try some more.

Watching the immigrant women laughing and dancing, and their men standing red-faced and beaming about the fires, Adam marvelled at the change that had come over the weary, despondent travellers who had made a sullen camp only hours before.

It was not only the men who were drinking the Texan whisky. A number of women were also drinking more than was good for them.

One of these appeared to be Nell Plunkett. During one of the fiddler's brief and infrequent rests, she and Hec Bowie returned to Caleb Ryan's fire, flushed and laughing. Slapping Eli heartily on the back, Hec Bowie's deep voice boomed out: 'Eli, you couldn't have brought these people here on a better day. I can't remember when I enjoyed a fourth of July more.'

Cheers from nearby camp-fires provided proof of the carrying power of Bowies voice. 'Now, where's that whisky? It's time for a toast. To America! God bless her.'

This brought another roar from the men who had crossed the river with Hec Bowie. Lowering the half-empty jug from his mouth, Hec Bowie eyed the men about the firelight and his gaze settled on Adam. 'Hey, you . . . you're English, ain't you? I didn't see you raising a jug to drink the health of the United States.'

In the silence that followed Hec Bowie's belligerent words, someone sniggered nervously. The sound was cut off abruptly and an unnatural silence fell on the camp as men and women awaited Adam's reaction.

Willie Godden, the fiddler, had not heard Hec Bowie's words, but he had played his fiddle in many dance-halls and saloons. He knew that all too often such a silence was the prelude to a fight. He also knew that fights were rarely confined to two opponents. Most wound up as pitched battles, involving all the men present – and often many women, too. Calling on everyone to resume dancing, he tucked his fiddle beneath his chin and struck up a lively tune.

A few children responded; the adults were far too interested in what was happening about Caleb Ryan's camp-fire.

Quieter this time, but with more menace in his voice, Hec Bowie spoke again to Adam. 'I said, I didn't see you drink the health of the United States of America, Englishman. I could be mortally offended if I put mind to the matter.'

Adam had drunk more whisky than he was used to. It pushed him to the verge of bravado. 'In that case I'll be happy to drink the health of America. Caleb, pass me some whisky.'

Reluctantly, Caleb Ryan handed Adam a half-filled jug of whisky. His acquaintanceship with Adam went back only a short time, but it was long enough for him to know that Adam was not about to bow meekly before the other man's demands. 'Take it easy, Adam,' he said, in a low voice, but Adam was not listening.

Raising the jug in a half-salute to Hec Bowie, Adam said: 'I drink a toast – to America, and all her people.'

There were a number of loud and derisive hoots from the watching Texans, and Adam did not miss the expression of contempt on Nell Plunkett's face. As the noise of the camp began to build up once more, Adam raised a hand and called for silence.

His heart began to pound as the surprised Texans and their hosts obeyed. When the only sound was the determined fiddle-playing of Willie Godden, Adam called loudly: 'As this seems to be a night for toasts, *I'm* proposing one now. I give you the lady who has worn the crown of Great Britain for little more than a year. To Queen Victoria. May God bless her.'

Willie Godden's fiddle scraped to a halt just as Adam began to announce his toast, and a sudden hush descended upon the immigrant camp. It was broken by Caleb Ryan. Stepping forward, he took up a jug of whisky.

'The Irish have little cause to love England, but I'll not hear a word said against the young Queen. I say, God bless her. May her reign bring peace, prosperity and understanding to *all* her people.'

Caleb took a quick swig from the whisky-jug before staring belligerently around the circle of camp-fires, his glance missing out none of his countrymen. Looking mildly embarrassed, they one by one rose to their feet and, with varying degrees of enthusiasm, echoed the toast.

Nell Plunkett expelled her breath in a small, angry explosion as she rounded on Caleb Ryan. 'Have you forgotten how many Irish men, women and children have died at the hands of the English? I don't care whether there's a king or a queen on the throne, I'd as soon spit on my own father's grave than drink the health of an English sovereign.'

Disgusted at the actions of her countrymen, and at the lack of response to her passionate outburst, Nell Plunkett walked out of the circle of firelight. Hec Bowie stood watching her uncertainly, not sure whether to go after her. Adam was hardly aware of her words. He had not eaten yet and the whisky was a furnace in his belly. But there was something he had to do before he allowed the whisky to dull his senses too much.

Taking a determined step towards Bowie, he said: 'I drank the health of your country. Now I'm waiting for you to drink to my Queen.'

Hec Bowie opened his mouth to voice a refusal when something sharp penetrated his shirt and pricked the back of his perspiring body, just above the waistband of his trousers. From the shadows behind him, Eli whispered a warning that was for the Texan's ears only.

'Don't say it, Hec. Just pick up that whisky, nice and easy, and do as Adam wants.'

Hec Bowie hesitated, then gasped as the point of the knife sank a quarter of an inch into his flesh.

'Do it, Hec. Do it now – and make it look good, or I'll cut your kidney out before you have time to scream. It's your own knife I'm holding against you, Hec. The one made for you by cousin Jim. You're fond of bragging how sharp it is, and how it's killed two men. If you want to make it *three*, you go right ahead and say what you was going to. If not, just bend down, pick up that jug and say something nice about the Queen of England. Do it with a friendly smile, Hec, but do it – now!'

The knife-point sank into flesh again, and Hec Bowie was sure he could feel blood chasing the perspiration down inside the waistband of his trousers. He knew Eli Varne well enough to believe he would carry out his bloodthirsty threat.

Reaching down slowly, he picked up the jug at his feet. The onlookers could see little more than Eli's grin as he stood behind Bowie, hidden by the shadows.

Raising the jug to his lips, Hec Bowie mumbled: 'The Queen of England . . .'

'God bless her, Hec – and make it loud.'

'*God bless her*!' Hec Bowie shouted the words, although they threatened to choke him.

'Great!'

The knife had disappeared when Eli stepped forward and clapped the Texan on the shoulder before relieving him of the whisky. Holding his hand high, Eli called: 'I'd like to propose one more toast before we get to dancing again and I expect every man, woman and child to be on their feet. I give you *Texas*. Our country!'

The shouts of the Irish and Scots immigrants were as loud as those of Hec Bowie's companions, who a few minutes before had toasted America so enthusiastically. The tension was broken and, as Willie Godden scraped out his music once more, couples began to drift back to the beaten-earth dancefloor.

Hec Bowie had not moved from his spot by the fireside, and he stared long and hard at Adam. Reaching down beside him for a long twig with which to light his pipe, Eli said softly: 'You aiming to take things any farther, Hec?'

For a moment, Hec Bowie said nothing. Then he shifted his gaze to Eli. 'I've got no quarrel with you, Eli – you're running things here and you don't want trouble – but the Englishman won't always have you to wet-nurse him. No one calls Hec Bowie out and gets away with it.'

'Don't underestimate him, Hec. He's his own man. But you're right about one thing . . . I'll have no trouble here. You want to dance, you're welcome to stay. If you've got anything else on your mind, then you and the others better get across the river right now.'

Hec Bowie looked to where Nell Plunkett had reappeared from beyond the wagons. She was watching the dancing, sullenly clutching a light shawl about her head as protection against the mosquitoes that lurked beyond the heat and smoke of the fires.

'There'll be no trouble.'

Having given this assurance, Hec Bowie walked off without a backward glance, heading for Nell Plunkett.

Adam was having some difficulty focusing on what was happening about him, but he followed Bowie's movements clearly enough. He saw the big man cross to Nell Plunkett. The two stood talking for some minutes, their heads close together. Then they turned and walked away, Nell shrugging off the Texan's hand when it rested upon her shoulder.

Adam reached for the whisky-jug once more. He had taken only a mouthful when a wild-eyed Scots woman ran towards him, calling for her husband. She was in a state of near hysteria, but there would be no help from her man. He sat against the wheel of a nearby supply-wagon, head back and eyes closed, a trickle of saliva escaping from the corner of his mouth.

'Tom! Tom! Will you wake up. Something's happened to the baby. Wake up, will you?'

Tom was a young man, unused to Texan whisky. The only result of his wife's efforts was to push him sideways to the ground.

There were a number of other settlers nearby, all in various stages of drunkenness. The world was beginning to swing about Adam, but he still had the wit to know the young woman was frantic. Pushing himself to his feet, he called upon all his willpower to gather his swimming senses.

'You won't get much help from your husband tonight. Is there something I can do?'

The young Scots woman continued to shake her prostrate husband in mindless desperation until Adam laid a hand on her arm. 'Tell me what's wrong. I might be able to help.'

'It's my baby . . . she's gone! I left her asleep in the wagon when the dancing began. I've just been to check and . . . she's gone!'

Suddenly, Adam's mind conjured up a picture of something he had witnessed, whilst sitting drinking earlier. He had failed to recognise it as being anything out of the ordinary at the time, but he did now. He had seen Peggy Dooley coming from one of the wagons, carrying a baby in her arms.

'Is that your wagon over there? The one with the water-barrels lashed to the tailboard?'

'Yes, the baby was in the front, behind the seat. . . .'

'Don't worry, we'll get her back. Have you seen anything of Peggy Dooley lately?'

The young woman was puzzled by the question. Then her eyes opened wide in alarm. 'You don't think she took her? But . . . she's half-crazed!'

'She'll not have harmed your baby.' As he spoke, Adam looked for Peggy, but she was nowhere to be seen within the circle of wagons. Taking the young mother's arm, Adam led her towards a gap between two of the wagons. He ignored the smirks on the faces of some of the Texans they passed on the way.

At the gap, Adam hesitated. 'I think she came out through here, but where would she go?'

In front of them the sluggish waters of the river gleamed like frosted mud in the moonlight. Looking at it, the young mother put a hand to her mouth. 'Oh my God! You don't think . . .?'

Her voice broke and she never completed the sentence. Adam never answered her. His mind was working well enough, but his legs were acting independently as he stumbled over the rough ground.

At the water's edge, the young woman suddenly clung to his arm. 'Listen! There's someone over there.'

Adam heard the sound, too, and he hurried towards it. As he drew closer he heard the breathless moaning of a woman. Then he heard another sound, the animal grunting of a man. He stopped quickly and grabbed the young mother as she tried to rush past him.

'That's not Peggy, or your baby.'

The woman struggled in Adam's arms, not listening. Before he could stop her, she called: 'Peggy? Is that you?'

There was a startled squeak of surprise in the darkness, then Adam heard a low whisper in a woman's voice: 'Who is it? Ask them what they want.'

'How the hell should I know who it is?' a disgruntled Texan voice snapped back. 'I don't even know who *you* are.' In a louder voice he called: 'Whoever you are out there, get the hell away from here. Find your own spot, farther along the bank.'

'Come on.'

This time the young mother needed no persuading. She had recognised the woman's voice and was deeply shocked. The woman's husband was one of the men rapidly drinking himself insensible at the camp-fire she herself shared.

When Adam and the young Scots mother had searched almost half a mile of river bank without success, he suggested they should return to the wagons. There would be a few men sober enough to make up a reliable search-party.

They had almost reached the wagons when Adam came to a sudden halt, putting out an arm to stop the young Scots woman.

'What is it?'

'Sh! I heard something – there!'

It was impossible positively to identify the sound, because of the noise coming from the nearby dancers, until Willie Godden drew the bow across his fiddle strings in a long, sliding note that ended discordantly. In the ensuing brief silence, it was possible to recognise the sound Adam had heard as a woman's voice, crooning a low lullaby.

It came from the edge of a nearby clump of cypress trees. Leaving Adam's side, the young Scots mother ran towards the trees so fast she was halfway there before Adam set off in pursuit.

Peggy Dooley was sitting on the ground, her back against the trunk of a tree. She cradled a small bundle in her arms, and there was a strong smell of whisky about her.

Neither Adam nor the baby's mother tried to conceal their progress through the long, coarse grass, and Peggy Dooley paused in her crooning to hold up a finger.

'Sh! I've just got Michael to sleep. He was crying. The noise of the dancing, you see.'

'Michael, be damned! That's my baby you've stolen, Peggy Dooley. If you've harmed her in any way. . . .'

Before Peggy Dooley could stop her, the young mother snatched the baby away. The sudden violent movement woke the infant and she immediately began crying, demonstrating that her lungs, at least, had not suffered as a result of the brief abduction.

'Peggy Dooley, you shouldn't be near sensible people. You should have been sent back to Ireland from Velasco. Other people's children aren't safe with you around.'

'Why are you taking him from me? He's crying. Give him back, he's wanting feeding. . . .' Peggy Dooley slid a round, well-fleshed breast from her dress. 'Here, Michael. Come to your mummy. I'll feed you now.'

'Take the baby back to your wagon. I'll bring Peggy. The loss of her own boy has unbalanced her.'

The young Scots woman snorted angrily. 'I feel as sorry for her as anyone else, but stealing my baby isn't going to help. Besides, it's whisky that's unbalanced her tonight, not grief for her son.'

With this the young mother turned and hurried away in the direction of the wagons, holding the baby to her shoulder, patting its back and making soothing sounds in a bid to stop its cries.

'She's taken my baby from me. Why has she gone off with Michael? Where's Seamus? He won't let her do this to me.'

Adam knew from his conversations with Caleb Ryan that Seamus was the name of the husband Peggy had lost on the voyage from Ireland to Texas. He felt desperately sorry for her, but the immigrant women in the camp would know what was best for her.

He tried to lift her to her feet, but she refused to move. 'No, I'm staying here until Michael has been brought back to me.'

Suddenly, Peggy Dooley began to cry. Adam was at a complete loss, not knowing whether he should try to force her to return to the camp or leave her out here on her own. It would have helped had he been able to think clearly, but his head was throbbing angrily, making all thinking difficult.

Peggy Dooley felt about her on the ground and located a flagon leaning against a tree. It contained enough whisky for half a dozen men to drink themselves into insensibility. One of the Texans had hidden it beneath a wagon for later use, but Peggy had found it first. She took a long drink, then passed the flagon to Adam without a word. In the absence of any planned course of action on his part, Adam helped himself to a drink.

The flagon passed between them more than once before Adam spoke again. His voice sounded thick and unfamiliar, even to himself. 'You should come back to the camp, Peggy. It's not good for you, sitting out here alone.'

Peggy Dooley tried to focus her eyes upon Adam, a frown of concentration on her face.

'I'm not ... alone. You're with me.'

Now it was Adam's turn to concentrate, but he could find no argument to meet the logic of her statement. He nodded vigorously, and immediately wished he hadn't. It set the whole world swinging about him. 'Yes ... *I'm* here with you; but, if I *weren't*, you'd be on your own.'

He was pleased with the clarity of the statement, but its effect on Peggy Dooley was to start her crying again.

'I'm used to being on my own. Nobody wants me now. I'm an . . . an *embarrassment*.'

Peggy Dooley had great difficulty in pronouncing 'embarrassment', and it served to increase her unhappiness.

'Don't. . . . Please don't cry.'

'I've got nothing . . . nobody. I might as well be dead myself. And why not? Why *shouldn't* I be dead, too?'

Standing up with some difficulty, Peggy made off unsteadily, setting an uncertain course in the general direction of the river.

Adam got to his feet and went after her. Too drunk to be truly alarmed, he nevertheless had no doubt that Peggy Dooley's intention was to throw herself in the water.

Peggy had probably drunk even more whisky than Adam, but she was light and fleet-footed. She reached the river bank while Adam was picking himself off the ground after his second fall, and he saw her silhouetted in the moonlight at the water's edge.

'Peggy . . . don't.'

She turned her head towards him. Then some prompting of her tortured and befuddled mind told her she should remove her clothes before throwing herself in the water. She was wearing only a dress and a petticoat, but they were enough to save her life. She had difficulty removing the tight-waisted dress and, by the time she wriggled unsteadily free of her petticoat, Adam reached her.

His arms went about her as she was about to leap in the river. In spite of her struggles, he half-carried, half-dragged her away from the water.

She was still struggling when he tripped once more, carrying her to the ground with him. Peggy Dooley gave a gasp of pain as the brittle stalk of a fern scratched the bare skin of her back. Then she suddenly ceased her struggles, and Adam became aware he was holding a naked woman in his arms. He loosened his grip on her, but now their roles were reversed. Peggy Dooley's arms went about him and she held him close to her.

'Love me. . . . Please love me.'

She kissed him hard and long, and Adam tasted the sour taste of whisky on her breath. He brought up a hand to pull away the arm that was crooked about his neck. Instead, it came to rest on her breast, the nipple beneath his fingers. He kept his hand there.

Peggy Dooley gasped and writhed beneath him, her fingers plucking first at his shirt, then at his trousers.

For a brief, sane moment, Adam told himself this was madness; that he would deeply regret what was happening here.

Then Peggy Dooley's hand slid inside his clothing and her fingers ignited the whisky in his veins. Now it was his turn to writhe beneath her touch, his body contorting unnaturally as he struggled to remove his clothes without breaking the intimate contact of their two bodies.

When they were both naked, Peggy Dooley's body enveloped him and he strove to meet the ever-increasing demands she made upon him.

Suddenly it was all over, but Peggy Dooley held Adam to her with such strength it seemed she was trying to fuse their bodies into one. Her breathing was so noisy that it was some minutes before he realised she was whispering, close to his ear.

'Seamus! Seamus! That was wonderful. I think we've made ourselves another baby, Seamus. A sister for Michael, maybe. . . .'

Minutes later, his clothes a bundle beneath his arm, Adam kneeled at the river's edge and was violently ill.

As soon as he could, Adam rose to his feet, shakily anxious to escape from the deep, dark water. The whisky, as well as making him ill, must have addled his brain, causing the reflection of the moon in the water to play tricks on him. For a brief, insane moment, he could have sworn it was the grinning skull of Peggy Dooley's husband, issuing an invitation for Adam to come and join the remainder of her menfolk.

CHAPTER FIVE

THE following morning, Adam felt worse than he could ever remember. His head throbbed with the relentless power of a beam-engine. When he was careless enough to turn unexpectedly, the world recoiled from him as though it wanted no part of the guilt he felt.

Few of the immigrants felt any better. They went about their morning chores in a pained silence. Breakfast was a wasted meal for all except the children – and even they ate in dark-eyed silence, irritable from lack of sleep. There were a few Texans from the other side of the river, too. They sat beside the camp-fires, drinking coffee, sheepishly aware that the settlers knew they had been too drunk to catch the ferry back to the Brazoria settlements, not too many hours before.

'Come on, move yourselves. We've twelve miles to travel and a river to cross before sundown. You wanted a party, now's the time to pay for it. Stir yourselves, now.'

Eli was suffering as much as anyone else, but he was determined not to allow the immigrants respite for any reason whatsoever on only the second day out of Velasco. During the later stages of their long journey it was possible their very survival would depend upon the discipline he instilled in them during these early days.

Just before the wagons moved off, Adam turned from securing a wagon-tail and came face to face with Peggy Dooley. It was a meeting he had anticipated with a great deal of trepidation, since his first waking moment that morning. Adam tried desperately to think of something to say to her. Should he apologise? Explain it was all a mistake? If he did, would she make a scene – cry 'Rape!' perhaps? Or even demand that he make an honest woman of her?

Peggy Dooley cast a brief look in his direction, then passed on as though she had never met him before. Adam looked after her, his emotions an untidy mixture of relief and chagrin. Surely she *remembered*? Or had she *really* believed it was her dead husband who was making love to her? Perhaps she had not recognised Adam, she *had* been drinking heavily. Or had the incident been no more than a passing physical encounter, enjoyed for the moment, and as quickly forgotten?

The thought was a blow to Adam's masculine pride. He

watched as Peggy Dooley climbed over the high box seat of one of the rear wagons. Before she disappeared from view inside the hooped canvas, she turned and looked back at him for a moment. He knew immediately that she had not forgotten a thing. It *had* meant something to her. He also knew that Peggy would not use the drunken incident to make trouble for him. Suddenly his hangover seemed less severe. Mounting his horse, he set off after the leading wagons, already on the move.

Soon after noon, three horsemen caught up with the slowly-moving wagon train. They were Hec Bowie and two companions. One was Magnus Bergstrom, a Swede who spoke little English, but who loved to talk. The other was introduced as Rafael Mexia, a Mexican who had been rendered speechless by Indian torture, many years before.

The approach of the three men had been observed for almost two hours across the flat, featureless plain, and Eli and Adam dropped back behind the last wagon to intercept them.

'Hi, Eli.' Hec Bowie greeted Eli cheerfully, pointedly ignoring Adam. 'Thought you might welcome a bit of company along the way.'

Eli's welcome was less than enthusiastic. 'You've never sought my company before. If you think you've unfinished business with any of the settler women, you'll waste less of your time by turning around right here and returning where you came from. Most are either married, or spoken for, and that's the way they'll stay while I'm bossing this train.'

Hec Bowie spread his arms wide in a conciliatory gesture. 'We're not here to cause any trouble, Eli. Hell, we're doing you all a favour. Word came to Brazoria that there's Indian trouble along the Colorado river, just north of the settlements. I thought you'd be glad to have three good guns along.'

If Hec Bowie's information was true, the three men and their guns could make the difference between success and disaster, but Eli did not wholly trust the Texan.

'How did you get the news?'

'A messenger rode in from "Big Drunk". If you don't believe me, ask the great man himself. He's on his way down to Velasco from Washington-on-the-Brazos. We should meet up with him sometime tomorrow.'

'Sam Houston's on his way down-river?' Eli's anger at Bowie's use of the name by which General Sam Houston had once been known to the Cherokee Indian nation was forgotten in his delight at the news.

'That's right, the President of Texas himself. Do we stay, or do we turn right around and go back to Brazoria?'

'You can stay. We're crossing the river at Bell's Landing and making camp on the far side before nightfall. Go over with the first wagons. While you're waiting for the rest of us, you can start teaching Caleb and his people which end of a gun is the dangerous end. Make it a nightly lesson. You might go some way towards keeping them alive when they get to where they're heading. You'll find guns, powder and shot in the first two wagons.'

'How about him?' Hec Bowie jerked a thumb in Adam's direction. 'He's got a real fancy rifle – want me to teach him as well?'

'I can talk for myself – and work my own gun.' Adam bridled at Hec Bowie's derogatory offer. He had no doubt the Texan had intended it to be offensive.

'I'm repeating what I said to you before, Hec. I'm happy to have three extra guns with the wagons, but at the first breath of trouble you'll be heading back to Brazoria. Adam is my partner on this trip. Ride him, and you'll find it's me who's doing the bucking.'

Hec Bowie grinned. 'You won't have any trouble with us, Eli. We're just coming along to shoot Indians. Now we'll catch up with them wagons. I've a feeling there's someone who'll be mighty pleased to see me again.'

As Hec Bowie rode off, flanked by his two friends, Adam said: 'He's going to cause trouble, Eli. Hec Bowie's not a man who's used to accepting orders from anyone.'

'I can take Bowie if I need to – and he knows it – but I'll be keeping a close watch on his friends.' Eli gave Adam a searching look. 'How about you? You bothered about having him along?'

Adam shrugged. 'You're the wagon boss. I'll put Bowie straight about one or two things if I have to.'

'That's what I thought. Come on, we'll ride on to the ferry and make arrangements to get the wagons across.'

Crossing the Brazos River at Bell's Landing was completed more smoothly than Eli had dared hope. One of the inexperienced Irish wagoners forgot to apply the crude wooden-block brake to his wagon, and two of the four wheels rolled off the floating wooden platform. His wife and three of their young children were pitched into the river, but were quickly rescued. This proved the only untoward incident during the crossing.

Wagons were unhitched and manhandled on and off the ferry

and the animals were swum across the river, linked to the ferry by long ropes. It took five trips before the thirty wagons were on the western bank of the Brazos.

There was a small town, Columbia, a short distance from the river. It was here that Sam Houston had been inaugurated as President in 1836. The town had the distinction of being the Republic's capital for three months, but it lacked the facilities required for the administration of a new country. Columbia was now a thriving community, but Eli made camp that night on the river bank. The immigrants were too tired to have another dance forced upon them by the women-hungry men of Columbia.

Hec Bowie and his companions had not been given the welcome Bowie had anticipated. The night before he had shared a fire with Nell Plunkett and her relatives. Tonight the three newcomers crouched about a small camp-fire of their own. Nell Plunkett was seemingly too busy even to acknowledge the presence of the man who had partnered her throughout the previous night's dancing. Adam saw Bowie cast frequent glances in her direction, but she continued to ignore him. Finally, Bowie and his two companions persuaded some of the settlers to go to Columbia with them.

News that Peggy Dooley had taken a baby from its bed and gone off into the night had caused a stir among the immigrants. Later that evening, as Eli and Adam sat beside a small fire, lit not for cooking but to keep insects away, Caleb Ryan came across to ask Adam what had happened.

'Nothing,' declared Adam firmly. 'Peggy heard the baby crying while its mother was off dancing. She picked it up and quietened it. She was foolish to take the baby off so far, but with all the noise of the dancing around the camp it would never have gone to sleep again in the wagon.'

Caleb was satisfied with Adam's explanation and went off to allay the fears of the settlers. Some mothers were concerned that Peggy Dooley had become unbalanced by the tragedies that had befallen her since leaving Ireland. They believed she might pose a danger to their own children. A few had demanded that she be sent back, if not to Ireland, then at least to Velasco.

'Is that the truth of what happened?' Eli had listened in silence while Adam and Caleb were discussing Peggy Dooley. He did not ask his question until the Irishman was out of hearing.

'More or less.' Adam busied himself cleaning his long rifle, which had been accidentally dunked in the river during the crossing. 'Why?'

'I thought you might have a special reason for wanting Peggy Dooley to stay with the wagon train. I watched you go out of the camp last night, and I saw that girl return with her baby. I didn't see you or Peggy Dooley come back, and I was around for a long while.'

'Are you keeping a watch on me?' Adam snapped, the guilt he felt adding fuel to his unreasonable anger.

'That's right, and on Peggy Dooley, and on every other man, woman and child travelling with this wagon train. That way I hope to get everyone to where they want to go.'

'I'm sorry, Eli,' Adam apologised to the even-tempered Tennesseean. 'You've got a lot of responsibility. I know that.'

Eli shrugged. 'What you get up to is your own business; but if Peggy Dooley *is* unbalanced, I want to know. It could affect all of us.'

Adam hesitated, then said: 'I thought she was going to throw herself in the river when the baby was taken from her last night. She didn't. I think she'll be all right now.'

'Good.' Eli climbed heavily to his feet. 'I'm going to talk to a few folk. Some of them weren't looking too good when we made camp, and this is fever country. Coming along?'

'No, I'll finish cleaning my gun.'

When Eli passed from the firelight into the darkness beyond, Adam heard a sound from the vicinity of a freight-wagon at his back. Checking that his revolver was safely tucked inside his belt, he was about to investigate when Peggy Dooley came noiselessly into view and squatted down , keeping Adam between herself and the firelight.

'I heard what you told Caleb, about me taking the baby. I doubt if the women will believe him when he tries to tell them, but I'm grateful to *you*, Adam.'

'Well, wasn't it the truth? Isn't that why you took the baby?'

'I wish I knew. I got confused. The whisky didn't help. I'm not used to drinking.'

Adam said nothing. He was thinking of her words, spoken at the height of their lovemaking, when she had called him by the name of her dead husband.

'Would *you* have done ... what we did, if you hadn't been drinking?'

'I don't know,' Adam replied honestly.

'Does thinking about it trouble you?'

'Yes.'

'Oh!' Peggy Dooley looked down and began plucking at the

skirt of her dress. 'If it will make you feel any better, you can do it again now.'

Adam's mouth was uncomfortably dry and he felt the stirrings of desire to take Peggy Dooley as he had taken her on the river bank the previous evening. If he did, he knew he would be committing himself to a relationship that had no place in the way of life circumstances had dictated for him in Texas.

As though reading his thoughts, Peggy Dooley said: 'I'm not asking you to take on responsibility for me, Adam Rashleigh. Last night you filled a need – one I didn't even know was there. Somehow it's helped me to put myself together again. I. . . well, I just don't want you to feel bad because of it, that's all.'

'I don't regret what happened, Peggy. I just feel I took advantage of you, that's all.'

'Well, now you know you didn't. I have no claim against you and I promise I won't try to trap you into anything.'

Adam said nothing, and there was a long and uncomfortable silence between them. It was broken when Peggy Dooley said, in a low and carefully controlled voice: 'Do I take it you don't want me again, Adam?'

'It might be better . . . for both of us.'

'I see.' Peggy Dooley stood up and looked at Adam for some minutes. Then, leaning towards him, she kissed him gently on the cheek. 'I wish it were otherwise, Adam, but thank you for what you said to Caleb.' Turning away, Peggy Dooley fled into the night.

Much later, Adam was awakened by the sound of loud voices. Among them he recognised Hec Bowie and his now totally unintelligible Swedish friend. Adam turned over irritably and went back to sleep again.

In the morning, he learned that one of the Irishmen drinking with Bowie had been carried back to the wagons suffering from a knife-slash that had almost disembowelled him. It had occurred in a fight that began with a quarrel between Bowie and the Mexican employees of one of the Columbia residents.

The incident greatly angered Eli. He now had a wounded man to consider, and the fight might have antagonised the established settlers. Their goodwill was essential along the route he planned to take. Calling all the men together, Eli declared that until the wagon train reached its destination there would be no more carousing. The announcement provoked a noisy protest from the men, but Eli was adamant. While he was guiding the wagon train, he would make the rules.

54

Hec Bowie listened to Eli's directive, and to the reaction of the immigrants, with an ill-concealed contempt.

'You sound like one of those Methodist preachers, Eli. These are *men* you're talking to, not children. Try to keep a man from having himself a drink when he feels like it and he's likely to look around for someone else to take him to where's he's heading.'

'Do you reckon you're that man, Hec?' Eli spoke quietly and evenly. 'Perhaps we ought to find out where everyone stands before I make any more plans.'

Turning to the immigrants, Eli said: 'Hec Bowie doesn't like my way of running things. He believes he can do better. He's putting himself up for the job of taking you on from here. The choice is yours – but it's going to be the last choice you'll make. If you want me, then you'll do things *my* way until the last man among you gets down off his wagon to stand on his own land. If you want Bowie . . . well, that's up to you. I won't be around if you change your mind again. If that's understood, we'll get to voting. Who'd prefer to see Hec Bowie running things?'

Not until Hec Bowie's glance searched them out did two of the men who had gone to Columbia the previous evening raise their hands.

Eli nodded; he would remember both men.

'And who's in favour of me carrying on?'

Caleb Ryan's hand was unhesitatingly raised high. All but two of the new settlers followed suit in an impressive display of accord.

Hec Bowie shrugged nonchalantly in the face of such an overwhelming rebuff. 'It seems they like being wet-nursed. I guess that's their business.'

'It's yours, too, if you want to stay with us. You'll keep to the rules, just the same as anyone else.'

For a moment it seemed that Bowie might be inclined to argue the point. Instead, he scowled and walked off without a word, followed by Magnus Bergstrom and Rafael Mexia. The two Irishmen who had voted with him remained behind with the other immigrants.

This was not the end of Eli's problems for the day. Three men were missing from the meeting. Eli learned they were lying ill in their wagons with a fever. A quick check disclosed that two women and three children were also ill with similar symptoms. Complaining one minute of the heat, and then of cold, the victims tossed and turned on their blankets, sometimes threshing about in the grip of delirium and occasionally lapsing into unconsciousness. Their illness struck terror into the hearts of relatives who were convinced they would die.

No one among the immigrants had any knowledge of medicine, and the herbs of Texas were as unfamiliar as the fever they wanted to treat. Eli referred rather vaguely to 'marsh fever', saying it was common to all who came to the low-lying country along the great Texas rivers, especially during the hot summer months. He promised the immigrants that farther inland the fever would subside and there would be no new cases.

He was eventually able to persuade them to hitch up their horses and oxen, and move off from the river bank, but they had already lost a couple of hours.

Then, when no more than half a mile from the river, one of the sick children, a three-year-old girl, started having convulsions. A few minutes afterwards she was violently ill. Half an hour later she was dead.

It soon became apparent that the girl's parents had family links with at least half of the Irish immigrants. Wagon after wagon creaked to a halt as the occupants hurried to offer condolences to the bereaved couple. Most remained to offer comfort to the loudly wailing mother, or to join in her noisy lamentations.

Impatient to move on, Eli nevertheless gave the family of the dead girl more time than he felt they could afford, to accept the death of the child. The he suggested it was time for the Irish parents to make the effort to contain their grief and bury the child beside the track. There was a new life impatiently awaiting her brothers and sisters.

To Eli's dismay, the lamenting mother declared she would not be satisfied unless a service was held for her dead daughter. She also insisted that she be buried in a 'decent' cemetery, such as the one seen by the previous night's revellers in nearby Columbia.

Eli argued the case for going on as quickly as possible but when he saw the stubborn expressions on the faces about him he knew this was an argument he would not win. Eventually, he was forced to give way and send Caleb Ryan to Columbia to arrange for the burial. Three hours later a single wagon carrying the body of the three-year-old girl set off followed by representatives from every wagon and family in the immigrant train, all of them dressed in travel-creased Sunday best clothes.

'Funerals are big occasions in the lives of the Irish,' Adam explained, as the funeral cortège headed towards Columbia. 'I've heard of some where the mourning has gone on for more than a week.'

'This isn't Ireland,' retorted Eli. 'When they get to Indian country they'll need to learn to bury their dead as quickly as they can and get on with the business of staying alive. The same goes here. The lands this close to the Brazos and Colorado Rivers aren't healthy, especially for newcomers. The sooner we get away from here, the better it's going to be for everyone. If they spend all this time over every funeral, they'll end up with more bodies than mourners.'

As Eli finished talking, Adam heard an unexpected sound that he remembered well. It was the hoarse steam-whistle of Captain Lelean's paddle-steamer *Liberty*. The two men looked at each other in disbelief. Running to their horses, they galloped the short distance to the river bank. Forcing a way through the thick undergrowth at the water's edge, they looked down-river. At the river crossing recently used by the immigrants the ferryman was straining every muscle to haul his clumsy vessel into midstream. Nearby, the wheezing steamboat inched closer to the cleared strip of river bank, puffs of white steam escaping from the raucous steam-whistle into the hot, still air. Every inch of *Liberty*'s deck was crowded with men, horses and loaded wagons.

Alongside Adam, Eli clutched a flimsy-looking tree branch and hung precariously far over the muddy waters of the river. 'Who the hell can have hired a steamboat to come up-river with that lot – and where are they heading?'

Adam thought he knew the answer, even before he saw the slight, crippled figure of Philippe Tolsa standing on the deck.

'It's Don Manuel. It looks as though he's come prepared for a long journey.'

The two men made their way to the ferry landing, arriving as the first wagon rolled off the paddle-steamer. There was much shouting and gesticulating among Don Manuel's Mexican employees, but the disembarkation was taking place with impressive speed and efficiency. When Philippe saw Adam, he began waving wildly until restrained by his mother. But Dona Antonia could not control her small son's delighted smile when Adam waved in return.

'I'd say that little man's a mite pleased to see you,' commented Eli. 'Be careful. Being a small boy's idol carries a whole lot of responsibility. Before you know it, you're trying to be the man *he* thinks you are. A man can tie himself in knots that way.'

The wagons continued to roll ashore, with an increasing number of armed and mounted Mexicans milling about among them. The slight figure of Don Manuel Tolsa picked his way through the chaos to where Adam and Eli stood watching the busy scene. Impeccably dressed and unflustered, Don Manuel embraced Adam with undisguised warmth and shook hands with Eli.

Moments later, Dona Antonia, Philippe and Maria joined the men on the river bank. Dona Antonia had admonished her son and ordered him to behave with some decorum. Philippe did his best, but when Adam took him up behind him on his horse and they rode off after Don Manuel he clung to Adam and giggled like any other young boy when the movement of the horse almost dislodged his lopsided body.

To Don Manuel, Adam said: 'I thought you intended remaining at Velasco for a while?'

'That *was* my intention.' Don Manuel glanced towards his happy son and his dark eyes twinkled. 'But after you had gone Philippe bombarded me with reasons why we should leave for San Antonio immediately and catch up with your wagon train.'

Maria came along at that moment. The Tolsa living-wagon had just come ashore. Dona Antonia wanted her son to return.

Smiling at his son's unavailing protests as he went off with the *niñera*, Don Manuel led the two men along the river bank, away from the paddle-steamer. When he spoke again there was little mirth in his voice.

'You have heard of the latest Indian troubles?'

'No details. Only that there's been a raid or two along the Colorado River.'

'It is more serious than that. Many small Comanche raiding parties are active along the frontier, from the Brazos River to San Antonio. A message from my ranch informed me that eleven *peons* have been killed in the area, and women and children taken captive.'

'You're taking Philippe to San Antonio knowing all this is going on there?' Adam asked.

Patting Adam's arm, Don Manuel said: 'Do not fear for Philippe. I have eighty armed men with me – and four times that number to call upon at San Antonio. The Indians will not attack my house. Why should they, when they have such easy pickings elsewhere?'

To Eli, Don Manuel said: 'I suggest our two parties travel together for mutual safety.'

Don Manuel did not add that, without his men, it was doubtful whether the inexperienced immigrants would survive an Indian attack. It was this conviction, quite as much as concern for his San Antonio home and lands, that had prompted him to set off from Velasco so hurriedly. He had paid Captain Lelean a criminally exorbitant sum for the hire of *Liberty* to convey men, horses and wagons up-river as far as the Bell's Landing ferry, and so gain two days on the slow-moving ox-drawn wagons of the immigrants.

'Since leaving Velasco we've picked up three useful gun-hands from Brazoria – Hec Bowie, Magnus Bergstrom and Rafael Mexia. You know them, Don Manuel?'

Eli asked the question casually, but Adam felt there was more behind the query than was evident. His suspicion was confirmed by Don Manuel's reply.

'Bowie bears the name of a man I loved as a brave and gallant companion. I celebrated with James Bowie when he married the daughter of my friend. I mourned with him when cholera took his wife and children. When he died at the Alamo I wept and prayed for his soul. The door of my home is open for any man who claims kinship with James Bowie – but this man of whom you speak is a Bowie in name only. He boasts of having killed men in America and Mexico. It was natural that when he came to Texas he should make friends with Bo Garrett. Oh, yes, they rode together for a year. Then Bowie killed two of Garrett's men in a quarrel, somewhere on the Mexican border, and he rode off with Bergstrom and Mexia.'

Don Manuel broke off to brush dust from the leg of his tight black trousers, as a heavily laden wagon lurched by.

'Bowie has chosen suitable companions. Bergstrom was a sailor. He arrived at New Orleans in irons, charged with murdering the captain of the ship in which he sailed. He was convicted and sentenced to hang. Before the sentence could be carried out there was a mass escape from the prison in New Orleans. Seventeen prisoners broke free, among them three convicted murderers. Bergstrom was one. Since coming to Texas, Bergstrom seems to have kept clear of trouble, although it was rumoured he was involved in the mysterious affair of *Bartolomeu Dias*.'

Eli whistled softly through his teeth. '*Bartolomeu Dias* was a Mexican merchantman found drifting off Matagorda. Her crew and the passengers had been murdered, the women raped first. Everything of value had been stripped from the ship.'

After this disclosure, there was a brief silence before Adam asked: 'How about Mexia? Do you know him, too?'

'Yes, indeed. Rafael Cristobal Mexia. He first went to prison in Mexico for killing a man who expressed the opinion, quite truthfully, that Mexia had more Indian blood than Mexican in his veins. In fact, Mexia's mother is half-Apache Indian, half-Mexican. Mexia himself was born as the result of an attack on his mother's home village by a raiding party of Kiowa and Comanche Indians. His father could have been either. When Mexia was released from prison, he moved northwards and became a Comanchero. He traded with the Indians and acted as an emissary for the return of those Mexican child-captives whose parents could afford to pay for their release. It is said Mexia was very successful – unless the child he was returning happened to be a particularly attractive young girl.

'When a Mexican provincial governor announced he would pay a bounty on Indian scalps, Rafael Mexia discovered a new way to earn money. The bounty was intended to rid the province of renegade Indian warriors, but it is difficult to know whether a scalp has been taken from a man, a woman, or a child. Mexia's victims were women and children. He became quite expert. With two companions he once succeeded in trapping a whole foraging party of Indian women and children, scalping them all. Then, while stalking Indian women, Mexia was himself taken. Fortunately for him, they were Paiute Indians, not Comanche or Apache. They had not lost any of their women to scalp-hunters. They believed Mexia was stalking the women in the hope of snatching a wife for himself. However, he told his captors so many differing stories that they branded him a liar and split his tongue down the middle, so all Indians would know he was a man not to be trusted. That is why you will not hear Rafael Mexia talk today. He *can* talk, but only with great difficulty, and it calls attention to the reason for his disfigurement.'

Spreading his hands wide, Don Manuel said: 'There you have the stories of your three companions. Travelling with such men you will not need to go in search of trouble. I think it is lucky for you I decided to travel to San Antonio at this time.'

Eli nodded. 'Could be you're right. Tell your men to head up-river a way. They'll find the tracks of our wagons. We're camped a short distance beyond those trees you can see over there.'

'A camp? At this time of day?' Don Manuel looked sharply at Eli. 'I had expected you to be on the move for most of the daylight hours. You have slow, heavy wagons. You need to *gain* time, not lose it.'

When Eli explained about the sickness and the funeral, Don Manuel's reaction was the same as Eli's own had been.

'These people will need to learn that Texas is for the living. The dead must be quickly forgotten. As for the marsh sickness, I have a treatment that has never failed me. Peruvian bark. I will ask Dona Antonia to mix some for those of your people who are sick. But you must understand they will never recover while you are camped so close to the river. I am taking my wagons a few miles inland. Bring yours up by nightfall. Dona Antonia and I will expect you both to dine with us. Please bring the immigrant leader with you. We must talk of safeguarding his settlers when they reach their new lands in the hills beyond San Antonio.'

CHAPTER SIX

By the time the Irish mourners returned to the camp the waiting wagons were hitched and ready to set off after Don Manuel. The immigrants were relieved to know they would now be travelling with the Mexican landowner and his large escort. Don Manuel represented the class of man who had always taken care of them in their own countries and he had already supplied proof of his generosity in this vast new land.

Hec Bowie and his two friends were less pleased. They had returned from Columbia with the immigrants, but the alcohol on Bowie's breath was proof that most of his 'mourning' had been carried out inside a town saloon.

'We don't need no Mexican escort,' he said, for the third time. 'You know the Indian, Eli. Next to stealing horses, killing Mexicans is his favourite occupation. He'll ride for miles just to get his fingers tangled in a Mexican scalp.'

'Indians will think twice about attacking eighty well-armed men, whatever their nationality,' retorted Eli. 'I'm more than happy to have Don Manuel along. He's a well-liked and respected man. Having him with us should ensure we get all the co-operation we need from the plantations between here and the Colorado River. Or were you and your boys figuring on sweet-talking 'em for us?'

Hec Bowie flushed angrily. 'I may not be strong on the sweet-talking, but you won't go short of anything with Hec Bowie riding along with you.'

'There's a difference between "taking" and "being given". Now, seeing as you're here, you can keep the last of these wagons on the move. I want them at Don Manuel's camp in time for you to give the people some shooting practice before dark.'

Since Independence, Bell's Landing had become a busy river-crossing with good roads leading to the surrounding plantations. The immigrants reached Don Manuel's camp long before dark. He had chosen his site well. The wagons were placed in the shade of a rare grove of live oaks, the trees festooned with Spanish moss that hung to the ground in some places. Around the grove, Don Manuel had set armed guards. They would be doubled after dark. Indians rarely made their way this far east, but Don Manuel was not a man to take any chances.

Here, for the first time since leaving Velasco, the immigrants were untroubled by stinging insects. Dona Antonia sent a servant with a plentiful supply of Peruvian bark, and that night there was a more relaxed air in the immigrant camp.

When Hec Bowie assembled the immigrant men for instruction in shooting, the off-duty Mexicans of Don Manuel's escort gathered to watch. The ignorance of the newcomers when they handled firearms caused much amusement, even when an incident occurred that might have had serious consequences. One of the immigrants swung around with his musket, calling to Hec Bowie that the gun had jammed. In fact, he had been trying to pull on the trigger guard, instead of the trigger. Even as he called for help, his finger found the trigger. The weapon fired with a frightening report, and a choking cloud of black powder-smoke enveloped the Irishman.

The musket-ball sang only inches from Hec Bowie's ear and caused a number of watching Mexicans to dive for cover. When they rose to their feet, both Mexicans and settlers laughed uproariously – but Hec Bowie was furious. Snatching the musket from the hands of the open-mouthed Irishman, he swung the butt against the side of the inexperienced gunman's head, knocking him to the ground.

The laughter died away quickly as Hec Bowie turned to glare at the onlookers.

'There's been one funeral today. I'm not going to be guest of honour at another. These are *guns* you're handling. They're made to *kill*. If you doubt me, then one of you need only pull a fool trick like this again. I'll shoot him dead, right in front of your eyes.'

Bowie's belligerent glare ran over the crowd and stopped when it reached Adam. 'I hope you're hearing me, Englishman. Let's see how you handle a rifle. Give him a gun, someone.'

One of the settlers proffered his empty flintlock musket, but Adam shook his head. '*I* don't need the practice, but there are many here who do. I suggest you get on and show them how to shoot – and how to avoid accidents.'

'You suggest . . .?'

Hec Bowie saw Eli and Caleb Ryan approaching and did his best to swallow the anger that threatened to choke him. '*I* suggest you listen to what I tell these sod-busters. Indians ain't turkey, who'll gobble at you and run. They're mean savages who'll shoot you, knife you, lance you or club you to death, just as soon as look at you. That's unless they can lay hands on a man and torture him to death. Being *able* to shoot isn't enough. You've got to shoot *well*, and load fast enough to keep an Indian at a distance. That way you might survive in Texas. If you can't learn, and learn *fast*, you'll be better off going back to your own country and shooting at something that's running away from you.'

There were a few sly smiles in Adam's direction from the settlers. Some of them had been employed on estates and knew the shooting habits of English gentry.

'I'll remember your advice,' Adam promised. Then he left to head off Eli and Caleb Ryan. Together, the three men made their way to Don Manuel's cooking-fire.

The Mexican landowner travelled, as he did most other things, with considerable style. Squatting on the ground close to a fire, choking on woodsmoke, was not for Don Manuel Xavier Tolsa or his family.

His camp consisted of two canvas tents. One was the sleeping-quarters for Maria and Philippe, the other for Don Manuel and Dona Antonia. In front of the tents were ingenious folding chairs constructed from Osage orangewood and soft-cured buffalo hide. They were set around a cloth-covered table, put together from loose wagon-floor planks and trestles. The dining-area was a comfortable distance from the cooking-fire, and Don Manuel's servants ensured that the needs of the Tolsa family and their guests were speedily satisfied.

As well as good food, the Mexican landowner had a plentiful supply of drinks. If Eli had any feeling of guilt for imbibing, after denying drink to the immigrants, he did not allow it to spoil his enjoyment.

Caleb Ryan had brought a crude map with him. It purported to give the main features of the area to which the immigrants were headed. A shaded area indicated the block of land to which they held land deeds.

Don Manuel spread the map on the table in front of him and studied it for a while. Then he shook his head.

'This is not the most fertile of areas – and it is an even poorer map. It does not show the correct route of rivers and creeks. Neither does it indicate the hills – and this is very hilly country. Before we can discuss anything more we must correct the map.'

Calling a servant, Don Manuel sent him to find one of the escorts, explaining: 'He has spent much time hunting these hills. Years ago the buffalo would be there. Today you will find only deer and bear, but Pedro knows every hill and every valley.'

Pedro was one of the oldest men in Don Manuel's escort. Small and wiry, his face was a skein of deep creases. He puzzled over the map for some minutes. Then, under his patient direction, Don Manuel drew up a new map of the Hill Country. He included hills and valleys, rivers and creeks, and even the type of soil the settlers were likely to find there.

The map was an important document for the settlers. The men would now spend many happy hours on the long journey to the Hill Country planning the type of farm they would have there.

Later that evening, while the others were still talking, Adam left the Tolsa camp-fire to go to his bedroll. As he skirted the cooking-fires of the immigrants, he came face to face with Nell Plunkett and Peggy Dooley. The two women were carrying a kettle of water between them. Adam started guiltily at the chance encounter, yet he looked not at Peggy Dooley, but at her companion. For a brief moment, Adam thought he saw beneath the mask of hostile indifference she always wore in his presence. Before he could be certain, both women hurried by. Adam realised that Peggy had probably told Nell Plunkett what had occurred at the camp across the river from Brazoria. He found the thought that Nell knew about it strangely disturbing.

Hec Bowie's peace of mind was also being disturbed by Nell Plunkett. At the dance by the river he had lavished attention and snakehead whisky upon the fiery Irish girl, believing the course the night would take to be a foregone conclusion. Then the incident involving a toast to the English Queen had occurred. After that, the evening deteriorated. When they were in the firelight, in full view of everyone, she was fine – affectionate even. Yet as soon as he tried to get her out beyond the wagons, where there was moonlight and soft, inviting grass, she became as cold as a Panhandle winter night. Once, when Bowie guided her to the shadows and tried to hurry things along, she slapped his face with such force he could have sworn every tooth in his head had been shaken loose.

The following day, back in Brazoria, Hec Bowie had not been able to get the Irish girl out of his thoughts. He finally managed to convince himself that she was probably feeling the same way and had rejected his attentions only because he had drunk too much. He thought that if he called on her when he was sober it would be a very different story. This was when he had hit upon the idea of offering his services to the wagon train.

Unfortunately, this had not worked, either. Hec Bowie had not been invited to the cooking-fire Nell shared with her sister's family, and she had hardly spoken a word to him since his arrival. Hec Bowie was a confused and resentful man.

The wagon train got away to an early and trouble-free start the following morning, and the wagons trundled over passable roads, through rich and well-cultivated land. This was cotton-growing country. In the fields beside the road, Negro slaves worked steadily, hoeing between lines of cotton plants and cheerfully returning the waves of the immigrant children as the wagons passed by.

Their lively chatter and ready smiles made it difficult to appreciate that these were not farmhands going about their daily work, but were listed among the plantation-owner's chattels. As such they would be well cared for, but they could be sold or exchanged at the whim of the plantation-owner. He alone decided to whom they would be mated in order to produce a new generation of healthy, hard-working slaves for the house and fields.

While their parents worked, the Negro children were cared for by an aged slave woman who was coming to the end of her working life. For them, the passing of a large wagon train was an event not to be missed. Followed by the scolding old woman, they ran barefooted across the fields between the slave-cabins and the road. Standing in a diminutive line, they waved and shouted enthusiastically.

As a student, Adam had listened to the impassioned speeches of such anti-slavery orators as William Wilberforce and Thomas Clarkson. Their harrowing descriptions of the evils of slavery had done much to force through legislation making slavery illegal throughout Great Britain's worldwide territories. Seeing these well-nourished, apparently happy people, Adam could not help thinking that the abolitionists had deliberately misled the British people.

Shortly before making camp in the late afternoon, Adam's new thinking received a severe jolt. He was riding ahead of the wagon train with Eli when they saw a group of horsemen riding towards them. As they drew nearer, two figures could be seen on foot in the midst of the party. One was a well-muscled young Negro. He stumbled along at the end of a long rope, tied in a running noose about his neck, the other end secured to the pommel of a white rider's saddle.

The Negro's hands and ankles were secured with iron bands and short, heavy chains. The chain on his ankles was not long enough to enable him to take a full-length pace, and bloody grazes glistened through the dust on his heavily perspiring body – evidence that he had fallen more than once.

The other prisoner was a young slave girl. She, too, had a rope

66

about her neck, but her hands and legs were unfettered. Her light cotton dress was dishevelled and torn, and there was an ugly swelling over her left eye. She was a light-skinned girl and quite pretty, but when she looked up at Adam he was shaken by the hopelessness he saw in her eyes.

After greeting the horsemen, Eli inclined his head towards the two Negroes.

'Runaways?'

'Yep.' The leader of the horsemen was a pleasant, clean-shaven young man of about Adam's age. He was employed, with his men, by the plantation-owners. His task was to patrol the settlements, checking on the movements of slaves when they were away from the plantations on their owners' business. He also pursued runaway slaves. There had been more of them since Texas declared itself independent of Mexico. Once across the Rio Grande, the river that divided Texas and Mexico, a Negro was a free man.

Jerking the rope, the young man pitched the shackled Negro to the ground. 'This one's a thief, too. When he ran away he went over to Colonel Dance's plantation and stole this girl. Then the pair of 'em made a run for the Mexican border. Damn fool nigger didn't even know it's more than three hundred miles off. If we hadn't brought 'em back, the Indians would have got 'em, for sure.'

'Why did he take the girl?' Adam asked the question.

'I guess he took a shine to her when they both worked for Mr Sherman. She was only recently sold to the Colonel.'

'Mrs Sherman promised that Abraham and I could be wed. A proper wedding, with the preacher an' all. Mr Sherman knowed this when he sold me off to that Colonel Dance.' The slave girl had a shrill, high voice that grated on the ear.

'You hold that loose tongue of yours, nigger girl, or I'll teach you another lesson, right here in front of these folks. Mrs Sherman's been dead these six months. What Mr Sherman does with you is his own business.'

The speaker jerked on the rope that held her, choking off her words. She reached up to ease off the noose as her captor's horse danced in a tight circle, dragging her with it.

On his feet again, the chained Negro took an unwise step towards the girl and was immediately brought crashing to the ground once more. The rope was jerked hard every time the young slave tried to rise. Finally he ceased his struggles and lay on his back in the dust, blood oozing from a new graze on his shoulder.

'What will happen to them now?'

Two of the mounted men had kneed their reluctant horses dangerously close to the fallen man, and Adam asked the question unnecessarily loudly in a bid to divert attention away from him for a few minutes.

'We'll drop the girl in to Colonel Dance on the way to the Sherman place. The old man will give her a thrashing, but I've no doubt she'll be warming his bed again tonight. As for him. ....'
The slave was attempting to rise again, but a tug on the rope tumbled him back in the dust. 'I think he'll need to be gelded, or he'll be off after the girl again.'

Adam saw the look of sudden fear in the young Negro's eyes.

'It's a pity, really. He's got the looks of a good breeding nigger, but it's better than hanging him and losing him for good – and that's what will happen if he runs off again.'

Adam looked aghast at these men who spoke so casually of brutally emasculating or hanging another human being. Before he could say more, Eli called out a hasty 'Goodbye!' to the slave-hunters and slapped Adam's horse sharply on the rump, sending it along the road. When Adam looked back he saw the Negro being hauled roughly to his feet at the end of the rope.

'Were they serious about castrating him?' Adam had to ask the question, although he already knew the answer.

'You'd better believe it! Forget any sympathy you might have for Negroes until we're clear of the plantations. The landowners hereabouts are influential men, Adam. They represent the power behind the whole republic. Upset them and they're quite likely to order our wagon train to turn about. If they do, there's not a damned thing that we, or even Don Manuel, can do.'

'But that's a *man* they're dragging along on the end of that rope, not some wild animal! All he's done wrong is to go after the woman he was supposed to marry and try to take her some place where they can start a life together. For that he'll wind up being hung, or mutilated, and she'll get a whipping?'

'That's about the size of it. I'm not claiming it's right – any more than I'm saying it's wrong. It's just the way things are, here in Texas. I don't intend setting off on any crusade to change them, and you'd be wise to follow suit.'

'And I thought the reason for Texas taking her independence was to strike a blow against *Mexican* injustice!' Adam said disgustedly.

'Injustice to *white* men, Adam. Nobody went to war for the niggers. Hell, you think *they're* badly off? You wait until you see the way the Indians are treated. You'll soon realise the nigger's coddled by comparison. Even *talking* this way about Indians is guaranteed to make a man a damn sight more unpopular with Texans than a nigger-lover. Go back, now, and tell Caleb Ryan to head the wagons towards that patch of timber about a mile ahead. I'm going up to the house yonder to make sure it's all right for us to camp there. Don Manuel says it is but, like I said, it don't do to offend anyone around here.'

They made camp earlier than usual, and Hec Bowie's daily shooting lesson was achieving its usual lack of success, when Don Manuel suggested there should be a shooting match between more experienced riflemen. He thought it would demonstrate to the immigrants the standard they might one day achieve. To make it more interesting, he put up a flagon of brandy for the winner.

Every man of Don Manuel's escort was a good shot, but the shorter barrels of the Mexican muskets could not match the long rifles of the Texans and Eli for accuracy. Soon, Hec Bowie and Eli were shooting against each other for the brandy.

The target was a black knot in the centre of a piece of wagon planking placed fifty yards from the marksmen. The man who got his six shots closest to the knot would be adjudged the winner. Five of Eli's shots struck the board closer to the knot than any of Hec Bowie's, but the sixth was not on the board at all. The wagon-train leader flung his long rifle to the ground in disgust, while Bowie's two companions thumped their victorious champion on the back and Bowie pulled the cork from the brandy with his teeth.

'What went wrong?' Adam asked, as surprised as the immigrants at Eli's defeat.

'It was my own stupid fault,' bemoaned the unhappy loser. 'When I was loading paper cartridges the other evening, I had one that was a bit short on powder. I should have thrown it away. Instead, I thought I'd keep it and sort it out later. It must have got in with the good cartridges. I guess that was my sixth shot. There just wasn't enough powder to blow the lead all the way to the target.'

As the sorry tale came to an end, Adam looked up to see Hec Bowie watching him.

'I thought you fancied yourself as something of a shot, Englishman. Why didn't you join in? Could it be that you're just too good for us Texan country boys?'

Hec Bowie's smile did not extend to his eyes, and Adam

realised that the shooting victory had given Bowie the confidence to defy Eli's warning and begin pushing Adam once more.

When Adam did not answer him immediately, Bowie said: 'What's the matter, Englishman, the stakes too low? All right, I tell you what I'll do. I'll put up my saddle and the brandy against that toy gun you've got tucked in your belt.'

Adam knew that he had no alternative but to accept the challenge. Taking the revolver from his belt, he weighed it in his hand thoughtfully. 'Throw in that knife you carry and I'll take you on.'

Hec Bowie hesitated for only a moment. 'Done!'

Taking the wide-bladed knife from the back of his belt, he flicked it casually through the air and the knife buried itself in the ground between Adam's feet. Calling to his companions, Bowie said: 'Magnus, go fetch my saddle and put it here with the other things. Rafael, you guard them with your life until I come to collect my winnings.'

'Eli, over what range can I depend on the accuracy of this gun of mine?' asked Adam softly.

'Farther than you'll be able to see the knot in that piece of wood,' declared Eli. 'You know how well you shoot, boy. I don't. All I can say is that your gun will do all that's asked of it.'

Adam nodded. Hec Bowie's gun had an equally long barrel, but he was gambling that its accuracy could not match that of the Pennsylvanian rifle over a longer distance.

'Why don't we make the contest more interesting by moving the target back to, say, a hundred paces? Of course, if you don't think you can shoot well enough at that range, we'll leave it where it is. . . .'

Hec Bowie was taken by surprise. A hundred yards was a long distance for any marksman, but he had shot Indians at that range before now.

'Put the target where you like. It'll just mean walking farther to prove you've lost, that's all.'

The new distance was paced out and the old bullet-holes marked so no mistakes would be made. By now word had gone around the camp that there was to be a shoot-off between Hec Bowie and Adam. The immigrants were aware of the antagonism between the two men. They also knew that much of it had been sparked off by Nell Plunkett. By the time the target was placed in its new position, every man, woman and child had deserted wagon and camp-fire to watch the contest.

The Tolsa family were at the front of the spectators. Philippe was pale-faced and tense, fearful that Adam might lose before such a crowd.

At Adam's insistence, Hec Bowie fired off the first shot. The Texan took very careful aim before squeezing the trigger. When the cloud of smoke from the black powder drifted away, the chatter of the onlookers died down as the Mexican inspecting the distant target straightened up.

Holding up a hand, the Mexican spread his fingers wide. 'A hand's breadth away.'

Magnus Bergstrom thumped his friend on the back enthusiastically. It was a good shot from this range.

Adam advanced to the mark, raised the long rifle to his shoulder and aimed the weapon as carefully as had Bowie.

When the smoke cleared, the Mexican held up *two* hands, fingers spread wide apart. Bergstrom whooped again, and the immigrants muttered their disappointment. Most of them wanted Adam to win.

Frowning, Adam set off to inspect the target for himself. The bullet had struck the target about two feet low, but the line was good. Adam was satisfied with the shot. He would need to file the front sight down a fraction later. For now, he could compensate for it when he next took aim. The gun itself was remarkably accurate.

Hec Bowie's first shot had left the Texan feeling overconfident. He fired too quickly for his second shot, and the Mexican was bent over the target for a long time. When he stood up again he waved both arms, signalling a miss.

Now it was Bowie's turn to stomp off to inspect the target. After a brief angry exchange with the Mexican adjudicator, Bowie stalked back to the firing-point, his face flushed with annoyance.

Once again Adam took his time over the shot, and his patience was rewarded. The Mexican indicated that his shot was no more than two fingers' breadth away from the knot. Philippe could scarcely hide his delight – until Hec Bowie's next shot struck only a bullet's width from Adam's.

Each man's third shot was equally close, and Bowie's fourth was, if anything, a shade nearer to the knot. In contrast, Adam's fourth was as disastrous as Bowie's second shot had been. Adam knew it was a misfire the moment the powder exploded in the barrel. It came as no surprise to him when the adjudicator signalled a miss.

Confident once more, Bowie placed his fifth shot no more than a hand's width from the knot, but Adam's answering shot brought a roar from the watchers. It was a bull's-eye, almost driving the knot clear of the wood planking.

It marked the end for Hec Bowie. Thoroughly rattled, his last bullet followed the path of his second and failed to strike the board.

Adam's last shot was no less spectacular than the one that had gone before and sent the knot flying clear of the wooden plank.

The watching crowd went wild when the Mexican adjudicator held the knot high in the air to signify Adam's victory. Young Philippe shouted himself hoarse, as did Maria. Even the stiff Dona Antonia was smiling. Peggy Dooley also applauded loudly, but she stopped abruptly and turned into the crowd as she looked at Nell Plunkett's face.

A hush suddenly fell upon the crowd and Adam turned to see a party of some half-dozen men walking their horses towards him. In the lead was a giant of a man, wearing a check hunting-shirt, a buckskin jacket and stained riding-breeches of the same material.

Leaving his horse with the other men, the big man limped towards Adam. Grasping his hand, he said jubilantly: 'That was as fine a piece of shooting as I've seen for many a year, young man. If you've come to Texas looking for adventure, I can promise you a place with the Rangers.'

'My partner's already fixed up, General. He's helping me guide these new citizens to their lands, out beyond San Antonio.'

'Eli Varne! I might have guessed that if I found a good rifleman there'd be a Tennesseean close by. It's good to see you, old friend.' Eli and the newcomer pummelled each other on the back, grinning happily.

'You have more than one old friend in this camp, Mr President – or do we belong in the past now you have exchanged your gun for the reins of state?'

The big man turned from Eli, his expression one of uninhibited joy. 'Don Manuel! You know me better than to ask a question like that. I'm a man who'll acknowledge old friends until the day I die. Besides, those who fought beside me and still remain my friends are all too rare, as well you know.'

Caught in a grizzly-like hug, Don Manuel was robbed of all his Mexican dignity and swung around, feet off the ground, like a child.

This in itself was unusual enough, but Adam could not take his eyes from the other man. This big, informal, friendly man who exhibited such boyish exuberance at meeting with old friends was General Sam Houston, President of the Independent

Republic of Texas. A legend early in his own lifetime, Houston had thrown away the trappings of civilisation, together with the governorship of Tennessee, when his marriage came to a disastrous and mysterious end. He went to live among the Cherokee Indians, only to reappear in the capital of the United States of America as an emissary, to plead the already lost cause of the Indians.

Alternating between periods of drunken wretchedness and an almost childlike need to hurl himself headlong and noisily into the chilly waters of American society, Houston offered himself to Texas in her hour of greatest need. Appointed general of the untrained, untested and wilful army of the embryo republic, Houston led them to achieve the impossible. He routed the experienced and hitherto victorious army of Mexico's President, General Santa Anna, taking the President himself prisoner. By this single accomplishment, Sam Houston made the secession of Texas from Mexico a reality. What the leaders of many world nations had looked upon as foolish, rebellious acts against legitimate authority became the agonies of birth for a new and potentially influential nation.

When his feet were once more resting on the ground, Don Manuel said: 'I am happy you arrived in time to witness the prowess of our young English marksman, Mr President. I don't think you have yet been introduced. Allow me to present Adam Rashleigh.'

'An Englishman, eh?' Sam Houston grinned at Adam's formal bow. 'No matter, that offer of a place with my Rangers still stands. They have need of men who can handle guns as well as you do.'

'Adam is here on important business for his own government, in connection with land purchases made by British immigrants. He is also personally acquainted with Lord Palmerston, his country's Foreign Secretary.'

'Is he, be damned! Then I'm doubly pleased to meet you, young man. I only wish your Lord Palmerston were here in person. I have a lot I'd like to say to him.'

'I am quite certain Lord Palmerston will be interested in anything you have to say, sir. I have to send a report to London shortly. I will be pleased to pass on a message.'

Adam hoped he had not said too much, but he was confident that a message from the President of Texas, albeit unofficial, was more important to Palmerston than Adam's own observations or opinions.

'I'm afraid your Foreign Secretary has shown very little interest

73

in Texas so far, Adam. I sent a man to England nine months ago to ask for your country's recognition of our independence. Palmerston won't even see him.'

'Perhaps you would like to continue this conversation over dinner tonight. You will be remaining in the camp overnight, Mr President? My tent is at your disposal.'

'The ground has always been good enough for me, Don Manuel, and God's sky is the best canvas I know. Now, young man, I see Dona Antonia standing over there, waiting to greet me, together with that young son of Don Manuel's. He was mighty excited when you won the shooting match. Please excuse me now; I never like to keep a lady waiting for any reason but war. You and I will have much to talk about later, I promise you.'

General Houston walked to where Don Manuel's family stood. He bowed low and long over Dona Antonia's hand; then, turning to her son, lifted Philippe high in the air and swore he had doubled in weight since they had last met. When he put Philippe down again, he told the boy to stay close. Slapping the leg that had been wounded at San Jacinto, when he defeated Santa Anna, he jokingly added that they could just about muster two good legs between them.

Still overawed at such an informal meeting with a man of President Houston's stature, Adam turned away – and came face-to-face with the undisguised hostility of Hec Bowie.

'You don't get to be a marksman on Sam Houston's say so,' said the defeated Texan. 'There's a whole world of difference between shooting at a piece of wood and picking off Indians when they're shooting back at you. Big Drunk's been a squawman too long to know the difference any more.'

'I'll remember that when I'm downing your brandy,' retorted Adam. Then he grinned. 'But I'd enjoy it more if you were to join me in drinking it.'

Hec Bowie hesitated, and for a moment Adam thought the tough Texan might accept his offer of conciliation. Then Bowie looked past Adam and saw Nell Plunkett standing in the now thinning crowd. 'No, thanks. I reckon I'd never be able to enjoy the taste of good drink no more if I was asked to drink the health of that Queen of yours again.'

Nodding to where his stake for the shooting match was heaped, Bowie said: 'If I was you, I'd get to practising with that knife you've won from me. It pays to kill quietly when you're in Indian country.'

Bowie had taken no more than twenty paces when Adam

74

called to him, Bowie's knife balanced easily in his hand. Hec Bowie turned and his eyes widened as Adam drew back his hand to throw the knife. Adam flicked the knife expertly and it entered the ground only inches from Bowie's boot, in exactly the same way as Bowie had delivered the knife to Adam earlier.

'The knife wasn't invented in America, Bowie. I was taught how to do that by Spanish gypsies when I was ten years old. They taught me other knife tricks, too. I gave up using them when my father told me that gentlemen don't fight with knives. Keep it. I'll take my chances with the Indians.'

Shouldering the saddle he had won, Adam picked up the flagon of brandy and walked towards the wagon where his belongings were stowed.

Behind him, Eli grinned broadly at the discomfited Hec Bowie. 'I warned you not to underestimate him, Hec.'

He looked to where Adam was making his way through the crowd of immigrants, many of them reaching out to slap him on the back as he passed by.

'I reckon Dan Coutter would be proud to know where his rifle's ended up.'

CHAPTER SEVEN

DINNER that night, outside the Tolsa tents, was a lively affair. President Houston was travelling with Henry Smith, Secretary of the Texas Treasury, two more government officials and two colonels of the Texan army. None was a reticent or shy man, but it was Sam Houston who dominated the gathering. As the sun slipped below the haze of the far-distant horizon, the President insisted that the party adjourn to the cooking-fire, declaring that men became friends more quickly when they talked to each other in firelight.

Dona Antonia would have taken Philippe off to their tent, leaving the men to their talking and drinking, but the Texan president would not let her.

'If you and Philippe desert us now, Dona Antonia, the evening will pass unnoticed in a recitation of bawdy jokes and risqué stories. Time is too precious to be wasted in such a manner. Tonight I have an all-too-rare opportunity to sit beneath the stars with old and new friends, and talk of the hopes and fears of the people of this great new republic of ours. We men will be happy seated on the ground, but we must have a chair for you, dear lady. Come and sit here, by my side. It's been a long time since I last enjoyed the company of a beautiful woman. No, don't look towards your husband. He will enjoy your company for the rest of his life. He'll spare me an hour or two. Adam, you come and sit on my other side. We have things to talk about, too.'

Dona Antonia deferred to the wishes of the irrepressible President and she could not have wished for a more attentive companion, or a more entertaining one. Houston's flow of conversation was interrupted only when he raised a glass of Don Manuel's brandy to his lips.

The talk ranged from the desperate state of the Texas Treasury's finances, through speculation about Mexican intentions, to the pitiably small standing army of the Texan Republic. It had been reduced to a mere six hundred men only a year before, when, amidst increasing rumours of an army-inspired rebellion, Sam Houston had sent the remainder on indefinite furlough. It would have been more satisfactory to dismiss the ill-disciplined soldiers, but, as Houston explained, such a course of action would have put the Texas government under an obligation to pay the men all outstanding monies due to them – and the government coffers were empty.

Then Eli asked the President what he knew of the Indian troubles that had been reported in the San Antonio area.

Red-faced from a combination of brandy and heat from the fire, Sam Houston scowled and brandished his near-empty glass in admonishment. 'Rumour, Eli. Unsubstantiated rumour. There *are* a few Comanche raiding parties around, sure – but you tell me a time when there haven't been. The Mexican government is trying to stir up trouble among the Indians, too, but Chief Bowles has given me his word that his Cherokees won't fight against us. Others will follow his example, you mark my words.'

'Do you trust the word of an Indian?' The unexpected question came from Dona Antonia, who had said little until now.

'Of course.' Sam Houston smiled sadly. 'Dona Antonia, I've been lied to by a great many men in my lifetime, more especially since becoming President of Texas, but no Indian has ever told me a downright lie. There are *no* Cherokees raiding our settlements, and the Mexican government has succeeded in stirring up no more trouble than was here already.'

'Are you saying we'll find *no* Indian trouble up-river?' Eli took the pipe from his mouth to ask the question.

'No. All I'm saying is that it's no better and no worse than it ever was – or ever will be until a treaty's made that *we* are prepared to keep. I've already made friends with Chief Flacco. His band of Comanches don't bother Texans anymore. But there's a whole mess of Comanches out there we haven't even *tried* to talk to. I believe we should.'

There was a murmur of disagreement among his companions, and Sam Houston turned the conversation to talk of the plans he had for the new city of Houston, the latest settlement to be accorded the privilege of becoming capital of the infant republic.

As the evening wore on, the voices of the men about the fire became louder, and the occasional oath began to be heard more often. Dona Antonia announced that she and her son were retiring for the night. Her tone brooked no argument, not even from the President himself. As she left, the men rose to their feet courteously. General Houston bestowed a kiss on Dona Antonia's cheek, protesting that she was ruining his evening by leaving the party at such an early hour.

The Texan president had drunk more than any man present, but when he returned to his place there was no hint of intoxication in the look he gave Adam. As the talk and laughter about them passed the level it had reached with Dona Antonia present, Houston said quietly: 'Young man, I am now going to bore you by talking government business.'

A great guffaw of laughter all but drowned President Houston's words.

'We'll leave these men to their stories. No doubt you've heard them all. If you haven't, you soon will. There are few new humorous tales in Texas.'

Adam followed the tall President from the firelight and they walked together across the wide space within the ring of wagons. Circling the dying fires of the immigrants, the President stepped over the tongue of a wagon and stood motionless for a few moments, looking out into the night. Drawing in a deep breath of air that was scented with woodsmoke, he said: 'That smell always takes me back to my days with the Cherokee. I could ride along a valley at night and tell which lodge I was approaching by the smell of the woodsmoke. There are seven lodges and each burns a different type of wood. They were good days. *Healing* days. Do you know anything of Indians, Adam?'

'Nothing at all. I've hardly been here long enough to get to know the Texans.'

President Houston snorted. 'I head the government of Texas, but I'm damned if I understand them yet. An Indian, now, he's a different bundle of sticks. You know where you are with him. You're either his friend or his enemy. Either way, you won't be in any doubt about it for long. You take those men sitting about Don Manuel's fire back there. There's seven of them, each claiming he's my friend. Yet I'd put my trust in but two of them – Don Manuel and Eli. There's not one of the others wouldn't trip me up and stamp on me if he thought it would put him in good with the next elected President.'

The two men walked on in silence until they stood side by side at the edge of a sandy creek, split along its length by a narrow trickle of iron-grey, moonlit water.

'I don't mind confessing that I'm worried, Adam. I've got less than five months of my term of office left to run and we're no closer to a solution of Texas's problems. We fought hard for our independence and we won. Now we're stronger than ever. So strong that the Mexicans haven't the courage to attack us. If they did, they would suffer a bigger defeat than before. But our progress is painfully slow. We need money to secure our future, but before we can get money *we must have international recognition*. Yet not a single country in Europe will exchange ambassadors with us. It's a bitter pill to swallow.'

Turning to Adam, Houston pleaded: 'You've recently arrived

from England. What's the feeling about us there? Do we have the sympathy of the ordinary man? And your government, where do you think they stand?'

Adam wondered whether the President suspected his true reason for being in Texas; whether this questioning was no more than a devious attempt to trick him into incriminating himself. The idea was dismissed from his mind even before he began seriously considering such a possibility. Sam Houston was the President of his country. He had no need to play such games.

'I doubt whether most Englishmen ever think about Texas. Indeed, few of them will know where it is. Most care little for anything that occurs beyond the bounds of their own town or parish. Even those immigrants who are in the wagon train knew nothing of Texas until they landed here. It was just a name to them; a hope – and the chance to begin a new life, free from poverty and the threat of starvation. It could as easily have been Africa, or the Australian colonies, for all they knew – or cared. As for the government, I think they have enough to think about with corn shortages and the growing clamour for reform.'

Adam hesitated for a moment before continuing: 'However, I do recall one of my late father's friends expressing the view that it would be foolish to recognise Texas as an independent country when annexation by the United States of America was in the offing. Indeed, he felt it was quite unrealistic of your government to seek recognition from the rest of the world whilst proposing annexation to America.'

For some unaccountable reason, Adam felt a great reluctance to lie to the big, bluff man standing beside him. In quoting Lord Palmerston's words, he was glad that the British Foreign Secretary *had* been a friend of his father.

Punching a fist into the palm of his hand, Houston let out a loud sigh of annoyance. 'I *thought* that was the way of things. I've said so all along.'

Reaching out, General Houston grasped Adam's shoulder in a strong grip. 'Adam, do you know Lord Palmerston well enough to write him a letter? Would he believe you if you passed on a matter of some importance to him – and to Texas?'

'I believe so.' Adam had no doubt at all that Lord Palmerston would be *greatly* interested in any matter of importance that was a direct quote from the President of Texas.

'Very well: then you will be the first to know. I am sending Anson Jones as my minister to the United States. He will be instructed formally to withdraw the Texas Republic's offer of annexation. Texas is going it alone. You tell this to your Lord

Palmerston. Tell him also that I am looking towards Europe for backing. It could come from any one of half a dozen nations. I would much prefer it to be Great Britain. Write the letter tonight. I'll take it on with me tomorrow and send it to England on the first ship to sail from Texas. If the letter leads to recognition by your country, you'll have earned yourself a place in history, and you'll not find the Texas government ungrateful.'

The following morning the wagon train and President Houston's party set off in opposite directions. Houston rode towards the rising sun, while the wagons headed for an ominous dark curtain of cloud, occasionally rent by a web of serpentine lightning that hung in the sky above the horizon.

Houston had departed with Adam's letter in his pocket, and had issued a standing invitation for Adam to lodge with him whenever Adam was in Houston, or in Nacogdoches, where the President also had a home. It was a promising start to the mission of Palmerston's young protégé.

Far less promising was the approaching storm. On the flat, featureless plain it was possible to see that the storm blanketed an area about twelve miles across. For a while it seemed that the wagon train would be touched by only the fringe of the storm; then a sudden turn in the trail sent the wagons heading for the very heart of the lightning-torn darkness.

The rumble of thunder was almost continuous now, and Adam's horse was nervous and skittish. Ahead of the storm the wind gathered strength. As Adam rammed his soft-brimmed felt hat more securely on to his head, Eli sidled his horse up to him.

'Get on ahead. Close the wagons up on each other. Tell them to check their wagon-covers, make sure they're well tied down.'

The wind was howling about them now, and Eli needed to shout his last words.

Halfway along the long line of wagons, Adam passed one leaning at a sorry angle beside the track, its contents heaped untidily about it on the ground. A wheel had collapsed. Hec Bowie and his companions were among the small crowd helping to lift the wagon, while a Scots settler stacked stones beneath the axle, helped by three young sons.

Adam rode the length of the column, passing on Eli's instructions. Well back, he passed the Tolsa wagon. Philippe sat hunched on the wagon box, a heavy poncho clutched about his shoulders. He waved vigorously, and Adam grinned and returned the greeting but did not stop. Don Manuel's men had anticipated Eli's order and were checking the covers on all their wagons.

It had begun to rain now. Big, heavy drops stung Adam's skin and drummed a tattoo on the taut canvas of the wagon-covers, sounding a warning of the storm that now raced towards the wagon train.

It struck with a ferocity that left Adam gasping for breath. Caught between two wagons, he saw the wagon ahead of him suddenly disappear behind a solid, dark wall of rain. The deluge almost knocked Adam from the saddle, the rain bruising his body through the cloth of his shirt and trousers, the sheer volume of water causing him to fight for breath.

Adam's horse snorted in terror and tried to turn away from the viciously driving rain, but there was no escape.

Crouched low over the animal's neck, Adam drove the horse forward. Such was the ferocity of the downpour that it was impossible to see as far as the ground beneath the horse's feet. If it turned and stumbled, Adam was likely to be trampled to death beneath the feet of the oxen pulling the next wagon. As he moved on blindly, thunder crashed all about him, accompanied by the crack and sizzle of lightning.

Suddenly, Adam's horse shied. In front of him Adam could just make out the curved outline of the wagon ahead of him. It appeared to be at an awkward angle, and Adam realised it had slewed off the track that was now a quagmire. The rear flap of the wagon was blowing loose in the wind, cracking with the ferocity of rifle-shots. As Adam edged his horse closer he could see sacks of provisions inside, wet from the rain.

Cursing the settler's carelessness, he tried to secure the wagon-flap, but the rain was so fierce he needed to shield his eyes and the horse would not remain still long enough for him to thread the rope through the stitched eyelets in the canvas.

Reaching down, Adam looped the horse's reins over a hook at the rear of the wagon and tied them tight. Then, throwing his rifle ahead of him, he swung from the saddle into the wind-buffeted wagon.

'Who's that?'

Adam hardly heard the words above the noise of the storm. Inside the wagon it sounded as though he were inside a drum at the height of a band concert. The canvas was leaking in a number of places, but compared with conditions outside it was positively luxurious.

Struggling to secure the canvas flap, Adam shouted: 'Why

81

didn't you tie the wagon-flap? Do you want to ruin all your provisions?'

'What?'

The word was shouted in a woman's voice. Adam turned as someone wriggled along the wagon until she was beside him. Not until she pushed her face to within inches of his own did he recognise Nell Plunkett in the gloom.

Adam tied the wagon-flap before turning his attention to the Irish girl. 'Where's the man who should be driving this wagon?' Adam shouted the question and turned his head to catch the reply.

'Back along the track somewhere, helping one of the Scots to change a wheel. The rest of his family are in the other wagon. . . .'

Something in her voice made Adam peer at her more closely in the dim light. 'Are you all right?'

'I . . . I think so. The lightning. . . . I think it hit the oxen. It knocked me back inside the wagon.'

As she was talking, Adam became aware of increased buffeting about the wagon. At first he thought it was the wind; then he became aware of a new sound above the din of the storm and recognised the noise of a river running in full spate.

The track ran beside the gully Adam had noticed the previous evening. Then there had been only a thin trickle of water in the middle of the wide, empty river-bed. The ferocity of the storm had quickly changed this. The river was now a raging torrent extending from bank to bank and spilling over on either side. Even so, this should not be causing the wagon to shudder and groan as it was now doing – unless the oxen had strayed from the trail into the river gully!

Adam scrambled over the jumbled provisions to the front of the wagon. This flap, too, was unfastened, and Adam peered out over the high wooden seat. It was still raining hard, but the skies had lightened enough for Adam to see the two rear oxen attempting unsuccessfully to back away from whatever was ahead of them. Water swirled about their legs, and about the wagon, too.

When Nell pushed into the space beside him, Adam pointed ahead into the gloom. 'I think the oxen have taken you off the road. If we don't get them out quickly, they'll be swept away – and the wagon will go with them.'

Climbing over the high seat, Adam dropped to the ground. The water rose above his knees. He made his way carefully past the two rear oxen. The usually patient and placid animals were snorting their fear as they tried desperately, but in vain, to pull back from the noisy torrent. Ahead of them Adam found two more oxen, both half-crazed with fear. As Adam edged past he felt the ground giving way beneath his feet.

The water was almost up to his waist, the current pulling at him with a frightening strength. He could see beyond the second pair of oxen now and quickly discovered the reason for their fear. There should have been two more pairs of oxen ahead of them, but he did not doubt that the leading pair were as dead as the two animals behind them. It was doubtful if they had drowned. More likely they had strayed from the trail and been killed by lightning before the flash-flood had filled the gully. With dead oxen ahead and the wagon behind, the remaining four beasts had no chance of pulling free.

The river was still rising. If the wagon was to be saved, Adam would need to work fast. Usually, a long chain ran from the wagon to the leading oxen, each pair being linked to the chain at regular intervals. Adam gave thanks for the shortage of chain at Velasco which had dictated that it be replaced on most of the settlers' wagons by stout rope. If he cut this rope immediately in front of the second pair of oxen, he could free them from their dead companions.

Speaking softly in an attempt to soothe the frightened animals, Adam eased past them, at the same time reaching to the back of his belt for the knife he kept there. To his dismay, he discovered it was missing. He remembered it had been necessary to cut a knot from the rope before threading it through the eyelets at the back of the wagon. He must have left the knife inside.

Easing his way past the snorting oxen once more, Adam suddenly met Nell, wading out to find out what was happening.

'I need a knife,' he shouted. 'I left it in the wagon.'

'What's happened?'

'Four of the oxen are dead. I need to cut them free quickly. Move back.'

Adam spoke impatiently. He had to get to the wagon but dared not move out too far. If he lost his footing, he would be swept away by the waters which were gaining in strength with every second.

Instead of doing as she was told, Nell Plunkett reached down and hitched her skirt well above her knees. Strapped to her thigh was a sheathed knife. Drawing it free, she passed the knife to Adam, offering no explanation for being armed in such a fashion. This was not the time to tell him she had carried the knife since the day the soldiers had raided her home in Ireland.

Taking the knife from her, Adam waded back into the gully,

going out wider than he would have liked, in order to keep clear of the oxen's wide horns. Taking a deep breath, he plunged his head beneath the surface of the muddy river. He found the long rope at the second attempt. Nell's knife was sharp, but it took four more dives before the rope parted, helped by the frantic efforts of the live oxen to break free.

He did not need to coax the animals to pull away from the river, but he grabbed the horns of the animal nearest to him to prevent the oxen making too tight a turn and overturning the wagon.

The wheels had sunk in the softened ground and, with only half a team pulling, it proved tough going. The rain was easing now and visibility improving. Seeing Adam's difficulties, Nell climbed to the wagon seat and picked up the bull-hide whip coiled beneath the seat. With a suddenly acquired expertise, born of desperation, she cracked the whip over the backs of the straining animals, shouting to urge them on to greater efforts.

Painfully slowly, it seemed, the wheels of the heavy wagon began to turn, and Adam and Nell redoubled their efforts. The oxen slipped and splashed, but they were pulling hard now – and suddenly the wagon lurched free.

They were not safe yet. There was no high land anywhere and water swirled about the wagon to a depth of more than two feet on the trail, but it seemed to have stopped rising now.

In the lessening gloom, Adam saw a clump of trees nearby. Feeling the way with his feet as he went, he led the oxen towards them. There was no need to secure the animals. The trees broke up the power of the water swirling along beside the river and the oxen were content to remain here.

Now Adam could see many of the other wagons. They were scattered at all angles along the flooded trail. Most were safely turned away from the torrent that swept along the gully and spilled dark-brown water over the surrounding countryside for as far as could be seen.

Adam felt great relief and he grinned foolishly up at Nell. There had been moments when he was certain the wagon and oxen would be carried away by the river.

For a moment she looked at him with none of the hostility she usually showed, but when she spoke there was the usual belligerence in her voice. 'I'm not tempting fate by risking my death of cold in these wet clothes. You'd better come in the wagon, too.'

Turning, she crawled inside. Climbing up to the seat, Adam followed her.

Nell was on her knees, rummaging through a roughwood box of clothes when Adam crawled past her. He headed for the damp provisions at the rear of the wagon, where he had lost his knife.

'You'd better get out of those wet things.' Nell held out trousers and a shirt. 'They belong to my brother-in-law. You've saved his wagon and all his possessions. He'll not begrudge you them.'

'It's still raining. I'll go and see what's happened to the other wagons before changing into dry clothes.'

She shrugged and threw the clothing back inside the box. 'Please yourself, but I'm not staying in wet clothes a moment longer.' Lifting her dress awkwardly, she worked it up over her head and dropped it in a sodden mass on a box. Slipping the straps of the equally wet petticoat off her shoulders, she worked it down to her waist.

Nell Plunkett had a beautiful body. Her breasts were round and firm, and it was doubtful if she carried an ounce of excess fat anywhere. With a start of surprise, Adam realised she was a very attractive girl.

She shook out her dark-red hair and was reaching for a rough cotton towel when she looked up and saw Adam's eyes upon her. The hand froze in mid-air as his eyes held hers, and the other hand went up to her breasts. For some moments neither spoke. Then, in a deliberate gesture, she picked up the towel and began drying her hair.

In a quiet tone that might have been regarded as teasing had she been any other girl, Nell said: 'You'll not be telling me you haven't seen a woman's body before, Adam Rashleigh? *I* know better.'

Ignoring the allusion to Peggy Dooley, Adam said: 'I haven't seen *your* body before.' His mouth felt uncomfortably dry, but there were voices outside now, calling from wagon to wagon, enquiring whether all was well with the occupants. It was time to be going.

His rifle lay to one side of Nell, but as he made a move to retrieve it she lifted her wet petticoat and her hand flew to the empty sheath on her thigh.

Adam smiled. 'Is this what you're looking for?' He handed her the small knife with which he had cut the heavy draw-rope. 'Don't use it on me before I've picked up my rifle.'

He leaned forward and took up the gun, his eyes only inches from her nakedness. Slowly and deliberately she slipped the knife back inside its sheath and allowed her wet petticoat to drop back in place over her leg.

85

'I despise arrogant men, Adam Rashleigh – arrogant Englishmen most of all. You've put the Plunkett family under an obligation to you today. I won't rest until it's repaid – but I don't pay debts with my body.'

'Keep it hidden away and you won't need to explain that you're not putting it on offer.'

'You're a despicable Englishman, Adam Rashleigh.'

'I'll accept that as a "thank you".' Adam's grin served to fuel Nell's anger. Ignoring her now, he untied the flap at the rear of the wagon. Pulling his horse towards him, he freed the rein and swung into the saddle.

CHAPTER EIGHT

'MOTHER MARY! What kind of country is this we've come to, Adam? One day it rains as though the Lord's pulled the bung on heaven, then for a week there's not a cloud to be seen. This sun's hot enough to roast a pig.' Caleb Ryan drew a damp forearm across his glistening forehead and turned a red and peeling face towards Adam. 'Look at the land about us. It's so dry it might not have rained here for months.'

'It probably hasn't.' Eli leaned on the high pommel of his saddle and looked down at the Irishman from beneath the shade of his wide-brimmed hat. 'You can watch a storm cutting across these plains, beating everything down in its path. Yet, only ten feet on either side, plants will be dying for lack of water. Up in the high country a man on a fast horse can pick his way through a whole mess of storms without once getting himself wet.'

'You know Texas well, Eli.' Adam made it a statement, not a question. Stripped to the waist, he had been operating a pair of hand bellows for one of the immigrants, who was a skilled farrier. Both Eli's horse and his own had been in need of shoeing.

'I know it well enough. As far west as Apache country, that is. I'd have travelled farther, but the Apache are meaner than Comanche. They won't give a white man time to explain himself. They start killing him just as soon as they set eyes on him.'

'I thought all Indians would do the same.'

'That's a mistake made by most folk who don't know Indians – and by a hell of a lot of those who think they do. You might as well say that an Englishman is the same as a Spaniard, or a Frenchman, Dutchman, or Italian. Indian tribes don't just have different names, they're different nations, each with its own language and customs. You'll find good and bad Indians in each tribe. They're people, just the same as you find anywhere else.'

'It seems to me a lot of men in Texas wouldn't agree with you.'

'Most have never *seen* an Indian,' retorted Eli. 'They wouldn't know an Apache from a Seminole. Not that I give a damn who goes along with my thinking, or who doesn't. I'm not figuring on standing for Congress. I just tell things the way I see them.'

'I'd like to come with you when you next go out looking for Indians,' said Adam seriously.

'I don't go looking for 'em. I travel through their country and they usually find me. What they do then depends pretty much on which tribe they are. Mind you, there was a time when any Indian would be curious enough to want to talk to you, even if he came back later with his friends and tried to scalp you. These days they've met so many white men whose first words were either "Missed" or "Got him" that they're not so inclined to chat as they were. But what's all this talk of coming with me? I thought you and Nell would be all fixed up by now.'

One of the immigrant men had seen Adam leaving Nell's wagon after the storm – and he had also seen Nell, half-naked in the wagon behind him.

'Take no notice of him, Adam, my son.' Caleb Ryan took the matter no more seriously than Eli. 'You could do worse than to choose an Irish girl – and we've no shortage of them right here on this wagon train. Take little Kathie Rafferty now, as sweet a girl as ever walked this earth. Sure, she's cross-eyed and carries a lot of extra weight, but she's a nice girl, for all that. Would you like me to put a word in there for you? Mind you, you'd do better by going down on your knees and asking the Lord himself to put your case to her. He's closer to her than any of us down here.'

An extremely plain girl, the sixteen-year-old Kathie Rafferty was shy to the point of imbecility in the company of men. She carried a bible with her at all times, reading it whenever a spare moment occurred. Completely out of place in the rough, makeshift frontier world of the settler, Kathie should have installed in the safe, cloistered world of a European convent before her parents set off to find a new life in Texas.

'I don't think Kathie's the one for Adam. I'd say Nell is definitely Adam's type.' Eli addressed his words to Caleb Ryan.

'Ah, you're right, of course. There's fire in that girl. Mind you, I'd say she has a mind of her own.'

'Maybe, but I hear she'll let you examine the goods before you buy. There's no fairer trading than that!'

Mustering far more dignity than the comments called for, Adam said: 'I thought it was only Tennesseeans who were supposed to be able to grin a raccoon out of a tree. You'd both better watch your heads when we reach the forests.'

Adam led his horse away with the whoops of Eli and the others ringing in his ears. A week had passed since the storm, and Adam had spent much of the time hunting. At last the monotonous, flat country had given way to low, rolling hills, with more trees than there had been before. Game was plentiful, but there were many mouths to be fed.

In the evenings, Adam had begun teaching young Philippe to

shoot. The boy's enthusiasm and Adam's proven skill had finally overcome the misgivings of Dona Antonia. Now, when she watched them together, she was forced to admit to herself that her crippled son was happier than she had ever seen him. For this she would always be grateful to Adam.

His hunting trips gave Adam the opportunity to gauge the feeling of the ordinary Mexicans employed by Don Manuel about the changes that had taken place in Texas in recent years. Adam hoped such opinions might be of some help to Lord Palmerston in formulating his future policy towards Texas.

The opinions differed little, although some men were more guarded than others when they spoke to the English friend of their *patron*. All agreed there was now a direction in their land, an end to years of stagnation and uncertainty; but the Mexicans were resentful of the manner in which the declaration of a republic had been made. Most thought it displayed gross ingratitude for the Mexican government's generosity in granting the Americans lands in Texas in the first place. They also resented the certainty that, with the exception of one or two great landowners like Don Manuel, the Texan Mexican was destined to become a second-class citizen in the land of his birth. Nevertheless, they were unanimous that Mexico possessed neither the means nor the will to win back the vast new republic.

Twelve days after leaving Velasco, the wagon-train reached the well-rutted trail that linked San Antonio with the ports of Louisiana. There were still a couple of weeks of travel ahead of them, but the immigrants felt they were now within striking distance of their goal. There was a feeling of lightheartedness in the air.

For this reason Eli listened sympathetically to a request from Hec Bowie and some of the settlers when they asked if they could ride to the nearby town of Columbus and buy whisky for a celebration. The wagon train was almost clear of the settled areas now. The possibility of upsetting any of the established and influential settlers was no longer a matter of any consequence. Besides, there was still a long journey ahead of them. The immigrants deserved a break.

Don Manuel provided a light wagon and fast horses to make the return journey to Columbus and bring back all that was needed to ensure the success of the merry-making.

The Mexican landowner knew, as did Eli, that the worst part of the journey was yet to come. Between here and San Antonio there were no well-ordered settlements or plantations. These were all scattered well to the south, along the Guadalupe and

Lavaca Rivers. For the remainder of the journey they were far more likely to encounter Indians than white men. There would be no further opportunity for celebration until they arrived at Don Manuel's San Antonio ranch.

Magnus Bergstrom took the light wagon to Columbus. He was accompanied by two settlers, one being Nell Plunkett's brother-in-law. At the last minute, Dermot Casey, Nell's ten-year-old nephew, persuaded his father to take him along, too. Dermot and Philippe Tolsa had become friendly, and Philippe asked permission to go with him.

On the long wagon-trek, as never before, Dona Antonia had seen her son attempting and enjoying all those things that came naturally to normal, healthy boys. She came within a hair's breadth of giving her consent – but then changed her mind. The men on the light wagon would not understand Philippe's limitations, and she would be unhappy knowing he was with them. Ignoring her son's pleas, she refused.

When the light wagon had gone, the remainder of the slower-moving wagons continued on their way along the trail, making an early camp. When Adam shot a white-tailed deer not far from the camp, it seemed the success of the forthcoming party was assured.

It should have taken the light wagon about two hours to make the return journey to Columbus. When three had passed, the settlers began to grumble about the selfishness of the men who had probably remained in the town to have a few drinks before returning. When three hours became four, the grumbling became concern. Eli rode off to have a talk with Don Manuel. When he returned he sought out Adam.

'Saddle your horse and bring your rifle – loaded ready. You and I are going out to look for Bergstrom and the others.'

'What do you think has happened to them?'

Eli shrugged. 'Could be any number of things. My guess is that they've run into some of those Indians we heard about down-river.'

A combination of fear and excitement accelerated Adam's heartbeat. 'Are we taking some of Don Manuel's men with us?'

'No, They'd be more of a liability than a help. The more of us there are, the more tempting the target – and a wounded man is a responsibility I don't need. I want someone with me I can trust – and someone who can shoot. Don't waste any time, but don't say anything to anyone else. There's no sense in causing a panic until we know for sure what's happened.'

Eli and Adam rode along the trail for about a mile, until the road forked. There was an equal number of wheel-tracks and hoofprints going in each direction.

Pointing to the trail branching off to the left, Eli said: 'That's the way we'll be heading tomorrow. Columbus is the other way.' Pulling on his rein, he headed his horse along the other trail, and Adam followed him. As they rode, Eli's head was never still and he cast frequent glances over his shoulder. Every clump of trees and bushes received a thorough scrutiny. If they were exceptionally close, he rode off the trail to pass around them.

They were approaching one such copse of trees when Eli said softly: 'That's the wagon, up ahead.'

The light vehicle was standing in low scrub, almost hidden from view, about thirty yards from the trees. There was no sign of the horses, or of the three men and the boy who had gone to town.

Adam kneed his horse forward, but Eli leaned over and grabbed the reins before the horse could move off.

'Wait.'

When Adam looked enquiringly at his companion, Eli said: 'Just sit a while. Stay quiet and look and listen.'

The two men sat their horses for a full five minutes. The only sounds Adam heard were the never-ceasing drone of insects, the song of a catbird, and the occasional rattle of harness when one or other of the horses shook its head in protest at the flies bothering eyes and nose.

Eli drew his long rifle from the saddle holster. Following suit, Adam said in a tense whisper: 'Have you heard something?'

'No, but that doesn't mean there aren't Indians around. A Comanche has the patience to out-wait any white man. I'm going up to the wagon now. You'd better wait here, just in case. ...'

'I'll come with you'

'Then I hope you've got a strong stomach.'

They walked their horses forward slowly, the two riders knee to knee, rifles held at the ready. There was no sign of life as they neared the wagons, and Adam said hopefully: 'Perhaps the men aren't here. They might have had an accident and taken the horses on to town.'

'They're here, but I doubt if they're alive. Look up there.' Eli jerked a thumb skywards, without raising his head.

Adam looked upwards and saw a number of large, blunt-winged birds gliding in a lazy spiral above them. There must have been eight or ten of them, the lowest no more than fifty feet above the ground, the highest a descending black dot in the vast blue sky.

'Whoever is over by the wagon hasn't been dead too long, or them buzzards would be on the ground by now.'

Adam tried to cover twice as much ground with his eyes as before, but he could see nothing. Just then, Eli grunted and pulled his horse to a halt.

'You're sure you want to go on?'

Adam was not at all certain, but he nodded. 'Can you see something now?'

'Over by that bush – the big one beyond the wagon.'

Adam looked in the direction indicated by Eli, but it was a while before he could make out the indistinct, pale shape in the shadow of the bush. Only by using his imagination could Adam identify it as a naked body.

They were not far from the bush when Adam's horse suddenly shied and snorted in fright. As the horse backed off, Adam saw why. The animal had almost trampled on the body of Magnus Bergstrom.

The big Swede was stripped naked and lay on his back, arms outstretched, his eyes still registering the terror from which he had long since been released. His face had been rendered expressionless by the Indian who had removed his scalp with a thorough efficiency, releasing all muscular tension from the skin of his face. The unfortunate Swede had also been horribly mutilated.

The two immigrants had been killed in a similarly gruesome manner, with only minor variations on the brutal mutilation of Bergstrom.

'We'd better get these in the wagon,' said Eli grimly. 'We'll use our own horses to pull it away from here and leave the wagon in the trees back along the road a way. We'll send some of Don Manuel's Mexicans out to bury them. There's no sense in letting any of the others see them looking like this.'

Adam expressed his concern at the plan. Eli had been meticulously careful until now to ensure they would not be surprised by Indians; yet he was now suggesting they hitch their horses to the wagon, thus making escape impossible, should it prove necessary.

'The Comanches are long gone,' said Eli authoritatively. 'They never wait around when they've taken a prisoner. They'll be well on their way home by now.'

'You think they've taken Dermot with them?' Until that moment, Adam had forgotten the boy.

'Sure of it, and with the horses and the scalps they've got it's been a very successful raid for them. A small raiding party would light out before its luck changed.'

'What will they do to Dermot?'

'Bring him up as a Comanche.'

Adam was stung by Eli's apparent indifference to the fate of the boy. 'We can't allow him to grow up a savage! What are we going to do?'

'Right now we're gong to load these bodies into the wagon,' repeated Eli. 'Are you helping me, or are you going to stand there beating your brains out on something we can do nothing about right now? The boy's been taken by Comanches; this is their style. That's *all* we know for certain. The Comanches could be any one of half a dozen bands: Penateka, Tanima, Tanawa – or the Quahadi from the north. The quickest way to commit suicide is to follow them and try to find out. We'll get him back, but we'll need to do it my way. Now, get the other end of this body. . . .'

Helping Eli to load the three dead men into the light wagon, Adam tried unsuccessfully to avoid looking at the mutilations. Talking between clenched teeth, Adam expressed the bitter opinion that perhaps Texans were right. People who committed such atrocities could hardly be considered as human.

To Adam's surprise, Eli rounded on him angrily. 'Do you think it's only Indians who do this sort of thing?' Pulling up a clump of coarse grass, the Tennesseean scrubbed blood from his hand fiercely. 'You've seen the hatband Hec Bowie wears. Do you know what it is?'

Adam shook his head. He had noticed the hatband only in passing. Sun-dried and dirty, it might have been the skin of some desert snake, or a strip of smooth hide from some unknown American animal.

'It's stretched skin, taken from between the legs of an Indian woman.' Eli discarded the bloody grass and strode to his horse. 'You try to think of some "civilised" way Bowie could have got that.'

Backing his reluctant horse to the wagon and its gruesome load, Eli said: 'Some men call me an Indian-lover. I ain't. I've got more reason than most to hate 'em. Yet I don't. I've killed more Indians than a dozen Hec Bowies, but I've killed to stay alive, not for what men like Bowie call "sport". Because I intend to stay alive out here I've set out to try to *understand* Indians. It's not easy, but it's worthwhile. I've yet to meet the man who really understands Indians and still hates them. He'll be horrified, disgusted – revolted even, at times – but he'll never hate 'em, not even at times like this. But I'm talking too much. Let's get this wagon moving. I've got things to do.'

Before the two men had travelled a mile, they met up with a strong force of armed Mexicans, sent out from the camp by Don Manuel. The Mexican landowner was also familiar with the ways of Indians. The men had spades with them.

Leaving the Mexicans to the unenviable task of burying the bodies, Eli and Adam rode on to the camp. Here Eli broke the news of the fate of the three men and the boy to the waiting immigrants. A harrowing howl of grief rose from the relatives. As their friends closed in to comfort them, Hec Bowie tackled Eli. Adam's eyes went to the Texan's hat. The hatband was totally unrecognisable for what it really was, but the thought of its origins filled Adam with loathing for its owner.

'Did Magnus die fighting?'

'No. The Comanches took him and the others alive. That's why I've had them buried out there, instead of bringing them back.'

'Bastard Comanches! Include Rafael and me in the party to go after 'em. Is Tolsa giving us some of his Mexicans?'

'No one's going chasing after any Comanches. There's little chance of getting close to them now. If we did, they'd kill the boy before we had a chance to barter for his release.'

'You're not going to leave him with those savages?'

'No, I'll get him back my way – alive.'

Turning his back on Bowie, Eli took Adam's elbow and led him away from the others. Behind them the wailing reached new heights when the bereaved relatives learned that the dead men were being buried alongside the trail and would not be afforded an elaborate funeral.

'I can't say I go along with these people's idea of sorrowing. Out here grief is a quiet and personal thing. I guess they'll change when they've been living beside death day and night for a while. Right now I need to speak to Don Manuel. Find Caleb and bring him along to Don Manuel's tent.'

Eli and Don Manuel were in deep conversation beside the Tolsas' cooking-fire when Adam and Caleb arrived. A Mexican servant hurried from nearby, carrying cups. Ladling coffee from a large pot hanging over the fire, he handed the cups to Adam and Caleb.

Don Manuel nodded abstractedly at the newcomers and resumed his conversation with Eli.

'Are you quite certain this is the only way to get the boy back?'

'I'm sure only that three men are dead and that the boy has been taken by Comanches.'

Don Manuel lapsed into deep thought for some minutes, and then nodded his head in agreement. 'Very well, I will do as you say. I will take the settlers on to my ranch, to await your return. Caleb will hold himself responsible for their good behaviour.'

By way of explanation to Caleb and Adam, Don Manuel said only: 'Eli is going to try to get the boy back.'

'But you said chasing after the Indians would be suicide – for us and for Dermot Casey.'

'I'm not chasing after any Indians. I'm going to ask Chief Bowles of the Cherokee for his help. General Houston sent him west to speak to the Comanche last year. I'm hoping he'll send one of his Cherokees to find out about the boy, or give me a guide to go to Comanche country myself.'

'When do we leave?'

'*I'm* going right away. You'll stay here and help Caleb.'

'*He* doesn't need any help. *You* might.'

Eli shrugged. 'You're a free man. Bring provisions for five days.'

Don Manuel looked sharply at Eli. '*Five* days? It is more than two hundred miles to the village of Chief Bowles, much of it through hostile country.'

'Each extra day is going to be a long one for a small boy who's with the men who murdered his father. The Comanche aren't known for their kindness to prisoners.'

Don Manuel conceded that Eli was right. 'I'll have my men bring you two extra horses. Good luck, Eli. And to you, too, Adam. Our thoughts will be of you.'

Dona Antonia stopped Adam before he left the Tolsa camp. 'Bring the boy back safely, Adam.' Her usual calm manner had been badly shaken by the knowledge that Philippe had so nearly shared the fate of the men on the wagon. Unlike Dermot Casey, he would not have been taken prisoner. The Comanche had no use for a boy with only one good leg. 'Be sure you return safely, too. Philippe has grown very fond of you. His prayers, and mine, will be with you.'

CHAPTER NINE

FOR TWO DAYS Adam and Eli travelled through land occupied by settlers, but by the end of the second day the cabins were more primitive and set farther from each other, the occupants wary of strangers. On the third day even these crude symbols of civilisation were left behind.

Their way took them through countryside that Adam found a confusing mixture of forest and prairie. For hours they would ride in the shadow of towering trees that rose from the forest floor like giant cathedral pillars, their canopies of leaves keeping out the sun and forming a vaulted roof high above them. The air of religious sanctity and peace was heightened by generations of leaves which had fallen to the forest floor, forming a dense carpet that deadened all sounds.

As suddenly as they had entered the forest, they left it behind and came out on open, speargrass prairie, liberally sprinkled with hackberry and yaupon thickets and laced with deep, sandy gullies which had narrow streams and tributaries wandering through them. There were creeks, too, and wide, lazy rivers that divided around low mud flats and wound across the prairie from horizon to far horizon.

The pattern of forest and prairie was repeated a number of times along the journey and once, in the distance, they saw a long line of mounted Indians following the path of a river, heading eastwards across open country. Fortunately, Eli and Adam saw the Indians while they themselves were still in a forest. They did not leave the shelter of the trees until the Indians passed from view. Eli thought they were probably Caddo Indians, and might have been friendly, but in view of their recent experience he was not inclined to put his theory to the test.

On the fifth day of their journey, the two men entered a wide, sparsely wooded valley, and soon the horses were following paths with ever-increasing signs of settlement on either side. Before long they reached a small river that had been crudely but effectively dammed. The water backing off from the dam was channelled to irrigation-ditches, watering fields in which strong late-growing crops were looking healthy.

When Adam expressed surprise at finding such evidence of civilisation here and asked how long Texans had been settled in the area, Eli smiled. 'That's the sort of question I'd have expected *from* a Texan. This is Cherokee country. They built the dam and planted and irrigated the fields. Up ahead is one of their villages. I expect you'll find one or two surprises there, too. Most folks do.'

The village was set among trees from which all the lower branches had been stripped to give the occupants space to walk about. Only the leafy higher branches remained to give plentiful shade.

There must have been at least a hundred houses in the village; they were a mixture of log and adobe cabins, clustered around a large hard-earth square which was itself dominated by a larger building.

As they entered the village, a tall, slim man of about thirty-five came to meet them. His skin was much lighter than Adam had imagined an Indian's would be, his features finely etched. He wore buckskin trousers, a fringed buckskin shirt patterned with small, coloured beads, and a pair of soft moccasins.

Alighting from his horse, Eli greeted the Indian in his own language. The Indian replied in the same tongue and both shook hands warmly. Then, in English, Eli introduced the Indian as Yellow Bear, son of Bowles, Chief of the Texan Cherokee.

In good but unpractised English, Yellow Bear welcomed Adam to the Cherokee village.

'We're here to see Chief Bowles,' explained Eli. 'I'm hoping he may be able to help us.'

Yellow Bear nodded, and a smile made him seem years younger. 'He has known for some hours that you were on your way, but my father has reached an age when he hurries neither for men nor for the Gods. He is dressing for you. While we wait, come and enjoy a coffee at my fire.'

At a signal from Yellow Bear, a young Indian boy, naked from the waist up, came from a crowd of inquisitive youngsters standing nearby and took the reins of the horses. Walking with the soft tread of a woodland Indian, Yellow Bear led the way to a nearby hut. Pointing to two plaited rush mats outside the door, he signalled for them to seat themselves. 'There is a breeze from the east. You will find it cooler here than inside.'

When they were seated, Yellow Bear squatted easily on the ground opposite them. Immediately, a young woman hurried from the hut bearing small bowls half-filled with steaming hot, aromatic coffee.

For some minutes the men spoke together of everyday things – of the weather; of the journey Eli and Adam had just made; of crops; and of hunting. Adam was impressed by the open, easy manner of their host, and by his command of English.

An old woman came around the corner of the hut and said something in the Cherokee language. As Yellow Bear grunted an acknowledgement, Eli rose to his feet. 'Time to move. Chief Bowles is ready to see us.'

Accompanied by Yellow Bear, and led by the old woman who had been sent to fetch them, Adam and Eli skirted the cleared space in the centre of the Cherokee village and came to a large shelter. It was no more than a split-wood roof, supported by a number of stout saplings.

Beneath the shelter, in the centre of a semi-circle of Indians, a very old man sat erect on a cushion of blankets. White-haired and watery-eyed, he had a skin as lined and leathery as that of a turtle. He wore an embroidered deerskin shirt similar to that worn by his son, but his trousers were of good-quality linen. On his head was a silk scarf, wound in the manner of a turban. He also wore a bright silk sash across one shoulder, from which hung a sword. Adam later learned that the sword had been a present from General Houston and was the Cherokee chief's most treasured possession.

This was the Chief Bowles, also known as 'Old Bowl'. Eighty-two years of age, Chief Bowles had witnessed the disastrous decline of his people from a great and widespread nation. Twenty years before, he had led his own small band from the Appalachian Mountains of south-west America to east Texas, having first obtained the approval of the Mexican government. Here he had hoped his people would find a permanent home. Although he was then the 'War' Chief of the Cherokee, he had convinced his people that only by adopting the White Man's mode of life could they hope to survive and retain their identity.

Chief Bowles's peaceful stand had been recently shaken by the refusal of the Texan Congress to ratify the agreement he had made with General Houston two years before. Then Houston had promised to give the Cherokee title to their own lands. This was after the aged chieftain had undertaken a mission to the wild Comanche tribes of the central Texas plains on behalf of the Texan president. Chief Bowles had attempted to negotiate a lasting peace treaty between the Comanche and the newly independent Texas Republic. It had failed, through no fault of the Cherokee peacemaker but because of the intransigence of the warlike Comanche and the appalling record of broken treaties that could be laid at the door of the White Man.

Seated opposite the venerable old Cherokee, Adam thought at

first that Chief Bowles was either very weary or possibly suffering from senile decay. For many minutes the old Indian sat unmoving, with downcast eyes. Then he looked at Adam for perhaps ten seconds and Adam was left feeling that the eyes had probed the recesses of his very soul.

'You have journeyed far?' Chief Bowles spoke in Cherokee, his voice deep and firm.

'We've been riding for five days.' Eli's reply was short and direct.

With Yellow Bear whispering a translation into Adam's ear, Chief Bowles said: 'Then your business will be important, and not to be discussed on an empty stomach. We will eat.'

The old woman who had come to Yellow Bear's house had been waiting. Now she hobbled away, calling orders ahead of her in a shrill, thin voice.

There was a sigh of pleasure from the Indians seated about the Chief and half a dozen conversations were begun. It was always pleasurable to partake of another man's food, especially when that man was a chief and the meal was intended to impress strangers to the village.

'When last we met you were riding with The Raven – President Houston,' Chief Bowles addressed Eli. 'He has sent you to us?'

'No, Chief. I come here seeking a favour.'

Chief Bowles nodded, his expression giving away none of his feelings; but, as Yellow Bear translated, Adam fancied the mood of the men about him had suddenly become one of disappointment.

'My people have not seen you before and your skin has not seen a summer in this land. You come from the north?' Chief Bowles's question was directed at Adam.

'I come from across the sea. From England.'

Adam expected to have to explain his reply further but to his surprise the old chief nodded and his eyes probed Adam's face once more.

'It is many years since I last met an Englishman,' Yellow Bear translated. 'Your people and mine were once friends. Some of us fought the Americans with you – and we lost. Now the Cherokee are treated as a defeated people by all white men. Is it the same with your people also?'

Aware of Eli's amusement, Adam replied: 'No, we put the defeat by the Americans behind us and moved on to conquer new lands and new people.'

'Given good guns we might have done the same. Joined with the Comanche and the Kiowa to conquer Mexico, maybe.' The old chief shrugged. 'It would not have helped. The White Man would have followed us there to claim that Mexico was his land also.'

There was much nodding of heads in the group about Chief Bowles, and Adam saw no one smile.

Just then the old woman returned, ushering four younger women before her. Each was bearing a bowl of steaming stew.

Adam caught no more than a glimpse of the Indian girl who laid the dish before him before Chief Bowles was urging him to eat. The smell from the stew was good, and Adam discovered he was hungry.

'This is delicious. What is it?'

'When you're enjoying Indian food it don't do to enquire too closely into what you're eating.' Eli was not allowing doubts about the food's origin to affect his appetite, but Adam lowered his bowl uncertainly.

A few throaty chuckles from the men seated opposite as they witnessed Adam's discomfiture proved they had heard and understood the brief exchange and Yellow Bear explained it to his father.

'Do not heed the words of your friend, Englishman. He is deliberately confusing our ways with those of our brothers on the plains.' Chief Bowles smiled, advertising the fact that passing years had robbed him of a large percentage of his teeth. 'You are eating a deer that was shot by my son John only yesterday. Eat and enjoy the food.'

As he ate, Adam had the opportunity to observe the men who sat opposite him, and also the women who went among them serving food. Chief Bowles and the woman who appeared to be his senior wife were full-blooded Cherokees. The remainder of the men were a variety of shades and some exhibited European features.

The younger women were equally varied in colouring. Only one was unmistakably full-blooded Indian. This was the girl who had served Adam's meal to him. She wore waist-length hair parted in the centre of her head and tied in long plaits. Hanging over her shoulders, the plaits framed a face with high cheekbones and features more finely chiselled than her companions'. She was taller, too, and moved among the Cherokee headmen with a natural and supple grace that made a man forget he had just completed a gruelling, five-day ride.

Adam was brought back to earth by the arrival of a ceremonial pipe, wrapped in a buffalo-hide pouch. It was handed to Chief Bowles by yet another of his many sons. The pipe had an ornately carved stone bowl and a stem that was decorated with coloured beads and black-tipped feathers.

Lighting the pipe, Chief Bowles blew smoke carefully to the four winds before passing the pipe on. It went from hand to hand in what seemed to be haphazard order, but Adam quickly grasped that a strict protocol was being observed. Adam and Eli were included among the smokers, Eli receiving the pipe first.

When the pipe was eventually returned to him, Chief Bowles laid it carefully on a flat stone by his side. 'Now we will speak of why you have come to our village.'

Sitting cross-legged and comfortable on a blanket, Eli told the Cherokee chief of the arrival of the settlers and of their journey towards the land on which they were to settle. He was careful to mention that President Houston had visited the immigrants in their camp, and then he described the attack that had resulted in the killing of three men and the abduction of young Dermot Casey. When Eli arrived at this point, the Cherokee chief and those about him nodded. Now they knew why the two white men had ridden so far to speak to Chief Bowles.

'The warriors who carried off the boy . . . you saw them?'

'No, but they were Comanche. Quahadi, I'd say, but I couldn't be certain.'

Again Chief Bowles nodded. He knew of Eli's reputation. If he thought the raid had been carried out by the Quahadi band of Comanche, then it was probably so. It made the task of finding the boy very much more difficult. The Quahadi were a far-ranging band, the most nomadic of all Comanche.

'The Quahadi are known to have been raiding the settlements, but they travel far and fast. Who knows where they may be now?'

'I believe they headed for home as soon as they took the boy. It was only a small raiding party. They'd got a prisoner, taken three scalps and stolen three horses. They'd have been well-satisfied.'

Chief Bowles nodded. Eli was right. A small raiding party would have been highly delighted with such success. The Comanches would have returned home as quickly as possible to boast of their 'victory'.

'You want the boy returned to you? How much are you prepared to pay for him?'

'Whatever it takes. His father was one of the men the Comanches killed. He is all his mother has left. But these are poor people. They left their own country because they were starving. They have few possessions.'

When the conversation was translated to him, Adam said

quickly: 'That doesn't matter. Get the boy back and I'll see that his ransom is paid in full.'

Adam's words brought a murmur of interest from the assembled Cherokee council, but Chief Bowles sat deep in silent thought for several minutes.

Eventually, he said to Eli: 'My eldest son, John, knows the Comanche and their lands. He came with me when I travelled seeking peace for The Raven. He will find the boy.'

'I'll go with him,' said Eli immediately.

'No. The Comanche do not welcome white men in their country. They would kill you both. John will go alone. You will stay here until his return.'

'That could be a month!'

'It may be longer if the Quahadi have moved northwards. Does the thought of staying in my village for so long distress you so much?'

'I can think of nowhere I'd rather be – if I didn't have a job to do.'

'You go back to the wagons. I'll stay here and wait for Dermot.' Adam's offer was made on the spur of the moment, but when Eli began to argue he was able to justify the decision.

'Caleb and his people need you, Eli. You're the only one who can take them to where they're going. I'm just along for the ride. I might as well stay here.'

Eli realised that Adam's offer made sound sense. Chief Bowles's son needed first to find the Quahadi Comanche, and then to negotiate for the release of Dermot Casey. It could take a very long time. But Eli was concerned for Adam. He was new to Texas – and new to the ways of Indians. The Cherokee were the most civilised of the American Indian tribes, but they had their strict customs and taboos, too. If Adam, in his ignorance, offended against them, he might land in serious trouble. Eli had heard the Indian girls giggling among themselves about the qualities possessed by the two white visitors. It seemed they found Adam attractive, and this caused Eli more concern than anything else. He knew from his own experience that women were responsible for more trouble between white men and friendly Indians than anything else.

'You are reluctant to leave your friend in my village? Do you think my warriors are Tonkawa cannibals, perhaps, and will eat him?' Chief Bowles spoke slowly and sarcastically, and Eli realised he had offended the Cherokee chief.

'Hell, no. . . .' Eli shook his head at Yellow Bear, signalling for him not to translate his words to Adam. 'He is a young man who

102

does not know the ways of your people. I am concerned he might put the friendship of our peoples at risk.'

Much to Eli's relief, Chief Bowles smiled. 'The Englishman has come to us and smoked our pipe in friendship, knowing less of our ways than the smallest Cherokee child. We do not punish children for their lack of years.' Chief Bowles's smile widened. 'But my hearing is still sharp. I do not think our young women look at him and see a child. Do not fear for him. I will have it known that he is under my special protection. He will come to no harm.'

'Fine. Then, Adam will stay here and wait for John to return. I'll leave for San Antonio in the morning.'

When he finished speaking, Eli heard the excited chatter of the Cherokee girls standing behind him. They had been following the conversation with great interest.

Eli hoped he had not made a wrong decision.

CHAPTER TEN

For a while after Eli had left for San Antonio, Adam was acutely aware that he was a stranger in the Cherokee village. He had been given a hut, and an old woman to cook for him, but the woman spoke no English. She had a ready smile, but it was no compensation for the lack of conversation. He was grateful when Yellow Bear took pity on him and gave him a tour of the Cherokee village and the surrounding lands.

Adam was impressed by the standard of Cherokee husbandry. The fields and gardens were well tended and contained crops of a quality that might have delighted any English gardener. The Indians working the land were mainly women and children, although there were also one or two men in the fields. Adam was most surprised to see a few Negroes working beside them, until Yellow Bear told him that the Cherokees owned a number of slaves.

Inside the village, the Cherokees busied themselves in the manner of any other frontier community. Women scraped and stretched the skins of animals, and made pemmican – the dried meat that travellers found invaluable. They also cooked and cared for their families, and found time to chatter loudly to each other while doing all of these things. Everything in the village appeared to be well ordered and unhurried, and for the first time since leaving England Adam had the feeling of being in a settled and organised community.

It was difficult to equate such an ordered way of life with the low regard in which the Cherokee were held by the Texans.

Later that afternoon, Adam and his guide passed by the hut of Chief Bowles. Seated outside were the girls who had brought food for the men attending the council meeting the previous day. The girl who had served Adam was among them. In the full sunlight, Adam could see that her skin was not so much dark as copper-hued. It was easy to appreciate why the early explorers had given the native inhabitants of the New World the misnomer of 'Red Indians'.

The girl was working with a stone pestle and mortar held between her thighs, crushing corn to make a coarse flour. Adam had come around the side of the hut, so she could not have seen him, yet suddenly, almost as though he had called to her, she raised her head and turned to look at him. There were small beads of perspiration on her forehead and upper lip. Seeing Adam, she smiled suddenly, but before he could return the smile she resumed her work.

The same old woman who had been in charge of the girls on the previous day was standing in the doorway of the hut. Witnessing the exchange of glances between Adam and the girl, she cackled like an old hen and said something to the girl.

Without raising her head, the copper-skinned girl murmured a reply that sent the other girls into peals of amused laughter. Aware that he was the subject of their merriment, Adam walked on. Before he and Yellow Bear passed from view, he looked back and saw that the Indian girl was gazing after him. Raising a hand, he waved. For a moment he saw the smile again, then she bowed over the mortar once more and attacked the corn with renewed vigour.

'It seems you have found favour with my sister.'

Adam bit back a reply that the feeling was a mutual one. Instead, he asked: 'What's her name?'

'A-Gan Tiski Tiskwa.'

Adam blinked at the almost unpronounceable name, and Yellow Bear laughed. 'It means "The Rainbird". We call her Tiski. She is the favourite of my father. He will ask a high price for her.'

Adam chose to ignore the significance of Yellow Bear's remark and changed the subject, asking instead about the miniature rounded huts that resembled igloos, standing outside many of the Cherokee houses. Nevertheless, while Yellow Bear was explaining they were houses in which the family slept during hard winters, Adam's thoughts returned to Yellow Bear's copper-skinned sister.

That night the Cherokees held a dance in the clearing at the centre of the village. Adam realised it was probably being staged for his benefit, but it began so casually it could almost have been spontaneous.

Adam had been invited to eat with Chief Bowles. During the meal Yellow Bear translated stories of the days when Chief Bowles had fought for the British, telling with great pride of the battles in which he had taken part.

The dancing began shortly after the men had enjoyed a meal of roast venison, sweet potatoes and corn-bread. They were squatting outside Chief Bowles's hut drinking bowls of scalding black coffee when suddenly, in the middle of the clearing, a torch was applied to a prepared fire. As the flames quickly soared to the height of the houses surrounding the square, men and women began gathering. Alcoholic drinks were forbidden by Cherokee law, but such an unpopular ordinance was difficult to uphold. Many of the men and some of the women had been drinking. Their loud and uninhibited laughter dominated all other sounds until the music began for the dance.

The music was provided by a number of drummers who dictated the tempo of the dancing, and by a lone flute-player who tried valiantly to make the thin sound of his instrument heard above the din of the drums and the noisy whooping of the young men.

Slowly an ever-growing circle of Cherokees formed about the fire. When it almost filled the square, a second, smaller circle was formed inside them. By now the first circle of dancers had linked hands. Facing inwards they began advancing slowly in time to the music, stamping first one foot and then the other in swaying time with the drums.

The tempo first increased and then slowed again, and some young men broke free of the hands that held them on either side, leaping high in the air, uttering a shrill, high-spirited cry.

Suddenly, someone came between Adam and the dancers. He looked up to see Tiski standing before him. Holding out her hand, she said simply: 'Come.'

There was a sharp intake from near at hand. Glancing quickly about him, Adam saw disapproval on the faces of some of the senior members of the council who occupied their usual evening places at Chief Bowles's fire.

Returning his gaze to the girl who still held out her hand, Adam suddenly knew that his response to her gesture was of importance to Tiski. Reaching up, he took her hand and rose easily to his feet. A moment later they were both running towards the dancers. The circle broke to allow them in and, as Tiski laughed happily, Adam squeezed her hand. She looked at him quickly, then looked away again. Adam thought he might have unwittingly offended her, but a moment later the happiness returned as they advanced upon the men and women of the inner circle. Adam found himself facing a light-skinned Cherokee girl of obvious mixed blood. As she smiled at him with an invitation that crossed all language-barriers, Tiski tugged his hand. Their circle began to move around the fire, and a moment later the coquettish girl was gone.

The atmosphere of the dance was one of excitement, but it went on orderly enough for a while. The memory of the music, the blazing fire, the heat and the dust, the swaying, stomping Indians, and the slim, warm hand held firmly in his own would remain with Adam for ever. He wondered what had prompted Tiski to ask him to dance. Once or twice he knew she was looking at him, studying his face, but whenever he turned towards her she always looked elsewhere. Twice he leaned towards her, speaking her name, but each time she shook her head and danced with renewed vigour.

As the evening progressed, the atmosphere in the square underwent a subtle change. The singing, chanting and dancing went on, but most of the voices now were those of the women who stood around the edge of the square and there were many more men than women dancing.

Hardly had Adam made the observation than he felt a pressure on his hand. His dancing partner led him away from the circle of dancers and guided him back to his place outside the hut of Chief Bowles. Without a word of goodbye, she turned away and disappeared inside the hut.

There were fewer men of the Cherokee council about the fire now. Many of Chief Bowles's friends had retired to their blankets at the first opportunity. They were old men. The excitement of the dance stirred memories of younger days, but the blood no longer ran hot, and night breezes were notorious for chilling old bones.

The faces of those who remained, Yellow Bear among them, showed the same division of pleasure and disapproval as before, but Chief Bowles welcomed Adam's return with a smile.

'Now you have taken part in the dance, Englishman, you will always be part-Cherokee.'

Yellow Bear translated his father's words. Adam, flushed by his recent exertions, replied: 'I can think of many worse things to be.' As he talked, Adam was looking towards the Chief's hut, hoping his late dancing partner would reappear.

'You were wise to stop dancing. Our young men are becoming excited. Soon they will begin to sing of the glories of past battles. They will become warriors, for a while. A white face might provoke feelings that have no place among friends. It is better for you to go to your hut now.'

It was a dismissal, but Adam felt no resentment. Chief Bowles was right to be concerned. The young men had been drinking, some of them heavily. Even so, Adam knew he was safer here than a Cherokee would be at a Texan village celebration.

When Adam still hesitated, Yellow Bear said softly: 'My sister has gone to her blanket. It is time you went, too.'

Adam turned to leave, but Chief Bowles reached up to him. 'Wait. It is time I slept. Unless you are young the night is best spent in sleeping. Come, you are young and strong. Give me your arm.'

Leaning heavily on Adam, Chief Bowles waved away Yellow Bear when he would have followed. At the doorway of his hut, Chief Bowles reached out to detain Adam before he could walk away.

'You speak Spanish?' The Cherokee chief spoke the language well, and Adam nodded.

'You have made no arrangement to see my daughter again tonight?'

Even as the Chief spoke, Adam saw a young Cherokee couple leave the diminishing circle of dancers and slip away into the darkness of the trees beyond the firelight.

'We have made no arrangement.'

The grip on Adam's arm relaxed. 'Good. She has taken your hand in the dance, and her feelings and needs are those of any young girl – but she is not as they are. Seek out those young widows and divorced women who look long upon you, Englishman. Yellow Bear will point them out to you. Should you share your blanket with them, my people will be happy for you. It is not good for a man to sleep alone.'

Sleep was slow in coming to Adam that night. In the square, the dancing went on until the first rays of the morning sun struck false life into the ashes of the celebration fire. The singing that accompanied the dancing became increasingly discordant as more illicit whisky disappeared down the throats of the Indians. But it was none of these sounds that kept Adam awake. He was thinking of Chief Bowles's daughter, and of the intriguing words of the Cherokee chief.

When Adam did fall asleep, it was to dream of walking through the streets of London, hand in hand with a girl whose skin reflected the colour of the copper beeches in the Royal Park of St James.

Two days later, Adam took a walk along the river bank, downstream from the village – and here he saw Tiski again. She was one of a number of Indian women kneeling by the river bank, kneading and pounding the clothes they were washing. Unobserved at first, Adam watched for a long time as the girl worked at her task, skirt rolled up to her thighs, chatting and laughing with the others.

Not until two of the women completed their laundering and rose to go was Adam spotted. Immediately, the eyes of every Indian girl except one turned in his direction and there was a moment of consternation. Then one of the women said something to make the others laugh and they relaxed. The two women who were standing picked up their baskets of laundry and set off along the path that led to the village.

Passing Adam, both women smiled at him, showing even, white teeth. A few paces on, one of them called over her shoulder in rapid Cherokee and raised another laugh. A few minutes later all but two of the remaining women had completed their laundry and carried their baskets of wet clothes along the path, past Adam.

One of the two remaining women was Tiski.

Adam stood by the path for some time. Every few moments the girl working beside Tiski raised her head to look at him. When he finally left the shelter of the trees and began walking towards them, his movements were immediately reported with great excitement.

Still Tiski did not look in his direction, although she spoke at some length to the other girl. Adam could see uncertainty on the face of the girl who had been keeping him under observation. Then Tiski said something very quietly. Although she was turned away from him, Adam sensed her determination and authority. The other girl hastily threw her wet washing in a basket. Snatching it up, she fled towards the village without looking at Adam as she passed him by.

Adam walked to where Tiski kneeled on the river bank and stood beside her for a full minute while she kneaded a grey blanket that looked as though it had once been army issue. When she did not acknowledge his presence, Adam coughed noisily to clear his throat, but suddenly found himself tongue-tied.

'You should take a drink of water from the river. It is very good for a tickle in the throat.'

The words were spoken in a soft and gentle voice, but it was Tiski's command of English that took Adam completely by surprise.

Suddenly she looked up at him and he saw that she was trying very hard not to suppress a laugh. He saw, too, that she possessed remarkable eyes that were more tawny than brown.

'We both seem to be having trouble. I can't find the voice to speak to you – and your eyes don't seem to be able to see me when I'm near.'

Bowing her head over the washing, she said quietly: 'I saw you, Englishman. I saw you standing beneath the trees before the others knew you were there.'

109

'My name is Adam.' For some extraordinary reason, Adam felt strangely awkward in this girl's presence.

'Adam . . . Adam,' she repeated the name twice. 'That is a nice name. Your bible says it is the name of the first white man.' Looking up at him, she asked: 'You are surprised I know of him? For many years there was a trading post along the river from here. The man and his wife were Quakers. The trader's wife taught me for two years, until they both died of smallpox.'

'Can I call you Tiski? Yellow Bear told me your full name, but I won't attempt to pronounce it.'

'Tiski is easier,' she agreed. Smiling up at him once more, she asked: 'But why should you ask Yellow Bear my name?'

Adam countered her question with one of his own: 'Why did you choose me for the dance?'

'You are my father's guest. It is a daughter's duty to make a guest feel welcome.' Suddenly it seemed that her washing had assumed great importance to her.

'I was given the impression that your father doesn't entirely agree with you.'

'He spoke of me to you? What did he say?' Once more the washing lay forgotten, half-in, half-out of the river.

'No more than any father who loves his daughter.'

'I am the daughter of his heart only. His blood and mine are not the same.'

'I don't understand.'

'I am Kiowa. Many years ago there was a bad season. The rains failed and the buffalo did not come south. My people were forced to travel far and hunt new lands. They came here, to Cherokee country. But the Cherokee were suffering, too. They had no food to spare for others. The Kiowa and Cherokee fought each other. In one battle the Cherokee beat the Kiowa and I was captured. I was brought to Chief Bowles's village. As I rode in it began to rain. It was the first rain that had been seen for many seasons. Chief Bowles said it was a good omen. I was named "The Rainbird", and he adopted me into his family. He has been a good father to me, but the Cherokee are not my people.'

Tiski began gathering up the washing.

'Must you go just yet?'

Tiski gave Adam another of her warm smiles. 'Yes. Tahnay, my Cherokee mother, is a wise woman. She knows how much washing I brought to the river and she will have seen the others return. She will ask why I am not with them. They will say I am here with you.'

Remembering how concerned the aged Chief Bowles had been

for his adopted daughter, Adam said hastily: 'Then you'd better return to the village right away. I don't want you getting into any trouble because of me.'

Wringing out the last of her clothes and throwing them in the basket, Tiski stood up to go. 'Tahnay is also a very *understanding* mother. She will not come seeking me until we have had time to speak together, you and I.'

'Then I'll carry this for you until we reach the village.' Adam picked up the basket and they began to walk slowly along the path towards the village. They had gone only a few paces when Tiski stopped and looked out across the river. Beyond the deep, green waters, brought to life by the late-morning sun, a well-treed island provided shade for a motionless blue-backed heron, standing hopefully at the water's edge. Beyond the island the forest stretched to the distant hills. Thin columns of tell-tale smoke showed that the Cherokees had carried their flourishing husbandry beyond the river.

'Look, Adam, is this not a beautiful land?'

When Adam agreed it was, she continued: 'It is very different from the lands of the Kiowa. It is beautiful there, too, but in a harsh and cruel way. The land, like my people, needs to fight hard to survive. Here there is peace. It is a peace that has been passed on to the Cherokee people. The Cherokee women do not tremble when their men are away from home, wondering whether they will ever see them alive again.'

With her back to Adam, she asked: 'Is your land like this? Or is it like the lands of the Kiowa?'

Adam thought of London. Of its bustling streets and crowded markets; the carriages and fashion-conscious men and women; the backstreets and dark, menacing alleyways; pickpockets and footpads; thugs and gin-parlours. Its glittering salons and filthy, disease-ridden prisons; the palaces of its queen and its bishops, and the broken-down squalor of the hovels on the eastern outskirts of the city. Adam had seen all these things as one of Robert Peel's detectives. But how did he begin to describe them to a young, unsophisticated Indian girl living here, in the heart of a Texas forest?

'My country is much smaller than yours, Tiski, but there are towns where each house touches the next for as far as you can see.'

They began walking again and Tiski frowned as she tried to imagine such a place. 'I do not think I would enjoy living there. . . .' She paused. 'Do your women worry when their men are far from home, as you are?'

With a sense of delight, Adam realised Tiski was being coy.

'Only when they go off to war, but I have no one to worry about me.'

Tiski had been watching his face and was happy with what she saw there, but still she persisted: 'What of the child carried off by the Comanche? What is he to you?'

By the time Adam had finished telling her of the voyage from England, and of the settlers he was accompanying to their new lands, they had reached the village. Here Tiski took the basket from him.

'If John finds the child and you return him to his mother, will you make your home with his people?'

'I don't know. I haven't thought about it very much.'

'It is not unknown for a white man to settle among the Cherokee. The Raven – General Houston – enjoys coming to see Chief Bowles. He lived with the Cherokee people in the north for some years. I have heard it said he has a wife there still.'

'Are you suggesting I come to live here?'

There was a strange expression on Tiski's face as she said: 'You have agreed you think it beautiful. Would it be so bad?'

Adam looked eastwards from the river, across the lush green of the Cherokee cornfields, to where some of the older boys grazed cattle on a pasture carved from the forest. It was difficult to believe this was beyond the frontiers of recognised civilisation. It would not be a bad life – but he had work to do for Lord Palmerston. He had also seen the bustle and growth to the east, where the plantations were spreading out from the Brazos River. The immigrant train from Velasco was just one of many. White settlers were moving westwards. When they reached the Cherokees' haven the Indian way of life would be at an end. Adam had seen and heard what the new Texans thought of Indians.

He said nothing of this to Tiski. Instead, he asked: 'Would it make you happy if I were to make my home here?' Adam awaited her answer, but it never came. There was an angry hail from the village and the young couple looked up to see the solid figure of Tahnay, principal wife of the aged Chief Bowles, advancing determinedly along the path towards them.

The heavily built old woman was not used to hurrying. By the time she reached Adam and Tiski she was blowing like a winded horse. Twice she raised a finger to admonish Tiski, but when she opened her mouth words would not come. The third attempt was more successful. As her voice gathered strength, she gave Tiski a tongue-lashing that needed no translation.

Tiski stood before her adoptive mother, eyes downcast, saying nothing.

'Tiski. . . . Tell her it was my fault, that I kept you talking at the river.'

At the sound of Adam's voice, Tahnay gave Tiski a respite and rounded on him. Resting her knuckles on well-padded hips, she gave Adam a shrill-voiced dressing-down that would have drawn applause from the notoriously caustic-tongued women of London's Billingsgate fish-market. For Adam, much of the sting was removed from the tirade by the sight of Tiski standing behind Tahnay, her eyes laughing at him over the Cherokee woman's shoulder.

Doing his best to appear suitably chastened, Adam said to Tiski: 'Tell her I am sorry I kept you talking at the river . . . but I'm not saying it won't happen again.'

Trying hard to keep the delight she felt from showing on her face, Tiski translated at least part of what Adam had said.

Tahnay appeared slightly mollified, but she snapped a tight-lipped reply to Tiski, her gaze not shifting from Adam's face.

'She says if you were a Cherokee she would take you by the ear and lead you to your father to demand that he teach you how to behave with unmarried girls. However, as you are a guest of Chief Bowles and do not know our ways, she accepts your apology. Do not worry, Adam. Tahnay's tongue speaks only for the ears of others. If she said nothing of this, she fears my reputation would suffer. You see, white men have been to our village before. . . .' Suddenly Tiski smiled. 'I did not tell her you might meet me again at the river, but I will be there at the same time tomorrow. . . .'

Tahnay was no fool. She was watching Adam closely and quickly realised that Tiski had translated far more than had been said. Her voice rose again. Firmly grasping the arm of her adopted daughter, she propelled her along the path towards Chief Bowles's hut. Adam thought he caught the name of the Chief among Tahnay's words to Tiski. He remembered the warning he had received from the Cherokee chief the previous evening.

'Wait!'

Both women turned, and Adam hurried after them.

'Tell Tahnay to leave it to me to explain this to your father. It will be better.'

Tiski explained his request to Tahnay, and the anger left the Chief's wife. When she spoke again her face was expressionless and her voice quieter.

'My Cherokee mother says that Chief Bowles is the leader of the Cherokee people. He has more important things to think about than the actions of a foolish daughter. You will say *nothing* of this matter to him – and neither will Tahnay.'

Tiski gave him a warm smile. 'I told you it was her tongue speaking and not her heart. She likes you, Adam.'

CHAPTER ELEVEN

THE MEETING by the side of the river never took place. That same evening, when cooking-pots were bubbling over the fires of the Cherokee village, a young Wichita Indian boy, close to exhaustion, staggered into the village of Chief Bowles and was brought to the Chief's fire.

When a bowl of food was fetched and placed before him the boy ate ravenously. No more than fifteen years of age, he was short and stocky and much darker skinned than the Cherokees who surrounded him. Tattoo lines extended across his eyelids, and back from the corners of each eye. The backs of his hands were tattooed, too, but the design was obscured by so much dirt and dust that Adam was unable to make it out properly.

When he had wolfed down the bowl of food and belched appreciatively, a second was brought for him. Before he was allowed to resume eating, one of the men at Chief Bowles's fire spoke to him. The Wichita boy replied in sign language. Putting both hands on his head with fists clenched, he raised both forefingers to indicate curved horns. The sign caused a great stir among those who watched.

Amid the ensuing hubbub, the boy snatched up the bowl of food and answered questions either in guttural monosyllables between mouthfuls, or with hurried signs. More and more men joined the circle about the fire. As the excitement grew, men began to look towards Chief Bowles. The old Cherokee chief remained silent. He was well aware that the men of his village were awaiting a decision from him, but he was far too experienced to be hurried. When he did finally speak, it was to the Wichita boy.

For the first time since his arrival in the village, the boy showed some respect. Putting down the bowl he hastily swallowed the food in his mouth and answered Chief Bowles at great length, his speech elaborately supplemented by sign language. At one point something he said provoked a gasp from his listeners, followed by an 'Ah!' from many throats when Chief Bowles had him repeat his words.

When the boy finished talking, the Cherokee chief nodded permission for him to take up the bowl and finish his food. For a few more minutes there was a buzz of excited talk about the camp-fire. Adam could see there was a vast gathering of younger men and women in the dusk beyond the camp-fire. Gradually, the chatter died away. All eyes were upon Chief Bowles, an air of great expectancy hanging on the air.

For a long time the Cherokee chief said nothing, and Adam was aware of the noise made by the eating Wichita boy. Eventually the boy, too, became aware of the silence about him and stopped chewing, looking about him self-consciously.

Not until now did Chief Bowles speak. Calling out the names of some of his younger men, he gave orders, using his guttural words economically. Seven or eight men were sent away before the old chief signalled for two of his companions to help him to his feet. When he was standing he looked about him before moving off to the seclusion of his hut.

As the aged chief retired to bed, the Cherokee village erupted in a cacophony of whooping, ululating and cries of enthusiasm that far surpassed the excitement Adam had witnessed at the dance.

It was some minutes before Adam was able to reach Yellow Bear to learn what was happening.

Chief Bowles's son was as excited as his fellow-Cherokees. 'The boy is a Wichita, from the edge of the great plains. He brings word from my brother, John. On his way to the Comanche country he sighted a herd of many buffalo, two days' fast ride from here. We leave for the hunt at first light. It is many years since the buffalo last came so close – so long that for many young men this will be their first hunt. You are lucky, Englishman. Soon you will see Cherokee warriors at their best – hunting the beast that once provided for all the needs of our people.'

'If it's two days' fast ride, how did the boy get here so quickly? He arrived on foot.'

'He has done well. My brother promised the boy that if he reached us in time he would be given a horse. His people are few, and very poor. To bring a horse into his family a boy such as this one would be happy to run until he dropped.'

The Cherokee village was filled with noise and bustle long before the sun blinked at the world from beyond the eastern horizon. For perhaps half an hour Adam lay on the soft leather-thong bed in the darkness, listening to the sounds outside. He found himself wondering what part Tiski was taking in the activity. He had thought about her before going to sleep, too. Somehow he could not put the image of her high-cheekboned face and tawny eyes out of his mind. He found himself slipping into impossible fantasies about her – wild exercises far removed from the task given to him by Lord Palmerston.

His very presence here in the Cherokee village would take a great deal of explaining to the hard-headed Foreign Secretary who was footing all Adam's expenses. Adam thought he could explain the excursion in his next report as being necessary for 'urgent humanitarian reasons', the return of Dermot Casey being of immediate importance. However, Adam believed the British Minister would be no more understanding about a romantic involvement with Tiski than would Chief Bowles. Adam also knew that neither Lord Palmerston nor the Cherokee chief – nor common sense – would prevail when Tiski looked at him again.

When Adam could see the first light of dawn around the blanket hanging at the doorway of the hut, he threw off the bedding and washed in readiness to face whatever the day had to bring.

Outside, the grey morning light revealed a scene that was busier than any Adam had witnessed since his arrival. Cherokees, horses and dogs were everywhere. Many of the horses were drawing travoises, a form of load-carrying frame adopted from the Indians of the plains. Two long poles were crossed and tied behind a horse's neck and secured with strips of rawhide. The long ends of the pole dragged on the ground behind the horse, kept in place by a cross-piece. Behind this cross-piece was a platform to which was secured all the cooking-pots, household goods and blankets needed by a family on a hunting trip such as was about to be undertaken. Some of the travoises were fitted with a wickerwork frame resembling a cage. Inside this would travel the small children, secure against bumps and spills.

There were more Indians than usual about the village. Adam guessed correctly that the men he had heard receiving their instructions from Chief Bowles the previous evening had been sent to surrounding Cherokee villages to bring men together for the hunt.

His breakfast consisted of scalding coffee and rough corn-bread. Adam was left feeling he was lucky to get this. Every able-bodied man and woman was going on the hunt, together with most of the children. Only the old men and women would remain in the village to tend the fields.

One old man who would not be left behind was Chief Bowles. In his eighty-third year, he was already up and about, inspecting the bows, arrows and lances of the young experienced hunters, giving them the benefit of his wisdom and long experience of the hunt. He would be riding with his people. He would not be one of the hunters, of course, but they all knew he would stay close enough to see who did well, and who fell short of the high Cherokee standards. Chief Bowles would also act as adjudicator, should disputes arise over the ownership of a felled buffalo.

By an hour after sunrise, the first of the Indians were on the move, fifty warriors providing the vanguard. Next came the women riding the horses drawing travoises. Many of them carried young babies in their arms, snug inside hide cradleboards. Behind them on the travois, some had two or three more children, secure inside their wicker cages.

Adam looked for Tiski but could not see her in the mêlée of horses, travoises, women, children and mounted and armed warriors.

Securing his bedroll behind the saddle of his horse, Adam slung saddlebags containing shot and powder on the horse's back before checking his guns and mounting. He was to ride with Yellow Bear. Chief Bowles's son had told him to stay close until the Cherokees had grown used to seeing a white man riding with them. Many of the hunters had been called in from outlying villages and family units. Not all were well disposed towards white men. A few had ridden with Comanches on their raids into Texan settlements. They had taken white scalps. It was necessary for these warriors to accept that Adam was travelling under the protection of Chief Bowles.

There was little order to the progress of the buffalo-hunting party. The two hundred or so warriors rode ahead or behind the column, seemingly as the mood took them. In between were probably another three hundred horses bearing women, children and provisions. The whole party cut a broad track westwards.

They forded two rivers that day, each crossing being so chaotic that Adam was amazed no children were lost. In spite of this they made excellent progress. That evening they camped among a forest of widely spaced oaks after a day spent crossing lush grassland.

While the women made shelters from brushwood, long grass and blankets, Adam and Yellow Bear, together with a dozen other Cherokees who had brought firearms, went off seeking game. They did not need to travel far from the camp. This was an area rarely visited by men. Game was both plentiful and unafraid.

With the aid of his long rifle, Adam was able to shoot and kill three white-tailed deer, each with a single shot, while the Cherokees were still debating the best means of stalking the beasts. These shots alone were sufficient to establish Adam's skill as a hunter.

Then, on the way back to the camp, Adam shot and killed a fat black bear while it was running from a clump of undergrowth to the shelter of a rocky outcrop. The bear was moving fast, and the Indians never even had time to prime their older rifles before Adam downed his quarry. This kill assured him of a place in the camp-fire tales of the Cherokee hunters for many years to come.

Back at the woodland camp, Adam found to his surprise that a brush wickiup had been prepared for him, his bedroll neatly laid out on a bed of long grass inside the flimsy shelter. His surprise turned to delight when he learned that the shelter had been provided for him by Tiski.

Adam found an opportunity to thank her while she prepared parts of one of the deer for cooking on a spit over the fire.

'It is good that I have given you pleasure,' said Tiski. 'But there are many others who would do as much – or more – for you. It has been seen that you are a good hunter. The family of any girl who shared your blanket would never go hungry.'

Tiski spoke the truth. She knew from the chatter of the other women that there were many who would share Adam's blanket, given the opportunity. The Cherokee had a very free-and-easy attitude towards marriages, or other 'arrangements' made between a man and a woman. A girl's first marriage was attended by some ceremony, and usually accompanied by gifts from the bridegroom, but many marriages were of only short duration, and the tribe paid no attention to the liaisons of a divorced woman. Tiski, however, laboured under a double handicap. She had not yet been married – and she was the adopted daughter of the chief of the Cherokees. Anything she did was observed and commented upon and might bring discredit upon Chief Bowles. She was aware of all these things, and the knowledge made her unhappy. Adam would not wait for her for ever.

'It would please me if you could prepare my wickiup each night.'

Tiski nodded without looking up. At the fire, Quaty, Yellow Bear's wife, said nothing. She had been listening to the conversation and knew just how much Adam's request meant to Tiski. Tahnay was too old to come on the hunting trip so, as the wife of her son, Quaty was in charge of Chief Bowles's household. But Quaty was still a young woman and very happy with her own husband. Tiski would find her a very sympathetic chaperon.

The next day Adam rode with Yellow Bear and the Wichita

boy, ahead of the main body of Cherokees. For some fifteen miles they picked their way carefully through woodland before coming out on grassland that extended twenty more miles. Beyond this they reached timber country once more. But the trees were spread further apart here, the countryside full of bluffs and irregular, broken valleys.

They followed the course of a river along one such valley for a few miles until it opened out in a huge, natural amphitheatre, fringed with trees. Here Yellow Bear decided they would make camp. Sending the Wichita boy back to guide the others to the spot, he set off for the top of a nearby treeless bluff. He made a careful study of the countryside about them. When he was satisfied he climbed down and slaked his thirst from a spring that flowed into the river.

'This is a good spot for a camp, Englishman. But we are nearing Comanche country. There is need to be cautious. We are too many to fear attack, but they would steal our horses and take any women and children who strayed away from the others.'

'I thought the Cherokee and Comanche were at peace.

'No one can be at peace with *all* the Comanches at one time. There are too many small bands, each going its own way. My father tried to bring them together to make a peace for The Raven, but the time is not yet right. The Comanche raid the farms and villages of Mexicans and Americans as they will. Sometimes they lose a warrior or two, most times they do not. They take the scalps of the men, use the women and carry off the children. Why should they want peace? When they have fought the White Man as the Cherokee once fought him, and seen the blood of their young men turn the grass to the colour of a High Plains sunset – then they will want peace. Not before.'

Mounting his horse, Yellow Bear said: 'Come, Englishman. I wish to see if your rifle can keep my people from hunger tonight, too.'

Once again they were in luck. Adam killed a good-sized buck and a wild hog. In addition, he and Yellow Bear killed six turkeys between them.

Looking at the bag, Yellow Bear said: 'We hunt well together. I hope we do as well with the buffalo.'

Touching the large buck with his foot, he said slyly: 'Tiski will be so busy with this she will have no time to make a wickiup for you.'

'Should I give the buck to someone else, then?'

'Not unless you wish to shame Tiski. No, tell her she may give away the meat, keeping only what we need. Then *she* can tell someone else to skin the buck and give her back the hide. That will be all right.'

Adam shook his head. 'I doubt if I'll ever fully understand the ways of your people, Yellow Bear.'

'You will – because you wish to please my sister.'

Adam lifted the saddle from his horse and dropped it to the ground beside the spoils of the hunt. As his horse cropped the long green grass at the river's edge, Adam said: 'I think I could learn to please Tiski all right, but Chief Bowles warned me off in no uncertain terms on the night of the dance.'

Yellow Bear's angular face broke into a smile. 'My father does the same thing to all young men of the village.'

He suddenly became serious. 'There was a time when he hoped to return Tiski to her own people in exchange for their friendship. That was many years ago when Tiski was still small and had not yet captured my father's heart. I have not heard him speak of this for a very long time, although he still uses it as an excuse to keep Tiski by his side.' Laying a friendly hand upon Adam's shoulder, Yellow Bear said: 'Do not despair, Englishman. When a man wants a woman and she wants him, it takes more than a father's warning to keep them apart – even if that father *is* Chief Bowles of the Cherokee. See, he comes now. Do you see a man to strike dread into a lover's heart?'

Along the river's edge, Chief Bowles rode at the head of his people. After two days of steady but mile-consuming riding, the Cherokee chief was looking more like a man of advanced years than at any time since Adam had first met him.

Yellow Bear ran to help his father from the saddle. The proud old chief, aware of his son's concern, refused to dismount until his people had chosen the sites for their cooking-fires, and Yellow Bear had been able to satisfy him that all necessary precautions had been taken against a surprise attack by hostile Indians.

The next morning the Cherokee hunting party was once more on the move at dawn. Adam was disappointed that there had been no opportunity to talk to Tiski during the night stop, but she had been kept busy looking after Chief Bowles. Determined not to allow advancing years to interfere with his duties, he kept those about him busy.

As they followed the river, the broken country gradually gave way to rolling coarse-grass prairie with a mauve-shadowed mountain range in the far distance. Clear of the forest, the sheer space of the plains gave Adam a vague feeling of unease. He would not like to be alone here. There was nowhere for a man to hide.

There was nowhere for a buffalo to hide, either – but there was still no sign of the great herd that had been reported by John. The Cherokee hunters spread out in a long line across the grassland to search for signs, but not until noon did one of the Indians, far out on the seemingly endless grassland, call excitedly to the others. He had found the unmistakable trail of a buffalo herd. Chief Bowles was called and the buffalo wallows examined. Eventually, agreement was reached. The herd had passed through here two days before, heading southwards.

The long column of Cherokees swung in pursuit and gradually spread over an ever-widening area of prairie. The warriors of Chief Bowles harangued the stragglers, urging them to close up on the leaders, but with indifferent success. A woman, mounted on a horse, drawing a travois loaded with three or four children and a variety of household goods, could not match the pace set by an eager and unencumbered warrior mounted on a fit hunting pony.

Late in the afternoon the buffalo were sighted, and Adam felt the thrill enjoyed by countless Indian hunters before him. It was a very large herd, containing upwards of thirty thousand animals.

For this day, establishing contact with the herd was enough. The Cherokee hunters found a spring bubbling from the ground on a hillside, flowing down to a shallow creek. Here they made camp.

The excitement the Indians had shown since they first saw the buffalo dominated the camp. Men sat about camp-fires, listening to the stories told by men who had hunted buffalo before. They were calculated to enhance the skill and bravery of the storytellers, and the buffalo became an animal of giant proportions, great courage and infinite cunning.

The tales were related in the Cherokee language, none of which Adam understood. He was already feeling bored when he saw Tiski pick up a skin bucket at the fringe of the firelight and disappear into the darkness in the direction of the spring. A few moments later Adam also left the fireside and headed towards the gurgling water of the spring.

There was no moon yet in the star-dusty sky, and Adam almost fell over Tiski as she knelt beside the water.

'Is that you, Adam?' Her voice was a whisper.

'Yes. How did you know?'

'I knew you had seen me come for water. I hoped you would follow.'

'You *hoped* . . .?'

'Yes – to talk about tomorrow's hunt. It is the Cherokee way that a buffalo killed by a hunter is skinned and cut up by his woman. You have no woman. Would you like me to do this for you?'

'Yes . . . if you don't mind.'

'It will make me very happy.'

Adam stood beside Tiski for what became an awkward silence, neither knowing what to say next.

'I must return with the water.' Tiski reached down for the bucket.

'No. Wait!' As she straightened up, Adam reached out for her. Gripping her arms, he drew her clumsily towards him. She stood with her body against his and he could feel her trembling. Then his arms went about her and he crushed her body hard against his until the trembling stopped.

For a long time they had no thought of anyone else, until a roar of laughter went up from the men about Chief Bowles's fire as one of the warriors ended a hunting story that was more bawdy than funny.

The sound made Adam start, and Tiski moved in his arms.

'Adam. . . .'

'Sh!' Their faces were close, and now he brought his lips down upon hers. Her mouth was soft and moist, and he kissed her with a controlled gentleness that he found desperately hard to maintain.

When the kiss ended, she kept her face tilted up towards his. In the faint light of the stars he could see her expression of wonderment.

'I have never done that before. Touching each other like that – it is as though you have started a fire inside my body.'

Adam kissed her again, but this time the hard passion would stay bottled inside no longer. Tiski resisted him for a moment, then her hands were on his back and she was pulling him to her.

Suddenly, from somewhere in the real world they had almost forgotten, they both heard a voice calling softly: 'Tiski? Tiski . . . are you there?'

It was Quaty.

Tiski pulled away from Adam hurriedly, grateful for the darkness. She was sure that the passion Adam had aroused in her must be obvious for anyone to see.

'Chief Bowles saw you and the Englishman leave the fire. He sent me to help you bring the water back.'

'It is here.'

Quaty came forward and took the skin bucket from her sister-in-law. 'I will wait for you between here and the fire. Do not be long or we will both be in trouble.'

When Quaty left, Adam tried to take Tiski in his arms again, but she twisted free.

'No, Adam. When I return to the fire I must try to act like a girl who has done no more than fetch water. I can not do that if you put your mouth on mine again.'

She took his hand and tangled her fingers in his. 'There will be other times.'

'Yes.' Adam kept hold of her hand when she tried to pull free. 'I think I've fallen in love with you, Tiski.'

'Hush! Say nothing you might regret when the sun rises. It is enough for now that you want me.'

'Do you want me, too?'

Tiski had to bite back the words that threatened to tumble from her heart. The words that would tell him she was so full of love for him that she felt she would burst.

'I want you, Adam – but the daughter of a chief can not behave as do other girls. Not even if she is only an *adopted* daughter.' Rising on the tips of her toes, she touched his lips with hers, but moved away again before he could take hold of her. 'Come, we must go now.'

They walked hand in hand to where Quaty waited patiently for them. Squeezing Adam's fingers for a last time, Tiski released his hand. 'Good hunting tomorrow – my man.'

Not wanting to return to the fireside so soon after Tiski, Adam flung himself down on the soft grass beside the spring. Lying on his back, hands linked beneath his head, he stared up at the stars and wondered where his life was leading him. He *was* in love with Tiski. Adam knew this. He had known for some time. She loved him, too, he was certain of this now – but what could they possibly do? Chief Bowles had already warned Adam off. Would he still object if he knew how Adam felt about Tiski? Even if Chief Bowles accepted him, how would Adam and Tiski plan their future together? She would be made miserable if he took her to a white settlement. She would never be accepted by the settlers while there were men like Hec Bowie in Texas. Adam could no doubt remain with the Cherokees, but he would never be wholly accepted by them and would live the life of only half a man.

Adam had no idea how long he lay by the spring pondering on

his problems before he became aware of an alien sound. It rose above the bubbling of the water, but was almost lost in the laughter and chatter of the men about the Cherokee fires.

Sitting up, Adam strained to identify the sound. It was a moment or two before he recognised the desperate breathing of two men locked in combat. It came from the place where the horses were tethered, the bridle of each horse tied with a loose knot to a long rope. Standing up, Adam could hear the horses snorting and fidgeting and thought he must have been mistaken. The sound might merely have been a horse. Then he heard it again as a horse whickered in fright. Two men were having a desperate battle among the horses. Wading the small stream, Adam headed for the horses at a run, drawing his revolver as he went.

He had covered no more than half the distance when he heard a sickening thud, followed by the gurgle of a man whose throat had suddenly filled with blood.

The moon had risen clear of the horizon now. It was no more than a quarter moon, but the air was clear and free of cloud. Adam saw an Indian rise from the ground, leaving a crumpled shape behind him.

'Who are you? What are you doing?' As Adam called, the Indian turned towards him. For the first time in his life, Adam found himself facing up to a Plains Indian, the streaks of white paint across his face plainly visible in the moonlight. Visible, too, was the upraised tomahawk in his hand.

Adam fired, but at the last possible moment he hesitated, and aimed low.

The Indian dropped to the ground, then rose again. Crouching low, and obviously in pain, he stumbled away. Adam fired again, more to ensure that the Indian kept going than for any other reason. The shot caused the Indian to change direction. He had been running across the slope, now he went downhill.

The sound of shouting came to Adam from around the Cherokee fires, and warriors came running towards the horses. Among the first to reach the spot was Yellow Bear. In as few words as possible, Adam told him what had happened. Yellow Bear shouted orders towards the camp, and Quaty and a wide-eyed Tiski came running, carrying blazing branches of dead wood. Tiski's eyes found Adam, and he saw her relief before Yellow Bear ordered two of the men to take the torches, sending the women back to the fireside.

The Cherokees pushed their way through the horses to where an Indian lay face down on the ground. When he was turned over, the voices of the warriors rose in a howl of anger. Adam had seen the same collapsed muscles on the faces of Magnus Bergstrom and his Irish companions. The Cherokee had been scalped.

'Did either of your shots hit the man who did this?' Yellow Bear asked Adam fiercely.

'Yes, I hit him in the leg. He made off down that way,' Adam pointed to where he had last seen the raiding Indian.

Yellow Bear rapped out orders to the men holding the torches and they ran off down the slope. There was a whoop of satisfaction from them when one of the Cherokees found blood glistening on the grass. Then the warriors grouped together. Howling loudly, they followed the trail of blood until it led them to the wounded Indian, and the noise of their jubilation reminded Adam of a pack of foxhounds that had just cornered their prey.

Adam made his way slowly back to the fire. Here he found Chief Bowles standing with Yellow Bear.

'You have done well, Englishman,' said the Cherokee chief in Spanish. 'But for you we would have lost our horses. Our hunt would have become a great disaster.'

He said no more because at that moment the Cherokee warriors returned. Two of them were dragging the painted Indian between them. He had been shot in the thigh and the wound was bleeding badly. When his captors released him he slumped painfully to the ground.

'Comanche!' Yellow Bear spat out the word as though it explained everything. He stood before the prisoner and, although Adam could not understand his words, he knew Yellow Bear was questioning the wounded man closely.

The Comanche said nothing, his expressionless gaze fixed upon Chief Bowles. For almost ten minutes the fruitless questioning continued. Then Yellow Bear snatched a gun from one of the Cherokee warriors. It was an ancient flintlock, and Yellow Bear made a great show of checking the powder in the pan.

He again spoke to the Comanche and, by way of a reply, the Indian loosened the cord at the front of his buckskin shirt. Pulling the shirt open, he tapped his bare chest, above the heart.

Yellow Bear looked across to where his father sat watching. Chief Bowles nodded his head. Without another word, Yellow Bear placed the muzzle of the musket on the spot indicated by the Comanche prisoner – and pulled the trigger.

Adam was standing close to Yellow Bear when the cloud of

acrid black smoke cleared. A sound like a sigh escaped from the throats of the watching Cherokees. The Comanche lay on the ground, a dark powder-burn on his chest, framing the hole from which spouted the Indian's lifeblood. The Comanche's eyes were fixed upon Yellow Bear, and twice he tried to raise his head, his mouth opening noiselessly, as though with a belated urge to speak. Then his head fell back and he died.

Adam was horrified by the summary execution, but when he voiced his thoughts to Yellow Bear the Indian bent over the dead Comanche and pulled something from his belt. Thrusting it into Adam's hand, he said: 'Tell your words to the widow of the man who lost this – or to his children. The man was a Comanche, and a would-be thief. His body will be left here as a warning to other Comanches. It is the way.'

Looking down at the object he held in his hand, Adam saw he was holding the gruesome trophy hacked from the head of the Cherokee who had been guarding the horses.

CHAPTER TWELVE

THE FOLLOWING MORNING it was as though the attempt to steal the horses, and the deaths of two men, had never happened. The camp was broken early and the excited hunters set off along the trail of the buffalo herd. When he looked back, Adam saw the spreadeagled figure of the Comanche lying on the grass beside the shallow grave of his Cherokee victim. For some, the hunt had already proven costly.

The Cherokee hunters caught up with the buffalo three hours later. The great herd was grazing over more than a ten-mile stretch of prairie. On a slight rise, overlooking the grazing herd, Chief Bowles discussed tactics for the forthcoming hunt with his warriors. Meanwhile, the women unloaded their travoises in preparation for the hard work to come. Before then they and the children would enjoy a grandstand view of the hunt and the deeds of their menfolk.

Only one woman and her four young children took no part in the hunt preparations. The widow of the lately killed Cherokee took her bewildered offspring to a spot well away from the others. Here she sat with the youngest child at her breast, rocking backwards and forwards in silent grief. The excitement of the hunt had robbed her of the sympathy she would otherwise have received from her friends.

Chief Bowles quickly decided upon the tactics that should be adopted for the hunt. The warriors would close in upon the buffalo in two mounted columns and force the great animals to run eastwards, into the sun. The front riders of each column would then ride in front of the buffalo and attempt to turn them in upon themselves. When the confusion was at its height the Cherokees would break their lines and charge into the herd. From this point it would be every man for himself. Each Indian would strive to kill as many buffalo as possible, at the same time trying to keep himself and his horse clear of the horns and hoofs of the formidable beasts, some of which weighed close to two tons.

Adam was to be a front rider with Yellow Bear. He was a riding arsenal, but his main armament would be the short double-barrelled rifle. It would be easier to handle during the forthcoming mêlée than the longer-barrelled Pennsylvania rifle which nestled in its saddle holster. Adam also carried the five-shot revolver, but its small calibre would render it ineffective against the tough hide of the buffalo.

All went just as Chief Bowles had planned – at first. The Indian horses closed in on a large group of buffalo and were almost alongside them before the large animals began running. It was not the panic-stricken galloping Adam had been expecting. Instead, it was an easy, mile-consuming run that did not extend the horses beyond a comfortable canter.

It was apparent that the buffalo did not appreciate the danger they were in until Adam, Yellow Bear and the other leading riders swung ahead of the herd and began firing at the foremost buffalo. Adam was the only man using a gun, the Cherokees preferring arrows and lances.

Adam downed two buffalo cows with his first two shots. While he reloaded, the Cherokees released arrow after arrow, most of them striking home, but few proving fatal to the buffalo. However, the sudden onslaught succeeded in turning the leading animals – and suddenly the scene was one of utter confusion. The Indians had been riding around the outside of the herd; now they plunged in among them, approaching each selected beast from behind and attempting to send an arrow into a vital organ of the body from behind the great ribcage.

The prairie erupted in a series of personal encounters, one man versus one buffalo. As the herd broke up in utter confusion buffalo were going down all about Adam. So, too, were horses and men. Adam downed two more buffalo and, as he paused to reload once more, he saw Yellow Bear close by, bending low over the neck of his horse, aiming an arrow at a prime young bull. Just as he released the arrow another bull with four or five arrows embedded in its great body crashed into Yellow Bear's horse from the far side, bringing horse and rider to the ground. The wounded bull also fell, but regained its feet quickly, glaring from bloodshot eyes at Yellow Bear, who had lost his bow and lay winded on the ground.

Adam had not completed reloading his short-barrelled gun, and there was no time now. Snatching the long rifle from the saddle holster, he brought it to his shoulder and fired, just as the wounded bull buffalo lowered its head and charged. The shot slammed home and the bull's nose dropped to the ground only inches from Yellow Bear. As the animal's rear came over to complete an ungainly somersault, the Indian rolled clear.

Yellow Bear's horse was badly hurt, leaving him in a precarious situation, surrounded by stampeding buffalo, galloping horses and arrow-firing warriors. Holstering the long rifle, Adam drove his horse on to where Yellow Bear crouched. The buffalo were now so thoroughly angry and confused that they were attacking anything that moved, including each other. When he reached Yellow Bear's side, Adam reached down a hand. The Indian took it and swung up behind Adam. There was no time for words. The hunt was still on, and Adam skilfully manoeuvred his horse clear of the herd. There were a number of riderless horses here, and Yellow Bear slipped to the ground and secured one of them.

The hunt was losing momentum now, the plain littered with dead and dying buffalo. Adam killed two wounded buffalo, including one with its thick neck transfixed by a long Cherokee arrow. Swinging its head angrily from side to side, it was trying to gore the buffaloes on either side, blaming them for the pain it felt.

Cherokees were moving through the downed animals now, dispatching the occasional wounded animal. The hunt had become a slaughter. Already the women were running to the scene, eager to find the animals killed by their own men. Identification was made by means of the arrows, each hunter having his personal design scored on them. Here and there a quarrel developed when a buffalo was found with the arrows of two hunters in its body. If it could not be proved which arrow had actually caused the beast's death, the dispute would be referred to Chief Bowles.

Tiski had no such problems. Adam was the only hunter using a rifle. He met her as she approached the herd, her eyes bright with the excitement of the hunt.

'I was watching you, Adam. You hunted well. Better than any other man, I think. I am going to need help with all the buffalo you have killed. Shall I find a widow? She will expect to receive meat – a hide, too, perhaps, if you are feeling generous.'

Adam looked up the hill to where a woman and her children huddled together, a tragic group, totally removed from the activity on the plain below them.

'Ask the widow of the man who died guarding the horses. Tell her that half of all I've killed is hers.'

Tiski's eyebrows shot up. 'That is *too* generous.'

Adam shook his head. 'But for the fight put up by her husband, I would never have heard the Comanche. There would have been no hunt, and we'd by walking home now. I'd say donating a few buffaloes to his widow is the least we can do.'

'Yes, Adam.' Tiski was aware that Adam's gesture of gratitude and sympathy was open to misinterpretation. A gift of such magnitude might be regarded as a bid for the widow herself. It was a common way of establishing a liaison, without either side being bound by the ties of a Cherokee marriage.

Tiski would ensure that the true reason for Adam's gift was known to the tribal gossip-makers. That way it would serve to increase Adam's standing with the tribe. Such generosity was usually the province of the tribal chief.

When Tiski had gone, Adam sat his horse for some minutes. The scene before him would be painted upon his memory for as long as he lived. Almost a thousand buffalo had been killed. Around them were many Cherokees, including children, all milling about the great brown bodies that littered the prairie like giant mole-hills. Beyond the scene of recent slaughter the remainder of the great herd grazed the rolling prairie as before, with no discernible decrease in its numbers.

Eli had once told Adam that in the high country the buffalo sometimes travelled in herds stretching as far as a man could see. A tribe travelling in the wake of such a herd possessed a never-failing store. A hunter had only to ride out and shoot a buffalo. The one animal provided the hunter and his family with all their needs. In addition to food for immediate needs, there would be ample left over to make pemmican. The hide of the buffalo provided material for food and clothing, tepee covers, bedding, robes, saddlebags and pouches and thongs of all descriptions. The paunch provided water-buckets, and cooking-utensils, cups, ladles and powder-flasks were fashioned from the horns. Glue was made from the hoofs and arrowheads from the bones, while the hair of the animal provided material for personal decoration and was useful for stuffing and padding. There was hardly a scrap of the great animal that was not utilised in some manner. Little wonder that the tribes looked upon the buffalo as a gift from the Gods.

Turning his horse up the slope, Adam reached the spot where those few not actively engaged in the hunt or its aftermath sat surveying the busy scene. To Adam's great surprise, Chief Bowles climbed stiffly to his feet to greet him. As Adam stepped down from his horse, the Cherokee chief enfolded him in a warm embrace.

'Englishman, my eyes were upon you today. I saw your skill with the gun and I watched you save the life of Yellow Bear.' With tears trembling in his eyes, Chief Bowles added: 'When I saw Yellow Bear fall and the buffalo turn to attack him, my heart cried within me. I believed I was about to lose a son. Instead, I have gained one. Englishman, yesterday you saved our horses. Today you saved my son. From this day you and Yellow Bear are brothers. Your enemies are his enemies, your sorrow as his own. Your joy will give him happiness; his home – and mine – will always be open to you.'

The Cherokee chief embraced Adam once again. 'Come, we will camp on the next rise, beyond the buffalo. There are trees there, and a deep creek. It will be a good place for the women. This is their time; they have much to do.'

The camp that night was a makeshift affair. The wickiups were constructed by the men, while the women took the hides from the buffalo and cut up the meat. They worked hard and long. By nightfall an incredible amount had been achieved. Buffalo hides were pegged to the hillside about the camp, and strips of buffalo meat were being prepared with herbs and hung on high rawhide drying lines, out of reach of the many dogs accompanying the hunting party.

That night, buffalo tongue was on the menu. The hunters, stomachs uncomfortably full, sat about the many fires, reliving the exploits of the day. It had been a good hunt. Three horses had been killed but, apart from a few minor scratches and bruises, the only serious injury suffered by the men was a broken leg. It was a simple fracture and the injured man sat with it stretched out in front of him, tightly splinted, as he cheerfully accepted the good-natured jibes of his fellow-hunters.

There was much talk, too, of Adam. His prompt action in rescuing Yellow Bear was praised by all who had witnessed the incident. Yellow Bear himself was unstinting in his praise, especially when Tiski was within hearing.

Later, Adam accompanied Yellow Bear on a tour of the guards, posted to prevent a recurrence of the attempt to steal the horses. There was less likelihood of its happening again, but Yellow Bear was taking no chances. The horses were tethered and hobbled, a deep creek at their back and the hunting camp sprawled in a loose semi-circle about them.

Puffing contentedly on a hardwood pipe, Yellow Bear looked about him at the low-burning cooking-fires, then up to the sky where a crescent moon climbed slowly towards the stars. Taking the pipe from his mouth, he said: 'At times like this I envy our people who live on the plains: Comanche, Apache, Kiowa, Cheyenne. Such freedom is theirs to enjoy every day.'

'Then why do they put their freedom at risk by raiding settlements and wagon trains? Sooner or later the people of Texas are going to put an efficient army together. Then the Army will come out here and carry the fight to the Plains Indians. They will enjoy little freedom then. Every time they make a camp they will need to look over their shoulder, knowing they are liable to be attacked.'

'Fighting and raiding are as much a part of their life as breathing, Englishman. They have fought everyone who has ever settled near their lands: your people, the Spanish, Mexican – and now those who call themselves "Texans". If there were no white men they would fight each other. Because of this they may keep their freedom when all other Indians have lost theirs. It is only fear of the Plains Indians that keeps white settlers from their country.'

'You and your people have both freedom and a way of life that doesn't bring you into constant conflict with the Texans.' Even as the words left his mouth, Adam thought uneasily of the immigrant wagons, pouring westwards from the coast.

When Yellow Bear spoke again, he chose his words very carefully. 'You have not been in this country long, Englishman. You have travelled with Eli Varne, and met The Raven. Both are friends of the Cherokee. There are few white people who think as they do. Most see no difference between us and the Comanche, or the Apache, or Kiowa. We are all "Indians", to be feared and hated, and kept as far as possible from the White Man's lands. The home of the main Cherokee nation is many miles to the north, in America. Many white men lived among us there, marrying Cherokee girls. The chief of these northern Cherokee has hair the colour of a cooking-fire, and his eyes reflect the winter sky. His people farm and have schools for their children, who carry names like Mary and John, James and Mollie. They pray to the White Man's God every Sunday. Yet even such "civilised" Indians as these are not safe. They are still *Indians*. What is more, they are living too close to the White Man, so they must be moved westwards. Even now they are being rounded up by soldiers and imprisoned in stockades until they can be escorted many miles to the west. Their lands and homes are being "won" by white men, who draw lots for them.

'We broke away from the main Cherokee nation many years ago. We came here to Texas because the Mexican government promised that the land where we made our homes would be ours for ever, while we lived in peace. They said they would give us papers to prove that the land was ours. They never kept that promise. Then, when the Texans began their war against Mexico, The Raven came to see my father. He promised that if the Cherokee did not take sides with the Mexicans and remained

133

peaceful, the new Texans would give us papers for the lands that are already ours. Because The Raven is known to our people, my father agreed. He has kept his word; The Raven's people have not. The lands where we live are still not ours. Now many more white people come to Texas. They look at our fields and our crops with envy. We are *Indians*. Why should we enjoy what they want? Today The Raven stands between his people and the Cherokee, but soon there will be a new Chief of the Texans. What will happen to us then? The Mexicans let us live in peace; I fear that the White Man who comes from the north will not. He even drives the Mexicans before him. What manner of man is he, my English brother? Why must those whose skins are not as pale as his own either become his slaves or be driven from his sight?'

Adam remained silent. He was no more able to provide an answer than was the man who stood beside him.

Yellow Bear's pipe had burned low while he talked and now he replaced it in his mouth, working hard to bring it back to life. When it was burning to his satisfaction, he smiled ruefully. 'My people are enjoying a hunt such as they have not had for many years, yet I can speak only of our troubles. Perhaps it is because you are a Cherokee now. Come, we must return to the fire if we are not to make my Kiowa sister anxious.'

As they walked, Yellow Bear asked: 'What are your thoughts of Tiski, now you are one of us?'

'I haven't allowed myself to think beyond this one visit to your people. I have work to do that is going to take me to many parts of Texas. From what I've seen so far, Texans aren't as hospitable as Cherokees. Tiski wouldn't be made welcome everywhere we went – and I wouldn't want to do anything to make her unhappy.'

Yellow Bear looked at Adam sharply. 'I do not say you should take her from our village. That you should think in such a way tells me much. But if you make her your woman she will be happy to remain with her people.'

The Indian rested a hand lightly on Adam's shoulder. 'You have found favour with my father. For you, all things are now possible.'

All that evening, whenever Adam glanced to where Tiski worked, he felt again the excitement of Yellow Bear's words. But he did not have the opportunity to speak to Tiski at any length that night, or for many nights afterwards. There was much work for the women during the five days and nights they remained at the scene of the buffalo kill.

When they began the long journey back to the Cherokee

village, things improved. The horses were heavily laden with buffalo hides, dried meat, and all the spoils of a highly successful hunt. Most women and children were forced to walk. As a result, they made slow progress. Occasionally, Tiski accepted a ride on Adam's horse, and as he walked beside her they talked – but of nothing in particular. He wanted them to be alone when he pursued the thoughts that Yellow Bear had put into his head, and the opportunity never occurred. There was now an escort for the women when they went to fetch water. A Comanche war-party was travelling close to the Cherokees. Never farther than a mile away during daylight hours, the Comanches posed a constant threat.

On the third evening of their journey homewards, a horseman galloped into the Cherokee camp. It was John, Yellow Bear's brother. Clinging behind him, on the same horse, was Dermot Casey.

At the sight of so many Indians crowding excitedly about him, the young Irish boy paled and tried to hide his face in the back of John's buckskin shirt. When John swung him down from the horse, Dermot saw Adam. For a moment his face registered total disbelief. Then he ran to Adam and flung his arms about his waist, and Adam held the young boy to him.

'It's all right, you're safe now. I'm here to take you home to your mother.'

Dermot Casey clung even tighter and suddenly he began to cry, huge, gulping dry sobs racking his thin body.

Adam let him cry for a while, until Dermot almost had the sobbing under control, then he ruffled the boy's hair in a gesture of affection and said gruffly: 'Come on, let's find some food for you. You've had a bad time, but it's over now.'

When Dermot raised his head he saw the Cherokees gathered about him and his grip on Adam tightened once more. 'The Indians killed Pa. They caught him and ... and made him scream. Then ... they killed him.'

'I know. Try not to think about it. John has rescued you from the Comanche. These are his people. You have nothing to worry about now.'

It was a long time before Adam could persuade Dermot to release him. The boy behaved as though he feared Adam would run away unless he stayed close. Even when he was eating Dermot looked terrified whenever a Cherokee warrior came near.

Dermot was hungry. He ate with all the greed of a young puppy, and later the combination of a full belly, the heat of the fire and his recent tiring ride had their effect. In spite of his determination to remain awake, Dermot fell asleep leaning against Adam.

Tiski had built a small grass shelter close beside Adam's wickiup, and Adam placed Dermot here, removing his heavy Irish-bought boots and covering him with a blanket. Looking down at the face of the sleeping boy, Adam felt a sudden deep sorrow for the dead father who would not see his son grow to manhood.

'The boy behaved well.'

Adam turned to see John standing behind him. 'He was beaten by Comanche boys and he fought back without tears. They taunted him with the scalp of his father, yet still he would not cry. Today we were chased by Comanches, but he kept his tears for you. It is good. He is too young to be a warrior all the time. He should enjoy the life of a child for a year or two more.'

Later, as Adam sat with Chief Bowles and his two sons at the camp-fire, John told them how he had located the Irish boy so quickly. Dermot had been taken by a mixed raiding party, comprised of about thirty Quahadi Comanches and a number of Kiowa warriors. As Eli had surmised, the Comanches had headed for home after killing Magnus Bergstrom and the others.

The raiding party was still many miles from their village on the Llano Estacado, the 'Staked Plain', when they met up with the remainder of the Quahadi Comanche. They were following the buffalo which, as the Cherokees had learned, were well to the east of their usual grazing-lands in this summer of 1838. The buffaloes the Cherokees had hunted were only a fragment of a much greater herd. It was this herd that the Quahadi Comanches had followed almost to the edge of the Great Plains.

John had spent a few days with the Comanches, bargaining for the boy's return. During this time they treated Dermot particularly harshly, hoping to increase John's anxiety for the boy and persuade him to pay a higher price for the boy's release. In part, the ploy was successful. John had not travelled this far, only to have the boy killed by the Comanches before negotiations for his release could be completed.

The price that was finally agreed was fifteen ponies. The Comanches and their Kiowa allies would come to collect the animals from the Cherokee village at some future date. John looked at Adam, to see whether the high price was in order.

Adam nodded. 'Give them the horses. Send an escort with me to San Antonio and I will see you are given fifteen of the best horses in Don Manuel Tolsa's herd in return.'

John was well satisfied. Don Manuel's horses were renowned

throughout Texas. His journey to the Comanches would be profitable for him. 'I will come with you. We will take only twenty men and ride fast. It will be best if we leave tomorrow. The Quahadi Comanche and Kiowa have ended their buffalo hunt and have joined with the Penateka Comanche for a raid into Mexico. It is the biggest raid for many years. While they are gone, the Texan settlements will have a time of peace and we can ride in safety. If the raid does not go well, they will return to show the settlements their anger. If we leave tomorrow, you can warn your people to be ready for them.'

John's arrival had cut across all Adam's own plans. It had been his intention to talk to Chief Bowles about Tiski upon their return to the Cherokee village. First, he wanted to be certain it was what Tiski wanted. Now he would be lucky if he were able to spend more than a few minutes talking to her before setting off with Dermot.

Immersed in his own thoughts, it was a few minutes before Adam became aware of the silence about the fire. John was expecting a reply. There could be only one answer. The lives of the settlers might be at stake.

'We'll leave in the morning.'

Adam looked for Tiski that evening. Incredibly, she was nowhere to be seen. By the time he had been to the camp watering-place half a dozen times in the vain hope that she would see him and meet him there, the camp-fires were burning low. Feeling thoroughly miserable, Adam finally decided that Tiski did not want to meet him. He would have to discuss matters with Yellow Bear in the morning and ask him to speak to her.

Dermot was in a deep, exhausted sleep. After pulling the blanket closer about the boy, Adam lay down in his own wickiup and gazed out at the stars through the open end of the flimsy, temporary structure.

He had been lying awake for no more than ten minutes when a shadow came between Adam and his view of the stars. Adam automatically reached for the gun lying beside him. As his fingers closed around the shaped butt of the Colt revolver the figure ducked inside the wickiup and Tiski whispered urgently: 'Sh! Say nothing. Sounds carry far here.'

A moment later, Tiski startled Adam even more by slipping beneath the blanket beside him. 'What have you been doing, Adam? I feared you would never lay down to sleep.'

'I was looking for you at the drinking-place. I thought you might see me and come there.'

'Would you rather we went there – or stayed here?'

137

Instead of replying, Adam drew her to him and kissed her. When the kiss was ended, Tiski clung to him. 'Quaty told me you must leave in the morning. It is so soon, Adam. There is so much in my heart that I wanted you to hear when we returned to the village.'

'There's a whole lot I need to say, too.'

Tiski cut him short by putting her lips to his. Between kisses, she whispered: 'We will leave it unsaid, Adam. You have put the fire inside me again. Do not waste the night in talk.'

Trying hard to control the desire Tiski had aroused in him, Adam held her from him for a moment. 'We *must* talk, Tiski. I want to know whether you love me enough to be my wife. . . .'

Tiski pressed herself against him and kissed him again with a ferocity that bordered on desperation. 'We do not have to think of marriage. Among the Cherokee it is not so important to be married. A man does not pay for a woman as he does among my own people. She can choose her man and decide whether or not they will marry. It is a good way.'

'That isn't what Chief Bowles said. . . .'

She kissed him yet again, almost angrily now. 'No more talk. I have chosen you to be my man tonight. If you do not want me, I will go and you will forget you ever met a Kiowa girl in a Cherokee village.'

'I'll never forget a single thing about you, Tiski. I love you.'

Tiski sat up in the cramped wickiup. With a quick movement she pulled her deerskin blouse over her head. In the dim light from the stars through the open end of the wickiup, Adam saw the firm outline of her body and it seemed to him that the thumping of his heart must be heard in every wickiup the length and breadth of the camp.

Beneath the blanket, Tiski wriggled free of her skirt and came to Adam. As her hands found his body beneath the rough shirt he wore, she whispered: 'Love me, Adam. *Please* love me.'

Tiski's hand, caressing his body, drove all other thoughts from Adam's mind. Soon there was no thought of anything but the girl whose body was seeking his own, and whose ardour released the passion he had held back for so long.

They made love in a wild, savage heat that left them both gasping for air. Then they made love again with a gentleness that was as magic as the moonlight outside the wickiup.

Afterwards they lay side by side, looking out at the moon. Adam could not believe that the world about them could possibly still be the same as before.

'I *want* to be married to you, Tiski.' He had been the first man for her, he knew.

Her fingers found his and they entwined painfully. 'We will talk of this if you return to our village again. For now, it is enough that you know I am your woman. My heart will always be yours, wherever you are and whatever you do.'

Something in her voice made him rise on one elbow and look down at her. He saw the tears in her eyes and, with a finger, traced their course down her face.

'There is no need for you to cry, Tiski. I'll come back – as soon as I can.'

'Hold me tight, Adam. Hold me very, very tight.'

Adam held her close and they lay together, her tears wet upon his shoulder before he went to sleep. When he woke the sun had climbed above the horizon and the camp was already busy.

Tiski was gone.

CHAPTER THIRTEEN

THE JOURNEY to San Antonio was swift and uneventful – until they came to the mission town, site of the battle where Davy Crockett, Jim Bowie, William Travis and 184 men fought and died for Texas.

Word had gone ahead of the party that they were approaching. They bypassed the town but when they reached a river-crossing a mile from San Antonio they found a party of well-armed Texans lined up to bar their way. The Texans were not inclined to allow the Indians across the river, even when Adam explained they were Cherokees and had rescued Dermot Casey from the Comanche. Only when the name of Don Manuel was mentioned did the Texans grudgingly allow the Indians to cross.

Once clear of the armed men, Adam said to John: 'They are likely to give you trouble on the way home. It might be as well if you kept well clear of San Antonio.'

'We will stay clear of *all* white men. It is safer.'

The Cherokee chief's eldest son was a taciturn man. During the journey he had spoken little, preferring his own company to that of his fellows.

'Another few hours and we'll be at Don Manuel's ranch. He'll make you welcome and you can choose your horses at your leisure.'

'We will choose the horses today and leave before dawn.'

'I'll give you a letter to say the horses are yours – just in case you meet up with more Texans. I'd also like you to take a message to Tiski. Tell her I'll be back to marry her, just as soon as I can.'

John blinked in surprise, momentarily shaken out of his usual indifferent manner. 'Marry Tiski? It is not possible!'

'Why not? I won't be the first white man to marry a Cherokee.'

'Tiski is a *Kiowa*. Her brother is a Kiowa war chief. He rides with the Comanche against the White Man. He was with those who took the boy. He wants Tiski returned to her own people. My father has agreed.'

Adam remembered the last night, in the Cherokee camp.

'Does Tiski know of this?'

'I told her myself, when I returned with the boy.'

Adam was stunned. Now he knew why Tiski had come to him

that night. Why she would not discuss the future with him. He remembered her tears. . . . But John had not finished talking.

'There is more. Tiski's brother, Metete, rides with Ten Trees, a Quahadi Comanche chief. Tiski has been promised to Ten Trees as his second wife. He will come to claim her when two moons have come and gone.'

Adam's dismay turned to anger. 'Tiski has been brought up as a Cherokee – as your own sister. You agreed to this?'

Unmoved, John pointed to Dermot Casey. Tired after days of hard riding, the small Irish boy drooped in the saddle of his horse. 'Would you rather I had left him with the Comanche? Tiski has been my sister and I love her as a sister. My father loves her as a daughter, but by giving her back to her brother it is a chance to gain peace with the Kiowa, and with the Quahadi Comanche, too. Yes, I agreed. So did my father. So, too, did Tiski.'

Adam looked at John in disbelief. The dream he had carried with him since leaving Tiski had suddenly become a nightmare.

'It is for the best, Englishman. You will find a white woman.'

'Do Comanche men have no women of their own . . .?'

Adam bit back the bitter words that welled up inside him and urged his horse on. He needed to think. He was certainly not prepared to allow Tiski to pass out of his life in such a manner. Yet the Cherokee village was many days' ride away – and Adam was committed to carrying out an important mission on behalf of Lord Palmerston. He had wasted a great deal of time already. . . .

'How much farther is it?' Dermot Casey's question broke in upon Adam's thoughts.

'I don't think it can be very far now. You see that line of trees ahead? That will be the river. Don Manuel's ranch is on the river bank, somewhere among the trees.'

They reached Don Manuel's house thirty minutes later. The Mexican landowner maintained a good lookout and he had been aware of their approach. His men had come out to meet the Indian horsemen, advancing cautiously until Adam was recognised.

Don Manuel awaited them in the huge courtyard of his house, and his welcome embraced both Adam and the Cherokees.

'Adam! Welcome to my house – and you have the boy, too! You have done well.'

'Don Manuel, I would like you to meet John, the son of Chief Bowles. He is the man who deserves all the credit for Dermot's safe return. He rode alone into Comanche country to bring him back. The price was fifteen horses. . . .' Adam pushed thoughts of the *additional* cost to the back of his mind. 'I told John you would give fifteen good mounts. I am certain the settlers will repay you in some way. If they can't, I'll meet the cost of the horses. . . .'

Don Manuel waved him to silence. 'There will be no talk of payment. I own more than two thousand horses. The son of Chief Bowles will take twenty – and ten more as a present for his father. The choice of horses will be his.'

Extending his hand to John, Dan Manuel said: 'Welcome to the Tolsa ranch. We have met before, you and I. When I visited your father with General Houston.'

'We have met,' John agreed. He shook hands gravely, hiding the pleasure he felt that the Mexican landowner should recognise him. Hesitating for only a moment, he said: 'The Comanches of Chief Ten Trees have another prisoner, a Mexican girl. The boy spoke to her and she told him you were her uncle. Her name is Eleanor.'

Don Manuel's eyes closed tightly and his face contorted into an expression of great pain. '*Madre mio*! We prayed she was dead.' Opening his eyes, he said: 'Could you not have brought her, too?'

John shrugged. 'Girl prisoners are not treated kindly among the Comanche – the Quahadi are the worst of all. She is no longer a child. Sometimes such a girl is not welcomed home by her family.'

'Get her back. For the love of God, get her back for us!' Don Manuel pleaded hoarsely. 'Promise the Comanche *anything*. I will pay.'

'I will try when Ten Trees comes to our village for his woman.'

It was Adam's turn to wince as John's words reminded him of the plans made for Tiski's future by those about her.

John declined Don Manuel's invitation to enter the Tolsa ranch-house, preferring to remain outside with his men, but he accepted the Mexican's offer to have food prepared for them.

While Don Manuel arranged for their needs to be met, Adam lifted Dermot from his horse and carried him inside the house. The Irish boy was close to exhaustion. A plump Mexican housekeeper clucked over him like a hen with a helpless chick, promising him a meal of as much as he could eat, followed by a hot bath and a soft bed.

Relieved to have handed responsibility for Dermot to someone else, Adam returned to the courtyard just as Dona Antonia and Philippe, with an escort, returned from a trip to San Antonio.

Their open carriage had hardly rolled to a halt before Philippe clambered awkwardly from the vehicle. His crutch tucked firmly beneath his arm, he swung his way to where Adam stood in the doorway of the house. Long before he reached Adam he was calling: 'Did you save Dermot? Have you brought him back?'

'He's safe. Not only that, I think he's to share your room tonight. Go in and speak to him; he's been looking forward to meeting you again.'

As Philippe tapped his way through the house towards the kitchen, Dona Antonia arrived at the doorway. To Adam's surprise, she kissed him on the cheek. 'No doubt Philippe will have told you how relieved we are at your safe return. You will have much to tell us at dinner tonight. I look forward to that, Adam.'

Contrary to expectations, dinner that evening was a difficult meal, filled with long silences and many unasked questions. Don Manuel was tortured by the plight of his captive niece, and Adam by thoughts of Tiski.

Don Manuel had already told Adam that Eli had taken the settlers to their lands, north-west of San Antonio, and Adam had said he would take Dermot there the next day. As quickly as politeness would allow, Adam left the dining-table, using the excuse that he was tired and wished to speak to John before retiring.

John and the Cherokees were camped beside the river, and Adam made a last plea for John to intercede with his father on his behalf.

'I cannot do this, Englishman. When I gave my word to Metete I gave him the word of my people. Tiski is an Indian; she understands this. You must also learn to understand.'

'On the day of the buffalo hunt your father told me I, too, was a Cherokee, and I have given *my* word – to Tiski. I'll be back in the village to claim her before any Comanche chief arrives.'

'You will bring trouble with you, Englishman.'

'Only if Chief Bowles insists on marrying Tiski to a Comanche. But this must not stand between us, John. You have been a very good friend. Without you we would never have recovered Dermot. This is a present to you, from one Cherokee to another.'

Adam handed John the double-barrelled rifle he had used on the buffalo hunt. The Cherokee had admired the gun on the journey to San Antonio.

John took the gun in a matter-of-fact manner, as though such a gift was offered to him every day. He tried very hard not to show his delight with the gift, but his eyes betrayed him.

143

'I will tell my father of your feelings for Tiski – as a favour from one Cherokee to another.'

Returning to the house, Adam was crossing the darkened patio when Don Manuel's voice called his name softly: 'Adam. Do not go inside yet. I wish to talk to you.'

Adam saw the glow of the landowner's lighted cheroot in the shadows of the patio. When he went closer he saw that Don Manuel was seated at a table in an arbour, a drink before him. Adam took a seat across the table from his host.

'The Cherokees have all they need?'

'Yes. They have chosen their horses and intend leaving during the night. They don't trust the Texans in San Antonio.'

'They are right to be cautious. It is regrettable.' After a pause, Don Manuel said: 'You did well to bring back the boy. If only John had done the same for my niece. . . .'

'I'll see what I can do when I'm next in Chief Bowles's village.'

'You will return there? Why?'

'I . . . I was happy there.'

'Ah!' Don Manuel gave a sigh of understanding. 'I thought something troubled you. There is a girl . . . an Indian girl?'

'Yes.' Now it had been said, Adam felt a great relief. He realised he felt guilty about being in love with Tiski – and he did not want to feel guilty. Unnecessarily belligerent, he explained: 'She's a Kiowa girl, captured by the Cherokees and adopted by Chief Bowles. I intend marrying her.'

It was a long time before Don Manuel spoke again. 'I, too, once loved an Indian girl. They are easy to love, Adam, and you are an honourable man. But think long before you marry this girl. What might be honourable in England and Mexico is not viewed in the same way here. Think carefully of what is best, for you *and* for the girl. Whatever you decide to do, please return to us here. We have grown fond of you. Myself, Dona Antonia and Philippe – especially Philippe. You have brought much happiness into his life. I would not like him to lose it now. The next few years will be difficult ones for all of us. We have been told that he cannot live longer than another three years.'

Escorted by some of Don Manuel's men, Adam set off with Dermot at dawn. John and the Cherokees had already gone.

In spite of his weariness, Adam had been unable to sleep, his mind a tortured turmoil as he thought of Philippe and of Tiski. Eventually, he spent the remaining night hours penning a long letter to Lord Palmerston. Skimming over his visit to the

Cherokees, Adam brought the British Foreign Minister up to date on the Texan situation, as given to him by Don Manuel.

The campaign for the Texan presidential election was hotting up. Those who favoured a continuation of the policy begun by President Houston had just been dealt a body-blow from which it was doubtful if they could recover. Houston himself was unable to stand again at this election, the Texan Constitution not allowing a president to serve for two consecutive terms. Houston had chosen a fellow-lawyer, Peter Grayson, to succeed him and continue the policies he had pursued during his own term of office. It had been thought that Grayson stood a good chance of taking over from the first President of the Republic of Texas, but news had reached Texas that Grayson had inexplicably committed suicide in Tennessee, the state Houston had once governed.

As a result, the front runner for the highest office in the land was a man who bitterly opposed Houston's policies. This man was Mirabeau Buonaparte Lamar.

In many ways, it would probably suit Great Britain to have Lamar as President of Texas. He was considered anti-American, in that he was a declared opponent of the annexation of Texas by that country. But he was also dedicated to the retention of slavery, was impractical, reckless, and likely to provoke renewed fighting with Mexico, thus making American intervention in the dispute between the two countries far more likely.

Adam brought these views to the attention of Lord Palmerston, urging him to grant recognition to Texas, thus securing Lamar's friendship and giving him a direction in which to look for advice.

Adam addressed the letter to one of Palmerston's friends in London. The letter would be passed on, unopened, to the Foreign Secretary. Don Manuel had promised to send the letter with one of his men to Velasco, for onward transmission.

Adam and his escort wasted no time on the journey to the Hill Country, where the new settlers had their land. By noon they were surrounded by well-wooded hills and splashing through the wide, shallow creeks that followed most of the valley bottoms. There was an abundance of tall cedars, oaks and other trees, together with a wealth of plant life, yet when Adam looked more closely there seemed to be very little earth to support them, the pale soil having the appearance of crushed limestone.

There was no shortage of wildlife in the area. More than once Adam saw the white tail of a deer flicking provocatively as the animal ran away through the trees. There were turkeys, too.

Sometimes they could be seen, but more often the travellers only heard their throaty calls from the cover of the long, coarse grass.

In the late afternoon they reached a wide green-water river. The Mexican guide told Adam, in Spanish, that Dermot was almost home. When Adam passed the information to the boy, he immediately straightened in the saddle, eager for the first glimpse of his mother and their new home.

They saw the smoke from a fire when they were a mile away and soon afterwards heard the steady rhythm of an axe biting into wood. In a clearing, close to the river, a number of people were engaged in the construction of a cabin. From the outline it appeared it would have two rooms, each about thirty feet long by fifteen feet wide. Both rooms would share a common gabled roof, with an open passageway between the two. One room was complete and already in use. The smoke Adam and Dermot had seen came from a mud-and-stick chimney protruding from this half of the cabin.

Caleb Ryan was on the roof, securing wooden shingles to stout log beams. Fifty yards away, Eli wielded an axe. An impressive number of short, white-topped tree-stumps bore witness to his industry, but Adam did not miss the long rifle propped near at hand against a standing tree. Eli had lost none of the habits he had acquired as a frontiersman. One of Caleb's young daughters was busy trimming the side-branches from the fallen trees with a billhook, and Adam was surprised to see the trimmed logs being hauled to the partly constructed cabin by Peggy Dooley and Nell Plunkett. Eileen Ryan, Caleb's wife, was washing at the river edge, but there was no sign of Kathie Casey, and Dermot looked at Adam anxiously.

As the mounted men came closer to the cabin, all work ceased. On the roof, Caleb shielded his eyes against the sun in order to see the visitors more clearly.

Edging his horse close to Adam, Dermot was close to panic when he said: 'You promised my ma would be here. . . .'

He broke off as Adam nodded in the direction of the cabin. Kathie Casey had been preparing the evening meal when the rhythm of the axe came to a sudden stop. Then she had heard the jingle of horse harness.

Each morning when she opened her eyes, Kathie Casey would pray that this would be the day when her son was returned to her. Eli had warned her many times against undue optimism, but it made no difference and he refrained from telling her that white children taken captive by the Comanche were seldom seen again. The search had never been abandoned for the three Parker and

Plummer children, taken two years before when Kiowas and Comanches raided their home, leaving five men dead and two women dying. Eli could have cited many similar abductions, but they would not have extinguished Kathie Casey's hope.

Now she stood in the doorway of the unfinished cabin, and the moment she saw the mounted Mexican escort she knew why they had come. Then the Mexican ranks parted and she saw Dermot. She began to run as fast as her legs would carry her. Dermot hardly had time to slide from his horse before his mother reached him. Sweeping him up in her arms, she hugged him to her, calling him her 'baby', her emotions a confused mixture of laughter and tears.

'Nice going. I didn't expect you back for another couple of weeks at the earliest.'

Adam looked down from his horse at Eli as Kathie Casey, unwilling to release her son for even a second, carried him to the cabin, his thin arms crooked tightly about her neck.

'John found him with a hunting party, not too far from where I was out after buffalo with the Cherokees.'

'And you . . .? How'd you make out with the Cherokees? You have any trouble with 'em?'

'Trouble? I was so well thought of that Chief Bowles made me a Cherokee. One of his own sons, at that.'

Eli switched his gaze from his own calloused hand to Adam's face. He had been playing at being a settler for a week or two, but he had lost none of his acumen.

'That's not an honour Chief Bowles would give away lightly. What did you do?'

'It's a long story. Right now I could eat this horse I'm riding. Do you run to another cook? I don't think the one you've got will have a hand free for the remainder of the day. Dermot's had a bad time with the Comanche, but John said he stood up to them like a man. He's earned the right to be a small boy for a few hours. He'll get precious little opportunity to remain a child for long, living out here.'

'I'll go along with that – but here's a man who won't agree.'

Caleb had climbed down from the roof of the cabin and was advancing upon Adam, beaming happily. 'It's good to see you again, Adam – and the boy, too. You've made Kathie the happiest woman in the whole of Texas today. There's none of us will be forgetting it, I promise you.'

When the Irishman grasped his hand, Adam could feel the callouses he had acquired since reaching his destination.

Grimacing, Adam said: 'You've acquired a new strength in

147

your arm, Caleb. Having your own place agrees with you. I see you have plenty of help here, too.' He nodded to where Nell and Peggy had just come from the cabin, leaving Kathie Casey and her son alone for a while.

'A woman without a man can't run her own place out here. Kathie, Nell and Peggy will stay with us here. There's more than enough land for everyone. More than I can make use of right now. We'll build cabins for them here and they can decide later what to do with their own lands.'

'What happened to Hec Bowie and his Mexican friend? Have they returned to Brazoria?'

Caleb's good-humour disappeared abruptly. 'I wish they had. They're up in the hills somewhere, putting out markers on land they won playing cards. They'd do well to stay there.'

Eli spat derisively on the ground at his feet. 'What Caleb isn't saying is that he gave Hec Bowie a thrashing he's not likely to forget in a hurry. Bowie was lucky at that. If I'd got to him first, I'd have killed him.'

'What happened?' Adam could not remember the steady Tennesseean showing such anger before.

'Bowie caught Nell off somewhere on her own, the day the wagon train broke up. Seems he thought she'd been leading him on. He tried to collect what he thought he had coming to him. He did, but it wasn't quite what he was expecting. She produced a knife and damn near cut off two of his fingers. We heard the hollering, along with everyone else on the wagon train. I went to see what it was about, but Caleb got there first. He didn't take to being told to mind his own business and roughed Bowie up a little.'

'What was Mexia doing while all this was going on?'

'Bowie had left him as some sort of lookout. He had a mind to take a hand when Bowie hit the ground for the third or fourth time, but he changed his mind when I slapped him behind the ear with a rifle-butt. Afterwards we ran 'em off. If they've got any sense, they'll stay well clear of the settlement. No one liked the way Bowie got his land. After the business with Nell, he'll not be welcome anywhere around her people.'

'Are you remaining here in case Bowie has another try for Nell, or is there something you haven't yet told me – partner?'

Eli's embarrassment gave Adam his answer, even before the Tennesseean replied.

'If you're thinking there's something between me and Nell, you've got it all wrong. If I wanted a woman to take with me on the trail, to shoot and trap and take her turn at standing guard,

I couldn't do better. But I take a partner along for them duties. My idea of a woman is someone who runs a clean and comfortable cabin, who'll give a man a reason for coming home, and who makes him forget the time he's spent away. Now, Kathie – Dermot's ma – is a woman like that.'

Eli saw the amused glances exchanged by Adam and Caleb. He blurted out: 'Hell! I'm just as human as anyone else. A man's got to look to the future – especially when his partner's likely to go off and ranch for a rich Mexican at any time. I don't know what it is you've got, but Don Manuel and that wife of his have bought it. They think you're the greatest thing to happen to Texas since the Spanish brought horses.'

Now it was Adam whose mood changed. 'You can forget all such talk, Eli. I'll no doubt be visiting Don Manuel often enough, but a lot has happened since you rode out of Chief Bowles's village.'

Eli had been watching Adam's face closely as he talked. Suddenly serious, he said: 'I knew that as soon as you rode in. A man grows up pretty fast when he's around Indians. I hope that what's happened to you has nothing to do with them Cherokee girls. They've a way of getting into the bones of a man, but being serious about one of 'em is the surest way *I* know of finding trouble – and I mean *big* trouble.'

CHAPTER FOURTEEN

THAT EVENING, Adam sat in the cedar-log cabin and related those experiences of his time with the Cherokees he cared to mention. The cabin was typical of ten thousand others scattered throughout the sparsely populated frontier regions of Texas and America. With a dirt floor, and not particularly roomy, it had no windows and was built with future expansion in mind. The women sat on crude wooden benches made from the planking of the Casey wagon and there was a table in the room from the same source. The Ryans' wagon was kept outside, intact, retained for the day when Caleb would have produce to convey to the San Antonio market. The men and children, Dermot Casey and Caleb's two young daughters, sat on the hard-packed earth floor, the men passing round a whisky-jar, a present from Don Manuel. Set about the cabin, home-made tallow candles spluttered and flickered, casting moving shadows on the crudely finished walls.

Don Manuel had been generous to the settlers before sending them off to claim their lands. Each family had been given at least one horse, and they had enough oxen between them to plough all the land they were likely to clear in the course of the next two or three years. In the lean-to shed behind the Ryan cabin was tied a milking-cow and four goats – three nannies and a billy. Other settlers had pigs. As the animals produced offspring the system of barter would ensure that every settler gradually built up his stock of animals.

The land up here, in the Hill Country, was well stocked with game, and there were fish in the rivers. Mulberries, wild plums and cherries grew in the valleys, and the family of a settler who had chosen his land well would never go hungry.

The deepest concern was felt over the threat of Comanche raids. Indians had not been sighted since the arrival of the settlers, but this was land to which the Comanche claimed a right. No one doubted there would be trouble.

Adam repeated what John had told him about the Comanche raid into Mexico, and Caleb declared he would put the brief respite to good use. The cabins had been built with defence in mind and Caleb would add to this by building a stockade to contain his own cabin and those he would build for the others.

'What will you do now?' Caleb put the question to Adam after his wife had packed the reluctant children off to bed on the half-width sleeping-platform that took the place of a ceiling, leaving the adults sitting about the sparsely furnished but cosy room.

'I'm not certain yet. I'll probably spend a few days riding around the hills, checking on the lands your people have settled, before going to Houston to see the President. Then I'll be going back to Chief Bowles's village for a while.'

'As you don't seem to have any plans to return to England, you might be interested in something Peggy has to say to you.'

Peggy Dooley rose from a wooden seat close to the fire. Looking more than usually self-conscious, she advanced to where Adam sat on the earth floor, his back to the wall. She thrust a roll of stiff parchment tied with a dull-red ribbon at him.

'We've talked among ourselves, all of us here and the others who came with us from Ireland and Scotland. We'd like you to have this. It's a "thank you" for everything you did for us at Velasco and . . . and afterwards.'

Peggy Dooley suddenly coloured up, and Adam knew she, too, had remembered what had occurred on the night of the dance. It seemed a long while ago now.

'It's especially for bringing Dermot back to Kathie. I know just how she was feeling. . . .'

Peggy Dooley faltered, and for a moment it seemed she might flee from the cabin into the night, but Adam reached out and took her by the hand. He had just untied the ribbon and opened out the document. It was a deed, granting Seamus Dooley 640 acres of land, inside an area defined by a number of quoted landmarks. The document was dated 1836.

'I can't take this, Peggy. It's yours. It's your land.'

'And what would I be wanting with any land? Caleb and Eileen have given me a home. In return I'll help out with their family, and the farm they're making. I have no use for any land. Kathie wanted to give you hers, but that's Dermot's inheritance, from his father. It would be wrong to give it away.'

'It's good land, Adam,' Caleb said. 'It borders my own, just along the valley. On the other side of the river are two lots belonging to Eli. A large part of his is treed and sloping, but he says that's what he wants. Yours is mostly good bottom land. You *must* take it, Adam. It's what we all want for you – and we'd like you for a neighbour. Peggy will be quite happy here, with us.'

Adam was still not certain he should accept the gift, but Caleb closed the argument. 'Take the deed. You don't have to think about living there right away. Just remember it's yours to come home to.'

Greatly moved by the generous gesture, Adam thanked Peggy Dooley warmly and she beamed her pleasure.

Later, feeling in need of some coffee, Adam went to the kitchen in the next cabin. Nell was there. She stood beside the coffee-pot, but seemed disinclined to move aside for him.

'Have you decided yet whether you'll take the land and stay here?'

'Not yet.'

'It's something that would please *all* of us, Adam.'

'I thought you couldn't live close to an Englishman.'

'So did I – but don't goad me, Adam. Otherwise I'll say something I don't really mean. I've made trouble for you in the past, with Hec Bowie, and I'm sorry. There was no reason at all why you should have risked your life to bring back Dermot, but you did. None of us will forget that.'

Adam remembered that Dermot was Nell's nephew. Even so, this was unlike the girl who had tried to draw a knife on him, in the wagon on the day of the storm – and who had cut up Hec Bowie when he attacked her.

'Do you think I'd be happy here, trying to scratch a living as a farmer?'

'There's more than one sort of farmer, but ... yes, you'd be happy setting up home here, among friends.'

The thought of setting up a home brought Adam's thoughts back to Tiski, and he spoke more sharply than he intended. 'I'm grateful for your concern, but I haven't yet decided what I'm going to do.'

'I think you have, Adam Rashleigh. You'll return to your Cherokee village.' There was a moment's hesitation, as though Nell was choosing her next words with great care. 'You can bring her here, you know. Caleb and Eileen would welcome her. I'd make sure the others did, too.'

'Bring who here?' Adam's reply was instinctively defensive and his throat felt dry at the idea of setting up house here with Tiski.

'The girl you've met while you've been away. She's Indian, isn't she? No, you don't have to answer me; I could see it in your eyes when you talked about the Cherokees, back there in the other cabin. You've fallen in love with a Cherokee girl. It isn't going to make life easy for you, Adam. Not for *you*. But if you bring her here you can promise her *one* friend, at least.'

Nell's unexpected words threw Adam into confusion as hope

152

and common sense vied for supremacy. The conclusion he reached was never really in doubt. Tiski was an Indian. When the Comanche plundered the settlements, killing men, burning property and carrying off women and children, the wrath of the survivors would turn upon her. It would not matter that Tiski had been brought up as a Cherokee, one of the five tribes designated by the White Man as 'civilised'. She had been born a Kiowa – and Kiowa warriors rode on the bloody trail through the settlements knee by knee with their Comanche brothers. Tiski would be a target for both whites and Indians, and Adam would not always be around to protect her.

By the time Adam had worked all this out in his own mind, Nell had gone, leaving Adam wondering about the strange complexity of the Irish girl.

The land given to Adam by Peggy Dooley was all that Caleb had claimed it to be. Adam accompanied the Irishman and Eli on a tour of the property the next afternoon. The three men had spent the morning working on Caleb's cabin, completing the roof soon after noon. Then they set off to explore the valley. As they rode on to Adam's land, Eli spotted a fine deer and promptly shot it. They hung it in the fork of a tree and left it dripping blood from its soft mouth, to await their return. They saw more deer as they wandered beside the river, but made no attempt to shoot again.

Adam noted, as he had before, that while the grass looked strong enough it was sparse, the ground about its roots a dusty white. Caleb took a handful from the hillside and allowed it to trickle through his fingers. Half of it blew away as dust.

'It will be fine as long as there's no shortage of water, but it's better grazing-land than growing-land – at least, on the hillside. Goats and sheep will do better than cattle here. The land by the river is better. You'll be able to grow all you want there. I don't say it's land I would have taken had there been a choice, but it will do . . . it will do fine.'

Caleb had the faraway expression of a man with a dream. Adam never doubted for a minute that he would do well here, in the Hill Country.

The men spent an hour walking Adam's land, but Caleb became increasingly restless. When Eli suggested they cross the river to inspect his holding, Caleb excused himself on the grounds that he needed to continue the work on his cabin. He set off, promising to retrieve the deer on the way.

'Caleb is a natural farmer,' commented Adam, as the Irishman passed from view. 'I doubt if he's ever been happier than he is now.'

'Then we'd better make sure he stays that way.' With no further explanation, Eli set off at a fast pace for the horses, forcing Adam to a trot in order to keep up with him.

'Are we going somewhere special?'

'We are – and you'd better check those guns of yours before we cross the river.'

Mounted on the horses, they reached a wide shallows. Here the otherwise sluggish water speeded up as it broke on shale and rocks. At the edge of the water Eli stopped. 'If you don't want this partnership broken up by sudden death, you'll need to learn to question everything you see, as soon as you see it. Take a look around you now. You see anything we ought to take a look at?'

Adam scanned the hills. Immediately, he saw what Eli had observed many minutes before – buzzards. Usually seen singly, or in pairs circling lazily in the warm air high above the hills, the broad-winged birds were gathering in a descending spiral above a break in the hills. More of the broad-winged birds, not designed for fast flying, were flapping to the scene, attracted by the unusual activity.

'It could be a deer – or even one of the settlers' sheep that's wandered up there to die.'

'Could be, but there's no settler with sheep on that side of the river. If it's a deer, I want to know how it died. But I've a feeling in my belly that it's no deer lying dead up there.'

The two men put their horses to the shallow river. As more buzzards put in an appearance, Eli urged his horse to a trot. Adam followed suit.

About a mile from the river they broke from the cover of the trees and a dozen birds lumbered awkwardly along the ground and took to the air, protesting at the untimely end to their grisly feast.

Left behind on the ground were four lacerated bodies, two of them obviously children. They had been so badly savaged by the birds that Adam turned away in sudden revulsion.

'Who did this – Comanches?'

'Hell, no. These *are* Comanches. It looks as though they were a family passing through to trade with Mexicans near San Antonio. They probably didn't know about any settlers being hereabouts now.'

Adam forced himself to look at the bodies. He saw that Eli was right. Their dress, together with what was left of their hair, was sufficient identification. There was little else left to tell him anything about them, other than that they had once been two men and two children.

'Who killed them?'

'Hec Bowie's land begins at that tree over there.' Eli indicated a fallen cedar that lay between two rocks, looking like a piece of giant artillery. 'His partner, Mexia, used to be a Comanchero. Indians are often blamed for their handiwork. These Comanches were a small family unit. I'd say they had no more than a bow and arrows between them. Certainly no gun.'

The buzzing of flies around the bodies had increased in volume now the insects no longer had competition from the buzzards.

'What do we do now?'

'I guess that depends on how you feel about things. We can bury these bodies and then go after the woman; or go after the woman and come back and bury the bodies; or bury the bodies, forget the woman, and go back to Caleb's place. But, whatever else we decide, we've got to bury this mess. If we don't, the first Comanche party through here will find the bodies and word will go back to the plains that Caleb's folk and the Comanche are just naturally at war. I want to avoid that, even though there's many who'll say I'm wasting my time. ....'

'*What woman?*' The question would wait no longer.

Eli shook his head despairingly. 'There are times when I *know* you'll never be the partner that Dan Coutter was. Look here.' Eli walked beyond the four bodies. The mud was churned up so badly here that it meant nothing to Adam, but Eli read it as clearly as though it were spelled out for him in a book.

'There are the signs of three horses here – Indian horses. Unshod. One of them was pulling a travois. That's where the kids would have travelled, together with everything else the family owned. This is what *your* eyes should be telling you. Three horses mean *three* Indians. Now, there's no Indian I know who'll travel with two young children and not take a woman along. Her body's not here, so I reckon she must be with whoever killed her family. That brings us back to the alternatives I suggested. Which of them do we take?'

'We go after the woman.'

'That's what I thought you'd say. First help me drag these bodies to the trees, then we'll cut off some undergrowth and cover 'em up. Otherwise there won't be a lot left to bury. You take the kids, I'll bring the others.'

Adam felt he should pick the children up – neither of them could have been older than seven or eight – but he could not bring himself to get so close to what remained of them. Following Eli's example, he dragged their small bodies to the shadows cast by the trees.

The grim task completed, Adam asked: 'Where do we find Bowie and Mexia?'

'I'll show you soon enough, but not until you've got a grip on yourself and we've decided what to do when we find 'em.'

'Do? They've just killed four people, two of them little more than babies. No one thought twice about what they had to do to Bo Garrett's men, in Velasco.'

'They killed *white* folk. Bowie ain't done nothing but rid the world of a few Indians. Out here four dead Comanches will guarantee a man a night's free drinking in any saloon. No one will question whether or not an unarmed warrior, one old man and two kids make a man a hero. In this part of Texas *any* Indian is vermin. You saw how that runaway Negro was treated, back in Brazoria? Compared to an Indian he was *human*. That's the way things are here.'

'We're wasting time. Let's go and find the woman.'

'We're wasting nothing. These Comanches have been dead for three hours, at least. Bowie and Mexia will have done whatever they intended to the woman by now. If she was good enough, they'll keep her for a day or two more. If she wasn't, they'll have killed her already.'

'Are you coming, or do I have to go and find her by myself?'

'Hell, boy. There ain't a grain of reason in that head of yours. When this is over you'd better tell me what happened while you were with Chief Bowles and those Cherokees of his. All right! All right! I'm with you. I just wanted you to know what we're heading into.'

Adam had been sickened by the task he had just performed and was angry with the men who had carried out such wanton slaughter. The thought that they were holding an Indian woman appalled him. He had no plan for when he met up with Hec Bowie and his Mexican partner, but it was a confrontation that was long overdue. It had been in the offing since Adam and Bowie had first met.

'You'd better let me lead the way,' Eli suggested, as Adam scouted around the spot where the bodies had lain, in a vain bid to learn which direction Bowie and Mexia had taken with the Indian woman. 'We don't need to track 'em. I know where they'll be. Bowie's got a dug-out shanty about a half-mile from here. If we cut over the hill, we'll come out above them.'

Turning his horse up the slope, he explained: 'When a man's got neighbours like Hec Bowie and Rafael Mexia he makes sure he gets to know as much about them as he can. Now I'm going to save my breath. You'd better do the same. It's a stiff climb up ahead.'

Leaving their horses just short of the ridge, the two men scrambled up the final feet of steep, treeless shingle. Once there, Eli crouched low and ran for the cover of some trees, an equal distance down on the far side. From here, Eli pointed out Hec Bowie's shanty.

It was an unprepossessing dwelling. Taking advantage of a shallow cave, Bowie and Mexia had extended the living-space with a timber frame, over which had been stretched animal skins. The door was a blanket, swinging in the light breeze.

Near the dug-out shanty was a roughwood corral containing a number of horses. When he saw them, Eli frowned. 'There are seven horses there. Three will have been taken from the Indians. Either Bowie's got himself two more animals since I last came looking, or he's got company. Do we stay up here until we've made sure, or do we go down?'

'We go down.'

The two men made their way cautiously down the slope, using the trees and occasional hollows as cover whenever possible, sometimes losing sight of the primitive home, but always moving closer.

They were crouched behind bushes no more than eighty yards away when a great roar of noisy amusement came from inside, accompanied by the shrieks of a woman in pain. Then someone shouted a warning. A moment later the blanket door was thrown aside and a naked Indian woman ran out. Hec Bowie was close behind her and the woman had gained no more than ten yards when he grabbed her, both falling heavily to the ground. The woman struggled violently until Hec Bowie straddled her and cuffed her into quiescence.

Behind him three men came from the hovel, and Eli drew in his breath sharply.

'This game's going to get rough,' he murmured. 'Those two with Mexia are Bo Garrett's boys. You've seen them before, at Velasco. The little one is Hondo Keller. He's wanted for two murders in Tennessee – and three or four more in Louisiana.'

Adam nodded without taking his eyes from the men gathered about the dug-out door.

'What we gonna do with her, Hec? She ain't worth keeping. There ain't no life in her at all till she sets off to running.'

'I'll put some life in her. Mex, kick that fire and get it flaming, then pass me a piece of wood when it's burning well. Wes, you hold her arms. Get her legs apart, Hec. I'll set fire to the fuzz she's got there. If that don't get her moving it, nothing will.'

The suggestion was made by the man Eli had identified as Hondo Keller.

Hooting with laughter, the three men did as they were asked. When Hec Bowie had the wildly struggling Comanche woman's legs prised apart, Rafael Mexia pulled a charred and flaming piece of wood from the fire and held it towards Hondo Keller. Meanwhile, the Indian woman had realised what was intended and was redoubling her struggles.

Adam had seen enough. Before Eli could prevent him, he had raised his rifle and fired. The burning wood flew from Mexia's hand and he crashed backwards, to fall across the fire. He may have had difficulty in talking, but he could scream well enough.

Eli was not pleased. With an explosive 'Damn!' he stood up, his rifle pointing to where the three men outside Bowie's shanty looked utterly confused.

'Hold it right there. Bowie . . . Keller . . . all of you. Stand still. Don't move a muscle.'

The three men turned to face Eli as Adam reloaded his rifle. Meanwhile, Mexia had squirmed clear of the fire. He lay with his clothes smouldering, nursing a shattered shoulder.

As Adam and Eli advanced slowly down the hill, Bowie called: 'There was no call to shoot Mex that way, Eli. We was just having a little fun. It's just some little old squaw. . . .'

'I saw where you'd had some "fun" over the hill. I didn't think much of that, either. As for Mexia being shot – well, that *was* a mite premature. I'd intended waiting until *Keller* had that there piece of wood in his hand. Then I was going to kill him deader than a whorehouse at breakfast-time.'

While they advanced, the Indian woman had been crouching on the ground, uncertain of what was happening about her. Eli and Adam were still twenty yards away when she suddenly sprang to her feet and ran to where Hondo Keller stood with his back to her. Before anyone else realised her intention, she snatched a broad-bladed 'Bowie' knife from its sheath at the back of his belt and plunged it handle-deep into his side, just above the line of his trousers. Keller screamed and grabbed the Comanche woman by the hair, bending her head back as she worked the knife from side to side, shrieking at him in incoherent Comanche.

The diversion was all that Bowie and his remaining companion needed. Both were men who had been in tight corners before – and both had survived to boast of their escapes.

158

Bo Garrett's man carried a single-shot pistol in his belt, and it was drawn and cocked in the time it took Eli to line up his rifle and squeeze the trigger. The man was knocked back two paces by the force of the large-bore lead ball and the pistol was fired harmlessly into the ground by an already dead man.

While this was going on, Hec Bowie sprinted for the dug-out shanty, the Indian woman between Adam and his target for most of the time. Adam snapped off two quick shots from his revolver as Bowie dived in a roll that took him through the blanket-covered opening, but then the blanket fell back in place and Bowie was inside.

Wasting no time on recrimination, Eli reloaded his rifle before running forward and checking Keller and Mexia for weapons. He took a gun from Mexia's belt, but it was doubtful whether the Mexican would have used it. His gun arm useless, Mexia was near-delirious with pain. Hondo Keller was unarmed. He was also dying. As he lay on the ground, his body sawn open by the Comanche woman, his life's blood turned white limestone ground to red about him.

The Comanche woman crouched to one side of the camp-fire, rocking back and forth, moaning softly as though it was all too much for her. All this Adam took in before Eli pulled him to the ground behind a low, scrubby bush.

'Do you think you hit Bowie?'

'I couldn't be certain. It all happened too fast.'

'Then we've got to get him out of there. Any ideas?'

'No – but I think *she* has.'

Adam shouted the words as the Comanche woman suddenly stopped her noisy rocking and rose to her feet. She walked slowly to where Hondo Keller lay still, surrounded by his own blood. Almost casually, she pulled the knife from his side and turned towards the shanty.

'I should have known she wasn't bemoaning her fate. That was the Comanche death-song she was singing to herself. Either she or Bowie is going to die – and she don't give a damn which way it goes.'

Both men rose to their feet as the Comanche woman pushed aside the blanket and was lost to view inside the dug-out. There was no shot. For a full minute, as Adam and Eli waited, there was no sound at all. Then a blood-curdling sound that began as a scream and ended as a sob filled the air.

Both Adam's shots had hit Bowie, one passing between two ribs to lodge in his right lung, the other striking him in the right forearm – and it was this shot that cost him his life.

Bowie was an experienced frontiersman. He kept a rifle fully loaded inside the dug-out for just such an emergency as this. He held it pointing towards the doorway as the Indian woman pushed the blanket aside. Three times he attempted to cock the gun, but his arm was bleeding profusely and the blood flowing down his hand caused his thumb to slip. He succeeded just as the Indian woman reached him, but it was too late. The powder in the brass pan of his flintlock rifle had been ruined by his own blood. The gun misfired. As Bowie reached for the back-up gun he had laid at his side, the Indian woman kicked it out of reach.

Too weak to defend himself, Bowie looked up at the woman and knew he could expect no mercy at her hands. He had shot her husband and slit the throat of her two sons as she looked on helplessly, pinioned by two of his companions. Then Bowie had been the first to rape her as she lay on the ground only an arm's length from her dead family. When they returned to the dug-out he had raped her again.

Now, with Hondo Keller's knife, the Comanche woman ensured that, even if a miracle occurred and Hec Bowie lived, he would never rape another woman.

Eli and Adam pushed through the blanket-door together and saw Bowie lying against the earth wall at the back of the dug-out shanty. The Indian woman still kneeled over him, the bloody knife in her hand.

His face contorted with excruciating pain, Bowie looked up at them accusingly and panted: 'All this ... for ... an Indian woman? Why, Eli ... for God's sake. ... Why?'

As Bowie's head dropped sideways in merciful unconsciousness, the Comanche woman grasped Bowie's hair and raised the knife in her other hand. Eli grabbed her wrist to prevent her from taking Bowie's scalp. The Comanche woman shrieked and tried to break free, but Eli shook the knife from her grasp and pointed to her clothes, which lay crumpled in a corner of the makeshift home. Snatching them up, the woman ducked out through the blanket opening.

Eli first checked Hec Bowie's wounds, then threw a blanket over his mutilated body. 'With any luck he won't come round again. Either way, he'll be dead by nightfall. Let's go look at the Mexican.'

Rafael Mexia was still moaning, but when Eli stirred him with his foot he struggled to sit up, succeeding eventually with Adam's help. When he saw the Comanche woman his frightened expression proved he had missed nothing that had happened since the shooting first started.

Making no pretence at gentleness, Eli examined Rafael Mexia's shoulder. His inspection completed, he said: 'He'll live – and more's the pity. With Mexia dead this whole mess would have had a clean ending. He could make trouble. The only thing in his favour is that he can't talk, and I doubt if he can write. I'll send him off in the direction of the Mexican border. No doubt he'll find a doctor somewhere along the way, or one of his own kind, to treat that shoulder. If he doesn't. . . .' Eli shrugged. 'He'll be no loss to the world.'

'What about the woman?'

'She can return to her people and tell whoever is her chief of what's happened here today. He might be grateful enough to leave us alone. There'll be other Comanche bands who *won't*, but it'll be a start.'

Crossing to the woman, who sat hunched beside the fire, Eli squatted down before her and began talking, his halting Comanche supplemented by skilful use of sign language. For the most part, the woman's replies were no more than a series of monosyllabic grunts, but occasionally she carried on a lengthier dialogue in a throaty, emotion-filled voice. During one such discourse, she pointed in Adam's direction and a fleeting grin crossed Eli's face.

When Eli rose to his feet and returned to Adam, he looked well pleased with himself. 'Adam, we've just scooped ourselves a man-sized kitty. That old man killed by Hec Bowie was the brother of Muguera, one of the most important chiefs of the Penateka Comanche. We've just avenged his death. This means old Muguera owes us one big favour. There's been a lot of killing here today, but we've probably saved more lives than we'll ever know – that's if we can persuade her to go back to her people and tell them what's happened.'

'What does that mean?'

'It means that we've saved her life, so we have first claim on her. She's offered herself to one or both of us for as long as we care to keep her.'

Adam looked at the woman who sat staring into the embers of the fire. There was a smear of dried blood at the corner of her mouth, a souvenir of the beating she had received for attempting to escape. Her hair was a mess and matted with earth and dirt, while her eyes reflected the tragedy and degradation she had suffered. Yet she was only a year or two older than Adam, and not unattractive. Then Adam remembered what she had done to

Hec Bowie. Bending down, he picked up Bowie's hat from the ground. Without a glance at its grubby, unrecognisable hatband, he threw it on the fire.

'The sooner she goes, the better.'

An hour later, both Mexia and the Comanche woman were gone. She took her own horses, plus those that had belonged to the dead men. She also carried away everything from Hec Bowie's hillside home that was movable. It was a poor exchange for the family she had lost, but her new-found wealth would ensure she had no difficulty in finding another husband very quickly.

Slumped painfully in his saddle, Rafael Mexia had ridden off in the direction decreed by Eli, after indicating wordlessly that he was being sent off to a certain death. Bluntly, Eli told Mexia that if he did not head straight for the border his fate would be equally certain at Eli's hands.

Adam and Eli dug a single grave for the two dead men. Before the task was completed, Hec Bowie also died. He was buried with them.

Finally, Adam and Eli put a torch to the dug-out shanty and walked over the hill to where they had left the horses. Then they returned to the place where they had first discovered the bodies of the Indians and buried them, too.

Their unwholesome tasks completed, Eli said: 'I think we've done enough for the dead for one day. Now it's time we gave a bit of thought to the living. I've got a gallon jar of good corn whisky hidden in a hollow tree down by the river. I come across and get acquainted with it when I've had too much of folks. Today I don't need to look for an excuse. We've earned ourselves a whole bellyful of whisky.'

It was long after dark when Adam and Eli crossed the river and made their unsteady way to Caleb's cabin. They found it crowded with settlers, each man carrying his gun.

Nell was the first to greet them. 'Adam! Eli. Where have you been? Angus Coutts came along to say his boys heard shooting earlier. We thought you might have run into trouble.' She stopped suddenly, her nose wrinkling suspiciously as Eli gave way to a sudden bout of coughing. Leaning closer, she said: 'You've been drinking!'

'We've been ... *drinking*,' Eli agreed, beaming about him benevolently. 'My partner and I have been drinking.'

'Well! There's everyone sick with worry and all set to start a search for you, and all you can say is "We've been drinking"!'

Nell stood before them, hands on her hips, her exasperation mixed with relief. 'You've made a fool of Caleb and . . . of *all* of us.'

Behind her, the settlers were grinning broadly, belying Nell's words. Their relief was tinged with envy. Whisky was a scarce commodity here in the newest Texan settlement.

Turning around quickly, Nell was in time to see their amusement. 'What are you all here gawping for? Do you have no homes to go to? You've spent an hour eating poor Eileen Ryan out of house and home while you talked, and did nothing. Now there's nothing for you to do. Away with you, before your wives need to come out looking for *you*.'

Nell shooed the shuffling, grinning men out through the door as though they were so many hens. Behind her, Caleb said good-humouredly: 'I can't ever remember seeing Nell so agitated before. She must be mighty fond of one of you.'

When the door slammed behind the last of the departing men, Nell picked up two letters from the heavy wooden shelf over the fireplace and brandished them beneath Adam's nose.'Here, these came for you this afternoon, sent on by Don Manuel. They look important, so if you're as drunk as you look you'd best leave them until the morning.'

Adam took the letters. One bore the heavy seal of the British Foreign Office. The other carried an equally large seal, but it was not one Adam recognised.

'I'll read them tonight.'

'Then you'll need to take a candle with you. You and Eli are bedding down in the lean-to, with the animals.'

In the lean-to barn, the entrance of the two men caused momentary consternation among the animals penned there. Sheep, horses and cows were all partitioned off from each other and there was one empty stall with two blankets laid on clean, dry grass. Eli lay down on one, while Adam took the candle clear of the dry grass and settled down near the door to read his letters.

The letter with the unfamiliar seal was from General Houston. Great Britain was still delaying recognition of the Republic of Texas, but it seemed that Palmerston had approved a limited trade agreement. Houston declared it was a stride forward. Rightly or wrongly, he attributed the agreement to the letter Adam had sent on his behalf. Houston said he would be in Nacogdoches for some weeks and asked Adam to join him there. He had some ideas on the future of Texas that might be of interest to Lord Palmerston. He wanted to discuss them with Adam. Then, if Adam felt inclined to oblige a friend once more, Houston said he would like Adam to forward them to Great Britain's Foreign Secretary.

The second letter was from Palmerston himself. In an informal note he thanked Adam for his most informative letter and congratulated him on gaining the confidence of the Texan president after such a short time in the country. He suggested that Adam pursue the acquaintanceship, bearing in mind Great Britain's future interests. He also thought Adam should engineer an introduction to the man who was tipped to succeed Houston as President of Texas and keep Palmerston closely informed of any change in the direction of Texan policy. Lord Palmerston enclosed a second letter, from one of his officials, which Adam was at liberty to show to Houston.

The official letter was written in more formal language. It noted Adam's comments about the importance of recognising Texas as an independent republic, but pointed out that there were a number of matters that required clarification before serious consideration could be given to the matter by Her Majesty's government. Houston's assurance that Texas would no longer seek annexation by the United States was welcomed. It was suggested that Texas could best further her interests by expressing readiness to sign a treaty providing for the suppression of slavery in the lands and waters it claimed as its own. The letter went on to mention other matters, such as Mexico's huge debts to British merchants, payment of which might be held up if Texas was recognised by the government of Great Britian. However, if the slavery issue could be satisfactorily agreed, and Texas showed its ability to stand alone, Great Britain would feel able to recognise Texan independence, and use its considerable influence to persuade Mexico to follow suit.

It was a politician's letter, containing, as it did, many vague half-promises. Yet Adam had no doubt that General Houston, desperate for international recognition, would seize upon the letter as a pointer to the future of the country he had done so much to create.

However, Adam reserved his own excitement for the last paragraph of Lord Palmerston's personal note. It helped him to justify the decision he had already made. The Foreign Secretary mentioned a report he had received from the Mexican ambassador to Great Britain. The ambassador claimed that Mexico was massing an army on the Texan border and was about to reclaim its errant province. It was claimed that, when the time came to strike northwards, all the Indians in Texas would rise in support of the Mexican army. Adam was asked by Palmerston to check the veracity of the information.

It was not entirely the whisky he had drunk that made Adam feel lightheaded as he burned Palmerston's note before extinguishing the candle and retiring to his blanket bed, surrounded by the noises and smells of Caleb's animals. He would go to Nacogdoches to talk to President Houston. Then he would head for Cherokee country, to the village of Chief Bowles – and Tiski.

BOOK TWO

CHAPTER ONE

THE TOWN known to old Spanish settlers as Nuestra Señora
del Pilar de Nacogdoches was proud of its antiquity. Its Indian
burial-mounts were ancient when the area was visited in 1687 by
the ill-fated expedition of the French trader and explorer René
Robert Cavalier, sieur de la Salle. In 1716 the settlement of Our
Lady of the Pillar of Nacogdoches sprang up about a mission,
founded in the same year by the Spanish founder of so many
missions, Captain Domingo Ramon.

In those early days, Nacogdoches was at the end of El Camino
Real, 'The King's Highway', linking the far-flung mission
stations with the provincial Spanish capital of Monclova, a
distance of more than five hundred miles.

After the American War of Independence and the rapid and
energetic expansion of the United States, the sleepy Spanish
settlement underwent a dramatic change. With the purchase of
Louisiana by America in 1812, Nacogdoches found itself at the
crossroads of the increasingly travelled land routes between the
American states and the towns and settlements of east Texas.

Nacogdoches saw cotton planters from the fields of Georgia
emigrating to Austin's promised land of Brazoria: wealthy, soft-
spoken men with their families, wagons – and slaves. There were
also merchants, traders who saw rich pickings to be made in the
lands south of the Sabine River; and adventurers, frontiersmen
trying to stay ahead of the ensnarements of civilisation, and
fugitives from the certain noose of justice. Most passed through
Nacogdoches, many to brand their names upon history. Some
stayed to offer what talents they possessed to the cosmopolitan
community that was Nacogdoches.

General Sam Houston was one of those who took up residence
upon his arrival here. Swashbuckling ex-soldier, ex-Governor of
Tennessee, honorary citizen of the Cherokee nation, emissary of
the Indian nation to the Great White Father in Washington, ex-
trader – and ex-drunkard, Houston took his place among the
gentry of the town. In Nacogdoches he practised law with such
men as Vicente Cordova, whilst buying and selling land for
considerable personal gain. Never quite certain himself whether
he was a politician or a soldier, Sam Houston was to have the best
of both worlds here. Always in the political arena during the

heated exchanges that led to the Texan Declaration of Independence, he was elected to represent Nacogdoches in the State Convention of 1833. Two years later the sharp tongue of a politician was exchanged for the accoutrements of a soldier. He was made commander-in-chief of the troops of the Nacogdoches area, in what was now a revolution in all but name. As it became clear that revolution would soon become war, Houston was made major-general of the rebel Texan army – such as it was.

Houston commanded a fragmented 'army' of volunteers, militia and 'one-man units'. Used to fighting as rugged individuals, the Texans were in the habit of obeying orders only if they happened to agree with them, and then rarely without argument.

After suffering a number of decisive, albeit occasionally glorious, defeats at the hands of the disciplined Mexican army, Houston was left with no more than nine hundred men under his command. Convinced that their brief bid for independence was over, Texan settlers were in full flight, heading for the American border, the trails behind them strewn with possessions, abandoned in their headlong flight.

Then, on the plain of San Jacinto, General Sam Houston and his outnumbered army won a single battle – and by that battle won a war. General Santa Anna, President of Mexico, was captured and the cream of his army lay dead about him, many slaughtered as they floundered in the waters of the bayous about the battlefield. It was grim retribution upon the soldiers who had offered no quarter to the Texan defenders of the Alamo mission at San Antonio.

Six months after his victory, the forty-three-year-old general took office as President of the Independent Republic of Texas.

This was the man Adam and Eli rode into Nacogdoches to meet in October 1838.

They found the town of almost two thousand inhabitants augmented to the point of overflowing by the ragged Texan militia, which made no pretence of wearing a uniform. Vicente Cordova, once General Houston's colleague in the High Court of Nacogdoches, had led an ill-timed, ill-planned and badly executed rebellion against the government of Texas.

Cordova occupied an island in the San Angelino River, which ran close to Nacogdoches. His 'army' of almost six hundred men contained many Mexicans who were not prepared to accept the status of second-class citizens in the new republic. Its ranks were also swollen by many Indians of various tribes, any one of whom would have welcomed the opportunity to become a Texan citizen of whatever standing.

From his island headquarters, Cordova sent a defiant message to General Houston, proclaiming his rebellion against the Texan government.

It was a short-lived insurrection. By the time the Texas militia arrived at Cordova's headquarters, the Indians were long gone and Cordova and his untried army were fleeing southwards, on their way to Mexico. However, the brief, uneventful rebellion proved profitable for the business of the Nacogdoches saloon-keepers. The Texas presidential elections were imminent. With more voters in town than any political agent could possibly have envisaged, calls of 'Drinks on the house' and political back-slapping went hand in hand.

But one drinking man in Nacogdoches was not sampling the noisy conviviality of the saloons. Adam and Eli found Sam Houston at home in a large, ramshackle cabin, drinking with a few of his closest government associates. He was in an unusually morose mood, although he brightened up considerably when his two visitors were announced.

Rising from the seat where he had been sprawled, Houston shook Adam's hand warmly and embraced Eli, saying with a wry smile: 'It will be good for me to meet men who aren't either buttering me up or putting me down, depending on who they're backing in the election.'

Houston found seats for them by moving a variety of outdoor clothing from a camp-bed. Dressed in dirty buckskins and moccasins, and sporting a beard that was in need of a trim, Houston looked every inch a frontiersman – but there could have been few more unlikely presidents.

Pouring each of his newly arrived guests a gigantic whisky, Houston said: 'Drink it down; you've got some catching up to do. From what I hear you deserve every drop. That was a fine thing you did, rescuing that young settler lad from the Comanche.'

Placing a great hand on Adam's shoulder, Houston boomed: 'You've made your mark on the Cherokee nation, too, young man. By saving the life of Chief Bowles's son you've earned the undying gratitude of a great chief and his people. I'm telling you, an Indian will remember his debt to you for longer than any white man.'

Houston's hand dropped away. Striding to the window, he flung it open. A wide variety of sounds entered the room from the town's bars and saloons. Singing, great roars of drunken

171

cheering and shouting – and just before the window was closed once more they all heard the unmistakable crack of a pistol-shot.

'You hear that? Do you know what they're celebrating? They're drinking to my departure from office and the election of that self-important little jackass, Mirabeau Buonaparte Lamar. The Texas Napoleon. He's promised them he'll extend our borders as far as the Pacific Ocean, conquering every Indian and Mexican along the way. He sees himself as a ninteenth-century *conquistador*. If he read history more carefully, he'd learn what happened to those *conquistadores*. They came here with the same idea. Lamar was a good man with a sword in his hand at San Jacinto. A *brave* man. I hear he's just as expert with a fiddle. He should have settled for one or the other, and kept his nose clear of politics.'

General Houston topped up his glass from a whisky-bottle.

'Lamar and his party of strutting turkeys would have stood no chance at all against either Peter Grayson or Jim Collinsworth. You remember Collinsworth, Eli? A good old Tennessee boy. He was my Chief Justice, right here in Texas – and a damned good one. He committed suicide, a week or two back. Drowned himself down near Galveston. Peter Grayson did the same up at Ben's Station, in Tennessee. You'll know that place, Eli. Can you imagine anyone wanting to commit suicide in Tennessee? Grayson did. Wrote a note apologising to the innkeeper for the mess he was about to make, then blew his brains out.'

Houston knocked back his whisky with a speed that awed Adam. Wiping the back of his hand across his lips, Houston shook his head sadly.

'Two good men and true. Two men who had served Texas well and had so much more to give. Either could have been President of Texas before the close of the year. Instead, they're rotting in their graves, lost to Texas and the world for ever.'

General Houston set his glass down on the table in front of him and looked across the room to where the two newcomers sat.

'Adam, I'm in need of some air. Join me and tell me how my Indian brother, Chief Bowles, is making out. The rest of you make sure you save some of that whisky for when we get back.'

Outside the cabin, General Houston took a deep breath of warm evening air.

'There's something about Texas that intoxicates me more than all the whisky in the world. One day soon I'll take more of one, and less of the other.'

Turning his back on the noise that emanated from the heart of Nacogdoches, the Texan president led Adam out of town, along a path that followed a narrow creek. The country hereabouts was still well treed, but the ground had been cleared for farming more than a century before and the soil was dark and rich. Adam could not help contrasting it with the shallow, impoverished soil of the San Antonio Hill Country.

'You received my letter? Your country has agreed to allow Texas ships and their cargoes to enter British ports on the same footing as vessels from Mexico.'

'I don't think I can claim credit for even such a small token of recognition.'

Adam marvelled at Houston. Only minutes before, in the cabin, he had appeared to be as drunk as any man deserved to be after drinking whisky for most of the day. Yet his mind was now working on the problems of his administration, as though he had been drinking tea with his government advisers. Adam wondered how many men had underestimated General Houston during his renowned drinking bouts.

'I've no doubt your letter helped, no doubt at all; but Texas needs more than trading concessions, Adam, important though they are. We need your country to recognise us as an independent republic – and quickly. Only Great Britain has the influence to negotiate with Mexico on our behalf; to convince them that our independence is *de facto*. Nothing Mexico can do, now or in the future, can alter our status. Mexico has an army, of sorts, and might be capable of the occasional raid into Texas – no more. It is more of an irritant than a threat to our existence. While in office, I have accepted it as such, but from the end of this year there will be another man occupying the office of President. If it is Lamar – and it seems that little can stop him – the Mexicans will find him short on both patience and diplomacy. What's more, his vision of self-grandeur will prove dangerous to both Mexico and Texas.'

Adam dipped into his pocket and pulled out the letter he had received from the Foreign Office in London. 'I think the British government is concerned about relations between Texas and Mexico. I received this at the same time as your letter. You'd better read what it says.'

Adam had thought the letter contained nothing optimistic for the future of Texas but, much to his surprise, Houston read the letter with increasing enthusiasm. When he had read the letter through twice, he said: 'This is a *definite* step forward, Adam. It shows that your government is at last taking the question of Texan recognition seriously.'

'Only if you are prepared to give certain assurances, surely? Even then, there is no guarantee. . . .'

'Diplomatic jargon, Adam, no more.' Houston made a small gesture of impatience. 'If only you had arrived in Texas a year earlier – or I had another year in office! With this letter I would have carried my Congress along with me – and chosen my successor in office. Now I'm a yesterday's man. Nobody will go along with me for fear of displeasing a President who won't take office for another three months.'

He shook the letter despairingly. 'I'd like to keep this, Adam. Just in case I might do something worthwhile, even at this late hour.'

Adam nodded. 'But remember, it's not an official document – and it's addressed to me.'

'I won't forget – but will you do another favour for me? Write to Palmerston again. Tell him of my reaction to his letter. . . . Oh, I know it hasn't *officially* come from him, but I don't doubt he's familiar with its contents. Tell him that everything he asks is possible. I am no lover of slavery. As for Mexico's debt to Great Britain, Texas will accept it as the price of freedom – if he can assure us of Mexico's recognition in return. But Palmerston must be made to understand the need for urgency. If there is no formal peace with Mexico when Lamar takes office, then it will be *war* with Mexico. That will benefit no one. On the other hand, if Great Britain recognises Texas and takes the initiative in negotiating a peace with Mexico, your country will have gained a powerful and lasting friend in the Americas.'

'You don't have to convince *me*, General Houston, but I'm not the British government. I'll write and tell Lord Palmerston what you've said and endorse your words with my own views, for what they are worth. Recognition will come. It *must* come, but I can't promise that Lord Palmerston will take immediate action.'

'I realise you're doing your very best for Texas, Adam, and I'm grateful – both as the President of Texas and as plain Sam Houston. When this business is finally settled I'll take you up to the Red River and show you some land I own there. It's beautiful country, you'll love it – and a thousand acres are yours for the choosing.'

Murmuring his thanks, Adam remembered Lord Palmerston's private letter. 'Perhaps you'll introduce me to Lamar sometime. After hearing both you and Don Manuel talk about him, I'm curious to see what manner of man he is – and, from what I hear, he's not going to be approachable if he gets the presidency.'

'He's not President *yet*, but when he does make it, come to Houston for the inauguration. I'll make sure he shakes your hand, at least.'

Farther away from Nacogdoches the path entered woodland – the high, silent world of a pine-wood, with an age-old carpet of needles underfoot, and a sky held at bay by the high canopy of gently waving branches.

'This reminds me of parts of the Cherokee country I knew so well as a boy. They were happy days. I seem to be thinking about them more lately than ever before. Something to do with the cares of office, I suppose. Sometimes, on a particularly bad day, I'll forget where I am, what I'm doing, and my memories take me right back to the forests. In those days my cares didn't go beyond winning the affections of a particular girl, or wondering where I was going to get hold of another book when I finished the one I was reading. I was a great reader in those days. If I had any ambition at all, it was to do my damnedest to read every book that had ever been written. I don't think I reckoned on there being more than a dozen or two.'

The Texan president paused at a spot where the creek doubled back on itself, the path continuing on the far side of a rickety wooden footbridge.

'What did you think of the Cherokee and their way of life, Adam?'

'I think they're a wonderful people. As for their way of life – well, I intend going on from here to stay with them for a month or two.'

General Houston raised an eyebrow. 'A month or two . . . ? Is there a girl involved in this plan of yours?'

'Yes, a Kiowa girl. Chief Bowles's adopted daughter.'

'Rainbird? A mighty handsome girl. Mighty handsome. Does she know you're on your way back to her?'

'I promised I'd be back.'

'I'm damned if I don't envy you, Adam. Had you come to me *after* the presidential election and told me where you were going, I'd as likely as not have come with you. God Almighty! Why did I ever get into politics? I'm no politician. I'm a backwoodsman, that's what I am – and a man has a right to be where he's happy, hasn't he?'

Suddenly General Houston grimaced. Rubbing a hand over his unshaven face, he said: 'You don't need to answer any of those questions, Adam. Come on, let's get back to the cabin. I hope Eli and the others haven't finished off my whisky. Tomorrow I'll be heading back to Houston and the burden of state duties – while you'll be on your way to Chief Bowles and an honest, simple way of life.'

CHAPTER TWO

ADAM knew something was wrong, even before he and Eli entered Chief Bowles's village. Along the way they had passed a number of children working in the fields outside the village. Instead of waving, they took to their heels as though they had seen the Devil.

In the village, too, the arrival of the two white men caused some consternation. Those Indians who were there seemed in a great hurry to be somewhere else. No one came out to meet them, and the two men dismounted uncertainly before the cabin of Yellow Bear.

It was a few minutes before Quaty, Yellow Bear's wife, put in an appearance. Taking their horses, she welcomed them nervously. When Adam asked about Tiski, she replied: 'Yellow Bear will come soon. He will tell you.'

Thoroughly alarmed, Adam demanded to know what was wrong with Tiski, and why Quaty had evaded his question.

'Tiski is well, but it would have been better had you not come here at this time.' Yellow Bear had come up behind Adam, unnoticed. After embracing Adam, he shook hands gravely with Eli.

'What's going on around here?' Adam demanded once more. 'Everyone is behaving as though I've got smallpox. I thought I was supposed to be an adopted Cherokee, this village my home. What's happened to change things? Is it to do with Tiski? Where is she?'

'You are a man with many questions, my English brother. I can give you a simple answer to them all. My father has other guests. Metete, Tiski's brother, and the Comanche Chief Ten Trees are camped by the river with their warriors and families. They came early for Tiski. Because you are of our family you are *both* welcome, but it might have been better had you not chosen this time to return.'

'He's right, Adam. The best thing we can do is turn and get the hell out of here. I've heard of Ten Trees – and of Metete, too. I'd as soon share a cave with a family of grizzlies as stay in the same village as them.'

Adam had paled when he heard that Ten Trees was already here, but the blood suddenly rushed back to his face. 'You leave if you want to. I'm staying. Yellow Bear, I want to see Chief Bowles right away. Tiski is not going to be the second wife of any Comanche chief.'

Eli groaned. 'All these years I've managed to hang on to my scalp. Now I look like *giving* it away, and all because of an Indian girl and a stubborn Englishman.'

'It is not good to talk so lightly of dying,' chided Yellow Bear. 'But my English brother would be wise to listen to the other things you say. My father is seeking lasting friendship with the Comanche and Kiowa. It is no place for a young man whose blood is hot for a woman who has been promised to them.'

'Will you take me to see Chief Bowles, or do I find him for myself and risk walking in on a meeting with Metete and this Ten Trees?'

Stiffly, Yellow Bear said: 'Not even a son can walk into the house of his chief unless he is asked to enter. I will go and speak with him. Perhaps he will wish to see you. Perhaps not. The Chief of the Cherokees will decide.'

'I'm sorry, Yellow Bear, I'm not out to make things difficult for you, or for Chief Bowles – but I've come here for Tiski, and no murdering Comanche is going to stand in my way.'

Yellow Bear's expression softened. 'You speak from your heart. That is how it should be between brothers. I will speak for you with my father, but I fear it will change nothing. While I am gone, Quaty will take you to a cabin.'

When the Indian had left, Eli gave Adam a strange look. 'I just wish you could have heard yourself speaking back there, talking of some "murdering Comanche". You sounded just like a Texan. I seem to remember that the last scalps we saw were lifted *from* Comanches – by white men.'

'That's right. We killed *them*, too.'

Thoroughly alarmed, Eli said: 'Now, you just wait a minute, Adam. Don't you get any damn fool ideas in that hot head of yours now. . . .'

Adam was not listening; he could see Quaty returning. Removing his rifle from the saddle holster and shouldering his saddlebags, he handed the reins of his horse to a young Cherokee boy who had been patiently waiting nearby, and went to meet Yellow Bear's wife.

'Quaty, I want to speak to Tiski. Where is she?'

As though she had heard nothing, Quaty said: 'Come, I will show you to your hut.'

Taking her arm, Adam brought her to a halt: 'Quaty, I asked

177

you a question. You're closer to Tiski than anyone else. How is she?'

'It will be better to talk when we are inside the hut. Many eyes are watching us here.'

Adam dropped his hand from her arm and followed her to the cabin he had occupied on his earlier visit. Once inside, Quaty wasted no time acquainting Adam with the situation. Tiski was well but, although deeply unhappy about the arranged marriage, she would be leaving the village with Chief Ten Trees, as his second wife. Chief Bowles had explained the reason why he wanted the marriage, and Tiski had agreed for the sake of her adopted father and the Cherokee people.

'How important is this treaty to the Cherokee?'

'In the days when the lands of the Cherokee were great and touched those of the Kiowa and Comanche, it was important. The Cherokee and the Kiowa were enemies. They fought whenever they met. Those days have gone – but not for Chief Bowles. His dream has always been to make peace with the Kiowa. It is important to no one else. But a daughter cannot tell her father this – and Metete *is* Tiski's brother.'

'I must speak to Tiski.'

Quaty shook her head. 'It cannot be. Tahnay will not leave her side until she is given to Ten Trees. Now you are here, Tiski will not leave her hut. What happened between you may be a secret from the men, but it is known to the women.'

'Then you'll have to speak to her for me – and tell her I want an answer from her *heart*. I must know whether things are the same between us. I don't want to know about her duty to Chief Bowles, or what is best for the Cherokee people. All I want to know is whether her feelings towards *me* have changed – and I need to know before I speak to Chief Bowles.'

'I will go now.'

Quaty passed Eli in the doorway. As the Tennesseean threw his saddle and bags on the floor, he said: 'She left here in an almighty hurry. You say something to upset her?'

Adam shook his head.

'Well, I don't mind admitting you've got me worried. Camped on the other side of that shallow river out there is the meanest bunch of Indians you'll find anywhere between the Canadian and Mexican borders. If you're planning on stirring 'em up, I'd be obliged for a day or two's warning. I'd like to put some distance between us.'

'Then you can consider yourself warned. I aim to stop Ten

Trees taking Tiski away with him. The stirring starts just as soon as Chief Bowles will see me.'

Once again Eli groaned. Giving Adam a rueful look, he said: 'Damn you, Adam. You didn't have to call my bluff that way. You could have tried sweet-talking me around to your way of thinking. Now, since you seem set on throwing dirt in the teeth of Chief Ten Trees, I think you'd better tell me what you got in mind. I'd like to know what part I play in this plan of yours.'

'There's no plan, Eli. At least, I haven't thought of one yet. If you come up with something, let me know. I'm going to take a walk.'

Leaving the hut, Adam walked along the river to the spot where the women did their washing. There was no one here today. Well upstream, beyond the Cherokee village, he could see the tepees of the Comanches and Kiowas. There must have been seventy or more of the conical, hide-covered tents, and there was a lot of movement around them. Adam watched for a while, before his thoughts returned to the immediate problem that faced him.

Adam was still sitting hunched on the river bank when Yellow Bear found him, an hour later.

'My father will see you now,' he said, when Adam raised tired eyes at his approach. 'The tribal council sits with him. It is an honour, to show you that whatever you have to say is of importance to the Cherokee people.'

Adam nodded. He would have welcomed more time to think things out in some detail, but he knew what he had to do.

As Adam approached the gathering of the council, Chief Bowles was helped to his feet and he greeted Adam with an embrace. Eli was already here and he eyed Adam warily.

Waiting until Chief Bowles had seated himself on his buffalo robe once more, Adam squatted facing the aged chief across a low-burning fire.

'You have eaten?' The question came from Chief Bowles.

'No, I've had other things on my mind.'

'We will talk of your thoughts later, after we have eaten and smoked together.'

Curbing his impatience, Adam answered Chief Bowles's polite questions about his journey, the weather and General Houston. Then food arrived. A number of Cherokee girls served the food, but Tiski was not among them. Quaty brought Adam's food to him. As she leaned low over him to place a bowl in his hand, she whispered: 'I have spoken to Tiski. It is the same between you.'

Then Quaty was gone. Only Eli knew that a message had been

179

passed and he kept his head bowed low over the bowl that had been placed before him.

When everyone about the fire had eaten, Yellow Bear brought a deerskin pouch to his father, carrying it carefully. Chief Bowles took it from his son with equal care. When he opened out the deerskin there was a sigh of surprise from the assembled council. Exposed to view was a beautiful pipe with a large, carved redstone bowl.

'You'd better believe what's said here tonight, Adam. I've heard of this pipe, but I've never seen it before. It comes out only when there's something very special to be decided or talked about. This is so no one will be in any doubt that whatever's decided here is final. I only hope *you're* as sure about what you're doing.'

Eli murmured this information to Adam as Chief Bowles offered the pipe first to the dying sun and then to the four points of the compass before applying a twig to the tobacco and sucking the pipe into life. Passing the pipe immediately to Adam, Chief Bowles intoned something that sounded remarkably like a prayer, to which the members of the council responded with a passable 'Amen'.

'The chief called for this meeting to be blessed with truth and friendship. He also asked that whatever is decided here might be for the good of the Cherokee people,' explained Eli in a low voice. 'If he'd added good wishes for me, I wouldn't have taken it amiss.'

When the last member of the council had smoked the pipe, it was handed back to the Cherokee chief. Knocking the still hot ash into his hand, Chief Bowles scattered it in four directions, then gazed into the fire for many minutes without speaking. It was almost dark now, but beyond the firelight Adam could see many of the villagers gathered to hear what was being discussed about Chief Bowles's fire.

Looking up, Chief Bowles fixed his gaze on Eli. 'We will speak in the tongue of my people. You will tell the Englishman what is being said.'

Shifting his gaze to Adam, Chief Bowles began to speak in the guttural Cherokee language. Pausing occasionally to think out a particular word, Eli translated: 'It is known why you have come to us. Because we know, our hearts go out to you. A man may seek all his life yet never find the woman he wants above all others to share his life. To find her, only to learn she can never be his, is to lose all but life itself. Yet this is how it must be for you, as I told you when you first came to us.'

As the tribal council nodded their agreement, the Cherokee chief continued: 'Many years ago I had a dream. I dreamed I saw white men coming from the sea like a great flood. They were so powerful that even the trees fell before them. Then, when I looked more closely, I saw they were not trees at all, and that they all had faces of friends who had fallen in battle beside me over the years. I trembled to see them.'

His words caused considerable consternation among the Indians about him. To dream of dead companions was an ill omen. To talk about them was to defy all the ancient tribal taboos – something that only the bravest, or most foolhardy, of men would dare to do.

'Then the flood that was white men came to a great forest. Here the trees stood close together. When it tried to pass through, the trees barred the way of the flood. Time and time again the flood tried to sweep through the trees, but it could not find a way. If a tree was felled by the water, those beside it held the tree in place. After a while, the flood that was white men tired and it went back from whence it had come.'

Once again the listening Cherokees reacted to their chief's words, this time with expressions of approval.

'When I looked at the forest I saw that these trees were Indians also, young, strong warriors: Cherokee, Kiowa and Comanche – all standing side by side, as do the trees of the forest. I thought much about this dream and wondered why it had been sent to me. There were few white men here then, and Cherokee walked apart from Kiowa and Comanche. Then came the bad year when the rains did not come. The ribs of our cattle and horses were as sticks laid side by side on a rock, their bellies filled only with wind. It was the same on the Great Plains, and the buffalo did not come from the north. Indians travelled far from their hunting-grounds in search of food. Cherokee met Kiowa and Comanche, and they fought. During one battle, a small Kiowa girl was captured by my warriors and brought to this village. Many of you who listen now will remember the day well. As the girl was lifted from a warrior's horse, rain began to fall. Soon the land was green again, our people contented. I took the Kiowa girl into my house and called her A-Gan Tiski Tiskwa, "The Rainbird". When I had my dream again I knew she had been sent to our people to fulfil a great promise. That time is here. Metete, brother of The Rainbird says the Kiowa will never fight the Cherokee again. When she is married to Chief Ten Trees of the Quahadi Comanche, his people will also be our friends. Together, perhaps, we can hold back the white men who come from the east and look with greedy eyes on our lands. I tell this to you, Englishman, because you have the respect of my people, as does the man who rides with you. It is a story that has been told to no other outside the tribe. Now you see why you cannot have the girl I have been happy to call "my daughter".'

The translation came to an end. With the excited hum of conversation all about them, Eli added his own comments, in a low voice.

'You've got a losing hand, partner. Tribal prejudice can be overcome, and you might put up a mighty good argument against an alliance, or two – but you can't buck the dream of a chief like Old Bowl. Forget the girl and let's go home. My scalp's beginning to feel uncomfortable, as though it don't belong to me anymore.'

Adam's face felt taut and drawn. He did not need Eli to tell him of the difficulties he faced, but he was not ready to accept defeat. He was grateful for the hours he had spent talking to Eli, on the journey from San Antonio. He had learned all he could about Cherokee customs, their beliefs and superstitions.

Across the fire, his face expressionless, Chief Bowles sat waiting to hear what argument Adam would use against the plan to marry Tiski to Chief Ten Trees. Adam bided his time. The excited chatter about them died down, but he said nothing until the expectancy began to drift into impatience.

'A man must heed his dreams. They are sent to him as messages from the spirits. But a chief must never forget that *he* is a man and not a god.'

Chief Bowles sat quite still, a blanket about his shoulders, his expression giving away none of his thoughts.

'Because he is not a god, a man must examine his dreams very carefully if he wishes their meaning to be made clear to him. Chief Bowles has done this. It is the wish of the spirits that Cherokee, Kiowa and Comanche should stand together, even as the trees of the forest.'

The statement brought a surprised blink from the Cherokee chief, but from the corner of his eye Adam saw Eli look anxiously at him before interpreting his words. The Tennessee frontiersman was convinced that Adam's own words had destroyed any remote chance he might have had of winning Tiski. By his next statement, it seemed Adam was determined to stack the odds in Chief Bowles's favour even more.

'When The Rainbird came to the Cherokee people she brought with her the gift of rain from the Spirits. Now, because of her, Kiowa, Comanche and Cherokee share the same water. Their smoke rises from the cooking-fires and is made one by the winds. The fulfilment of Chief Bowles's dream is very close.'

All about them, heads were nodding agreement, but Chief Bowles's eyes were upon Adam's face and only he was not taken by surprise at Adam's next words.

'This is why it saddens me to see the Cherokee chief making such a serious mistake.'

The heads stopped nodding, and the gasps of surprise quickly swelled into a rumble of anger. Beside him, Eli spoke from the corner of his mouth: 'You'd better have something to back up them words, or there'll be trouble, for sure.'

Adam was not listening. Across the fire, a grudging smile crossed the face of Chief Bowles and he held up a hand for silence. 'The Englishman has said nothing to give me offence. He has learned our ways well. I would hear more.'

'Comanche and Kiowa warriors are camped across the river. They have shared your fire, just as I do now. Have you shared a pipe and talked of peace between your people and theirs?'

'The time is not yet right. I have the word of Metete that his people and ours will be as one family, even as The Rainbird has been as my own daughter.'

'I don't doubt that Metete is a man of his word, but he does not speak for all the Kiowa people. Chiefs Eagle Feather, Little Mountain and Satank are all more important Kiowa chiefs than Metete.'

The names of the Kiowa chiefs had also been supplied by Eli, when he and Adam had discussed the standing of Tiski's brother among the Kiowa.

'When you look across the river, how many tepees do you see? Sixty? Seventy, perhaps? Most belong to the Comanche. Only a few are Kiowa.'

Seeing he now had the undivided attention of his Cherokee audience, Adam pressed home his advantage. 'Has Ten Trees *promised* that his people will stand beside the Cherokee as trees in a forest?'

Angered at the way Chief Bowles was allowing Adam to dominate the meeting, one of the younger members of the council answered him, determined to put Adam firmly in his place: 'Chief Ten Trees does not need to speak of such things. You do not know our ways. An Indian does not go to war with his wife's family.'

'The family of The Rainbird are Kiowa,' retorted Adam brusquely. 'She was taken in war – and what kind of a treaty is it that will stand or fall on the success of a marriage? Ten Trees already has a wife – a *Comanche* wife. The Rainbird will be the second woman in his tepee – an *inferior* wife. In the eyes of the women of Ten Trees' people she will always be second to a Comanche. If Ten Trees favours The Rainbird above his first wife, will the Comanche wife's family swear everlasting friendship to the Cherokee? And what if she does *not* please her Comanche husband? Will he then think kindly of the people who brought her up? Perhaps she will find herself another man and shame Ten Trees. Will he still love the Cherokees from whence she came? Does he understand that Cherokee women are not the same as those of his tribe? That a Cherokee woman is not the *property* of a man, like his gun, his horse, or his blanket? Here, among the Cherokee, The Rainbird has learned that a woman is free to love a man – or to leave him if he makes her unhappy. Can she change so much?'

There were murmurs of agreement from the women on the outer fringe of the circle about the fire, but Adam had more to say. His voice dropping even lower, he asked: 'Tell me, Chief Bowles, what would Ten Trees say if he knew that The Rainbird loved another man? That this man had already been more of a husband to her than any Comanche will ever be?'

The gasp that rose from the Cherokees was one of genuine shock. Since the tribe had become settled in its ways, Cherokee women enjoyed far more sexual freedom than did Comanche women or any other Plains Indians, but such matters were never the subject of public debate.

'This is not true. The Rainbird has always behaved as should the daughter of a chief. She has known no other man.'

Adam was not proud of what he was doing, but there was no other way. 'There is one who can tell you if what I say is the truth.'

It was the first time Adam had pierced the inscrutability of the Cherokee chief. For a moment he saw an old man, clinging to little more than natural dignity and the comfortable familiarity of the old ways.

'Bring The Rainbird to me. I would hear what she has to say.'

There was no containing the eruption of excitement now. It consumed the crowd that had gathered about the fireside meeting and spilled over on the council. Only Adam and Chief Bowles sat quietly awaiting the arrival of Tiski, Adam successfully concealing the apprehension he felt at what he was doing.

Seated cross-legged beside Adam, Eli shook his head in bewilderment. 'You've stirred up a whole mess of hornets here.

184

I only hope you'll come out of it without getting yourself stung too bad.'

The excited chatter about them rose to a crescendo – then stopped abruptly, as though gagged by a giant hand. Behind Chief Bowles, Tiski stepped from the hut and walked to the fire, looking neither to left nor to right.

The crowd knew immediately who it was, but recognition came as a shock to Adam. Tiski had a drab blanket draped about her shoulders. The beautiful hair of which she was so proud had been inexpertly hacked off, leaving behind a ragged mess, the parting daubed with a bright-red dye. Painted designs of the same colour adorned both cheeks and circled her eyes, and lines were drawn from her chin to her ears.

Tiski had been transformed into a Comanche woman, in readiness for her forthcoming wedding.

Stopping in front of the Cherokee chief, her back to Adam, Tiski stood with downcast eyes, waiting for her adopted father to speak.

'A-Gan Tiski Tiskwa. This is the name I gave to you when you came to my village as a small child. I took you into my hut and you became my daughter. Today you stand before me as a woman soon to be married. Yet you are still my daughter and I have heard things of you that greatly disturb me. It is said you do not wish to marry the Comanche chief, Ten Trees.'

'I will obey my Cherokee father's wishes.' The words were spoken so quietly as to be inaudible to most of those about the fire.

'You will marry the husband I have chosen for you?'

Adam willed Tiski to say 'No!' but after a lengthy pause, without raising her eyes from the ground, she said: 'I will marry Chief Ten Trees.'

'Aah!' The long-drawn-out sound came from the throats of the Cherokee listeners.

Eager to prove there had been nothing between Tiski and Adam, Chief Bowles said: 'Things have been said tonight that I do not believe are true. The Englishman has claimed you will not marry another because your heart is for him.'

Once again, Tiski repeated: 'I will marry Chief Ten Trees.'

Adam could not see the face of Chief Bowles because Tiski stood between them, but when the Cherokee chief spoke again there was triumph in his voice.

'Then tell me I have not been mistaken in my faith in you. Tell me the Englishman has not known you.'

Speaking only loud enough for his voice to carry across the fire to Tiski, Adam said: 'Speak the truth, Tiski. Tell him you love me as I love you.'

For a moment, Adam thought Tiski had not heard him or, if she had, that she would ignore his words. Then, raising her head, she looked first at the Cherokee council, next at the blurred faces of the people beyond the firelight, and finally at Chief Bowles. Her adopted father saw the tears that ran down her face – and he knew he had lost.

'You have told me that by becoming the wife of Ten Trees I will secure the friendship of the Kiowa and the Comanche for the Cherokee. I love you as a father and the Cherokee as my own people. Because of this love I will become the second wife of Chief Ten Trees – but my heart will not live in his tepee. It has been given to the white man who saved the life of Yellow Bear. He does not lie. His body has known mine.'

Tiski spoke in Cherokee, and as Eli made a rapid translation Adam sagged with relief. He had feared Tiski would not be able to make such a confession before Chief Bowles and the whole Cherokee village. He realised how alone she must be feeling right now.

But there was someone else whose pride and dignity had been all but destroyed, and it was to Chief Bowles that Adam now spoke. 'I believe The Rainbird will still be the means by which the dream of the Chief of the Cherokees will be fulfilled – but not by marrying Ten Trees.'

As though he had not heard what Adam had said, Chief Bowles rose to his feet. Brushing off the hands that reached out to steady him, the aged Cherokee chief towered above Tiski.

'We have talked enough for tonight. Tomorrow there will be a council with Chief Ten Trees and Metete. The Englishman will also be there.'

As Tiski followed Chief Bowles from the meeting, she glanced at Adam and he saw fear in her eyes. Whether it was for him, or for herself, he could not know.

CHAPTER THREE

THE MEETING with the chief of the Kiowa and Comanche band was a serious affair. To Adam, it seemed more in the nature of a trial. Chief Bowles and the Cherokee council were already assembled when Yellow Bear came to the hut to lead Adam and Eli to their allotted places. So, too, were Ten Trees and Metete, with their warriors seated behind them.

Cherokee warriors were here in strength, brought in from every village and community for miles around. They were kept well back from the council and formed a great circle inside the village.

When the two white men appeared, a disapproving hiss went up from the assembled Kiowas and Comanches. These warriors were the scourge of the High Plains, spreading terror in every settlement from the Arkansas River to the Mexican border, and beyond. The fierce tribal merger carried violent warfare to the White Man wherever he could be found. Never before had two white men walked among them and attended a council meeting. The Ten Trees–Metete alliance did not attend peace talks with white men.

Chief Bowles was the first to speak. After outlining the reasons why he had welcomed the marriage of Tiski and Ten Trees, he proceeded to tell the Comanche chief of what he had learned the previous evening. He spoke in Cherokee with his son John acting as interpreter for the Comanches and Kiowas, while Eli gave Adam the gist of what was being said.

The anger of the Comanche warriors was clear, and Adam wished he had his revolver tucked in his waistband when the hate-filled glances were turned in his direction.

Chief Ten Trees was also angry, but his was a cold, controlled anger – and more deadly for this. A thickset, ugly man of about forty, Ten Trees wore the full-feathered headdress of a Comanche Indian of rank, and he carried himself with the dignity his position demanded. He had earned his chieftainship in battle, leading the men who backed him now.

When Chief Bowles ended his explanation, Ten Trees looked arrogantly at Adam for a full minute before making a reply. Adam had to wait impatiently until the words were first translated into Cherokee and Eli could be certain of their meaning.

'He's asked what punishment the Chief has lined up for you. ... Chief Bowles is replying that he can't punish you; that it all happened before the wedding was fixed up. He's also telling Ten Trees that you saved the life of his son and so are as entitled to the pick of Cherokee girls as anyone else.'

'Chief Bowles said that?'

'More or less. I might have skipped a word or two, here and there. Now he's asking Ten Trees whether the marriage is still going to go ahead.'

'Make sure you don't miss any of his reply.'

Pointing to Adam, the Comanche's reply was brief.

Eli grunted. 'I don't need any translation of that. He's making trading talk. He wants to know how many horses you'll pay him by way of compensation for taking whatever you took from Tiski.'

'Do I get her instead of him?'

'Not the way Ten Trees sees it.'

'Then he'll get nothing from me.'

'I think Chief Bowles realises that. He's saying that, if Ten Trees feels aggrieved, *he'll* settle the bill on your behalf.'

'Damn!' Before Adam could say more, Eli waved him to silence. Ten Trees was talking again.

'He's asked for the girl to be brought here. Yellow Bear's been sent to fetch her.'

When Yellow Bear returned to the meeting, Tiski walked behind him. She was still made up as a Comanche woman, but there was a defiant pride in her walk that was entirely her own.

When she would have halted before the Cherokee chief, Yellow Bear took her arm and led her to where Ten Trees sat.

Rising to his feet, the Comanche walked twice about Tiski, his eyes taking in her body and the neat, bead-embroidered dress she had made herself. Finally, he took her chin in his cupped hand and moved her face to examine it from various angles.

'You'd think he was buying a horse,' commented Eli drily. Adam said nothing. He was seething at the disdainful manner in which Ten Trees was examining Tiski. Her life would not be a happy one if the Comanche took her as a wife.

His inspection over, the Comanche chief spoke to Chief Bowles in short, abrupt sentences.

'He says he'll take her for a wife – but only to please his pal Metete, and because he's ridden a long way to collect her.'

Chief Bowles anxiously asked a question, and the Comanche shrugged.

'Chief Bowles asked if taking her is a sign of friendship

between their tribes. Ten Trees says he can't speak for the Kiowa, but there's nothing here interesting enough to bring a Comanche all this way.'

'Tell Ten Trees I don't like to see him go away disappointed. I'll give him three horses for the girl. Then he can go back to his village and boast of getting the better of a white man in a trade.'

'What the hell you trying to do? You want to insult Ten Trees in front of everyone here by saying his bride isn't worth three horses? No, Adam. . . .'

'*Tell him!* If you don't, I'll have someone else do it for me.'

Eli was inclined to argue further until he saw the cold determination on Adam's face. He still thought Adam had taken leave of his senses, but he did as he was asked.

As the translation was given to him, Ten Trees looked sharply at Adam, his nostrils flaring angrily. Behind him there was a ripple of movement among Ten Trees' followers, who shared his anger.

Standing alone, Tiski dropped her head in shame. She had not expected to hear such words spoken by Adam.

When Ten Trees replied, he spoke slowly and deliberately, his eyes fixed firmly on Adam's face. His look did not waver through two translations.

'Ten Trees says it seems that the Comanche learn good manners at a younger age than white men. He suggests that, if Chief Bowles is going to adopt you as a son, he'd better get one of his old women to take you in hand and teach you the ways of an Indian, as they are taught to a small child. He also says that, if you're so free with your horses, you'd better give some to Chief Bowles, to make up for those he's lost as a bride-price for Tiski.'

Eli followed his translation with a warning. 'Leave it there, Adam. You got away with it that time. Don't push your luck with a man like Ten Trees.'

'I'm only just beginning,' retorted Adam. 'Tell him it's a pity he feels insulted by my offer; it was made because I feel sorry for him. But no doubt a cast-off woman is good enough for a Quahadi Comanche chief.'

Eli's jaw dropped open and he stared at Adam in disbelief. 'I can't say *that*! It would start a war, right here and now.'

'I know what I'm doing, Eli, believe me. If you can't do it, I'll walk across there and say it to Ten Trees, face to face. I can see by their reactions that one or two of his warriors understand English. I don't doubt they'll tell him what I'm saying.'

With a gesture of despair, Eli said: 'I can't believe I'm doing this. I never thought I'd wind up with a partner who has a death wish. All right, I'll tell him. But I hope you *do* know what you're doing. A Quahadi massacre ain't a pretty sight at the best of times. Being part of it don't figure in my ambitions.'

The Tennesseean had trouble persuading John to pass the message on to Ten Trees, until it became evident that some of the Comanches understood at least part of what was being said. They began shouting and gesticulating angrily, and John hurriedly acquainted the Comanche chief with Adam's insulting words.

Ten Trees leaped to his feet, but his words could not be heard above the howls from his warriors. When it seemed the Comanche and Kiowa warriors would be contained no longer, Ten Trees held up his hand and succeeded in silencing his furious followers.

The Comanche chief began to speak again, but this time his words were directed at the unhappy Chief Bowles. The Comanche and Kiowa warriors whooped with delight as Eli licked his lips nervously. 'If I've got what he's saying, I don't think you're going to like this. . . .'

When John began translating for his father, Eli twice interrupted to put forward an argument of his own. Standing alone, apparently forgotten by everyone, Tiski's face expressed her own concern.

'Are you supposed to be translating, or working out some deal of your own?' Adam could stand the suspense no longer.

'Both,' retorted Eli. 'Ten Trees says you've gone beyond bad manners. You've insulted him. He says that if Chief Bowles doesn't kill you he will. I've said you intended no insult. That you'll apologise. . . .'

'Damn you, Eli! Mind your own business. Tell Ten Trees it's easy to talk like a brave man when there are a hundred warriors behind you. Tell him *that* – and don't add any of your own ideas.'

Belated enlightenment came to Eli, but it did nothing to allay his concern. 'You *want* to fight Ten Trees? Don't be a fool, Adam. He's probably killed more men than any other Indian in Texas. He's a proven warrior. A war chief.'

'So was the Duke of Wellington, but I wouldn't back him in single combat. Start translating.'

The reply from Ten Trees was immediate and what Adam had been working for. Ten Trees would fight Adam, man to man, with knives.

'I'd have preferred guns, but I called him, so the choice of weapons must be his. Is it understood that the winner gets Tiski?'

Tiski had been growing increasingly agitated as arrangements

190

for the duel were discussed. Now she broke into a passionate plea. Chief Bowles listened in silence and did not deign to reply.

'She's trying to get the old man to stop the fight,' said Eli. 'She says she'll go with Ten Trees and make him a good wife if he agrees not to fight you. Dammit, she's got a sight more sense than you! Back down, Adam. No one's going to think badly of you. There isn't a man here who would take on Ten Trees. . . .'

Eli broke off to translate the Comanche chief's latest comment. Scorning to consider the possibility that Adam might win, he said he would take Tiski anyway, but the fight was not over a woman. It was to avenge an insult.

'I'm not interested in his reasons for fighting.' If Adam was scared, it did not show. 'Go and fetch my guns, Eli. The long rifle, my new double-barrelled hunting-gun and the Colt revolver. Bring them here and put them down in front of Ten Trees.'

Past arguing, Eli hurried off to carry out Adam's instructions. When the guns were laid at Ten Trees' feet, he looked down at them, then cast a questioning glance in Adam's direction.

'Tell him I'm willing to make a side-bet with him. Those three guns against the Mexican girl prisoner named Eleanor, Don Manuel's niece. I also want a promise that the Quahadi Comanche and the Kiowa will live in peace with the Cherokee, whoever wins today.'

For the first time since the meeting began, Chief Bowles looked directly at Adam. There was understanding in his look, but he said nothing.

A great deal of animated conversation began among the Comanche and Kiowa warriors as the guns were passed among them. The Colt revolver attracted the most interest, but Ten Trees was particularly taken with the long rifle. He weighed the gun carefully in his hand, held it to his shoulder and squinted along the long barrel. Then he ran his finger over the silver filigree decorating the stock. Finally, he grunted an order to one of his warriors and the man jogged off in the direction of the Comanche camp. Scorning the interpreters, Ten Trees nodded acceptance of Adam's terms.

'I hope you're ready, partner. It seems Ten Trees is in a hurry to get this business over.' Eli passed the glum message on to Adam as Ten Trees removed his feathered headdress and pulled his fringed buckskin shirt over his head. His squat, barrel-chested body was well muscled, but it was the scars on his body that brought gasps from the watching Cherokees. There were scars from bullets and arrows, as well as two from Mexican sabres that must once have laid open the great muscles of his back.

Adam stripped off his own shirt. He could not match the bulging muscles of the Comanche chief, but he looked hard and fit. Eli was most concerned about Adam's lack of fighting experience, but when he tried to offer advice Adam silenced him.

'I've handled a knife before, Eli. As a boy in Spain I spent much of my life with Spanish gypsies and I think they might teach your Indians a trick or two.'

'You ain't going up against Ten Trees to practise "tricks",' retorted Eli brutally. 'You're going out there to kill a man, or to be killed yourself. Have you ever faced a man who intended killing you?'

'Once or twice. Texas isn't the only place in the world where men kill each other. As one of Peel's detectives in London's East End I arrested more than one murderer who knew he had only the gallows to look forward to. Each of them was prepared to fight as hard for his life as any man in Texas.'

'They weren't Comanches. A Comanche warrior thinks killing is the only reason for being alive – and Ten Trees is especially good at it.'

At that moment the Comanche who had been sent to Ten Trees' camp returned, pushing ahead of him a young Mexican girl who could have been no more than twelve years of age. Something about her face made Adam think of Philippe, but the resemblance ended there. The tattered, dirty dress she wore was much too short for her and was probably the dress she had been wearing at the time of her capture, two years before. Her face, arms and legs were only fractionally cleaner than the dress, and were covered with ugly sores and scars. Her hair was uncombed and tangled – but it was her eyes that held Adam. They were the eyes of an old, old woman, for whom life had become an intolerable burden.

'Eleanor? You are Eleanor, the niece of Don Manuel Tolsa?'

The use of her name brought a startled response, and a brief flash of hope crossed her face, but it disappeared again as she was pushed on towards the Comanches gathered about Ten Trees.

At a word from Yellow Bear, the Cherokees, who had been watching developments from a distance, now surged forward. Jostling and pushing to gain a good vantage-point, they formed a large circle about a hundred feet in diameter, around the assembled men. At the same time, the Cherokee council members, the Kiowa and Comanche warriors and the others about them abandoned their places and took up positions in the front rank of the great circle.

Wishing Adam a gruff 'Good luck!', Eli reluctantly went with them.

Only Ten Trees, Adam and Yellow Bear remained inside the circle. Calling the two men to him, Yellow Bear held up two knives by the tips of their blades, one in each hand. Moving with deceptive speed, Ten Trees snatched one of the weapons, even as Eli screamed at Adam to grab a knife. Grasping his weapon firmly, blade pointing upwards, Ten Trees barred Adam's way to the second knife.

Adam tried circling cautiously around the Comanche, but Ten Trees moved with him. There was anguish on Yellow Bear's face, but he could do nothing. To attempt to get the knife to his defenceless friend would have been an act of partisanship that would not have been tolerated by Ten Trees' warriors. He could only stand helplessly by and hope that Adam could somehow reach him without being disembowelled.

The two combatants feinted first one way and then the other, but the situation remained the same. Ten Trees had a knife. Adam had none.

Adam tried another tactic. Backing away from Ten Trees, he folded his arms and waited for the Comanche chief to come to him. He got his wish, but gained no advantage. Crouching low, Ten Trees moved closer, darted in, slashing at the air, then retreated again, still between Adam and the knife.

For many minutes the two men continued the deadly serious game, one seeking to keep his advantage, the other unable to reach the knife.

Then, as his warriors shouted for him to kill Adam, the Comanche chief did his best to oblige them. He made another crouching advance upon Adam, but this time did not back away again. Coming in close, he suddenly shifted the knife to his left hand and lunged forward.

The blade struck Adam's rib as he twisted away. It skidded off harmlessly, leaving only a bloody and painful cut across Adam's left side. It had been a narrow escape, and when the two men drew apart again Ten Trees still blocked the way to Yellow Bear and the second knife.

It seemed that Ten Trees had made up his mind to end the fight quickly now. He came in again, this time passing the knife from hand to hand, and at last Adam's luck changed. Backing away, he suddenly stopped and lashed out with his foot. It was not a hard kick, but it struck home when the knife was in the air, causing Ten Trees to miss his catch. The knife dropped to the ground. As Ten Trees swooped to pick it up, Adam charged

193

forward, bowling him over. Then he was past him and his hand closed about the knife held in Yellow Bear's hand.

The howls of chagrin from the supporters of Ten Trees were drowned by the shouts of the Cherokees. They had forgotten that Adam was a white man, forgotten the peace treaty Chief Bowles wanted to obtain. This was a contest between Comanche and Cherokee – and Adam was their representative.

Inside the circle, the two men feinted and slashed, advanced and backed away, neither man prepared to make an all-out attack. They both drew blood. Adam received a second gash across the front of his chest, and Ten Trees a stab wound in his right arm.

Twice the men came to grips, wrestling desperately with each other, free hand grasping the wrist of the other's knife hand, using all the strength each possessed in a bid to gain ascendancy over the other. However, despite their disparate physiques, one tall and slim, the other short and heavy, there was little to choose between them in the matter of strength.

The fight lasted for half an hour. Then, as they circled each other at the edge of the ring, they passed the spot where the meeting had taken place. There was a small fire here, provided so that the Indians might light their pipes. It appeared to be out, but as Adam's foot dragged through it the ashes glowed red.

When Ten Trees passed the same spot, he suddenly snatched up a handful of the hot ashes. Ignoring the pain, he darted forward and flung them in Adam's face. Temporarily blinded, Adam stumbled backwards into the crowd, at a spot where Comanche warriors outnumbered their Cherokee counterparts.

Gleefully, the Comanches threw Adam back into the arena, but their action proved the undoing of Ten Trees. Leaping in for the kill, he collided heavily with Adam and the two men crashed to the ground, Adam on top of his opponent.

Peering through his smarting eyes, Adam saw Ten Trees as no more than a blurred image, but his hand went instinctively to the wrist of the Comanche's knife hand. Adam's own wrist was immediately seized in a similar grip, and for some minutes the two men wrestled together in a desperate tussle, rolling over and over on the ground, each seeking the advantage that would bring the fight to an end.

When sight began to return to his red and painful eyes, Adam felt the heat of the fire close to the fingers clasped about the wrist of Ten Trees' knife hand. The Comanche felt it, too, and tried to shift his position, but Adam held him firm. Straining every muscle and ignoring the increasing heat on his fingers, he forced

Ten Trees' hand down through the grey ashes and into the glowing heart of the fire.

The Comanche chief made no sound, but his body writhed beneath Adam. Still Adam held on and finally he felt the other man's fingers twitch as his grip was broken and the knife dropped into the fire.

Releasing his grip on Ten Trees' wrist, Adam shifted his position to sit astride the Indian's chest. Clenching his left fist, Adam punched Ten Trees twice, once to the side of the temple, and once to the jaw. As the onlookers screamed encouragement, Adam felt the grip on his right wrist slacken.

A moment later Adam held a knife to Ten Trees' throat, and the helpless Comanche chief looked up at Adam, awaiting death. There was no fear in his eyes, only a black malevolence.

For what seemed eternity, the two men stared at each other. Then, with a quick movement, Adam drew the knife across the Indian's throat. Standing up, he turned his back on Ten Trees and walked to where Eli stood waiting for him, Adam's guns in his hand. On the way, an inconsequential thought crossed Adam's mind and he wondered what the Foreign Secretary of Great Britain would think of his 'government observer' if he could see him now!

Behind him, Ten Trees sat up. His hand went to his throat and came away stained with blood. Adam's knife-blade had left a thin, bloody line from ear to ear, but the cut was no more than skin deep.

Eli shook his head vigorously. 'You've just made one of the biggest mistakes of your damn fool life. You've made an enemy who isn't going to rest easy until he's killed you – or unless he's died in the trying.'

Adam did not answer. His hand held to his ribs in a vain attempt to stem the bleeding, he was scanning the crowd, looking for Tiski.

'You listening to me, Adam? You should have killed Ten Trees. You've stripped him of everything he lives for – his authority, his pride, and his standing with his people. Why the hell did you have to go soft when you had him? It was one of the best knife-fights I've seen for years. To let it end like that. . . .'

Tiski was no longer in the crowd. Adam did not see her again until he was taken to Chief Bowles's hut to have his wounds dressed. The Cherokee chief's senior wife first checked his ribs, clucking over them but expressing more admiration for his bravery in the fight than concern for his injuries.

Then, suddenly, Tahnay was gone. She had been behind him,

tying the ends of a strip of rawhide that held a poultice of herbs in place, when other hands took over the task.

Adam knew who it was before he turned around, recognising the fragrance Tiski mixed with her buffalo-fat soap. Ignoring her protests that she had not finished tying the rough bandage, he turned and pulled her to him. For a moment she struggled against him, protesting that he would start the wound on his ribs bleeding again. Then her arms went about him and she clung to him as though he might vanish if she let him go.

When he stopped kissing her she leaned against him.

'I thought I would never speak to you again. That I would be taken away by Ten Trees and spend the rest of my life as a Comanche, fearing to look whenever he brought home a scalp, in case it was yours.'

Suddenly she stepped away from him and looked at him seriously.

'You should not have allowed him to live. He will hate you for every minute of every day because he has been shamed. It would have been better for you had he died.'

'So everyone tells me. You, Yellow Bear, Eli. . . .'

He murmured the words, his face against her hair, which was still damp after being hurriedly washed in a bid to remove the red dye. The paint had been washed from her face, and a beaded band encircled her forehead, keeping her shortened hair in place.

'Forget about Ten Trees. I want to talk about us. You and me. When can we be married?'

'You do not have to marry me. We have shared a blanket – you told everyone so. You have fought for me, and won. I am now your woman.'

'I want more than that, Tiski. That would be enough if I lived here all the time – your people would see us together and know that all was right between us – but I'll be spending a lot of time away. Before you know it, tongues will be wagging. They'll tell you that I've probably got a wife somewhere else.'

Tiski smiled up at Adam. 'How can you know this? Are white women and Cherokee women so alike? It does not matter if you do take a white wife. I will still be your Indian woman. I will wait for you and make you happy to return to me.'

'I don't doubt it, but I want your people and mine to know you're my *only* woman. Isn't there a mission anywhere near here?'

'No – but there has been a man preaching to the Cherokees in one of the villages down-river from here. He came from the Cherokee people in the north. I don't know if he is still there.'

'I'll go and find out. If he is, he'll marry us.'

'I would like that.' Tiski's eyes glistened. 'For Cherokee women many things are better than they are for Kiowa women, but taking a husband is not so important for them. In this, I am still a Kiowa.'

'I'm glad. That's the way I want it to be for both of us.'

There were sounds outside the cabin, and Eli entered.

'You got those cuts bound up? You'd better get your shirt on and come outside. The Comanches and Kiowas are packing up and moving out. They'll be coming through the village here soon – and with a new leader. Ten Trees is out, and Metete's in. That puts him in a pretty strong position. The Kiowa from other bands will follow him now; so, too, will the Comanche if it ever comes to a big war.'

'The Apache, too, perhaps,' said Tiski. 'The Kiowa have many blood ties with them. My sister is married to an Apache war chief.' She spoke hesitantly; she was not yet sure of Eli. Although he was Adam's friend, he looked and dressed like the many white men who had passed through the village of Chief Bowles in the past. Eager only for an Indian woman to share their blankets, such men did not like women to join in their conversations.

Eli whistled through his teeth. 'Now, there's an unholy alliance! Kiowa, Comanche and Apache. If they got together, backed by the Mexicans, they'd stand Texas on its ear! But come out and watch these Plains Indians on the move. It's a sight not to be missed.'

Adam and Tiski followed Eli into the bright sunshine. Down-river, the tall tepees were coming down quickly, the long poles on which the skins were laid being pressed into service as travoises.

Within an hour of the end of the knife-fight, the Kiowa–Comanche band were on the move. At their head rode the new war chief. He was a splendid sight, wearing a buffalo-horn headdress, bedecked with eagle feathers that hung in a double row down his back.

Behind Metete rode the man he had deposed. Ten Trees also wore a splendid headdress of eagle feathers, and he carried a warrior's lance. More than eight feet in length, the lance was decked out with beaded hide, and from it dangled a tuft of bear's fur, adorned with more eagle feathers.

Metete rode past at the head of half his warriors, looking neither to left nor to right. Ten Trees tried to do the same, but for a moment he wavered in his intent and his glance shifted to

Adam, standing between Tiski and Eli. The look was so filled with hatred that Adam felt a chill pass through him.

'Where did you put the guns?'

'I'll go fetch 'em.' Eli had also seen the look.

At the edge of the village, no more than a hundred paces from where Adam stood, Ten Trees pulled his horse out of the line and sat motionless, watching the procession of Plains Indians riding past him.

After the warriors came the women, children and older men, all riding in single file, their worldly goods packed on the travois pulled behind each horse. Dogs trotted around them, growling and bristling at their Cherokee counterparts. Finally, the second half of the warrior force brought up the rear.

Eli returned with the guns and handed Adam the revolver and long rifle. Both were carefully checked.

As the last of the Comanche warriors rode past Ten Trees without acknowledging his presence, the ex-chief of the Comanches shifted the balance of the lance in his hand. Letting out a cry that released all his frustration and anger, he wheeled his horse and urged it to a trot, heading back through the village.

It was the last desperate gesture of a fiercely proud man who had nothing else left to him. When the trot became a canter, the metal tip of the lance was lowered menacingly. Then the trot became a full gallop and a Comanche war cry left the throat of Ten Trees.

Adam held his fire until the very last moment, hoping the Comanche was putting on a final act of bravado. Not until it would have been impossible for the pony to be brought to a halt did Adam pull the trigger of his long rifle. The heavy lead ball knocked Ten Trees backwards from his horse. He was dead before he hit the ground. As the wiry pony swerved to pass by Ten Trees' intended victim, the long lance slithered along the ground and came to a halt at Adam's feet.

By the time Metete and his leading warriors returned to the spot, the body of Ten Trees was surrounded by excited Cherokees, many of them angered by the incident.

At a curt command from Metete, the Comanche and Kiowa warriors kneed their horses into the crowd, contemptuous of the Cherokees. A number of warriors jumped to the ground and lifted Ten Trees' body across his horse, tying hands and feet together beneath the animal's belly.

'Tell Metete there was no other way. Had I not killed Ten Trees he would have killed me.'

Tiski spoke to her brother while he stared arrogantly at Adam.

His expression unchanging, he replied through Tiski: 'It does not matter. Ten Trees was already dead. By beating him in the fight you killed him as surely as if you had plunged a knife in his heart.'

'There is still peace between you and the people of Chief Bowles? The death of Ten Trees changes nothing?'

The arrogance became disdain. 'This is a treaty made between Indians. It is not a White Man's treaty. *We* will not break it. The Kiowa and Comanche follow the paths they have always trod. It is the Cherokee who walk the way of the White Man.'

'Tell your brother I intend marrying you. Ask him if you come to me with his approval.'

The conversation between brother and sister was a lengthy one. When it ended, Tiski was close to tears.

'Metete says I marry you as a Cherokee, not as a Kiowa. Our marriage is a matter to be settled between you and Chief Bowles.'

Metete called to his sister and said something more. This time, when she turned to Adam again, Tiski was smiling through her tears.

'Metete says he will tell our mother I am to marry a great warrior. It will make her very happy.'

Metete, war chief of the mixed Comanche and Kiowa band, inclined his head almost imperceptibly in Adam's direction. Swinging his horse about, he rode off without a backward glance.

CHAPTER FOUR

THREE DAYS after the departure of Metete, Adam and Tiski were married. The ceremony took place outside Chief Bowles's hut, conducted by the Reverend Hywel Morgan. Sent out from England by the Wesleyan Methodist Society, Morgan was visiting American Indian tribes in order to assess the feasibility of sending Wesleyan missionaries to work amongst them. The reception afforded him by the northern Indians and by the the established missionaries of other denominations had fallen far short of expectations. So he had crossed the border and entered Texas, seeking tribes who were neither claimed by existing missions nor disillusioned to the point of animosity by those who had gone before.

The Reverend Hywel Morgan had enjoyed little success here, even among the easy-going Cherokee, until today. He was determined to make the most of the opportunity that he was certain had been engineered for him by the Almighty. It did not matter that more than three-quarters of his vast congregation did not understand a word of his sing-song, Welsh-accented English. Hywel Morgan was preaching the word of God to His heathen peoples. The Lord would ensure its message was not wasted.

Eli acted as Adam's best man and wore a new buckskin shirt and fringed trousers, made especially for the occasion. Chief Bowles was giving Tiski away. He stood beside her, tall and erect, and slightly bored with the proceedings. Chief Bowles was not a Christian, but he had needed neither to welcome nor to discourage missionaries from his lands. They simply had not come to work among the Cherokees of Texas.

The whole of Chief Bowles's tribe were in attendance at the ceremony, moved entirely by curiosity. They also looked forward to the feast being provided afterwards by Chief Bowles. No fewer than ten of the Chief's own cattle had been butchered to celebrate the occasion.

As they kneeled before the Wesleyan preacher, Adam cast a sidelong glance at Tiski. She had made a determined attempt to restore her hair to some of its former beauty. Tahnay had cut it more evenly, and a beautiful new beaded band about her forehead held it in place. She was wearing an embroidered dress of pale, soft doeskin, with moccasins and leggings of the same material. Adam thought he had never seen a lovelier bride anywhere.

Tiski was aware of his look and she was happy. Being married to a white man would pose many difficulties, she knew, but Tahnay had told her she must put such thoughts aside. Tiski and her Cherokee mother had talked until well into the night on her wedding eve. Tahnay had said that the whole tribe knew Adam had eyes for no one but Tiski. Had he not fought for her? Tahnay had known it from the first night Adam had come to the village, when his eyes had been not for his food, but for the girl who was serving it to him. After the dance, Chief Bowles had told Adam to choose a widow or a divorced woman. That he had not done so was further proof of his love for Tiski.

The old Cherokee woman also told Tiski that if she worked at keeping her man happy she would be the envy of every Cherokee girl in the village. This advice was not necessary. Tiski returned Adam's love and she was determined he would never regret taking her for his bride.

When the ceremony concluded, the newlyweds were escorted to the open space in the centre of the village where the cattle donated by Chief Bowles were being cooked over great spluttering fires. Here they occupied the place usually reserved for the Cherokee chief himself. It was a recognition that this was *their* day. Today there was no one more important in the whole Cherokee tribe than Tiski and her husband.

While the newly married couple and the members of the council were eating, the dancing began. It would last all the day and most of the night. The Reverend Hywel Morgan was enjoying the celebrations as much as anyone else. One of the women had coaxed him to join the dancers, and he soon showed he did not lack enthusiasm, returning to his place only infrequently, to mop his brow and gain sustenance from the excellent beef.

Adam and Tiski did not see the festivities through to the end. Towards late afternoon, Adam whispered that it was time for them to leave. When Tiski asked why, and where they were going, Adam signalled for her to keep quiet and to follow him. Mystified, Tiski took Adam's hand and went with him to the edge of the village. Here Yellow Bear waited with two grey horses saddled ready for riding. There was also a pack-horse, with bulky bundles slung across its back.

They were mounted and out of the village before the celebrating crowd missed them, but the howls of disappointment reached them as they rode away.

'Where are we going?' Tiski asked the question again when the sounds of the village had faded far behind them.

'We're going on a honeymoon; but, first, there's something I've been dying to do all day.' Pulling her horse to a halt, he leaned across and kissed her. Tiski clung to him fiercely until a restless movement of Adam's horse forced them apart.

'What is a "honeymoon"?'

'It's something we will share with no one else. We can kiss and do other things all day and all night long, with no one to see or hear. It's a time for you and I to really get to know each other, Tiski.'

'Where do we find this . . . honeymoon?'

'No more than five miles from here. It's at the end of a creek – the Cherokees call it "Hidden Creek". Tahnay and Quaty, with some of the Cherokee women, have spent two days there, building us a special honeymoon house.'

'So *that* is what they have been doing. Every time they looked at me they had a secret smile. I thought it was the way married women look at other women when they are about to be married, too – but how do you know the way?'

'Yellow Bear brought me and I chose the exact spot for our honeymoon home. It's a large wickiup. It will be a good home – a happy home – for all the time we are there.' Adam reached across and took her hand and they rode with hands clasped for the remainder of the way.

When they reached the creek they rode towards its source through a fragrant-smelling pine-forest. The forest floor was a soft carpet of brown pine-needles deposited by many generations of trees. Before long the land closed in about the creek, rising on either side in sheer-faced bluffs. Then the pine-trees gave way to broad-leaf oaks, ash and walnut, with here and there a patch of grassland dominated by a wide-spreading magnolia. There were flowers here and many berries. Honeysuckle and partridge berry; Viburnum, elderberry and woodfern underfoot.

Soon after they had left the pine-forest behind, the creek circled around the edge of a prominent bluff that captured all but the very early-morning sun. It was at the foot of this that Adam had selected the site for a wickiup. Nestling in a small grove of oaks, it was a cabin in everything but name and permanency. The door was no more than twelve feet from the shallow creek that ran over clear, stony shallows. Downstream, about thirty yards away, the creek narrowed to a deep, cool pool, ideal for bathing and swimming.

Tiski took in the wickiup and its setting, aware of the thought behind its siting and construction. Drawing Adam's hand up to her breast, she whispered: 'This is beautiful, Adam. We shall have a wonderful honeymoon. I can feel it here.'

'I can feel it, too, Tiski.' Adam dismounted and lifted her down from her horse. 'I wish we could spend the rest of our lives here, without ever coming across any other person. Life won't allow us to do that, so let's make the most of things while we can.'

He kissed her, and as her lips moved beneath his the warmth they both felt became a fire and Adam picked her up and carried her inside the wickiup.

Much later they lay inside, Adam's arm about his bride, Tiski's head resting on Adam's naked shoulder, her fingers tracing the line of the partially healed wound caused by Ten Trees' knife. Outside the shadows lengthened, and when Tiski eventually raised her head and saw how late it was she moved to rise, but Adam pulled her down to him again.

'I must make a fire and cook you some food, husband. And there are the horses . . . they need to be unloaded and tethered. No! You must wait. . . .'

Her unconvincing objection came as his free hand smoothed the soft flatness of her stomach, before rising to meet her ribs and finally close gently about her breast. He felt the nipple harden beneath his touch and turning towards her, his lips brushing the soft skin of her neck, he murmured: 'The horses won't go far. There's good grass up here and none in the forests. As for the food . . . the only thing I'm hungry for is you.'

For a few moments her ardour matched his own. Then, with an unexpected, lithe movement, she slipped from his embrace and rose quickly to her feet.

'That was downright sneaky,' he protested, rising on one elbow. The protest died on his lips as he gazed at her naked body. The sunshine of the dying day slanted through the open door of the wickiup, bringing her copper-coloured skin magically alive. Suddenly his love for her welled up inside him and threatened to choke him.

She saw his expression change and was aware of the reason. Dropping to her knees, she drew his head to her. 'I love you, too . . . husband.' She held him to her for a long time, and as she stroked his face, her head bent over his, Adam could feel the strong beat of her heart against his cheek.

'We should move, Adam.'

'I know.' He lifted his head and kissed her breast. 'We have many nights and days ahead of us.'

Outside, he unsaddled the riding-horses and unloaded the

provisions from the pack-animal before setting them free. As he had told Tiski, they would not go far. The wickiup was at the far end of a canyon. There was all the water and grass the horses needed, and a shaded, grassless forest between them and the outside world. The canyon was in the heart of Cherokee country and there was no fear of anyone, Indian or white man, arriving unexpectedly to threaten the total privacy and security they enjoyed.

The two weeks Adam and Tiski spent in their honeymoon retreat passed all too quickly, their days spent swimming, walking, making love, and talking. They talked sometimes far into the night, telling each other of their thoughts and hopes, fears and dreams. They spoke of their childhoods, and families and friends, until each understood far more about the other.

Gradually, Tiski learned to overcome many of the inhibitions she had inherited from her Kiowa background and Cherokee upbringing. She was no longer ashamed to stand naked before Adam after they had been swimming in the deep, cool waters of the creek, and making love in the light of day no longer brought a half-hearted protest from her. She delighted in Adam's body, just as he enjoyed hers. In their honeymoon canyon, two minds and two bodies achieved a fulfilled oneness.

On the last night of their stay in the canyon, they went swimming at dusk, then returned to the wickiup to make love with a fierce awareness that never again would they enjoy such uninhibited freedom. Afterwards, as they lay quiet, side by side, each remembered a particular highlight of tenderness or passion that had occurred during the two weeks they had spent together.

When Tiski stirred and turned her head towards him in the darkness, he felt her breath soft against his cheek as she whispered: 'I wish our honeymoon could last for ever. There has been so much happiness in me, here with you. I never imagined that belonging to a man would be like this.'

'It's been much the same for me, Tiski. I knew I loved you – I have since I first saw you – but I never realised how much until we came here.'

She hugged him, trying to ignore the nagging fears she felt for their future. 'If we always feel this way, our life will be a honeymoon even in the village, but we will not be able to swim together without clothes, or make love on the creek bank.'

'Then we must make the most of it while we can. There's a beautiful moon out there, water inviting us to jump in for a swim, and a creek bank just waiting for us to make love. Come on!'

Ignoring her laughing protests that they had made love too

many times already, Adam held her hand and ran with her to the creek. Jumping in the water together, they did all the things she had said would be impossible when they returned to the village.

The next morning they packed and loaded the horses in an unhappy silence. When the task was completed Adam would have thrown a burning stick from the fire inside the wickiup, but Tiski stopped him.

'One day perhaps you will bring me here again. For a day or two we will once more be on a honeymoon and say the things that may be forgotten when others are around us. . . .' Tiski faltered unhappily and then suddenly she was in his arms, unable to control the tears that had been threatening since they woke.

'I will never forget to say "I love you", Adam,' she whispered. 'Even when others are about us and I cannot speak with my tongue, my eyes will tell you. When you are away from me I will say it to the stars and the moon and the wind and the sun. They will be able to tell you, wherever you are, that I love you every minute of the day and the night. This is how love will be for us.'

A feeling of unease came to Adam as he and Tiski rode through Chief Bowles's village, and he was reminded of the last time he had entered the village with Eli. All appeared to be as it should, yet he sensed that something had changed. Warriors who would have given him a happy greeting before his marriage turned away as he approached.

They passed the cabin of Paint, a warrior he had come to know well on the buffalo hunt, and the tribal humorist. Immediately before Adam's marriage, Paint had passed up no opportunity of making him the subject of crude but good-humoured jokes concerning the forthcoming wedding. Paint was seated outside the door, casting musket-balls for the ancient matchlock he owned. Adam braced himself for the witticism he felt sure would come. Instead, when Paint looked up and saw Adam he appeared to be embarrassed and hurried inside his hut.

Adam frowned. Something *was* wrong. Then he looked at Tiski riding beside him and his expression softened. So eager was she to catch a first glimpse of the cabin that had been built for them, she had noticed nothing out of the ordinary.

'See! There it is.' She reached across and gripped his arm, pointing with her other hand to where a cabin stood among the trees. Constructed of split logs, their flat sides forming the inside walls, the exterior was heavily plastered with mud, much of it still only half-dry. The roof was also of logs, covered with a loose thatching.

Unable to contain her eagerness, Tiski kneed her horse on ahead. Sliding to the ground outside her new home, she was immediately surrounded by her friends and the younger female members of Chief Bowles's family. Chattering excitedly together, they led Tiski inside to show her all the furnishings, pots and other precious possessions they had donated to the newlyweds.

Quaty was among the women, but before she went inside with the others Adam was able to draw her to one side.

'Something's going on, Quaty, I can *feel* it. Everyone is on edge and embarrassed at seeing me. It's just like the last time I arrived. Has something happened to Eli – or to the Mexican girl?'

Quaty shook her head. 'No, they set out the day after your wedding. She will be safely home now.'

Adam waited for Quaty to say more, but she allowed an uncomfortable silence to come between them. More convinced than ever that something was wrong, Adam pressed Quaty to tell him what it was.

Yellow Bear's young wife looked desperately ill-at-ease. 'It is not for me to discuss matters decided by the council of the Cherokees. Yellow Bear will speak of it to you.'

Quaty had said all she intended on the matter. Turning away, she went inside the cabin to join Tiski and the others.

Adam had unloaded the horses by the time Yellow Bear came visiting. After telling Tiski she had the colour of happiness on her cheeks, Yellow Bear greeted Adam, grimacing as the laughter and chatter of the women in the cabin rose to a new crescendo. 'This is no place for men to talk, my brother. We will walk by the river.'

Adam nodded and picked up his rifle. Deer often came to drink at the river, sometimes quite close to the village. He and Tiski would need meat.

The two men walked in silence until they came to the shade of the green-leafed trees along the river bank. Yellow Bear suddenly stopped and said: 'One of the children has told of seeing an alligator on this part of the river. There has not been one here for many years. The women say they will stop coming here to wash clothes if the men do not soon find it.'

'There is more than an alligator in the thoughts of your people, Yellow Bear.'

'You have been told?'

'I have been told nothing at all, and it's worrying me. Whatever is wrong must concern me – and can't be good.'

'You are my brother, the Cherokee are your people, and now you have taken Tiski for your wife your heart will remain with us wherever you are. But you are also a white man. The Cherokee have been asked to fight the white men in Texas. If the council agrees, you will be a man tied to two horses, each going a different way.'

Adam looked at Yellow Bear in disbelief. 'Cherokee fight . . . ? After all these years of peace? Why? It doesn't make sense.'

They had arrived at the spot where the women did their washing. Yellow Bear sat on the flat, raised rock where the women stood their baskets. 'We have had a visit from Mexican soldiers. There were eight of them, with two Apache guides. They left only yesterday, after speaking to the council.'

The news of Mexican soldiers this far north astounded Adam. Chief Bowles's village was more than four hundred miles from the Mexican border. Between the two was either the hostile Texan Republic or the lands where the Comanche roamed, depending on the route taken by the Mexicans.

'One of the soldiers was an important man, a colonel. He came to ask our help to fight the Texans. He said the Mexicans are making a great army ready. Soon they will cross the Rio Grande. When they do, they will ask us to help them take Texas back. Then they will give us papers to say these lands where we now live are ours for ever.'

Adam snorted derisively. 'There's no way Mexico will ever take back Texas. General Houston beat the Mexican army at San Jacinto with only nine hundred men. Now he can raise ten times that number – twenty, perhaps. The Mexicans have been so busy fighting among themselves they no longer have an army worth talking about.'

'I know this is true, but the Mexican colonel spoke words the council wanted to hear. When he said the Comanche, Kiowa and Apache would rise with us the council were in favour of joining them. Only my father said the time was not yet right, even though the council reminded him of his dream.'

'I hope the council listened. The Mexicans can give you only empty promises. I doubt if their army will ever set foot in Texas again. They know this. They're simply out to stir up as much trouble as they can. When it comes they'll still be home in Mexico. Afterwards, the Comanche, Apache and Kiowa will ride back to the High Plains. All the anger of the Texans will be directed against the Cherokee. They'll leave you with no homes and *no* lands. You'll be lucky if you still have a Cherokee people. For God's sake don't let the council vote for war. I'll speak to them, if you like.'

Yellow Bear shook his head. 'Not yet. There are those who say we will lose our lands anyway. That it is more honourable for the Cherokee to die fighting than to bow our heads like the White Man's sheep and be driven from our homes.'

'General Houston would never allow that to happen. . . .' Even as the words left his mouth, Adam realised there would soon be a new administration in Texas. Houston would be able to do little to help the Cherokee. It seemed Yellow Bear was also aware of this.

'The Raven's heart is good towards us, but he is not an Indian chief. His word is not sacred to *all* his own men. He once promised to give us the papers for our land, but his people would not let him do this. Soon there will be a new chief in his place. It is said the new man hates *all* Indians, just as some men hate snakes. He has already promised his people that the Cherokee have reaped their last harvest in Texas.'

'White men say many things they don't mean when they are seeking office,' explained Adam, wishing he was able to speak the words with more conviction. 'The new President of Texas will learn that his country has problems enough, without stirring up trouble with the Cherokee. On the other hand, if your people go along with this Mexican plan he'll have all the excuse he needs to carry out his election promises.'

'For the Cherokee people the day is almost ended, my brother. We took the White Man's trail all those years ago – I believe we were wrong. The Comanche and the Kiowa will still be riding paths unknown to the White Man when the laughter of the Cherokee is no more than a trick of the wind.'

'Your words hurt because there is truth in them, Yellow Bear, but while there is hope you must prevent the council from leading your people to certain destruction. I will go to see General Houston. He might have an answer. I must also tell him of the Mexicans' plan. The settlers have to be warned. For this reason I *beg* you to persuade the council not to back the Mexicans.'

Yellow Bear rose to his feet. 'By telling you of this I have placed a heavy burden upon you. Do not allow it to break you. The fate of the Cherokee people was decided by the Gods many years ago. I think it is too late to change it now. Come, you have spoken of going to see The Raven. My father has a message for him.'

Chief Bowles was in his hut. He sat wrapped in a blanket, and it was difficult to know whether he was dozing or thinking. When he eventually spoke, his voice was that of an aged, weary man.

'My son has told you of the visit of the Mexicans, Englishman?' Chief Bowles spoke in Spanish.

208

'He has. It is bad. You were wise to tell the council so. They, too, are interpreting your dream through the eyes of men. I believe that if all the Indians in Texas stand together and *talk* to the Texans it will achieve far more than trying to fight them. You know that if your people stir up trouble when Houston goes an army will be sent here to destroy the Cherokee.'

'The council is the government of the Cherokee people. Although I am their chief, my voice is but one of many, strengthened only by the wisdom of years.'

'My English brother goes to speak to The Raven. He says he must tell him of the Mexican plan.'

Chief Bowles nodded acknowledgement to his son. 'Of course. How could a man live with himself if he allowed his own people to die because he said nothing?'

The Cherokee chief's voice faded away and for some minutes he sat hunched in his blanket, his mind far away. Then he looked up at Adam. 'You remind me of the man The Raven once was. He, too, took a Cherokee bride. Because of her, the troubles of the Cherokee people became his troubles. Acting on their behalf he went to speak to the man they call the "Great Father". The Cherokee loved him as a brother, and he worked hard for them. When he drank too much whisky, so he might forget what had been in his life before, and walked with the unsteady steps of a very young child, still they loved him. When he left to return to his own people, they were glad for him. They knew that the pain he felt was healing. The people of the northern Cherokee listened for news of him and were happy to hear of each great deed he performed. None was more proud of him than Tiana, his Cherokee wife. Two days ago a messenger came from the Cherokee nation of the north. He brought news for The Raven. I give you his message, Englishman. Tell The Raven that Tiana is dead. She had a chill that became so bad she could not breathe. She was proud of her husband to the end. Tell The Raven this.'

'Can I also tell him you will persuade the council not to help the Mexicans? That the Cherokee will remain at peace with the people of Texas?'

'I will do what I can. Tell him it will not be the Cherokee who begin a war between our peoples. Go now, and walk in peace.'

Outside, Yellow Bear asked: 'When are you leaving?'

'Tomorrow. The warning must go out to the settlers to be on their guard.'

Adam thought of the plans he and Tiski had made for their return to the village. When he thought of her disappointment his

209

resolve wavered – but there were too many lives at stake for him to delay any longer. He *had* to warn General Houston of the activity of the Mexicans. He also wanted to send an urgent dispatch to Palmerston. It was just possible that the British Foreign Secretary might use Britain's influence with Mexico to bring a halt to the plan to stir up the Texas Indians.

Yellow Bear broke in upon Adam's thoughts. 'You will not want the company of Quaty and the other women tonight. I will come with you to your cabin and tell them to return to their own homes.'

When the two men reached the cabin, Yellow Bear spoke a few low words to Quaty. Within minutes the cabin had emptied, leaving Adam and Tiski together.

Bewildered, Tiski wanted to know what had happened. When she saw his face, she knew.

'Something is wrong. You are going away?'

'Yes.'

Tiski had always known that being married to Adam would not be the same as marriage to a Cherokee man. Adam would need to go away from the village often. She had resolved she would make no fuss whenever he left her. It was the price she must pay for having the man she loved. Tiski reminded herself of all these things as she stood forlornly before Adam. She tried hard to be as brave as her resolve, but once the first tear escaped she knew she had lost the battle. When Adam reached out for her, she clung to him and wept unashamedly.

Later that night, when the sounds of the village had died away, Tiski lay with her head cradled within his arm, her body pressed hard against his. She studied the shadowed contours of Adam's face as a log shifted and flared in the stone-circled fireplace and she saw his eyelashes move.

'You are still awake?' she whispered.

He answered by tightening his arm about her.

'You should sleep now. Tomorrow you travel a long trail.'

'All trails will be long until I return to you, my wife.'

She gave a small wriggle of pleasure. 'It is good that you miss me, but do not miss me *too* much.' She raised herself on one elbow. Looking down at him she traced a soft pattern on his chest with a finger. 'This journey you make is a very important one?'

'Yes. It could mean life or death for many Texans – and for the Cherokee, too.'

'You will return when you have spoken to The Raven?'

'First I'll need to warn Eli and our friends that the Mexicans are stirring up the Comanche. I'll return just as soon as I can.'

Still looking down at him in the flickering light of the fire, she said: 'My life will be more like that of a Kiowa woman than a Cherokee. Kiowa warriors spend much time away from home. I am proud of what you are trying to do for the Cherokee, Adam. My head tells me there is no other man who can do this – but my heart wants you to stay here with me. With you I am a woman. Without you I can never be whole again.'

CHAPTER FIVE

When Adam rode off early the next morning, he found Yellow Bear waiting for him at the edge of the village.

In reply to Adam's question, Yellow Bear replied: 'I thought I would ride part of the way with you.'

'Do you always carry a war bow and arrows when you ride with a friend?'

'You have the mind of an Indian, my brother. No doubt I will hunt along the way.'

'You don't fool me, Yellow Bear. You are expecting me to run into trouble. Is it from the Mexicans who were in the village?'

Aware that further deception was futile, Yellow Bear nodded. 'They know you are a friend of The Raven. They also know you will have learned of their plans. I believe they will try to stop you reaching The Raven. Last night, Broken Knee, one of my father's warriors, left the village and has not returned. He once rode with the Mexican army as a scout for General Santa Anna. I believe he has gone to warn them.'

'You told me there are eight Mexicans and two Apache scouts. With surprise on their side these are pretty formidable odds.'

'There are two paths you might take. This means they will need to divide their party – and any surprise will be ours. John left the village before dawn. He will learn where they are hiding.'

'You're as wily as they come, Yellow Bear. I hope it runs in the family and John stays clear of those Apache scouts.'

Yellow Bear snorted as derisively as only an Indian can. 'This is Cherokee country. The Apache are warriors of the plains. John will be as a blade of grass or a tree. He will not be seen.'

Yellow Bear spoke with a confidence that brooked no argument, but Adam observed that his glance ranged the countryside from horizon to horizon, taking nothing for granted. Every odd-shaped tree, every misshapen rock or unexplained change of colour was noted and closely scrutinised until Yellow Bear was satisfied all was as it should be.

At first they chatted easily to each other, but as the sun climbed higher in the sky the knowledge they they were moving closer to probable ambush began to tell and they lapsed into silence. Adam's nerves jangled whenever a stone turned beneath the horses' hoofs, and the rattle of metal harness-trappings was a peal of bells in his ears. He found himself wondering whether John was as clever a scout as Yellow Bear had boasted. What if he had been caught and killed . . . ?

Adam's doubts were resolved when they reached a small grove of trees. John was here, his horse standing motionless in the shadows. When they reined in beside him, he said: 'They are ahead, in the pass. I have seen four Mexicans – three soldiers and a captain, but not an Apache or Broken Knee.'

'They might have gone with the Mexicans on the other trail.'

'Broken Knee, perhaps. Apache will be hidden among the rocks above the entrance to the pass. He will want to warn the Mexicans of your approach.'

'Can we get past them without being seen?'

John shook his head. 'First, we will need to find the Apache and kill him. Then we can get above the Mexicans when they show themselves and kill them, too.'

Adam shuddered. He still found it difficult to accept the almost casual manner in which men out here, Indian and Texan, spoke of killing their fellow-men, but he knew better than to reveal these thoughts to the two Cherokees.

Yellow Bear said he and John would ride on and deal with the Apache and then move on to take up positions above the Mexicans. He suggested Adam wait for an hour and then ride slowly through the pass. Adam agreed without comment.

'When you hear shooting in the pass, take cover among the rocks. John and I will be all right. We will be shooting down on the Mexicans.'

'With that?' Adam pointed to Yellow Bear's bow. 'If they see you first, they'll kill you before you can string an arrow.'

Unholstering the double-barrelled rifle that was identical to the one he had once given John, he flung it to Yellow Bear. It was followed by the pouch containing percussion caps, shot, and paper cartridges. 'Take this; it's a good gun.' He gave the Cherokee a weak smile. 'You should only need two shots. John will take care of the other two Mexicans.'

Yellow Bear's eyes gleamed. He had long envied his brother's ownership of the rifle. It was rare for an Indian to possess a modern gun. Those sold to them by traders and dealers were invariably at the end of their useful lives. He gave no thanks; it was not the Indian way. His gratitude would show in the use to which the rifle was put in the next few hours.

Adam gave the two brothers a long hour before he set off through the pass. Soon the path rose clear of the trees and he now rode through patchy, low brush, passing layered rocks sculpted in weird shapes by centuries of wind, baking sun and sudden, violent rainstorms.

Adam's nerves were as taut as bowstrings. He started suddenly when he heard a sound from the stony hillside, high to his right. A shower of small stones poured over a high ledge to the ground below, but when Adam looked upward he could see nothing. He stopped for a few minutes and allowed his horse to crop at a patch of coarse grass while he anxiously scanned the steep sides of the pass. He had every confidence in John and Yellow Bear, but no man was infallible. There might have been *two* Apaches, and not the lone Indian the brothers were expecting. Adam began to perspire as he tried in vain to scan every foot of the pass ahead.

He must have been halfway through the pass when the shooting began. It was not the four clean, quick shots for which he had been hoping, but a regular fusillade. In addition to the crack of the rifles he had given to the sons of Chief Bowles, he could make out the flat report of more than one older musket. The Mexicans had not been taken by surprise. John and Yellow Bear had a fight on their hands.

Adam rode on until he could see a pall of black smoke drifting above an area of broken rock. Slipping from the saddle, he tied his horse to a stunted tree and, rifle in hand, made his way stealthily towards the Mexicans' position.

At least two of them were still alive. They were firing at the slope above them as Adam worked his way closer. He could see nothing of the two Cherokees until there came the crack of a rifle-shot and he saw dark smoke seeping from between two boulders high on the canyon side. The Mexicans saw it, too, and a moment later a musket-ball gouged a shallow groove along the side of one of the soft stone boulders.

There was a shot from the heights on the other side of the pass – and now only one Mexican musket returned the fire.

Adam edged closer still and then something caused him to swing around. It might have been an almost indiscernible sound, a scent on the slight breeze – or pure instinct.

Crouching not ten feet away was the Cherokee, Broken Knee. Adam recognised him immediately as one of the warriors who had been close to him on the buffalo hunt. Indeed, they had both shot the same buffalo, Adam conceding it to the Indian. Broken Knee's wife had been one of the women in the cabin to welcome Tiski on her return from their honeymoon.

Because of this, Adam hesitated – and Broken Knee leaped at him, knife in hand, knocking aside the rifle as Adam fired. The shot went wide, and Adam felt a searing pain as the Indian's knife glanced off a rib and plunged deep into his body. Broken Knee wrenched the knife free to strike again, but by this time Adam had the revolver clear of his belt and cocked it with his thumb. He fired as the Indian returned to the attack. Broken Knee stumbled and fell. Looking at Adam with raw hatred in his eyes, he tried to rise. Adam fired again, and Broken Knee pitched forward on his face and lay still.

Adam looked down at the Indian for some moments. Then, to his utter astonishment, he found himself sitting on the ground, the revolver resting on his thigh, too heavy to lift. Adam stared stupidly at it for a moment, wondering why the gun had suddenly become so heavy. He had not found the answer when Yellow Bear appeared from the direction of the rocks where the Mexicans had been hiding.

'The Mexicans are dead,' he said, scarcely able to conceal his elation. 'John killed one, I shot three.'

'You missed Broken Knee,' said Adam unnecessarily. He raised a hand to point at the dead Cherokee, only to discover that his hand was now as heavy as the revolver.

'Broken Knee was a Cherokee. He hid himself well. So, too, did the Apache.' Yellow Bear made the admission grudgingly. 'We did not find him until he signalled your approach to the Mexicans. . . .' His elation died away as he saw for the first time the stain that was spreading across the front of Adam's shirt.

Yellow Bear dropped to his knees and opened Adam's shirt wide – then swung around to meet a sound from behind him. It was his brother John. Saying nothing, he held Adam's shirt open for John to see the blood flowing from the knife-wound.

'We must get him back to the village.'

'No!' Adam's own voice came to him as though from a great distance. 'Take me to Nacogdoches . . . to General Houston.' Talking hurt his chest. Lifting a heavy hand with great difficulty, he placed it on the ground beside him to support himself as he rose to his feet. Instead, he toppled sideways, puzzled and dismayed by his weakness. Then the steep slopes on either side of the pass began rotating about him and a roaring darkness that hurt his eyes enveloped him.

'He is too badly hurt to take to Nacogdoches. Even the village is too far.' Yellow Bear made the comment to John as he straightened Adam on the ground.

'There are white settlers not far from here, on Sweetwater Creek.' The creek was about five miles away and had been settled by immigrants from Europe for no more than a year.

'We are Indians. They will shoot us as soon as we come within range of their guns.'

'That is a risk we must take – unless you wish to return to our Kiowa sister and say her husband is dead. That he died because we failed to find Broken Knee.'

'We will take him to the white men.'

When Adam opened his eyes it took him a moment or two to focus in the dim light. Then he made out the dimly lit interior of a crude log cabin. There were no windows. The only light entered through a number of small chinks in the walls, and around the edge of an ill-fitting door. He moved slightly in an attempt to peer into the far corners of the cabin, but the movement caused pain in his chest and he began to cough. This hurt him even more, and he discovered he had a tight rough-linen bandage about his body.

When he stopped coughing, he groaned. Just then, the door opened and a big-boned, healthy-looking woman entered the cabin. Coming to the bedside, she smiled down at him.

'You are feeling better, yes?'

Adam placed the heavy accent as belonging to one of the German states.

'Where am I? How long have I been here?'

'It is lucky you are a strong young man. You should be dead now.'

'When did I come here?'

'Such questions!' The woman checked the bandage about his chest and nodded her satisfaction. 'Good. You have stopped bleeding. You will get better now, I think. When you came yesterday I thought you were dead already.'

The door behind the woman opened, and a giant of a man filled the doorway. His voice was as large as the frame from which it came.

'He is living, Henrietta, ja?' Coming across the cabin to the bedside, the giant beamed down at Adam. 'Hello. I am Gustav Miesenbach. This is Henrietta, my wife. It is good you are alive. When I find you yesterday I almost bury you on the spot. Instead, I carry you here.'

'Was I alone when you found me?'

'Alone? Ja . . . except for the Indians.'

'Yellow Bear and John! Where are they now?'

'Locked in the cowshed, behind the house. My neighbour Julius wanted to shoot them. He said he thought they had tried to rob you. I was not sure. We have had no Indian trouble here.

216

I say to him: "Why should they stay with you when they could have taken everything and gone?" So I lock them in the barn. Julius has gone to find Captain Dollar of the Rangers. He will know what to do, I think.'

Adam had met Texas Rangers. Raised primarily to protect the frontier settlements against Indian raids, they had become a law unto themselves in an otherwise lawless land. As a consequence, they had attracted many of the border ruffians and adventurers to their ranks. Adam could guess what the Rangers would 'do' with the two Cherokees.

'Those Indians saved my life. I was attacked by Mexicans and the Indians killed them.'

'Mexicans, here at Sweetwater Creek?' Gustav Miesenbach looked at Adam as though he were delirious.

'They were waiting in the pass between Chief Bowles's village and Nacogdoches. They had an Apache scout with them.'

'Apache ...?' Now the German knew for certain Adam had taken leave of his senses. The Apache lived far to the west. No one had ever seen them in this part of Texas. Nevertheless, he paled. 'Apache' was a word that struck terror into the hearts of every settler who heard it spoken.

'The two Indians who were with me are sons of Chief Bowles. I *must* see them.'

Gustav Miesenbach was a picture of uncertainty. 'I have had no trouble with Indians, but Julius lost his brother to Comanches. He knows more of Indians than I. He said I was to keep them until the Rangers came.'

'Do you have children?' Adam broke in on the German's rambling musing.

Gustav Miesenbach looked startled. He thought he must have misheard Adam. Then his face split in a happy smile. 'Children. ... Ja! Three.' He held up three fingers to emphasise his statement. 'Two good boys and one girl.'

'I was with a wagon train when Comanches killed three men and carried off a small boy. If it hadn't been for one of those Indians you've got locked away, his mother would never have seen the boy again. John went after the Comanches and brought the boy back. That's why I gave him that rifle leaning against the wall over there.'

Adam had seen the guns and pouches, together with Yellow Bear's bow and arrows standing in a corner of the cabin.

'I gave the other gun to Yellow Bear when he went off to attack the Mexicans lying in wait to kill me. He and his brother killed the Mexicans and the Apache, but in the fighting I got this.'

Adam was gasping for breath by the time he got to the end of his story, but there was more that had to be said.

'You've got two very important and friendly Indians locked away in your stable. Release them now and you'll have made two powerful friends. Let anything happen to them and you'd better leave this cabin and take your wife and kids somewhere else, because you'll be killed by their people for certain.'

Gustav Miesenbach was not a quick-thinking man. He looked uncertainly from Adam to his wife. Adam struggled to raise himself, and Henrietta Miesenbach hurried to hold him down, clucking disapprovingly. 'You must not move, or you will bleed again.'

'Release the Indians, or I'll get off this bed and release them myself, if it's the last thing I do. . . .'

'Lie down!'

Henrietta Miesenbach reached a decision more quickly than her husband. Gently but very firmly she laid Adam back on his pillow. As she held him down, she turned her head towards her husband. 'Let out the Indians and bring them here.'

'But Julius said. . . .'

'I *know* what Julius said. Can you not think for yourself? When he returns with those men you know what will happen. They will kill the Indians. Do you want the children to see such things? You have said Indians have never made trouble for us. Why let something happen that might change our good fortune? Bring them here.'

'You won't regret this. Yellow Bear and John are good men.'

'So is my Gustav – and Julius, too. There are good men among every people. Bad men, too. The Indians must go quickly, before Julius comes back.'

As she finished speaking the door opened, and John and Yellow Bear entered the cabin. Behind them lumbered Gustav Miesenbach, holding a scattergun menacingly before him.

John looked about the cabin in sullen anger, but Yellow Bear seemed mildly amused by the situation in which the Cherokee brothers found themselves.

'Do these people see us as a Comanche raiding party, my brother? Are we so fearsome that they must lock us away for a night and most of a day without food or water?'

Henrietta Miesenbach gave her husband a censorious look. 'You did not say they had no water.' Going to the back of the room, she picked up a wooden bucket and a ladle and set them down before the Indians.

'There is water. Drink. We will leave you to talk now. When you have done you must go – and please be quick.'

Gustav Miesenbach protested to his wife about leaving the Indians unguarded. She replied to him in rapid German and, flapping her apron, drove him from the cabin ahead of her.

'I'm sorry for what's happened to you and John,' said Adam to Yellow Bear, while John went to the corner of the room and picked up their guns. 'It's poor thanks to you for saving my life.'

'What has happened does not matter. Now I have seen you will live, we can return to the village.'

'First, you must go to the pass. Get rid of Broken Knee's body. The Rangers will be here soon. I'll send them to the pass to find the bodies of the Mexicans – and the Apache. If I don't, they'll chase all the way to the village after you – or whoever else they find along the way. Don't tell Tiski what's happened. I'm feeling much stronger already. In a couple of days I'll be on my way to find Houston.'

The effect of so much talking threatened to prove Adam a liar. He lay back on the pillow, close to exhaustion. 'Take your guns and leave now – and travel quickly.'

Yellow Bear reached out a hand and let it rest on Adam's shoulder for a few seconds. 'Get well soon, my brother.' John said nothing. Slinging the pouch over his shoulder, gun in hand, he followed his brother from the cabin. As the door closed behind them, Adam gave way to his tiredness and closed his eyes gratefully.

Outside the cabin, Gustav and Henrietta Miesenbach stood by the small corral that held the Indians' horses. Their three children were with them. They watched as the Cherokees caught their horses and secured the light softpad saddles. Gustav Miesenbach held the scattergun in his hands, still not convinced that the decision to release the Indians was the right one.

John and Yellow Bear led their horses from the corral and mounted. Before they left the small, cleared yard, between cabin and corral, Yellow Bear turned his horse towards the anxious family group. Ignoring the wide-muzzled gun that swung in his direction, he looked down with a serious expression and spoke to the older of the two boys. He was a tall, slim child of about ten years, who favoured his mother rather than his massively built father.

'You. What is your name?'

Before replying, the boy looked to his parents. Henrietta Miesenbach inclined her head.

'Hans. Hans Miesenbach.'

Yellow Bear unhitched the bow and the decorated deerskin quiver of arrows and held them down to the boy.

'Here, Hans Miesenbach. This is Yellow Bear's bow. It is a good bow, with true arrows. You will never go hungry if you learn to use it well.'

The small boy stepped forward and took the bow and arrows, all fear of the Indian forgotten in his pleasure at receiving the unexpected present.

As the two Indians rode away, the confused Gustav Miesenbach finally lowered the scattergun, while his wife smiled her pleasure and their delighted son showed his present to an envious younger brother.

CHAPTER SIX

ADAM AWOKE to the sound of men's voices raised in anger outside the cabin. It took him a while to collect his senses. Then he remembered where he was – and he knew the reason for the commotion. The door swung open, and a red-faced, bearded man strode across the cabin to the bed. Behind him, some twenty or more sweat-stained Rangers crowded inside the cabin.

'Mister, you'd better have a damned good reason for setting a couple of no-good, thieving Indians free after they'd been locked up by an honest, God-fearing Texan.'

'They saved my life. Can you think of a better reason?'

'That depends on whether your life is worth saving. Who are you, where have you come from, and what's your business hereabouts?'

The short beard jutted forward belligerently, and as the light from the doorway fell upon it Adam saw that the beard was as red as the face of its owner.

'I'm Adam Rashleigh and when I get up from this bed I'll be on my way to find General Houston.'

The beard lost some of its aggression as its owner asked: 'What's your business with the General?'

'That's between him and me.'

'You met him before?'

'Once or twice. The first time when I was travelling with Eli Varne.'

There was some movement among the men farther back in the cabin, and Adam caught a brief glimpse of a face that was vaguely familiar.

'So you're acquainted with Eli Varne, too, eh?'

'He would have been with me now if we hadn't rescued a Mexican girl from some Comanches. He took her off home to San Antonio. But you have the advantage of me. I don't think I caught your name.'

There was a murmur of interest from some of the men at the mention of Comanches. The bearded man merely raised his eyebrows. 'Sam Dollar. *Captain* Sam Dollar of the Rangers.'

Tugging at his beard absentmindedly, Captain Dollar gave Adam a searching look. 'I've fought alongside both Sam Houston and Eli Varne. They're mighty men in a battle, but they both have the same weakness. They're soft on Indians. I'm thinking you're the same, Rashleigh.'

'You might say that. I'd sooner trust my life to an Indian than to most white men I've met in Texas.'

The beard jutted forward again. 'If you were on your feet, I'd call you out for that remark. The Indians in this country are like an arrow in the arse. They need to be removed before a man can sit comfortable in his home, knowing his wife and kids are safe. It will be a good thing when Lamar is inaugurated as President; he'll sort them out soon enough.'

Adam was beginning to tire, but he had just recalled where he had last seen one of Dollar's Rangers.

'Like most operations, that's going to be dangerous, and a lot of blood will be lost. As for children being safe in this country, I saw a child killed within minutes of setting foot in Texas. The men behind the guns weren't Indians, they were your so-called Texans. I see you've got one of them right here, in your "Rangers". He and his friends were arrested in Velasco, but they escaped, killing two men on the way.'

During the ensuing hubbub, the man Adam had recognised tried to slip out through the doorway, but his way was barred by some of his companions. They pushed him forward to where Captain Sam Dollar stood at Adam's bedside.

'This the man?'

Adam nodded. 'That's him. He was one of Bo Garrett's "militiamen" then.'

The man looked scared. 'He's got it all wrong, Cap'n Dollar. Bo was collecting dues for Texas, that's all. The killing was kind of an accident.'

'You'll have a chance to explain that to Judge Williamson in due course. Take him outside – and keep him under guard.'

Returning his attention to Adam, the Ranger captain declared: 'This doesn't alter a thing as far as I'm concerned. You had two Indians released. I want to know why.'

Adam was having great difficulty in keeping his eyes open.

'Captain, I'm tired. I was ambushed by Mexican soldiers in a pass not far from here. They had an Apache scout with them. . . .'

Through his weariness he could hear the buzz of excitement that greeted his words.

'The Cherokees killed the Apache and the Mexicans – three soldiers and a captain. They were here to cause trouble. Their bodies, or what's left of them, will still be up in the pass. The Apache's high up by the north entrance, the Mexicans among rocks about half a mile in. I learned they were in Texas. . . . I'll tell Houston the details. . . .'

Adam's eyes would not stay open any longer, and when Captain Dollar pressed him for more details the voice came from a long distance, the words fading intermittently.

Henrietta Miesenbach had been standing in the doorway with her husband, listening to what was being said. Now she came to Adam's rescue.

'You have asked enough questions. He is a very sick young man. You will all leave my home now. If you wish to drink, you will find good water in the creek. If you have food, I will prepare it for you. Then you can go to find the Mexicans. Please to be quiet in the yard; our milking-cow is not used to so much noise. Out you go now. Shoo! Shoo! Gustav, hurry them along while I make the young man comfortable. He has gone to sleep, poor boy. So much talk has tired him.'

The Rangers left the cabin talking noisily, in spite of Henrietta Miesenbach's entreaties. Their disappointment at not having two Indians to lynch was forgotten. If there really were bodies of Mexican soldiers in the pass, it would cause more excitement in Nacogdoches than the death of two Indians.

Adam left the Miesenbach cabin five days later, ignoring Henrietta Miesenbach's warning that he was not yet fit to travel. Her husband accompanied him for half the sixty miles to Nacogdoches, but when they reached the old San Antonio road Adam was passed into the care of a party of United States Congressmen. In Texas on an unofficial fact-finding mission, they were eager to question him on his experiences, but by the time the party arrived in Nacogdoches their curiosity had become anxiety. Henrietta Miesenbach had been right. Adam was not yet fit to travel and he entered the town reeling in the saddle.

After finding a room for him in one of the establishments that rather grandly called itself a 'hotel', the Congressmen called a doctor, then rode on their way. The doctor declared that Adam had still not made up the blood lost after the stabbing. Adam was ordered to remain in bed for at least a week. The knife had pierced his lung, only an inch from his heart. The doctor also expressed interest in the scar left by the knife of Chief Ten Trees, but Adam refused to satisfy his curiosity.

Adam had hoped to find General Houston in Nacogdoches, but the out-going President was in the capital, winding up the affairs of his two-year-old administration. As had been predicted, Lamar had won a runaway victory in the presidential

223

election and was eager to take up his post as leader of the Texan Republic.

Nominated as Vice-President during Houston's term of office, Lamar had done little to relieve the President of any of the burdens of office. Indeed, for much of General Houston's presidency, Mirabeau Buonaparte Lamar had actively worked against the first man in the land, in order to secure his own eventual election.

While Adam rested in Nacogdoches, he compiled a lengthy report for Lord Palmerston. Adam appraised the British Foreign Secretary of the current situation in Texas and once more urged him to recognise Texas quickly. He warned Palmerston that if Great Britain did not act soon she would miss an opportunity to influence the policies Texas would pursue in the next few years. He again expressed his view that Mexico would *never* conquer Texas. Tardy recognition of this fact by Great Britain could only cause lasting resentment.

At night, when Adam should have been sleeping, he lay awake in his uncomfortable hotel bed, thinking of Tiski. He wished he had returned to her instead of coming to Nacogdoches after his partial recovery from the ambush in the pass. Had he known General Houston would not be here, he would have done so. However, his reasons for seeking the President in his last days of office still remained, and were growing more urgent. The country's settlers needed to be warned of a possible upsurge in Indian depredations, and Adam needed to ask Houston's advice.

Four days later, Adam packed his belongings, paid his bill and set off on the 150-mile journey to the Texas capital. The journey was accomplished in three days. Sometimes Adam rode with a companion, found along the way. More often he rode alone with only his thoughts and the cry of a high-circling buzzard for company.

Adam was tired but stronger when he finally arrived in the bustling town that Houston had become in the two years since independence. The main street was a succession of saloons and he watched more than one man step unsteadily from one, only to disappear inside the next.

Adam rode to the executive 'mansion' in the centre of Houston. Little more than a sprawling, two-storey log cabin, Houston's home was, nonetheless, one of the finer buildings in the raw capital. Newly fitted with floorboards on the ground floor, curtains now hung at the windows in readiness for its new, more fastidious occupant.

General Houston came out to the mansion yard to welcome Adam and expressed concern at his pale and wasted appearance.

'Come in, Adam. Come in.' He helped Adam inside. Ignoring his protests, he led him to a comfortable padded chair alongside the blazing log fire. 'I've had Captain Dollar here with some garbled story of you and two Cherokees fighting off Mexicans and Apaches. He said you were wounded and lucky to be alive. I thought he must have gone out of his mind; but, looking at you now, I don't doubt a word he said. Sit yourself down. . . . Elias! Where *is* that damned boy? I swear I'll leave him here when I go, just to spite Lamar. *Elias!* Ah, there you are at last, you deaf jackass. Rustle up a very large brandy for Mr Rashleigh – bring the bottle, he deserves it. I'll have the whisky here, too. Now, Adam, tell me the truth of what's been happening.'

Adam stretched out stiff and weary limbs and told General Houston what had taken place at Chief Bowles's village and afterwards.

'Damn the Mexicans and their sly ways!' General Houston paced about the room, a tumbler three parts filled with whisky in his hand. 'They know full well that it's the women and children who'll suffer most if the Indians are roused. Mexico will gain nothing at all.'

Pausing before Adam's chair, Houston said: 'Do you think Chief Bowles will be able to bring the Cherokee council round to his way of thinking?'

'He seemed confident enough. I have no reason to doubt him. He usually gets what he wants from them.'

'I hope you're right. Lamar has promised his voters he'll end the Indian problem, once and for all. He'll be looking for a quick and decisive victory over the Indians – any Indians. The Cherokee would fit his bill perfectly if there were so much as a whisper of their involvement with the Mexicans. Chief Bowles owes you a great debt for saying nothing about the Mexicans' visit to him.'

'I have my own interest in the Cherokee people. I'm married to Chief Bowles's adopted daughter now.'

Cutting short General Houston's congratulations, Adam said: 'That brings me to an unhappy piece of news. A message reached Chief Bowles from the Cherokee nation up north. Tiana is dead. From the few details he had, it sounds as though she died of pneumonia, although nobody called it by name. I believe she's been buried close to a place called Wilson's Rock. I'm sorry that I'm the one to bring you such news.'

General Sam Houston was, by nature, an emotional man, and

Adam saw deep grief on the President's face. Then the many years spent in politics came to his aid and he put on what his opponents called his 'Indian face'. Turning away abruptly, Houston gazed into the fire for some minutes before saying: 'She was a lovely girl, Adam. A rare beauty. I knew her for many years. . . . Many years. She saw me at my best – yes, and at my worst, too. I always needed her far more than she ever needed me, yet she was always there. The world is a poorer place for her passing.'

Returning to stand by Adam's chair, General Houston reached out and placed a hand, Indian fashion, on Adam's shoulder. 'I envy you, Adam. I envy you from the very depths of my heart. You have discovered the Cherokee way of life, and have a beautiful Indian girl who loves you. You are untrammelled by politics and politicians – and, if you've got the sense I think you have, you always will be. There are times when I wish to God I'd never let myself get mixed up with them. But I'm becoming maudlin. Where's that bottle? Tonight I'm going the whole damn hog.'

Refilling the glass that Adam had not even noticed being emptied, General Houston raised it in salute. 'A toast, Adam. To those we love, and have loved. God bless them all.'

Adam responded to the President's toast; then General Houston declared Adam must stay in the mansion while he was in Houston. 'You'll need rest – and there's not a quieter place in town than the home of a *departing* president.'

As the evening wore on, the number of callers gave the lie to Houston's statement, and Adam learned he had become something of a hero in the community. Word had reached the capital of his fight with the Mexicans, and of his earlier fight with Ten Trees which had resulted in the rescue of Don Manuel's niece. If the part Tiski had played in the drama was known, nobody mentioned it.

General Sam Houston drank a prodigious amount of whisky during the course of the evening, yet he was sober enough to stand outside the back door of the mansion house at the height of the party and discuss with Adam the policy Chief Bowles should adopt if the Cherokee were to secure a future for themselves in Texas. He said that the Cherokee chief and his council must be prepared to accept all the insults and goading that would come their way during the three years of Lamar's presidency. Houston told Adam to convey his promise to Chief Bowles that, if the Cherokee held out until then, he, Houston, would be back in office. His first task would be to right the many injustices the Cherokee had suffered over the years.

Adam doubted whether this would be enough to persuade the Cherokee council to pledge their loyalty to the Texans and he expressed his views to Houston. 'I haven't been in this country very long, General, but it seems to me there have been too many promises made to the Cherokee in the past. They are going to take a lot of convincing that new promises are any better than old ones.'

'True – but empty promises are preferable to loaded guns,' retorted Houston. 'They *have* to trust me. No one else can do anything for them.'

'I've written to Lord Palmerston again, urging him to recognise Texas and intercede on behalf of the Cherokee.'

'Palmerston would need to move quickly, but I don't think he will. British interests in Mexico take precedence with his government, especially now there is no danger of annexation by the United States. Great Britain's short-term interests are served well enough by the trading concessions Palmerston has given to Texas. Now he'll wait to see what Lamar plans to do before making another move. It's sound diplomatic policy, albeit stolid. Your Lord Palmerston is a "tomorrow" man. Texas is a "today" republic.'

When Adam pleaded exhaustion and retired to bed, the impromptu party was still in progress. He woke briefly to see dawn streaking the eastern sky as the last revellers fell out through the mansion-house door. Frugal to the last with the nation's meagre budget, Houston had squeezed enough from the near-empty Treasury coffers to make it easier for members of the departing administration to lay down their burdens of office.

General Sam Houston stepped down as the first duly elected President of the Republic of Texas on 10 December 1838. He possessed a great love of the dramatic, and had an actor's unfailing sense of occasion. Both were demonstrated to great effect on this momentous day.

Dressed splendidly, although the clothes he wore had not been fashionable for many years, Houston delivered a powerful speech. Justifying the decisions made during his presidency, he castigated Congress for not always supporting him in his bid to lay the foundation of a brave new republic. Before the huge crowd that had gathered outside the capitol building, Houston fired broadside after verbal broadside at his critics. Adam was listening and he was convinced that, had Houston called on the crowd to follow him in rebellion against the newly elected President, they would have done so to a man.

Mirabeau Buonaparte Lamar thought so, too. When Houston threw his arms wide and passed the Republic of Texas into the care of his successor, Lamar accepted the Chair of State, but was so overcome by nerves that he was quite unable to deliver his inaugural address. The speech was read out for him by his private secretary.

Houston had spoken of a glorious past, of his personal part in these glories, and of opportunities lost. Mirabeau Buonaparte Lamar made lofty promises for the future. He scorned any suggestion of annexation by the United States of America. Texas would become a great nation in its own right, without help from its northern neighbour. To Mexico, Lamar offered peaceful co-existence – but only on Texas's own terms. To the Indians, Lamar promised neither peace, co-existence nor hope. There was no place for them in Lamar's country. His sword had earned him promotion from private soldier to cavalry commander in a single skirmish before the battle of San Jacinto. Now he promised to carry that same sword to the Indians.

Aware that the British Foreign Secretary would expect a full report of Lamar's speech, Adam listened with an increasing sense of dismay. He had told Chief Bowles that politicians were notorious for saying things the electorate wanted to hear, rather than declaring honest policies, but it was clear that Lamar meant every word.

Forty years of age, Lamar had been born on his father's plantation near Louisville, in Georgia. An expert horseman and swordsman, he also received an excellent education, developing a great love for music, painting and poetry. Adam had heard him described as a weak man, governed by passion and prejudice, and unfit for the realities of the onerous duties of a president. To these observations, a wag at the inaugural ceremony now added that Lamar would need to barter his new capitol building in order to equip the army that would be required to carry out his stated policies – always assuming he could find men willing to fight without payment for their services.

Adam accepted Houston's invitation to attend the inaugural ball that evening. It was attended by members of both Houston's and Lamar's administrations, as well as by judges, generals, scholars and landowners. In fact, the occasion brought together the future élite of a land whose inhabitants had not yet settled into the social strata of larger, longer-established countries.

Adam had hoped he might have the opportunity to question

Lamar on his Indian policy during the course of the evening, but the new President was more aware of his status than his predecessor had been. When Adam was introduced, he received a polite, limp handshake and was promptly passed on to the next figure in the long line of Texan government officials.

Not everyone at the grand ball of the year was as niggardly with words as President Lamar. Soon after running the gauntlet of Lamar's hand-shaking administration, Adam heard his name being called. He turned to see Don Manuel pushing his way through the crowd towards him.

Don Manuel's affectionate hug of greeting caused Adam to wince in sudden pain and the Mexican landowner was immediately filled with concern. 'I am forgetting you have been badly hurt. You wish to sit down? Shall we find another room?'

'I'm all right. I can't take too many liberties with my body just yet, that's all.' Looking about him, Adam asked: 'Where is Dona Antonia?'

'She had a chill and could not face the ride from San Antonio. She remained with Philippe but insisted that I come here to represent the Tolsa family. It is important that we be seen to support the government of Texas. But where are my manners? I am deeply in your debt, Adam. Thanks to you, my niece will one day be able to enjoy dances such as this.'

'I'm glad Eli got her home safely. How is she?'

'Eleanor is still afraid to go far from her house, fearing Comanches will come and carry her off again, but she is improving. They say she has learned to smile again. Perhaps, one day, her father will smile, too. For now, there is only hatred in him for what the Comanches did to Eleanor.'

'There's a whole lot of hatred in Texas – and the new President owns his share.'

'Lamar?' Don Manuel looked at Adam suspiciously. Reassured that he was not being trapped into saying something he might regret, he said: 'He claims to love everyone except Indians – and Mexicans.'

'Can he make things very difficult for you?'

'Perhaps. Your Cherokees and I have much in common. We both have land coveted by the new Texans.'

Further conversation was made impossible by the arrival of one of Don Manuel's friends. Shortly afterwards, General Houston came to take Adam to meet a friend who had just returned from the capitals of Europe. He had been trying, unsuccessfully, to secure recognition, as well as a much needed loan, for the bankrupt republic.

Before the two men parted, Don Manuel told Adam there was a letter waiting for him at the San Antonio ranch. Adam made a quick decision. He wanted to return to Tiski, but the letter might be important. He decided to go to San Antonio with Don Manuel the next day.

CHAPTER SEVEN

THE TWO-HUNDRED-MILE RIDE to San Antonio was both fast and pleasant. Accompanied by a forty-man mounted escort, Adam and Don Manuel made the journey in four days along the well-defined road. They stayed the first night at the home of another wealthy Mexican rancher, who lived within sight of the Colorado River.

The family and their guests sat on the covered veranda, enjoying an evening drink, and Don Manuel and his host exchanged experiences they had shared during the early days of the Texan War of Independence. Not far from the house the Mexican ranch-hands were putting on a *fandango* for the benefit of Don Manuel's escort, and Adam wandered along the long veranda to listen to the singing and watch the hand-clapping, foot-stamping dancing.

He remained watching and listening to the Mexican merrymaking for some time, until he began wondering what Tiski was doing. She might be watching the same setting sun and thinking of him – or perhaps some young Cherokee warrior was talking to her, trying to persuade her that her white husband would never return to the village. . . .

Adam returned to the family party and signalled for a Mexican servant to bring him another drink.

The letter at the Tolsa ranch was from Lord Palmerston. Its contents were brief, and brutally to the point, leaving Adam with a feeling of deep despondency.

The British Foreign Secretary wrote that the British government had decided that the question of Texan recognition should remain in abeyance for the time being. With the annexation of Texas by the United States of America no longer a serious threat, Palmerston had decided that the wisest course for Great Britain at the moment was to do nothing. He believed that maintaining Great Britain's friendship with Mexico would benefit everyone in the long term. If Texas survived as an independent nation, this friendship would prove invaluable in securing ultimate Mexican recognition. The Foreign Secretary thanked Adam for his reports from Texas and informed him that he was now free to return to Great Britain at any time. However, Lord Palmerston added that he would deem it a personal favour if Adam remained in Texas and kept him informed of any new developments in the situation here. The British ambassador in Mexico and the consul in New Orleans had been instructed to issue Adam with whatever funds he might require.

It was a disappointing and discouraging letter, but not entirely unexpected. Adam was honest enough to accept that, since coming to Texas, his concern had been as much for the survival of the young and virtually unrecognised republic as for British interests. Lord Palmerston, on the other hand, had no such divided loyalties. He had devoted a lifetime to extending Great Britain's supremacy in the world, thus making his country truly 'Great'. No other consideration influenced his foreign policies.

With this in mind, Adam sat down that evening and penned a long and detailed report to the British Foreign Secretary. He reported President Lamar's ambition of extending the Republic of Texas from the Atlantic to the Pacific Ocean, thus establishing a powerful country that would outstrip its neighbours to both the north and the south. Adam added that he did not doubt such a dream might be accomplished. Certainly, Mexico was powerless to prevent the loss of her lands along the California coast, if Texas could muster an army to take them.

By offering recognition and help to Texas, Adam suggested that Great Britain would gain an ally far more important to her than revolution-torn Mexico. If Britain failed to act, then Texas would eventually be forced to turn to America, where there was much sympathy for the new republic. Houston had told Adam he intended going to America early in 1839. His idea was to turn that sympathy into tangible support, in readiness for a planned return to presidential office in three years' time. Given the dynamism of Texas, and the resources and population of the United States of America, they could sweep side by side to the Pacific Ocean and jeopardise the future of British colonies on the American continent. It was an awesome prospect for a Foreign Secretary of Great Britain to contemplate. Adam sealed the letter with a certain sense of satisfaction. He hoped it might persuade Lord Palmerston to think again about his policy towards Texas.

The next day, Adam left the Tolsa ranch and headed for the Hill Country. It was only a little out of his way on the route north to Chief Bowles's village, and Adam wanted to warn the settlers about the trouble being stirred up by the Mexican soldiers.

Adam travelled alone, having declined Don Manuel's offer of an escort. Thanks to the lessons he had learned from Eli, and

Adam's own experiences with the Cherokee, he was confident that he had the ability to find his way, and stay out of trouble on the way there.

He travelled fast, but cautiously. With their Mexican raid behind them, the Comanche would seek amusement elsewhere – and Caleb Ryan's settlers were closer to the traditional Comanche hunting-grounds than any other whites.

Adam saw the smoke the moment it began to rise above the trees on a hillside about four miles ahead, slightly to one side of his route. It was far too dense to be a cooking-fire, and more concentrated than a brush-clearing operation. Turning his horse off the trail, Adam headed in the direction of the smoke, exercising extreme caution as he drew closer. When he reached a low ridge, he dismounted. The source of the smoke was in the valley below him, hidden by a number of tall trees, but close enough for him to hear the crackling of burning timber.

Adam wriggled his way through the trees until he could see a cabin burning furiously. In front of it was a sight he had hoped never to see again. The scalped bodies of a white family. Adam studied the scene for some time. When he was satisfied no Indians remained in the vicinity, he went back for his horse and led the animal to the burning cabin.

As he approached, the horse began to snort and dance with fear. It might have been the smell of blood. More likely, it was the proximity of the fire, which had by now completely gutted the cabin.

There were four bodies. The mother and daughter had been stripped and raped before they were killed. This was the Comanche way. In all the time Adam was in Texas there was never a Comanche Indian attack involving white women, where the women were not raped. The bodies lay close to the corral. Nearer to the cabin were the bodies of the settler and his young son. Both had been savagely mutilated. Adam hoped it had happened *after* they had died. Looking down at them, he could well understand the hatred so many Texans had for Indians.

He was dragging the bodies to the cover of an unfinished barn when he heard the sound of gunfire coming from the direction of the river – where Caleb had his cabin. Leaving his gruesome task, Adam mounted his horse and headed for the river. There was more firing now, and it was evident that Caleb's cabin was under attack. Adam rode as swiftly as he dared, dreading that he might see the smoke of another burning cabin before he could reach the scene.

Adam did not ride into the clearing Caleb and Eli had made.

233

Instead, he took his horse away from the path, heading for a low bluff overlooking both cabin and clearing.

Gaining the vantage-point, Adam could see that the cabin was under attack by only eight Indians. Four were with the horses at the edge of the clearing. The others were sniping at the cabin as they worked their way slowly forward, using the cover of tree stumps left in the half-won fields. The Indians were Comanches.

Adam knew that once they reached the house they would start a fire and burn out the occupants. One of the Comanches was no more than thirty yards from the cabin when Adam shot him. The Indian dropped on his face and lay still. The others lost interest in the cabin immediately, turning towards the new threat from the bluff.

They had not decided whether to attack or to retreat when Adam fired again. Another Indian fell to the ground, but he regained his feet and, crouching low, ran for the horses. His companions quickly followed suit. One was brought to the ground by a shot from the cabin, but he, too, was only wounded. Dragging a leg behind him, he was able to reach the others and was lifted on his horse by a companion.

It was the end of the Comanche raid on the settlement. They had taken four scalps, but the death of their companion and the wounds sustained by two others had turned their victory sour. There was no thought of seeking out and killing Adam. The tide of fortune had turned against the Comanches. Their only thought now was to escape without suffering further loss.

Adam sent another shot after the departing Indians, in case they changed their minds, but it was no more than a gesture. They were already out of range.

When Adam reached the cabin, Caleb came out to meet him, a rifle resting in the crook of his arm. Behind him was Nell Plunkett, similarly armed. In the doorway, Adam could see Eileen Ryan and Kathie Casey, their children peering out from behind them.

Caleb's face was showing the strain he had been under during the attack. Extending a hand, he said: 'You don't know how good it is to see you, Adam. I don't think we could have held them off for much longer. There was only Nell and me shooting, with just the two guns between us. Had they rushed us we wouldn't have stood a chance.'

'At least you weren't taken by surprise. Your neighbours along the valley weren't so lucky. They'll need burying.'

There was an exclamation of distress from the doorway, and Caleb's mouth set in a tight, grim line.

'Where's Eli? It's not like him to be missing when he's most needed.'

'He went off after Peggy, five days ago. We haven't seen him since.'

'After Peggy? You mean . . . Indians have taken her?'

'We don't know. She'd been acting strange for a week or two, going off on her own all day, telling no one what she was doing. Then, six days ago, she just walked right out through the cabin doorway and no one has seen a sign of her since. One of the settlers came in and said he'd seen some Indians crossing the river, some miles to the north of here. Eli went off to check on whether they'd taken her – and that was the last we saw of *him*.'

'Has no one been to look for him? He could be lying hurt somewhere. . . .'

'I've been out,' replied Caleb. 'Every day. I found the river-crossing, but we'd had rain. There was no trail left to follow. Besides, I've needed to get back here before nightfall. . . .' He waved a hand in the direction of the dead Indian. 'You can see why.'

Adam nodded. 'You couldn't have done anything else. Right now, you and I have a few chores to perform before dark, starting with the Comanche. We'll talk while we're doing them.'

There was a sober atmosphere about the table in Caleb's cabin that evening. He and Adam had thrown the body of the Comanche in the river before going on to bury the settler family in a single, shallow grave, close to where they had died. The two children had been of a similar age to Caleb's two girls, and the families had been friends since first meeting on the boat from Ireland.

Adam told everyone about his time in Houston, in a vain bid to help them forget the events of the past few days, but only the children showed any real interest. As soon as he stopped talking, Kathie Casey blurted out: 'Why? Why did there have to be the killings today? Why won't the Indians leave us alone? I know they say we're on their land, but is that a reason for such a useless waste of life? This is a great big country with room for everyone.'

'That's the way the Indians thought, once,' replied Adam, aware that his reply was not what his listeners wanted to hear. 'I'm reminded of something Chief Bowles said to me, while I was in his village. It seems a very old Creek Indian summed it up, a few years ago. He had lived for a hundred years and witnessed countless talks between Indians and white men. He'd arrived at the conclusion that when you scraped away all the fine words and promises and got down to what was *really* being said to the

Indians it always amounted to the same thing: "Move on. Go farther away. You are too near me." I guess he was probably right. The Indians are fighting us in a desperate attempt to hold us back and give their children a few more years of the life they have always led. They feel if they don't fight they are going to be swept right off the face of this land, big though it is.'

'Does that mean there's nothing we can do to stop the slaughter of innocent men, women and children? People like us, who have no grudge against anyone, and only want to make a future for *our* children?'

'I didn't say that. I just wanted you to know that the Indian has a point of view, too. I don't like the way he puts it across any more than you do. Tomorrow I'll set off to look for Eli and Peggy. If I don't find either of them, I'll go on to see the Cherokee. I'll get one of them to take me to meet the Comanche. Perhaps I can make some sort of treaty between them and the people here, in the Hill Country.'

He might have announced he was going out to commit suicide. Caleb tried to dissuade him, and Eileen Ryan and Kathie Casey agreed it was too great a risk. Nell Plunkett kept her opinion to herself until Caleb called for her support.

'It's dangerous,' she agreed. 'But so is staying here and trying to carve a farm out of the forest. If I were Adam, I'd do exactly what he's planning to do.'

Nell's observation brought to an end the attempts to dissuade Adam from undertaking his journey. They had been merely perfunctory in the first place. It was clear to every settler that, unless the Indian raids ceased, there would be an exodus back to the east. The price demanded for their new way of life was too high.

Adam and Caleb sat beside the fire, talking softly, long after the women and children had gone to bed. Adam told Caleb about the Mexicans, and it was agreed that the day's attack could be the beginning of a Comanche campaign. Adam suggested that Caleb should push ahead with building a stockade around his cabin, making it large enough to hold all the settlers who lived nearby. Caleb promised to put the suggestion to a meeting of the settlers at the earliest opportunity, and call for their help.

Adam also gave Caleb details of the new Texan president. In return, Caleb brought Adam up to date with news of the new settlement. Before the Indian raid it had been the story of any other small community. There had been two births and no deaths. One family had left, not because of Indians, but because the wife had become ill and would need continuing medical treatment.

Caleb confessed that the work was harder than anyone had anticipated, but it gave them all a sense of common purpose. Each small step forward was magnified and hailed as a major success. The settlers understood how much effort went into achieving even the most minor goal. Listening to Caleb speak, Adam had no doubt that, given freedom from Indian troubles, the Irish and Scots settlers would build a happy and successful community.

He set off from Caleb's cabin the next morning and headed for the river-crossing where he knew Eli would have begun his search for Peggy Dooley. As Caleb had discovered before him, rain had washed away the tracks of the Indians. But Eli had started here, so Adam would do the same.

Adam sat his horse for a long time at the crossing, wondering why this particular crossing-place had been chosen by the Indians. Where was their destination, and from whence had they come? He finally concluded that it had been a large raiding party on its way back to the Penateka Comanche lands from Mexico. No doubt they preferred this route to one that would take them through the inhospitable and arid lands to the west of the well-watered Hill Country. It was probable, also, that the Comanches who raided the settlement had broken away from this larger band.

For two days Adam scouted the area about the crossing, in the vain hope that he might find some sign of Eli. As he expected, he found nothing. It would probably have been the same had the trail been fresh. Eli was too experienced a frontiersman to leave signs for an Indian to read.

Adam decided to head for Chief Bowles's village. He would make enquiries about Eli and Peggy Dooley when he visited the Comanche villages. If they had been taken, or killed, someone there should know something of them.

Adam did not take the direct route to the Cherokee village. Instead, he followed the Pedernales River, which would eventually join up with the Colorado. Near here was a small stockade known as Waterloo. This was where Mirabeau Buonaparte Lamar intended locating a new Texas capital, to be named Austin.

The country was new to Adam, and once he began heading eastwards he was pleased to find a ridge running in the direction he was taking. He rode just below the ridge. The trees were sparse enough here to make travelling easy, yet they offered cover from all but the keenest eye, and gave Adam a good view about him.

He had been riding for no more than three hours when he saw a thin wisp of smoke rising from a narrow cleft in the hillside. Dispersing quickly, even before it reached the treetops, the smoke could not have been seen by travellers following the creek in the valley below. Such a cleverly concealed fire had been lit by someone who did not want to advertise his presence to passing Indians. Someone like Eli Varne.

Cautiously, Adam made his way down the slope towards the fire. As he drew closer he could see just how clever was the concealed camp-site. It was a deep, shadowed fault, cut at an angle into the hillside to form a high, roofless cave. Scattered rock blocked the entrance, making it impossible for more than one man at a time to enter. It was a perfect defensive position.

When Adam was still fifty yards from the entrance, he glimpsed a movement a short distance to his left. Drawing his revolver, he turned quickly. He knew now that, whoever was occupying the cleft in the hillside, it was *not* Eli. The Tennesseean would have no reason to hide once he had recognised Adam.

For a full minute Adam watched the spot where he had seen the movement. Finally, he called softly: 'Come out of there, whoever you are – and come out slowly.' When his words brought no response, he repeated them in Spanish, and then in halting Cherokee.

At first his words had no effect. Then a head of greased black hair rose above a rock and a pair of dark eyes scrutinised Adam uncertainly. With his free hand, Adam signalled for the Indian boy to rise to his feet.

When he did so, Adam could see that he was no more than eight years of age. As naked as the day he was born, the boy carried a small bow and arrow in his hand, the taut string of the bow drawn back, an arrow pointing at Adam.

It was a tricky moment. The boy and his bow and arrow were all small, but Adam had seen similar combinations at practice in Chief Bowles's Cherokee village. Accurate enough to hit a target at forty paces, the half-size bows possessed sufficient power to put an arrow right through a turkey at that range.

Adam hesitated only a moment. Returning the revolver to his belt, he touched his hand to his heart and held it up, palm foremost, in a gesture of friendship.

The Indian boy did not ease his grip on either bow or arrow. Adam was wondering whether he might not have made a grave error of judgement, when from near at hand a woman's voice was raised in anger.

'Mocho! What do you think you're doing? Put that down this minute, do you hear me? Put it down now, I say.'

The words were in English, with a strong Irish accent. It was doubtful whether Mocho understood them, but their meaning was clear enough. The boy lowered the bow and eased off the bowstring without allowing his gaze to slip from Adam's face.

Adam had recognised the woman's voice immediately.

'Peggy! Everyone's been worried sick about you. Caleb and the others thought you'd been taken off by Comanches. What are you doing *here*?'

Peggy Dooley had not recognised Adam from the back. Now a whole series of conflicting emotions left her staring open-mouthed at him.

Her surprise was no more than Adam's own. This was not the Peggy Dooley he remembered from his first visit to Caleb's cabin, or from the weeks with the wagon train. Even in those days when her sanity was in some doubt, Peggy had always kept herself clean and neat. Now she stood before him barefooted, her clothes dirty and stained, and her hair lank and uncombed.

There was a sound from the rocks at the entrance to the cleft in the hillside as the Indian boy disappeared inside. Turning back to Peggy, Adam asked: 'What are you doing here? Are you being held prisoner?'

Peggy Dooley smiled, and suddenly Adam saw behind the stained clothes and uncombed hair. It was the smile of a contented woman.

'No, Adam. I'm not a prisoner. I've found myself a new family, that's all. People who *really* need me. Come inside and meet Wolf Alone and Ardilla. They're Mocho's father and sister. Come, there's no need to be afraid.'

Adam secured his horse and followed Peggy into the shadowed hillside fissure. He paused just inside, to allow his eyes to adjust to the reduced light, before picking his way between the rocks and boulders within. Soon one wall of the fissue became an overhang and it was here that Peggy Dooley had her new 'home'. Secure from rain and wind, it was as untidy as Peggy herself. There was wood for the fire piled against the rock, and the paunch of a buffalo half-filled with water lay beside it. Blankets, bows and arrows, berry-bags, horn cups and ladles, and a miscellany of gourds and clay pots were scattered about, and a tin cooking-pot sat atop the fire. The smell emanating from it made Adam wrinkle his nose in disgust.

Close to the fire, an Indian man lay on a bed of dry grasses, covered over with a blanket. He looked ill, but his eyes were alert enough and there was fear in them as Adam walked towards him.

'It's all right, Adam's a friend,' Peggy Dooley explained, but it was apparent that Wolf Alone understood her no more than did his son. There was a small girl here, too. A naked girl of no more than three or four. She was as frightened as her father was of Adam, and when Peggy Dooley held out her arms the girl rushed to them.

'This is Ardilla,' said Peggy Dooley, exhibiting as much pride as though the girl was her own.

'Ardilla . . . that's Spanish for "Squirrel". You speak Spanish?'

Adam put the question to the sick Indian and received a nod by way of reply.

'You can talk to him?' Peggy Dooley was filled with childish delight. 'Why, that's *wonderful*! He doesn't speak much English. Mocho is teaching me their language, but I haven't learned much yet.'

'What's wrong with him?'

'I think he's had pneumonia. He should have been better by now, but moving here took a lot of his strength and all we've had to eat are some roots that Mocho found.'

Looking more closely at the two children, Adam saw they were thin to the point of emaciation.

'Go and fetch the packs from my horse. There is pemmican there, and coffee and sugar – enough to ensure a decent meal. Later I'll go out and shoot a deer. They are plentiful enough in the hills about here.'

'God bless you, Adam.' Peggy Dooley set down the girl and hurried off.

'You have come to take the woman back to her people?' Wolf Alone put the question to Adam.

'I've been looking for her. So have her people.'

'I knew it would be so. She should not have come with us. I do not need trouble from white men. It is enough to be hated by the Comanche and by my own people.'

'You are *not* Comanche?' The Indian's statement took Adam by surprise. He had automatically assumed that Wolf Alone belonged to one of the Comanche bands.

'I am Tiskanwatitch – your people call us the Tonkawa.'

Adam had heard of the Tonkawa Indians, now no more than a few scattered remnants of a once great tribe.

'Why should the Comanche hunt you?'

Wolf Alone lay back and gazed up at the sloping stone 'roof' above him. 'You see me as a sick man. The Comanche know me as a scout who once led Mexicans to their lands, destroying their most important villages and killing many of their warriors. Because of this they kill Tonkawas wherever they find them. Now my own people hunt me, too. They believe that if they kill me the Comanche will leave them alone. It may be they are right, but I do not think so.'

Adam looked from the sick Indian to the two children huddled together against the rock wall of their primitive home.

'What will you do when I take the woman away with me?'

Wolf Alone did not shift his unemotional gaze from Adam's face as he answered quietly: 'We will die.'

CHAPTER EIGHT

ALL THE WAY to the proposed new capital of Austin, Adam wondered how Caleb Ryan and the other settlers would have reacted had he gone back and told them he had found Peggy Dooley living with a sick Tonkawa Indian and his two naked, half-starved children – and had left her with them! They would have been aghast, of this he was certain. He was equally certain it had been the right decision for Peggy.

He had stayed with Peggy and the Indian trio for two days. During this time he had shot sufficient game to last them until long after Wolf Alone was back on his feet and able to hunt once more. Adam had seen a marked improvement in the Indian's condition before he left.

During his stay, Adam had spoken at some length with Peggy and he had never seen her as happy as she was now. She told him that at Caleb's cabin she had been constantly reminded of the son and husband she had lost, and of the tragedy of their premature deaths. She had taken to going off alone on long walks, ignoring the warnings given to her by Caleb and the others. It was on one of these walks that she happened upon the young Ardilla, drinking from the creek. The child had run from her to the crude camp she shared with Mocho and her father. Peggy followed and found Wolf Alone lying sick in the camp. Ill though he was, Wolf Alone managed to move his camp almost a mile that night, but the next day Peggy found it again. This time she had brought food for the children.

Wolf Alone supplied Adam with the remainder of the story. The sick Indian tried to tell Peggy to go away and leave the small family alone, but she refused to understand him.

Wolf Alone had been placed in an impossible position. He knew the White Man held his women in as high esteem as an Apache – and Wolf Alone wanted no more trouble. Then came the day Mocho reported seeing Comanches passing nearby. Wolf Alone knew it was time to move to the hideout he had discovered almost a year before. He tried, but was so sick he would have died long before reaching the refuge had it not been for Peggy. He never knew for certain when she arrived on the scene. Stricken by bouts of delirium, it seemed to Wolf Alone that at one moment *he* was shepherding the children high into the hills, the next Peggy had charge of the whole family.

Once in the hideout he gradually became used to walking in the daylight and finding her there. When she was not cooking the few roots Mocho found, or feeding Wolf Alone, she would be seated with an arm about Ardilla, learning Tonkawa words from the child. Sometimes, at night, he would wake and reach out a hand to find that Peggy was sharing a blanket with her adopted family. Wolf Alone knew he and the children had a woman once more.

Adam had seen Peggy's happiness with the children, with Ardilla in particular. He could not carry her away. And so he had left her. It would be a hard, uncertain life for all of them, yet not so far removed from the precarious existence of many white families in the frontier settlements of Texas and America.

Riding up to the stockade that protected Joseph Harrell's tiny community on the south bank of the Colorado River, Adam marvelled at the optimistic vision that had prompted Mirabeau Buonaparte Lamar to site his new capital here. There were four families living inside the split-log palisade, and Adam received a warm welcome from them. He was astonished to learn it was Christmas Day. Dates, and even days of the week, had long ceased to be of any significance to him, and only the warmth or chill of the days and nights provided an indication of the season.

Adam stayed only one night at the proposed capital. Before he left he was shown all the prime sites that the present owners intended recommending for Lamar's administration buildings.

On his way from Lamar's dream city to the Cherokee village, Adam experienced a 'Norther', one of the incredible sudden falls in temperature so dreaded by even the most experienced Texan traveller. Adam was fortunate to find a sheltered gully, away from the full force of the bitterly cold wind. Here he built a great fire, not needing to concern himself that it might be spotted by Indians. He kept the fire going for two days and two nights, until the weather reverted to normal as suddenly as it had changed.

He reached the Cherokee village at the dead of night, setting up a clamour among the village dogs. After rubbing down his horse, he fed him a few handfuls of grain and turned him loose in the paddock with the other horses.

The cabin was in darkness when he pushed aside the buffalo-hide curtain, and there was not a break in Tiski's even breathing until Adam dropped his saddle on the floor in a corner of the room.

As he eased off his boots, she called: 'Who is there? What do you want?'

'I've come looking for my wife, but I must be in the wrong cabin. Perhaps I should try another one. . . .'

'Adam!' Tiski leaped from the bed and flung herself into his arms. 'I have been so worried. . . . When Yellow Bear told me you had been wounded I made him go back to the white man to see how you were, but you had gone.'

'Yellow Bear should have said nothing. It was a scratch, nothing more.' It was only a *small* lie, he told himself, and already his thoughts were of much more pleasant things.

There was a fresh, clean smell to her that made him forget he had just spent seventeen hours in the saddle. He had been so excited at the thought of seeing Tiski again it was impossible to make camp, knowing she was no more than a few hours' ride away.

Later that night they lay together, naked in the darkness, each contented in the nearness of the other.

'You have found no white girl you would like to take for a wife, Adam?' Tiski whispered the question while her head was lying on his chest and her fingers were caressing his face.

Adam's immediate reaction was to make a flippant reply, but he checked himself in time. He had realised early in their relationship that Tiski did not make, or take, jokes about their life together. She had a very real fear that Adam would one day find himself another wife among his own people. Although it would make her very unhappy, he knew she would accept such a situation.

Hugging her to him, he kissed her hard and long. Then he ran his hands gently over her body until she began to tremble beneath his touch.

'Tiski, every time I look at another girl I feel sorry for the man who will one day marry her, because she is not as beautiful as you.' As he spoke he kissed her eyes, her nose, her lips, chin and throat, and she writhed beneath his lips.

'Adam . . . you make my body sing a happy song. I am not truly alive when you are away. . . .'

He kissed each breast in turn and she pulled him to her. 'Love me, Adam. . . . Love me again. . . .'

When he awoke, the sun had climbed well above the horizon. Outside the cabin the village was well into its daily routine. As Adam stretched lazily, Tiski came in through the doorway.

'Ah! You are awake at last. Everyone is saying you must be sick to lie in bed for so long.'

Her happy smile took away every vestige of criticism from the words. 'I told them you had travelled by night and day to be with me and we had so much love to give to each other that you might sleep for a whole week.'

'I've still got plenty more love where that came from. Come here and kiss me.'

'Oh, no! Your kisses do not stay on the lips. They set fire to every part of me. This morning we eat before we do anything else.' Despite her words, Tiski came over to the bed and kissed him, but she pulled away when he tried to draw her to him.

'No, we cannot do that now. Your friend will be here to see you soon.'

'My friend . . . ? You mean Eli is *here*?'

'You did not know? That is good. Now I *know* you have come to see *me*.'

'How long has Eli been here?' Adam swung his legs from the bed and reached out for his shirt which was hanging nearby. 'All the settlers have been searching for him. They think he's been killed. I'm glad he's here. He can come with me to speak to the Comanche.'

Some of the happiness left Tiski. 'You are leaving to go to the Comanche? When?'

'I don't know yet. I'm hoping Chief Bowles will be able to arrange a meeting with someone like Chief Muguera for me.' He had seen her change of expression, and added: 'I *must* go, Tiski. Far too many people are dying for no reason at all. Someone has to try to call a halt to the killing.'

'Yes.' Tiski stood beside the bed, not looking at him. 'I will be very proud when praises are heaped on you for making such a peace, but I am afraid for you. I do not trust the Comanche.'

'Neither should anyone – at least, not until a Comanche's given his word. Then you can trust him up to the hilt.'

Eli followed his words through the doorway. 'What's all this talk of Comanches? Don't tell me you two are short of something to talk about already? Tiski, I'd just love a cup of that coffee I can smell.'

As Tiski busied herself producing coffee and food, Adam pulled on his clothes, talking as he dressed. He told Eli of the furore the Tennesseean had caused by going off without returning to Caleb's settlement first.

Rubbing his jaw, Eli said ruefully: 'You know, I had it figured them folk were becoming a mite too proprietary about me. That's what happens when a man stays in one place too long. I followed the Comanches' trail until I was certain Peggy wasn't with 'em.

By then I was closer to here than to there, so I came on to see if I might find you. You weren't here, but I knew you'd show up sooner or later. You know, you've got it made, Adam. You're as free as a swallow, yet when you show your face you've got the prettiest girl I know, waiting to give you a welcome you'll remember in every cold, wet, lonely camp along the trail.'

Taking the coffee from Tiski, Eli said: 'Tiski, if you had a sister, I'd go right out and marry her this very day.'

'Then you'd start envying Caleb's way of life, or someone else's,' declared Adam. 'Now, if I had *my* way, I'd forget the rest of the world and settle down here, hunting, sowing crops and raising a family.'

Taking a sudden interest in the fingernails of his left hand, Eli asked: 'Is there any *special* reason why you can't do just that?'

'More than one. At the moment it's Comanches. They attacked the settlement after you left. One family was massacred and Caleb's cabin attacked. I think it's time you and I had a chat with Muguera and the other Comanche chiefs. I want to ask them to stop warring against the settlers in the Hill Country.'

His fingernails forgotten, Eli looked at Adam to see whether he was serious. When he realised he was, the Tennesseean groaned. 'When we first met, I thought you'd make a good partner because you didn't have as many fool ideas as most men I knew. I was wrong – you have *more*! What makes you think the Comanche will listen to you?'

'Chief Muguera owes us. We gave his brother a decent burial, killed his murderers, then sent his brother's wife back home to her people. I'd say that's enough to get talks started, anyway.'

Eli grunted. 'We'll need to discuss this some more. Right now I'd appreciate an invitation to breakfast. I'm hungry enough to eat an angry skunk.'

Tiski looked up from where she was working dough made from her home-made cornflour. 'I thought Woya was looking after you during your stay here?'

Adam knew Woya by sight. She was an attractive young Cherokee divorced woman. During the short period since her divorce she had succeeded in turning the heads of half the young men of the tribe.

Eli looked vaguely embarrassed. 'So she is – and she's looking after me well, but I reckon I've learned why her husband divorced her. She could serve a man fresh melon and ruin it. If you folks don't mind, I'd appreciate eating with you, once in a while.'

When Adam spoke to Yellow Bear about arranging a meeting with the Penateka Comanche leaders, he was relieved to learn that Chief Bowles had succeeded in persuading the tribal council to reject the Mexican proposals. The Cherokee would not join in any uprising against the Texans. The *certainty* of swift and merciless retaliation by the Texans proved to be a stronger argument than the *possibility* of Mexican aid. The decision meant that Lamar had been deprived of an excuse to attack the Cherokee.

While Yellow Bear and Chief Bowles discussed the Cherokee role of mediators between the Comanche and Hill Country settlers, Adam took Eli for a walk alongside the river and told the Tennesseean about finding Peggy Dooley.

'Have you told anyone else?'

Adam shook his head. 'I didn't think it was a good idea.'

'Not a good idea . . . ?' Eli's eyebrows shot up. 'You even *hint* that a white woman might be happy with an Indian and you'll be run out of Texas so fast your feet will leave scorch marks. Will this Tonkawa keep her with him when he's up and about again?'

'I'd say so. His children have certainly taken to her. The girl thinks the world of her.'

'Poor Peggy. I think you'd better say nothing, but try to visit her from time to time, just to see how she's making out.'

'I was thinking along the same lines – but here comes Yellow Bear.'

The Cherokee chief's son told Adam that Chief Bowles had agreed. Yellow Bear himself would try to arrange a meeting with the chiefs of the Penateka Comanche. He would ride out later that day. There was no guarantee that a meeting with the Comanche would bring about a truce, but Chief Bowles agreed that it was probably the only hope Caleb and his settlers had for survival in their exposed frontier settlement.

Yellow Bear was away from the village for the first four weeks of 1839. Adam spent the time learning the ways and the language of the Comanche. His tutor was an old Cherokee who had ridden with the Penateka Comanche for many seasons. The old man was proud of his association with the Plains Indians. He claimed they enjoyed a freedom unknown by the Cherokee and the other Indians of the east. They were also a proud people, with a strong sense of valour and honour. Other Indians referred to the Comanche as 'The Snake People', but the Comanche called themselves 'People of People', acknowledging no other Indians as their equal.

When Adam was not learning Comanche ways, he went off hunting with Eli, ensuring that their cooking-pots, and those of Chief Bowles and Yellow Bear, were never without meat.

Each evening, Tiski taught Adam the elaborate and detailed sign language of the Indians. She taught him many other things, too, and sometimes, when she was with the women, their eyes would meet and they would smile as they shared a secret thought. It was a time of great happiness for both of them.

February came in with a fierce 'Norther'. The wind swept down through Texas, sending red men and white scuttling for shelter. In Chief Bowles's village, men and women spent their days huddled about cabin fires, blankets draped about their shoulders, talking of other 'Northers' they had known, some of which had left behind scores of dead men and beasts, frozen in sub-human temperatures. At night many of the Cherokees adjourned to their small 'hot houses'. These were particularly favoured by the very old and the very young. Low to the ground, and similar in shape and style to the igloo homes of the Eskimo, these 'hot houses' were heavily plastered inside and out with smoothed clay. When a fire was lighted inside, they retained heat in much the same way as did a clay vessel. Adam crawled inside one only once. He felt there was a very real danger of its occupants being choked by smoke from the low fire burning there, but it was surprisingly snug and warm.

Adam and Tiski preferred to spend the two days and three nights of the 'Norther' beside their cabin fire, or lying in each other's arms beneath the blankets and buffalo robes of their bed.

One morning the Cherokee villagers awoke to find that the 'Norther' had passed on, leaving behind a crisp, cloudless world that felt warm after the low temperatures of previous days. That morning, Yellow Bear returned to his people.

No more than ten miles from home when the 'Norther' struck, Yellow Bear had made immediate camp among rocks in well-wooded land. Here he built a roaring fire and kept it burning night and day, forgoing sleep and food in his determination to remain warm and alive.

Yellow Bear's mission to the Penateka Comanche had been only partially successful. Chiefs representing less than half the Comanche had agreed to meet with Adam. More encouraging was the news that only two chiefs of the various small Penateka bands and family units had expressed their determination to continue raiding the new settlers. The remainder would wait and see how any new agreement affected their brothers.

Chief Muguera was one of those who would meet Adam.

Yellow Bear confirmed that the senior Indian chief felt indebted to Adam and Eli for their part in avenging the death of his brother. Yellow Bear believed the old chief would prove a valuable ally.

Adam and Eli set out with Yellow Bear a week later for their meeting with the Comanche chiefs. Adam left with very mixed emotions. He was convinced he could obtain at least a partial treaty on behalf of Caleb Ryan's settlers and was excited at the prospect of meeting with the Comanche, but his heart was left in Chief Bowles's village, with Tiski.

The three men rode westwards, following the route taken when Adam had accompanied the Cherokees on their buffalo hunt, but they rode faster and travelled much farther than before. They rode across miles of flat, featureless grassland, bowing low in the saddle in homage to the constant wind. They sheltered from the driven rain in deep, weathered, grassless gullies, fording countless creeks coloured red with washed-down soil and tainted with enough gypsum to bring a man to the ground in stomach-cramping agony should he be foolish enough to drink the tainted water.

Yellow Bear was a good guide. He knew which streams had water that was pure and cool, and where a sheltered camp could be made, with fuel for a cooking-fire. It was not difficult to obtain meat. The plains were dotted with small herds of buffalo, driven south by severe weather to the north.

The three men rode into Chief Muguera's village early one morning, before the mist had left the river on which the village was located. Cleverly concealed in a shallow dip on the wide plain, the tepees of the Comanches were distributed along a single bank of the river, the crossed poles of the framework rising above the mist that hovered in the shallow hollow.

Their arrival took the Comanches by surprise, causing early consternation as they rode between the tepees. The occupants spilled from their homes as the white men passed by, looking at them in silence, no trace of welcome on their faces. Adam observed that there were few warriors present. Most of those who stared sullenly at them were women and small children, with a sprinkling of aged and wrinkled men, some so crippled by bullets or arrows that they would never again ride a horse.

'There is a raiding party out somewhere,' commented Yellow Bear matter-of-factly. 'We must hope our talks are ended and we have left before the warriors return.'

'Why? If Muguera isn't strong enough to guarantee our safety, he certainly won't be able to enforce any peace treaty.'

'Muguera will see that any promise to you is kept by his people; but, first, he will need to explain it to them. The return of a raiding party is not a good time to make such explanations. If it has been successful, the warriors will not want to give up a source that might provide them with horses, scalps and prisoners. If it has been a bad raid and warriors have been killed, their families will want vengeance. If there is *tiswin* in the village, the young men will drink. Those who did not kill on the raid will wish to prove that they, too, are warriors. It will be better if we are gone before their return.'

Chief Muguera thought the same. Almost as aged as the venerable Chief Bowles, Muguera no longer led his warriors on raids far into the settlements of Texas and New Mexico. Many of the younger warriors had always known him as the 'old' chief. He had not won their respect by courage and leadership as had some of the younger, lesser leaders.

Nevertheless, Muguera *was* the senior of the Penateka Comanche chiefs, and when he sent out for the others they came to sit at a meeting of his council. When a pipe had passed among them, Adam put his request. He told them that Caleb Ryan and his settlers had been forced from *their* own lands and had come to seek a new life, here in Texas. They meant no harm to any man, red or white. If a peaceful Comanche were hungry, he would be welcome to share whatever food the settlers had. If he were hurt, he could go to them for help. The settlers would take no punitive action against Comanches and they would be free to pass through the Hill Country, as they had before the arrival of the settlers. This was what the settlers would offer if the Comanche ceased their raids.

The Comanche chiefs talked among themselves for many hours, the argument going first one way, and then another. When he became bored with the talking about him, Muguera, a wizened, balding little man, said to Adam: 'When a man comes to ask a favour it is usual to bring presents. What have you brought for me?'

'I offer your people the greatest gift a man can give, Chief Muguera. The gift of lasting friendship.'

When Adam's reply was translated for him, Chief Muguera's gaze rested briefly on Adam's face, but he said nothing and, quickly losing interest in him, returned his attention to the other chiefs.

The argument between the chiefs was still raging when Adam heard excited shouting coming from somewhere beyond the village. Immediately, the large crowd of onlookers about the seated chiefs began to thin as children and women ran towards the sound.

Beside Adam, Eli sucked in his breath noisily. 'Adam, if you're a praying man you'd better put your hands together right now. We've got trouble – *big* trouble. Unless I'm very much mistaken that's the raiding party returning – and they're not screams of joy them Comanche women are cutting loose with.'

Around Adam and Eli, some of the Comanche chiefs and sub-chiefs began to stand, the better to see what was happening. At the height of the confusion, an impressive Indian rode into view. Wearing only a breech-clout and simple headband, he yet sat his pony with an unmistakable air of authority. As he drew nearer it could be seen that his face had been blackened, only the thin slash of his mouth and his alert, glittering eyes relieving the self-applied mourning.

Riding to where Chief Muguera sat, the Indian pulled in his horse and sat staring before him, saying nothing.

'Hears-the-Wolf has returned as a mourner and not as a victor. How many warriors have been lost?' Chief Muguera spoke the words as an accusation.

The mounted Indian looked first at Chief Muguera, and then at the assembled chiefs, saving his last and longest look for Eli and Adam.

'In the land across the Great River, all went well. We took many horses and two boys and a woman without a shot being fired at us. But as we returned across the river white men were waiting. They killed White Horse and Twin, and forced us back across the river.'

Yellow Bear explained in a low voice that the river to which Hears-the-Wolf referred was the Rio Grande, the border between Texas and Mexico. It seemed that Mexicans and Texans were able to forget their differences when both fought Indians.

'We rode many miles before we found another place to cross. On the way we had to fight Mexican soldiers. Little Buffalo was killed and some of the horses were lost, but we took two more women – and two men.'

A great crowd of Comanches had gathered about Hears-the-Wolf. As he named each of the lost warriors there was a sigh from the assembly, and a number of women set up an anguished wail. Gathering their children about them, they hurried away to begin a period of total – and extremely painful – mourning. Comanche women had a habit of cutting off their fingers to emphasise how much their menfolk had meant to them. One of the chiefs at the

251

meeting also rose, his face void of expression, and the crowd parted respectfully to allow him through.

'We couldn't have come at a worse time,' growled Eli. 'If it hadn't been for the Texans forcing Hears-the-Wolf and his warriors back across the Rio Grande, he'd have come back to a hero's welcome. There'll be no treaty made here today. We'll be damned lucky to ride away with our scalps.'

Adam looked to Yellow Bear for confirmation, and the Cherokee nodded.

Rising to his feet, Adam spoke to Muguera: 'It is not a good time to talk of peace when you mourn lost warriors. We will talk again tomorrow.'

Chief Muguera nodded unhappily. The presence of the two white men had become an embarrassment. But he owed them a debt. No harm would come to them while they remained among the lodges of his tribe. He snapped an order to a group of Comanche women standing nearby, and the woman Adam and Eli had rescued from Hec Bowie and his friends stepped forward.

'Wait! Do you speak Spanish?' Hears-the-Wolf put the question in the Spanish patois used by the Mexicans who lived along the border with Texas.

When Adam answered in the affirmative, Hears-the-Wolf looked down at him arrogantly. 'The Mexicans are to be given to the women of those who were killed. Come and see how well they die, White Man.'

Adam had heard many tales of the methods used by Comanche women to torture men to death. He had no wish to witness it for himself. 'At the end of it they'll be no more dead than the warriors *you* lost. I'm here to see if we can't keep men *alive*.'

Adam turned and followed the Comanche woman to the tepee that had been prepared for Yellow Bear and the two white men. He did not see the strange look that crossed the Indian's face as Adam left him.

Inside the tepee Eli said: 'Be careful how you speak to Hears-the-Wolf. He's young, but the warriors listen to him, and would follow him anywhere. Muguera might make peace with you, but if it's to be war instead, then it'll be delivered by Hears-the-Wolf, sure as hell.'

The Indian woman remained with them only long enough to satisfy herself that they had enough in the tepee to make them comfortable. After bringing them food she hurried away, anxious to miss none of the forthcoming 'entertainment'.

The torturing of the two Mexican men began soon afterwards,

preceded by screams of terror from the victims as they were stripped naked. The screams brought a roar of eager anticipation from the Comanches.

The ordeal of the Comanche's victims lasted for almost four hours, punctuated by alternate screams and tearful pleas from the suffering Mexicans, and accompanied by howls of approval from the Comanche audience.

The sufferings of the doomed Mexican prisoners did not come to an end until after nightfall, by which time Adam's taut nerves were stretched to breaking-point.

Suddenly the flap of the tepee was thrown back and Hears-the-Wolf stepped inside, the black mourning-paint washed from his face. Ignoring the other two men, he said to Adam: 'Come, we talk.' With this, he turned and walked from the tepee.

Adam followed Hears-the-Wolf as he made his way between the tepees, heading towards the river. On the way the two men crossed a large clearing lit by a number of great fires. Suspended over one of them, tied upside down on a wooden frame, were the bodies of the unfortunate Mexican prisoners. Squatting in front of the bodies were the widows, mothers and sisters of the dead Comanche warriors. Their hair was cut almost to the scalp as a sign of mourning, their half-naked bodies daubed with mourning-paint mixed with blood from self-inflicted wounds. They formed a hideous group as they stared in ghoulish satisfaction at the men upon whom they had wreaked their vengeance.

Adam shuddered. There was a raw primitiveness about the firelit scene that filled him with both horror and despair for the future of such people. Then he remembered Hec Bowie's hatband. Perhaps the two sides were not so far apart after all.

'What is the matter, White Man? Those men were Mexicans – your enemies. Why should you care what happens to them?'

'They are not *my* enemies. My country is far across the water. We are friendly with Mexicans and Texans – yes, and with Indians, too.'

'A White Man's country with friendship for Indians?' There was a great bitterness in Hears-the-Wolf's words. 'Then your country must be far away indeed. White men who come to Texas soon become like their brothers.'

'That's hardly surprising if they see scenes like that.' Adam jerked his head in the direction of the dead Mexicans without looking at them. 'It turns my stomach over – and I've seen Comanche handiwork before.'

'You do not like the Comanche people, yet you come here

seeking peace with us?' Hears-the-Wolf stopped walking and looked closely at Adam, the light from a nearby fire etching the fine bones of his face.

'I don't know enough about the Comanche people not to like you. I don't much care for some of the things you *do*. That's why I'm here. Once we've sorted *that* out I might find I like your people as much as I do the Cherokee.'

Hears-the-Wolf grunted. 'The Cherokee warriors are women. They have forgotten how to fight. One day the White Man will tell them to leave the land they share, because he no longer wishes to look upon their faces. What will the Cherokee do then? Chief Bowles's warriors have forgotten how to live like Indians. They have also forgotten how an Indian should die.'

'I hope it never comes to that. My wife is a Cherokee.'

'Your wife is Kiowa.' Hears-the-Wolf's knowledge took Adam by surprise. 'She can always return to her people and live like a true Indian – unless you intend taking her with *you*, to this land where all Indians are friends?'

Before Adam could reply, the Comanche began walking again. When Adam caught up with him, Hears-the-Wolf said: 'Chief Muguera says you have come to ask our people not to raid the new settlement near the town you call San Antonio. What do you offer us in return for this?'

'Perhaps an end to that.' From the clearing in the village, the Comanche widows were wailing noisily, each trying to outdo the other in a demonstration of grief. 'Your warriors will be able to ride through the settlement without stealth. No one will fire upon them when they are hurt. If your warriors or their women and children are sick, they can come to be helped. They will be given food – although the settlers don't have too much of that for themselves just yet.'

Hears-the-Wolf snorted scornfully. 'The Comanche have always ridden through the Hill Country and found food. We are many, your settlers are few. It will be better if they return to their own lands.'

Adam shook his head. 'They come from a part of my country where there is no longer food for them. Many have died on the way here. There is no going back. They have found a new home in the Hill Country. They will live there – or die there. If they die, others will come to take their places. The newcomers might not want to make peace with your people.'

The two men had cleared the Comanche village now. Before them the river curved away into the distance. Silver-grey in the moonlight, its banks were fringed with dark-shadowed trees.

Above them, from horizon to horizon, the soft, dark sky was peppered with stars.

'What if Chief Muguera *does* agree to what you ask? What if the Comanche stops raiding in the Hill Country? Will your people welcome us when we pass through after a raid, carrying white women and children as captives?'

Adam realised that Hears-the-Wolf was an unusually deep-thinking young warrior chief. An evasive answer would be a great mistake. He countered with a question of his own.

'What would the Comanche people do if white men rode through their villages flaunting captive Comanche women and children? You know the answer, and so do I. They would be angry. Your warriors would try to free the captives. My own people are no different. If there is to be a lasting peace between us, each side will need to try to understand the other.'

Hears-the-Wolf nodded. 'What of Mexican prisoners?'

'I have Mexican friends, and I've just seen what you do to them. If I could prevent such a thing from happening, I would.'

'It seems the Comanche has little to gain and much to lose by making peace with your people, White Man.'

'You don't really believe that or you wouldn't be talking with me now. Let me tell you something, Hears-the-Wolf. White men are like the stars up there in the sky. There are too many of them for one man to count in a whole lifetime. More and more of them are pushing out from the east. One day they will reach the Comanche, no matter how far you move away. Unless you can come to terms with them, "Comanche" will be only a word, remembered by fewer and fewer people. The time to make a treaty is *now*, while you're still strong. If you wait, you'll one day find yourselves so outnumbered you'll have to accept whatever you're given – and that will be *nothing*.'

The two men had slowed their pace as they talked and now they stopped, looking out across the moonlit river. Hears-the-Wolf was silent for a long time, and Adam feared he had offended the fierce pride of the Comanche. But when Hears-the-Wolf spoke again it was clear that he had given deep thought to Adam's words.

'You have said nothing I have not said to myself, many times. But I am a young man, a leader only on the raid. In times of peace my voice is no more than a whisper in the council of my people. When it *is* heard, the old men are quick to remind me of the other times we have made peace with the White Man. They say the peace lasts only until the White Man believes he is strong enough to defeat us in battle. Then the treaty means nothing. Some of the

Comanches made a peace with the man the Cherokee call "The Raven". They have since learned that the treaty was between the Comanches and one man only. When The Raven's people stopped fighting Mexicans they fought Comanches once more.'

'The Raven is no longer chief of his people. The new chief of the Texans does not understand the ways of the Indian. I cannot promise he ever will. All I can say is that a small peace with the settlers in the Hill Country will be a beginning. Friends of the Comanche people will use it to prove that white men *can* live at peace with the Comanche.'

'It will be a beginning for whom?' The bitterness returned to Hears-the-Wolf's voice. 'Only for the white men who put sticks in the ground to keep other men out, who cut down the trees and tear open the belly of the earth. For the Comanche it will mean the end of the life he has always lived, the freedom to roam where he will, following the buffalo.'

Adam wished he could offer Hears-the-Wolf some reassurance for the future of the Comanche people, but there was none to be given. Immigrants were pouring into Texas from the whole of the North American continent. Those already settled along the eastern coastal regions were raising large families. These children would grow to adulthood eager for lands of their own. The move to push the frontiers of civilisation westward was already gathering momentum.

The reputation of the warlike tribes of the central plains was all that prevented this tide of immigration from flowing out from the frontier and carrying 'civilisation' forward. But there were too few Indians to hold back the human flood for ever. Once it began, it would sweep the Indians away.

'What you say is true, Hears-the-Wolf, but it's something that neither you nor I can stop. While your people have lived an unchanging way of life for hundreds of years, white men have learned *new* ways and conquered new lands. It is the White Man's way to move forward, brushing aside those who do not go with him. He is strong, and he *knows* he is strong. His numbers are as the blades of grass on the plains. The Indian can never win a war with him. No matter how many white men are killed, ten times that number will come to take their places. Yes, the life the Comanche has known is coming to an end. If you are to survive as a people, you must make peace with the white men and learn their ways. It's not going to be easy, and I'm not claiming that making peace with a few settlers will save the whole Comanche nation, but you've got to start somewhere – and damned soon.'

Unexpectedly, Hears-the-Wolf said: 'I like the way you speak,

White Man. You do not hide your words because I may not like to hear them. Neither do you make promises you know cannot be kept. If it is a good peace between your settlers and my people, perhaps the new White Chief will want such a peace for all white men?'

Adam tried hard to hide the excitement he felt at Hears-the-Wolf's words. 'No man in his right mind would miss such an opportunity.'

'Then you will have your treaty. I will stand with Muguera at the council tomorrow. Not every chief will speak for peace, but I will let it be known that any attack on your settlers will be an attack on me, because *I* have given my word. Should this not be enough, and you have trouble from Comanches, you will let me know.'

Abruptly, Hears-the-Wolf turned and strode away, leaving a bemused Adam to return alone to the tepee and break the good news to Eli.

CHAPTER NINE

WHEN THE COMANCHE COUNCIL met again the next day, Hears-the-Wolf kept his word. The result was an agreement that the raids upon Caleb and his settlers should cease. Only the chiefs of two small Comanche bands dissented, but they quickly changed their minds when Hears-the-Wolf gravely informed them that he was personally underwriting the treaty.

Highly satisfied with the results of their peace mission, the three-man delegation said goodbye to their Comanche host and departed. Once outside the encampment they, too, parted company, Eli and Adam heading for the settlement, Yellow Bear returning to his Cherokee village.

Adam would have preferred to ride with Yellow Bear and return to Tiski, but Chief Muguera had taken the first unexpected step towards peace. Now Adam hoped to move the Texans closer to the Comanche. He would call on President Lamar after visiting the Hill Country.

When the two men reached the edge of the Hill Country, Eli asked: 'How far from here is the place where Peggy is living with the Tonkawa Indian family?'

'Not far, perhaps twelve or fifteen miles west. Are you thinking of paying her a call?'

Eli shrugged. 'Why not? It's a neighbourly thing to do. Besides, it looks as though they've had snow around here. They might have found hunting a little difficult. We'll take them in some fresh meat.'

There *had* been snow. Some of it still lay in shadowed hollows, but most had long since thawed, leaving the ground soft and wet underfoot.

Adam shot a deer when they were five miles short of the hidden hillside fissure and packed it in front of him as he rode along searching for remembered landmarks. Soon he found the creek that wound through the valley beneath the hill. The two men had been following it for half an hour when Eli kneed his horse alongside Adam. 'Some horses have been through this valley recently. See where they crossed the creek up ahead?'

It did not require a frontiersman's eye to see the spot where the hoofs of horses had churned up the earth on both banks of the creek.

'Wait here a minute, while I have a look.'

Without waiting for an answer, Eli urged his horse on. When he reached the crossing-place he slipped to the ground and examined the tracks. Beckoning Adam to come on, Eli called grimly: 'I don't think we're the first visitors Peggy's had. These were all shod horses, so they'd have been white men.'

'Caleb?'

Eli shook his head. 'The settlers don't own as many horses as have crossed here. I'd say there were upwards of twenty.'

He looked up the hill to where the narrow slit that was the entrance to Wolf Alone's cave could just be seen. 'They went up there and then returned. I'd say it was about two days ago ... maybe three. Probably following footprints. There would have been more snow about then, and footprints in melting snow can be seen a mile away.'

'Let's go up and find out whether anyone was home when they called.' Letting the deer slip heavily to the ground, Adam dug his heels into his horse's belly.

Peggy Dooley and her adopted family *had* been home when the horsemen came calling. The first evidence of this lay half-buried in a small snowdrift against the cliff-face, only yards from the fissure. It was Mocho, the Indian boy, his small bow still clutched in stiff, dead-frozen fingers. He had been shot through the head and body.

Wolf Alone was inside the narrow cave-house. He, too, was dead, his body riddled with bullets. It appeared from the scarred stonework about the entrance that his killers had fired a fusillade of shots from outside the cave.

There were no signs of Peggy or Ardilla.

'Whoever was here probably took them off with them,' said Eli.

'Perhaps. All the same, I think we ought to search around here before we go.'

Eli nodded his head to where Mocho's small body lay. 'What are we going to do with them? There are no tools around here for a burying.'

Eventually, Tonkawa father and son were buried together beneath a cairn of loose rocks, gathered from about the area of the makeshift home. Then the two men separated and began a search of the surrounding hillside.

They had searched for two hours when a shot echoed about the wooded hills and sent Adam pounding up the hillside to where he could see Eli's riderless horse.

Eli was pulling the thin body of Ardilla from a gap beneath a flat, leaning limestone boulder. It had been almost concealed by a deep blanket of windblown leaves.

Pale and angry, Adam began to say something, but Eli, his ear against the girl's thin chest, held up a hand for silence.

'She's still alive!'

Carrying the girl down the hill to the home where her father and brother had died, Eli got a fire started from the wood stored there, while Adam wrapped Ardilla in a blanket taken from the bedroll he kept tied behind his saddle. Ardilla wore only a crude dress made from a small deerskin. Her arms and face were dirty, and there were cuts and grazes on her legs, but the two men could see no other injuries. Hungry and tired, and too frightened to return to her former home, she had probably crept beneath the rock seeking shelter from the bitterly cold wind. She was suffering from exposure, but if Eli was correct, and the attack on her home had taken place two or three days before, she was lucky to be alive.

When the fire was going well, and Ardilla lay close to it in her blanket, Adam fetched the deer he had shot. Skewering strips of meat on the blade of his knife, he cooked them over the fire.

Before long Ardilla began to stir, as though waking from a deep sleep. Suddenly, her eyes opened. For a few moments her mind registered nothing. Then she saw Eli and was seized by a terror such as no four-year-old girl should have known.

'It's all right, Ardilla. No one's going to hurt you. Take it easy now.' Adam's arms went about her as she started up.

She understood nothing of what was said, but Adam's voice was calm and reassuring, and he had called her by name. When she recognised him both men could see her relief.

Pointing to Eli, words tumbled from her, but they were no more intelligible to Eli than to Adam until Eli suddenly offered an interpretation. 'I guess she doesn't like my beard.'

'You understand the language?'

'No. I've never met up with a Tonkawa before, and the language is like no other I've heard, but she used a Kiowa word – *senpo* – and touched her chin. It means "beard". I reckon the men who killed her pa and brother had beards.'

'Then they were Texans.'

'Or Mexicans. Either way, she don't like this beard.'

Eli rose to his feet while he was talking, and Ardilla cowered back against Adam. When Eli walked away, Adam removed his knife from the fire. Pulling a piece of meat from it, Adam handed it to Ardilla. It was so hot that it burned her hands and mouth, but she tore off chunks with her strong little teeth and bolted the meat down so quickly that Adam feared she would choke.

When Eli returned to the fire he squatted down self-consciously and helped himself to a piece of meat. He had been to the creek. Using soap and his hunting-knife, he had shaved off his heavy black beard.

Looking up from the fire, Eli saw Adam staring at him. Fingering his denuded chin, Eli said: 'Aw! What the hell. . . . A man needs reminding once in a while that he's human. Otherwise he'll wind up looking like a winter-coated bear.'

Adam was about to make a facetious reply when he looked at Ardilla. She was staring at Eli in wonderment. Suddenly she reached out her hand to his face and a tiny finger traced the line dividing brown, weather-tanned skin from that hidden by his heavy beard for so many years. She uttered a short sentence and smiled.

When it brought no immediate response, she repeated the words and smiled again. Breaking into a grin, Eli reached out and ruffled her thick, untidy black hair. 'I don't know what you're saying, girl, but it was worth losing a little hair to put a smile on that pretty face of yours.'

They stayed that night on the hillside of death. Once, in the dark hours of the early morning, Adam was awakened by the cries of Ardilla, caught in the throes of a nightmare. Before he could throw off his blanket, Eli reached her. Picking her up in his arms, he carried her back to his own blanket, and the little girl quickly snuggled down and slept once more. Adam smiled sadly as he pulled his own single blanket up about his neck. Ardilla had completely captured the heart of the tough Tennessee frontiersman.

When they broke free of the trees and rode towards Caleb Ryan's cabin, the two men could see that the Irish settler had company. There were at least twenty horses in the corral and a number of men lounged about the cleared yard, whittling wood, throwing sticks for Caleb's two dogs, or engaged in other pastimes born of boredom.

Patting Ardilla's arm reassuringly, Eli rode straight up to the cabin door and dismounted. He lifted Ardilla clear of the saddle, but did not put her down. Her arm about his neck, the Indian girl buried her face against his shoulder, shutting out faces she did not want to see.

As Eli turned towards the cabin, a thickset, florid-faced man with sandy hair and a short, red, aggressive beard came from within to block the doorway.

'Well, well, well! If it isn't Eli Varne, the Indian's friend – and without his beard, too. What you got there, Eli? That one of your own half-breed brats? Or are you going to fatten her up for Thanksgiving?' It was Sam Dollar, the Ranger captain, whom Adam had last seen at the home of Gustav and Henrietta Miesenbach.

'This little mite? No, sir, Captain. She's just a little survivor I picked up from the scene of one of them great battles you and your men fought against hostile Indians. You and twenty Rangers against one Indian and an eight-year-old boy, wasn't it? That's if you don't count this little girl. I got to hand it to you, Captain. You sure did show them hostiles that it don't do to tangle with the Rangers. I don't think a single bullet missed that Indian – but, then, he didn't have a weapon to spoil your men's aim, now, did he? Mind you, that eight-year-old boy *did* have a toy bow and arrow. I expect that's why only three bullets hit him. Now, get out of my way, Dollar, or I'll walk right through you.'

The Ranger captain's beard jutted forward, in the expression of anger Adam remembered, but before he could make a reply he was pushed aside and Peggy Dooley rushed from the cabin.

'Ardilla! Oh, my darling girl . . . you're alive! Thank God!'

At the sound of Peggy's voice, Ardilla wriggled from Eli's arms. The joy on her face as she went to the widowed Irish woman was beyond belief.

The discomfiture of Captain Dollar's Rangers as they witnessed the scene was evident and they looked to their captain to give them a lead. Caleb, his wife and family, with Nell Plunkett and Kathie Casey, had come from the cabin. They knew nothing of what had gone before, but the women were soon caught up in the joyful reunion of Peggy and Ardilla. Explanations could come later.

Caleb greeted Eli and Adam warmly. It had been feared in the small settlement that both men had been killed by the Comanches.

'Captain Dollar and his men brought Peggy back to us,' Caleb burbled happily, unaware of the ill-feeling between Eli and the Ranger captain. 'She'd been captured by Indians and was being held no more than a day's ride from here.'

Eli looked contemptuously at the Captain of Rangers. 'Sam Dollar found Peggy looking after a man and his two motherless children. Trouble is, Peggy isn't as clever as some folks. She didn't notice they were *Indians*. I guess killing the Indian and his boy was one way of making sure they got no sympathy from anyone else. They'd have killed the girl, too, if she hadn't run off and hid herself. She was near to freezing to death when Adam and me found her.'

Eli's words carried to Captain Dollar, but not to where Peggy stood with the women and children. Nell Plunkett was the only woman to hear his words.

Captain Dollar's face registered his anger. 'You've always been soft on Indians, Eli. They're vermin – and young vermin grow to be big vermin. What are you going to do with the girl?'

'What am *I* going to do with her? Nothing. I've brought her here. As far as I'm concerned, this is where she'll stay, if Caleb's got no objections.'

Caleb looked to where Peggy held Ardilla. The child was clinging to her while Eileen Ryan smoothed back the child's hair and murmured sympathetically.

'It would take a braver man than me to send the child away. That's the first time any of us has seen Peggy smile since she came back. Don't worry, Captain, the girl will be brought up as a Christian. She's young enough to forget her Indian ways.'

Captain Sam Dollar looked at Caleb scornfully. 'Yes, and I've heard of frogs turning into princes, too. She's an Indian and will never be anything else. Having her here will attract Comanches like wasps to a honey-pot. They'll never rest until they've taken her back.'

'The girl's a Tonkawa, of no interest to the Comanche at all.' Adam was appalled at Captain Dollar's ignorance of Indians, but hardly surprised.

Turning his back on the Ranger captain, Adam spoke to Caleb: 'You'll have no more trouble with the Penateka Comanche. They've agreed to leave the settlers alone. Tell the others to do nothing stupid, and keep clear of any Indians they see for a while. But there should be no more surprise attacks – unless the Quahadi Comanche come back this way.'

Adam's words brought murmurs of scorn and disbelief from the listening Rangers. Captain Dollar asked: 'Are you trying to tell us you've made peace with the *Comanche*?'

Some of the Rangers laughed, but before Adam could reply Eli touched him lightly on the arm. When Eli spoke it was to the Ranger captain, his voice soft, but Sam Dollar never missed a single word.

'The peace we've made is between the Penateka Comanche and Caleb Ryan's settlement, not with anyone else. I was right there in Chief Muguera's village when the peace was agreed.

263

Now *I've* repeated what Adam just told you. If you're thinking of calling anyone a liar, then make it me – but don't act surprised if I take it personal.'

Adam saw that Eli was holding his favourite rifle. Adam had not seen him slip it free of the saddle holster. Cradled in Eli's arm, it was pointing nowhere in particular, but every Ranger in Sam Dollar's troop was familiar with the ways of the frontier. With varying degrees of haste, they cleared the line of fire between and behind the two men.

Captain Dollar knew how well Eli could shoot and he had seen him in action. Adam's prowess with gun and knife was also being talked about wherever frontiersmen gathered. The Ranger captain was no coward, but neither was he a fool.

'What you so touchy about, Eli? I'm not doubting your word, or your partner's, either. You say you made a peace with Muguera, then I believe you. I just don't put any faith in a Comanche's word, that's all. If these folk have any sense, they'll stay on their guard and shoot to kill any Indian who comes within gunshot range. That's my recipe for remaining alive.'

'So I've noticed. I get edgy with men like you around me, Sam. I can't tell you to get the hell out of here because I'm not on my own place, but if you don't there's likely to be a nasty accident. You know how it is, my trigger finger being so itchy, and all? 'Course, it don't matter so much about you and me getting hurt, we're grown men, but with you and your boys here I'm feared for the children.'

Captain Dollar flushed angrily. 'Don't push me too far, Eli. I've got no quarrel with you and I see no sense in starting one. Me and my men will be on our way before nightfall. I shouldn't have been this way at all if I hadn't come with a message for your partner. It's from President Lamar. He wants to see you. He'll be at Austin – you might know it as Waterloo – until the middle of March. Then he'll be returning to Houston. No use asking me what it's about. I don't know. The President of Texas doesn't confide in me.'

The small red beard jutted forward once more. 'Now you've got your message and these folks have their woman back, me and my men will leave. Seems some Mexican troops have got into the habit of crossing the border down near Laredo and behaving as though Texas still belongs to them. We're going to teach them different.'

Captain Dollar raised his voice to pass on this information, and Adam had the feeling it was meant to impress one of the women. Whether it was Nell Plunkett or Kathie Casey was not clear.

Neither seemed particularly interested, and when the Rangers rode away an hour later no one left the Ryan cabin to watch them go.

CHAPTER TEN

Adam remained at the settlement for ten days. During this time he erected a crude cabin on his land. There was a current rumour in the settlement that unless a man could show he had 'improved' his land it was liable to be taken from him, and Adam had no intention of losing his land to the Lamar administration.

While he was working, a band of forty Comanches came through the settlement, causing great consternation among the settlers. The Indians rode through without incident, pausing only to water their horses at a creek. The incident gave the nervous settlers new hope that the treaty negotiated by Adam with the Penateka Comanche would hold.

Meanwhile, Ardilla was adapting to her new surroundings as though she had never lived anywhere else. Eli, too, seemed more relaxed in the settlement. Since he and Adam had returned from Chief Muguera's village, Eli was showing an increasing interest in Kathie Casey. The settlers were beginning to hint that the settlement might soon be having its first marriage.

With Kathie Casey spending much of her time with Eli, and Peggy totally involved with her young charge, Nell sometimes sought Adam's company. They talked together often when he was at Caleb's cabin, and when he was working hard on his own place she sometimes brought him a meal, often staying to help him lift a log or two into position, or to work on clearing a patch of land at the rear of the cabin that showed some promise of making a vegetable-patch.

Nell was a changed girl from the bitter, English-hating peasant girl who had sailed from Ireland a year before. The old hatred had not entirely gone, but learning of the atrocities that other peoples inflicted upon each other had helped to damp it down. Much of the conversation she had with Adam centred upon the Cherokee and the Comanche. She had an interest in the Indians that almost matched Adam's own, and she proved that the fire inside her had not died completely by complaining bitterly that she was kept from visiting their villages only because she was a woman.

The young Irish girl questioned Adam closely about Tiski. By her newly found sympathetic understanding, she came to learn more than any other person how deeply he loved his Indian wife, and of his happiness when he was with her. On many occasions

Nell urged him to bring Tiski to the cabin when it was completed. Nell assured Adam that Tiski would have the friendship of all the women who lived on Caleb's land.

Adam was tempted by the thought of having Tiski here, and of farming the land and raising cattle. But then he would remember Hec Bowie and Sam Dollar and his Rangers. He knew in his heart that it would never work. Not yet. He would worry about Tiski every time he left the cabin – and with just cause. There were too many men like Bowie and Dollar in Texas, and would be for many years to come.

Talking to Nell made Adam restless. It was time he left the Hill Country again. It was also nearing mid-March, the time when President Lamar would be leaving his future capital and returning to Houston. Adam did not want to have to chase the President across half of Texas. He decided he would go to see him, and then return to Tiski.

Eli did not come with Adam. For perhaps the first time in his life, Eli had a good reason for remaining in one place. Kathie Casey and her young son both worshipped the Tennessee frontiersman.

Leaving the settlement, Adam rode first to San Antonio, to call on Don Manuel. Neither the Mexican landowner nor his family were at home. His courteous Mexican ranch-manager informed Adam that the Tolsa family were 'away', hinting that the journey was concerned with the affairs of the government of Texas.

There was a letter at the ranch for Adam – from Lord Palmerston. Penned in a somewhat irritable vein, the letter reprimanded Adam for the 'alarmist' views he had expressed in an earlier letter. There was, Palmerston insisted, no possibility of the Texan government extending its jurisdiction to the Pacific coast. Indeed, Lord Palmerston's personal view was that Texas would have the greatest difficulty in surviving within its present ill-defined borders for longer than a few more months. Texan envoys were currently scouring Europe in an unsuccessful bid to raise a loan to prop up the tottering Republic. As for annexation by the United States of America, Adam had himself reported that Lamar was opposed to the idea. With anti-slavery factions dominating United States politics, there was little likelihood of another slave-owning State being admitted to the increasingly fragile Union.

However, Lord Palmerston expressed disquiet at reports reaching him of increased *French* interest in Texas. The French, in common with England and the United States, had a longstanding dispute with Mexico over sums of money owed to the three countries and their citizens. At the end of 1838, French patience had finally run out. After first bombarding the Mexican port of Vera Cruz, they sent landing parties ashore to blow up the city's defences. Somewhat belatedly, the Mexican government sent for the country's one-time hero, General Santa Anna, to save the day for them. In virtual disgrace since his humiliating defeat at the hands of Sam Houston, Santa Anna fared no better on this occasion. The Mexican general lost a leg in the fighting and the Mexicans were heavily defeated.

Although France had not yet recognised Texas, their victorious naval captains struck up a close friendship with their counterparts in the tiny Texan navy. It was hardly surprising; both were blockading the ports of a mutual enemy. French ships adopted the habit of slipping into Texan ports where their crews enjoyed the unstinting hospitality offered by the Texans. The French sailors, some with friends and relatives in high places, were fighting for their country far from home. The French people warmed towards those who offered their heroes a friendly welcome in the New World.

Although French influence in Texas was not so serious a matter as American involvement, it *was* cause for British concern. Lord Palmerston asked Adam to report on the extent of French influence in Texas. If the opportunity presented itself, Adam was also asked to suggest to Lamar that British recognition might be forthcoming if the new President expressed a willingness to move towards Great Britain on the slavery issue.

However, it seemed that Palmerston's regard for the rights of his fellow-men did not extend to the American Indian. In a curt final paragraph, Adam was informed that the government of Her Majesty had no intention of making the American Indian an issue in any negotiations on Texan independence. They were the sole responsibility of the *de facto* government of Texas, and Adam was 'strongly advised' not to involve himself in Texan internal affairs.

Adam burned the letter. As he watched the stiff paper blacken and curl, he pondered on the capriciousness of a government that refused recognition for Texas because of the country's policy towards one unfortunate race of people, yet deliberately ignored the plight of another.

Austin had grown in size since Adam's earlier visit and he had no need to enquire where he might find President Mirabeau Buonaparte Lamar. One house rose above all the others. A two-storey timber house, it was surrounded by an eight-feet-high stockade. Inside, on a flagpole as high as the house itself, flew a red, white and blue flag with a single large star emblazoned upon it. Although he had not seen the flag before, Adam guessed rightly that it was the new flag of the Texas Republic. He had also learned enough about Lamar to know that the Texan president would be found within a shadow's length of the flag.

His guess was confirmed when he tried to ride through the stockade gate, only to have his progress blocked by a musket-carrying soldier.

'This is the President's residence. No one goes in without the permission of Colonel Dawson.'

'Where will I find this Colonel Dawson?'

'He's in the house.'

'The house inside the stockade? Will you fetch him for me?'

'Sorry, mister. I'm on guard. It's more than I dare to do to leave my post.'

Adam leaned forward on the pommel of his saddle to ease the aching muscles in his back. He tried hard not to lose his temper. 'Soldier, I've ridden a long way to see President Lamar. Are you going to let me in, or do I sit here and whistle for the President to come out to me?'

'You got an appointment? The President don't see no one without an appointment, and I ain't been told to expect anyone.'

'President Lamar doesn't keep his appointment-book in the Hill Country beyond San Antonio,' Adam said wearily. His patience was beginning to wear very thin indeed when a tall, grey-haired man wearing an impressive uniform, complete with blue sash and sword, came from inside the gateway.

Stopping in the gateway, the Texan army officer looked from the mud-spattered, buckskin-clad figure slumped on the horse to the guard. 'Everything all right, soldier?'

'This stranger says he has business with the President. He ain't got no appointment. Hell, I don't go none on this "guard duty", Colonel. I joined the army to fight Mexicans and Indians, not to stand here dressed up like something out of a New Orleans shop window. . . .'

Ignoring the grumbling of the discontented guard, Colonel Dawson scrutinised Adam once again, this time taking in the two rifles in saddle holsters, the revolver tucked in his belt, and the bulging saddlebags and tightly rolled bed-blankets.

What he saw was a typical self-contained frontiersman, used to travelling far and living off the land in a frequently hostile environment. There were many such men in Texas. A few had talents the young republic would use. Many more were in Texas as refugees from United States justice.

'Call at the President's office tomorrow morning and state your business. One of my staff will deal with you.'

Annoyed by the Colonel's curt dismissal, Adam said: 'Things have become pretty fancy since General Houston handed over the presidency. He never cared much for guards, offices, and colonels in fancy uniforms.'

Colonel Dawson coloured angrily. 'A great many things have changed since Houston was replaced. President Lamar is the figurehead of the Independent Republic of Texas, and head of a responsible government. He conducts himself with the dignity demanded by such an office – not in the manner of a saloon-keeper declaring open house for all his drunken friends.'

Adam had ridden through a two-hour rainstorm shortly before reaching Austin. He was cold, wet, tired and irritable.

'I guess you could say I was one of those "drunken friends", Colonel. Perhaps you will be kind enough to inform the President of the Independent Republic of Texas that Adam Rashleigh called – as requested. If he still wants to see me, I'll be camping down the road only long enough to clean up and cook myself a meal. Then I'll be heading for the village of Chief Bowles.'

A young officer found Adam an hour later, in a camp beside a creek, at the base of a hill that was a carpet of spring-flowering bluebonnets. The officer tendered the President's apologies for the misunderstanding that had occurred and asked Adam to return with him to the President's residence.

Having eaten and changed into dry clothing, Adam was in a better temper. The officer shared Adam's coffee and told him of the changes brought about by Lamar since taking office. Most of Austin had already been laid out in lots. An extensive programme for free public schools throughout the country was also well into the planning stage. The young officer was even more enthusiastic about Lamar's promise to clear the Indians from the country and so throw open the road to the western expansion of Texas.

Adam said little, preferring to listen as he broke his brief camp and set off to meet President Mirabeau Buonaparte Lamar.

Adam was shown into a room in which a number of men stood about talking, and he saw Lamar immediately. The Texan president was at the centre of the all-male gathering, his words listened to with silent respect. Lamar was a small man, but well built and with a shock of long black hair. Elegantly dressed in a well-tailored suit, he was a marked contrast to his flamboyant but carelessly dressed predecessor. When he saw Adam standing in the doorway, Lamar excused himself from his companions and came across the room, a hand extended in welcome.

'Thank you for coming all this way to see me, Mr Rashleigh. It is most kind of you. *Most* kind.' Lamar's voice was soft and courteous, his manners those of a Georgia gentleman.

Adam was introduced to the other men in the room. Most were members of Lamar's administration. After Adam had answered a number of polite enquiries about San Antonio and the Hill Country settlement, Lamar led him to a smaller room, accompanied by a few of his officials. Here Adam was seated facing Lamar across a large desk, the others ranged about him.

Placing both hands on the desk in front of him, Lamar began to speak. 'You may be wondering why I have asked you to come here, Mr Rashleigh. The truth is, I understand you are acquainted with your country's Foreign Secretary, and that President Houston made use of this acquaintanceship to establish an unofficial link with Great Britain?'

Adam nodded; he had thought this was the reason why Lamar had sent for him. 'My late father and Lord Palmerston were friends – yes, General Houston did contact Lord Palmerston through me.'

The information brought a stir of interest to the men about the table, not all of whom had been in Lamar's confidence.

'Good!' President Lamar leaned back in his chair and beamed at the men about him. 'It appears to have been one of the few intelligent moves made by Houston during the course of his administration. Mr Rashleigh, will you continue to presume upon your acquaintanceship with Lord Palmerston on my behalf – for Texas?'

Once again Adam was being asked to adopt a role that should delight Lord Palmerston.

'I deem it an honour to help Texas in any way I can, President Lamar, but I don't doubt that Lord Palmerston will reiterate the conditions that must be met before Great Britain can consider recognition – conditions President Houston was unable to fulfil.'

'I trust you are not suggesting that, because Houston was unable to lead Texas to its rightful place on the international stage, my administration must also fail? Houston was an inept President. Brought face to face with a few problems, he was prepared to forgo that very independence for which so many brave men fought and died. He would have handed Texas to the United States of America as though it were some unwanted gift. You'll find Texas has a *real* administration now, Mr Rashleigh, led by men determined that the sacrifice of so many of their countrymen shall not have been in vain. I intend extending the borders of Texas to take in *all* men who value freedom, honour and opportunity. We are free and independent, Mr Rashleigh. While I am President we shall remain so. I am not *begging* for your country's aid; I am asking only that our independence be justly recognised. Any obstacles in the way of recognition can be removed – *I* will remove them – but it must be made plain to Lord Palmerston that I am extending the hand of friendship to Great Britain, not bending my knee in a gesture of servility.'

The other men in the room nodded agreement, and Adam grudgingly admitted that the new President of Texas would impress Lord Palmerston far more than had his predecessor. Lamar loved words. He seized the opportunity to make a speech whenever the occasion arose, always saying what the majority of his listeners wanted him to say, tempering his views to suit the occasion. For the sake of Texas, Adam hoped Lamar's administration contained enough able men to carry on the less spectacular, but more demanding, tasks of government, while Lamar played with words and enjoyed his dreams of grandeur.

'I'll pass on your views to Lord Palmerston, but I feel he will want some assurances on the slavery question before recognition can be seriously considered.'

'I'm damned if I'll give up my slaves – for Great Britain or anyone else. . . .'

The outburst came from a large, florid-faced man who represented the plantation-owners along the Brazos River valley. Lamar swiftly waved him to silence.

'The subject of slavery is an emotional one on both sides of the Atlantic Ocean, Mr Rashleigh. I myself am a slave-owner, and expect to remain one until the end of my days, but I don't doubt that Lord Palmerston and I can reach an agreement that will satisfy everyone. You may also inform His Lordship that I am trying to negotiate a permanent peace with Mexico. At this very moment a friend of yours, Don Manuel Tolsa, is in Mexico. I have authorised him to offer the Mexican government up to five million dollars as the price of our independence. Don Manuel has reported that the reception given to the idea is encouraging – and the government of the United States has expressed a willingness to mediate in the matter.'

Adam was surprised that Lamar had entrusted Don Manuel on such an important mission. The Mexican landowner's friendship with Houston was well known. As though reading his thoughts, Lamar said quietly: 'I, too, was at San Jacinto, Mr Rashleigh. Don Manuel and I fought together there.'

'Of course. I sincerely hope his mission will be successful. In the meantime I will write to Lord Palmerston and acquaint him with your views. I, too, am convinced that early recognition of Texas by Great Britain is in the best interests of both countries.'

'Good. I am glad we are in agreement. Now, shall we return to the other chamber? I feel the time is ripe to drink a toast to the success of our efforts. Regrettably, I must insist that it remain a *secret* toast. I feel our various ventures have more chance of succeeding if few people are aware of them.'

Returning to the larger room, Lamar called for drinks before questioning Adam closely about his background. The Texan president expressed envy that Adam had visited so many of the cultural centres of Europe and had listened to the music of the great composers played by trained, professional musicians.

'I sometimes wish I could cast off the cares of my office and travel to Europe – to walk the shaded paths trodden by Moore and Dryden, view the ruins of Rome as Gibbon did, or tramp the hills that inspired the writings of Scott. Ah . . . if only I had the talent to bring the heroism of the men of Texas to life in my own scribblings.'

'You have the opportunity to do much more, President Lamar. You hold the future of a country and its people in your hands. People of every colour. White, black – and red.'

Adam was angling to broach the subject of a peace with the Comanche, but Lamar's reaction was hardly encouraging.

'The red man has *no* future in Texas. None at all. But you are right, of course; the president of any country has an awesome responsibility – and he is at the mercy of future historians who possess the advantage of hindsight.'

'I was brought up to believe in a greater judgement than that of historians. . . . But there is also a Cherokee saying, "Men are merely arrows, fired from the bows of the Gods". If this is so, we needn't worry *too* much about Judgement Day. We can lay the blame for what we've done on whichever God we believe in, claiming his aim must have been at fault.'

'That must be a very comforting concept of life for an Indian. It excuses all his murdering and thieving habits. But we are talking about making Texan history, Mr Rashleigh. Indians have no part in this. As far as I am concerned, the Indians of Texas are a fragment of history that future historians may remember, if they so wish. I see them only as a problem to be firmly resolved and speedily forgotten.'

CHAPTER ELEVEN

ADAM'S RETURN to the village of Chief Bowles came as a welcome release from thoughts of the politics of Mirabeau Buonaparte Lamar and Lord Palmerston. In the Cherokee village life went on with little change from day to day. Men went hunting while the women washed clothes in the river or pounded corn into flour and cooked for their families. Together, men, women and children worked in the fields, weeding and irrigating, cultivating corn, yams and sweet potatoes.

Adam slipped easily into the orderly life that was free from obvious pressures. However, additional responsibility was not far away. Tiski was radiantly pregnant.

She gave Adam the news hesitantly, as though afraid he would be angry with her. Instead, Adam gave a whoop that would have done credit to a Comanche. Hugging Tiski to him, he swung her off her feet in his joy. He promptly set her down again, concerned that he might have harmed her.

'It's just wonderful!' How long have you known? When is the baby due?'

'It should be born before the leaves change to red. I knew about it when you were last here.'

'Why didn't you say anything then?'

Tiski would not look directly at him. 'Among my people, a man does not sleep with his wife while she is bearing a child. I do not know how it is with your people. I did not want to be sure too soon.'

'It is not the same in my country – and this is one time when I am going to insist that you behave like a white woman. When I come home to you we share the same blanket, no matter how pregnant you are. You understand?'

'I understand.' Tiski was both happy and relieved at his words. She thought she would never be able to sleep if she and Adam were under the same roof yet not able to touch one another at night. Other women would shake their heads and say that such taboos were not to be lightly disregarded, but they would accept without question that a woman must abide by the customs of her husband's people.

That night Adam and Tiski lay together, snug and warm on their buffalo-robe bed, and talked about the unborn child. The

274

news had made a lot of difference to Adam's thinking. Tiski would be happier in Chief Bowles's village until the baby was born, but then Adam would take them both to his cabin in Caleb's settlement. It would pose a number of problems, but none was insurmountable, and Adam did not want his child to know its father only as an occasional visitor.

Adam remained in Chief Bowles's village as Tiski blossomed towards the full bloom of pregnancy. When spring had changed to summer, a small herd of buffalo, no more than a dozen strong, was seen on the plains, seventy miles to the west. With Yellow Bear and a number of warriors, Adam set out to find them. He was gone only a week – but it was to be one of the most momentous weeks in the history of the Cherokees of Chief Bowles's tribe.

In accordance with President Lamar's declared Indian policy, more and more companies of Rangers had been formed and sent out to seek and destroy roving bands of Comanche Indians. They met with a mixed success. Comanches *were* found and killed, but so, too, were Rangers.

Then, in the third week of May 1839, a company of Rangers ran into a party of Indians no more than twenty-five miles from Lamar's new capital city. With the Indians was a Mexican, probably one of those who had visited Chief Bowles. The Indians were routed and a large quantity of powder and shot captured. Among those killed was the Mexican. He was found to be carrying a number of letters, the contents of which so excited the Ranger captain that he took them straight to President Lamar.

One letter disclosed the Mexican plan to unite the Texan Indians, including the Cherokee, against the Texans. Another spoke of a planned new uprising at Nacogdoches and promised that the Cherokee would fight for the Mexican cause when the time was right.

The letters were typical of many that passed between Mexico and their Texan sympathisers. No one believed in what was written, least of all the writers. They were sent only to bolster the flagging hopes of those who espoused the Mexican cause. A total divorce from reality had long been the *modus operandi* of successive Mexican governments, but the letter provided President Lamar with an opportunity he was quick to seize upon.

Riders were dispatched to call in the scattered units of the regular Texan army. Then, while Adam was away hunting, a commission from Lamar came to the Cherokee village to speak to

Chief Bowles. They ordered him to remove his people from Texas forthwith, taking the shortest route northwards, across the Red River.

For eighty-three years Chief Bowles had witnessed the inevitability of the changing seasons. He knew that summer heat would always follow the mild days of spring; that when summer ended the leaves would change colour and fall to the earth that had made them.

Now, with equal certainty, Chief Bowles knew this was the end for his people. It would not matter what he said, what he did, or wherever he tried to lead them. This was the end of the good life for which they had worked so hard, in the land where there had once been no white man to cast his disapproving shadow over them.

Chief Bowles knew all this, but he tried hard to put off what had to be. He told Lamar's commission that he needed time to consult with his council. The men of Lamar's commission nodded their heads and agreed that he should have time – not *too* long, but time enough to agree to remove from their lands peaceably. The Texans, too, needed time. The army of the Republic had not yet mustered in sufficient strength to enforce removal. The commission returned to Nacogdoches.

When Adam arrived at the village, the council was in session. He listened with dismay as one after another their long and colourful speeches ended with the single word, 'Tla!' – 'No!' The Cherokees declared they would not go. They would fight and die here, where they had their homes.

Adam knew nothing of the Mexican letters. He urged Chief Bowles to prevent his people from doing anything that might justify Lamar using force against them. John rounded on him angrily.

'Would you have us stand like the buffalo until we are all slaughtered? We are told we must leave our lands. Where can we go? We asked Lamar's men this question and they told us to go north, to the lands from whence our people came. Those lands are no longer open to us. The Cherokee who once lived there have been "moved", too. They were herded by the White Man as though they were his sheep – but with far less kindness. A whole nation, more than sixteen thousand people, was driven off by the white soldiers. Before they reached their new lands, four thousand had died. The Northern Cherokee call it the "Trail of Tears". There is not a family among them that does not mourn its dead. You have a Cherokee wife, Englishman. Would you like to think of Tiski being driven by soldiers to an unknown land?'

276

'I would like some of the council to come with me to Nacogdoches, to speak to the men of this commission. We'll try to have the removal threat held off until I've had a chance to speak to Lamar.'

In his cabin as he prepared for the journey, Tiski came to him. Kneeling before him as he cleaned his revolver, she took the tiny deerskin bag she wore on a leather thong about her neck. Holding it out to him, she said: 'You are going on a very important journey, Adam. I want you to take this with you. It will keep you safe and bring you back to me.'

Taking the gift from her, Adam asked: 'What is it?' He began to loosen the thong about the neck of the tiny bag, but Tiski put out a hand and stopped him.

'Do not open it or some of the power may be lost. It is a Kiowa medicine-bag. Strong medicine to protect the wearer. My father put it about my neck on the day I was born.'

'Then, *you* must keep it. ...'

'No, Adam. I wish you to take it with you. It is important to me – and for our child – that you return safely. If anything happened to you, I would not wish to live – and I have so much to live for.'

When Adam held Tiski close he could feel her trembling. Gently, he said: 'You must drive all unhappy thoughts from your mind – for the sake of the baby. These are uncertain times for Chief Bowles and his people, but nothing will happen to come between us. If Lamar insists on the Cherokee leaving Texas, I'll take you to the Hill Country right away. If you can't settle there, we'll go to England. Wherever it is, we'll be together. Man, wife and baby.'

The trembling ceased, and Tiski made a brave attempt to smile. 'We always *are* together, you and I, Adam. I feel my love go out to you when I am alone in the night. I know it is strong enough to reach you wherever you are and whatever you are doing. It will always be so.'

She kissed him, and the kiss held until they heard a sound outside the cabin. It was Yellow Bear. He would travel to Nacogdoches with Adam and the four selected members of the Cherokee council.

Half an hour later the six men rode from the village. So vitally important was the errand on which they were going that every man, woman and child in the village turned out to see them off.

Tiski stood in the doorway of their cabin, her hands resting on the bulge that was their child. Before passing from sight, Adam turned to look at her again. She looked so very vulnerable that he had an almost overwhelming urge to return to her. Instead, he raised his arm in a last, unanswered gesture of farewell before trees and distance hid her from view.

'It is always hardest to leave when it is the firstborn,' Yellow Bear said sympathetically, as he guided his horse alongside Adam. 'But she is a healthy girl and Quaty will take care of her.'

One of the Indians riding with them spoke at some length in the nasal Cherokee language. When he stopped, Adam had caught the gist of what had been said, but Yellow Bear gave him a full translation: 'He says that when you worry about your wife perhaps you will spare a thought for my father. You are concerned for the well-being of one woman, and the birth of a child. My father awaits the death of all his people.'

Nacogdoches was as busy as Adam had ever seen it before. A line of supply-wagons was drawn up at the side of the main street, reducing passing traffic to a single wagon-width and causing many a heated argument on the occasion when two wagons met head-on.

The saloons and hotels were crowded, and as Adam led the Indians through the streets of the town men gathered on the sidewalks to watch their progress. Adam was relieved when his judicious enquiries led him away from the centre of the town to a house some distance away. Here he found the four-man commission who had delivered President Lamar's ultimatum to the Cherokee.

The commissioners were not pleased to see Adam. At first they refused to talk to him and the Cherokee delegation. They eventually relented, but it soon became apparent that they had no authority to negotiate any change in the harsh conditions of the removal order.

Adam hoped to have the order held in abeyance – at least until after the harvest had been gathered in. By then it might be possible to effect a change in Lamar's policy towards the Cherokee. Even if Lamar refused to remit the order, the Cherokee would at least be taking the road to their uncertain destination with adequate supplies to keep them alive for some weeks. Without their harvest, the Texan Cherokee would have less chance of survival than had their northern brethren on the long 'Trail of Tears'.

Adam wished he could have turned to General Houston for help and advice, but the ex-President was in the United States of America.

For two days Adam remained in Nacogdoches, arguing the cause of Chief Bowles's people, but was finally forced to admit defeat. All he was able to obtain was a promise from the commission that no further action would be taken until new instructions were received from Lamar. Armed with this fragile assurance, Adam set off to appeal direct to the Texan president.

The commission would meet with Chief Bowles in ten days' time to receive official notification of the decision he and his council had reached about the removal. Given the usual time-scale for such negotiations, they were liable to drag on for months, perhaps years. The commissioners had told Adam they were authorised to offer compensation for improvements made to the Cherokee lands, although they would not pay for the land itself. Argument on this issue alone could delay the removal for many weeks.

Adam was concerned that the general bustle in the town heralded the build-up of a force to drive the Cherokee northwards. Much to his relief, the wagons and many of the men left before he did, heading along the San Antonio trail. It seemed the Penateka Comanche were now raiding in some strength and any wagon making its slow way along the country's trails needed company – and a large escort.

After seeing Yellow Bear and the four members of the Cherokee council well on their way along the trail to Chief Bowles's village, Adam set off to find President Lamar. Before parting company with them, Adam received an assurance from Yellow Bear that in the event of trouble Tiski would be taken to Caleb Ryan's settlement. Eli was there and would take care of her. Adam did not believe such a step would be necessary, but he felt better for making the arrangement.

Riding from Nacogdoches to Houston, Adam went over all the arguments he would use to persuade Lamar to change his mind about the Cherokee. The possibility of an effective peace with the Comanche *might* interest him, but it would have to be a peace with *all* the Comanche tribes, and Adam would need to negotiate it himself. It would be dangerous.

As it transpired, the argument was never put to the test. Adam reached Houston only to learn that Lamar had gone south, to the town of Victoria. He was not expected to return to Houston for at least a month.

Adam knew there was nothing for it but to ride on to Victoria. The small town was 125 miles away, and he battled torrential rain along the way. The rivers and creeks of the wide coastal plain spilled out over their banks, inundating hundreds of square miles of countryside. Adam was forced to spend three impatient days and nights sheltering in a small grove of trees on a rapidly diminishing island that had once been the top of a small bluff. When it seemed that even this meagre sanctuary would soon disappear, the floodwaters began to recede and Adam was able to resume his slow progress to Victoria.

The journey took him eight wet and weary days and he reached Victoria only to learn that Lamar had left for Austin a few days before.

Adam was exhausted. He had ridden through the night in his determined but unsuccessful bid to reach Victoria before the departure of the elusive Texan president. At the first boarding-house he found in the town, he put up his horse, booked an indifferent, shared room, and went to bed.

Adam did not open his eyes again for five days.

On the way through the flooded, low-lying country between Houston and Victoria, Adam had contracted malaria. As soon as he lay down on the hard, straw-filled mattress, fever took possession of his body.

His condition was not discovered for twenty-four hours. During the night his room-mate returned too intoxicated to pay any attention to Adam's tortured writhings and moaning. In the morning, the bleary-eyed drunkard took one look at Adam and, convinced he would die, stole all his possessions.

Had the boarding-house proprietress not grown concerned that Adam had ridden off without paying his bill, he would not have been found until it was too late to save him. As it was, Adam hovered in the uncertain world between life and death for days before the fever finally broke.

The first person Adam saw when he opened his eyes was the Victoria sheriff standing by the bed holding Adam's guns in his hands. Adam identified them with a nod of his head in answer to the sheriff's question. He received the confusing news that his late room-mate had died using Adam's revolver, attempting to outshoot a comparatively sober Texan.

They were all that had been recovered of Adam's missing property. His money and clothing were long gone.

Adam did not hear more than half the sheriff's words. Weak from his illness, he kept lapsing into the dark world of unconsciousness. When he came to, he was vaguely aware that he should be concerned with something of far more importance than the loss of his belongings.

The sheriff was still in the room when the doctor arrived, accompanied by the landlady of the boarding-house.

Brusquely, in a clipped Scots accent, the doctor ordered the sheriff from the room, telling him he would have ample time to talk to Adam when the patient was stronger. No sooner had the sheriff gone than the thin-lipped boarding-house owner began informing Adam that his illness had prevented her from putting prospective boarders in the room. She would have to charge him double rate – and she wanted to know where the money would come from.

The doctor brought her tirade to a halt as abruptly as he had silenced the sheriff: 'You'll get your money from Señor Benavides.'

The boarding-house owner's manner underwent a swift change. 'Señor *Victoriano* Benavides?'

'That's right. You'll be paid today. Señor Benavides wants this young man taken to his house as soon as he's fit enough to be moved. I would say that time is now. There are too many people with too much to say to him in this house. Look at him. All this talking has brought on his delirium again. Out you go now, woman. *Out*, I say.'

It was not delirium that had brought on Adam's sudden agitation. His memory had suddenly returned. He remembered where he was – and *why* he had come to Victoria. He struggled to rise from the bed, but it needed no more than a gentle hand from the doctor to restrain him.

'I've got to get up. I need to see President Lamar. It's . . . vitally important.'

'Nothing is more important than life itself, laddie – and that's what you'll be forfeiting if you try to stir from that bed before I tell you.'

'I *must* see Lamar . . . I *must*!' Adam's head was aching, and the room swam about him as he struggled to leave the narrow bed.

'Here, laddie. Get this down you.'

Adam groaned as the doctor put an arm about him and held a glass of foul-tasting liquid to his mouth. Alternately choking and gulping, Adam managed to swallow almost as much of the doctor's concoction as he dribbled down his chin. Gasping for breath, he was laid back on the pillowless bed.

'That should make you sleep for a while. The last thing we want is to have you getting all upset about something you can do nothing about just yet.'

Adam tried to tell the doctor that he had to do something for the Cherokee before it was too late, but no words came. Moments later he drifted off in a dreamless sleep that bordered on the unconscious.

Adam was pulled from his deep sleep by the sound of two voices speaking softly in Spanish. He realised immediately that something was different. The bed upon which he was lying was soft and comfortable, and beneath his fingers he felt fine linen. When he opened his eyes the overpowering impression he gained was one of a whiteness and cleanliness that hurt his eyes. He turned his head to look in the direction of the voices, and the sound stopped immediately.

Standing close to the bed were two girls. One was plump and dark, with a ready smile. The other was Eleanor Benavides, the girl Adam had rescued from Chief Ten Trees and his Comanches. But this was a very different little girl from the one pushed ahead of the Comanche warrior from Ten Trees' camp. Thirteen years of age now, Eleanor would one day be a great beauty, but her dark, serious eyes told of experiences that went far beyond those of a normal thirteen-year-old girl.

'So you have decided to live after all, Señor Rashleigh? Poor Dr Ewing will be most relieved. He has been to the house twice this morning already.' The older of the two girls had a warm smile.

'This morning?' Adam croaked. He found it difficult to bring time into perspective.

'You were brought here yesterday. My father would have fetched you sooner, but Dr Ewing said you were too sick to be moved. You have been very ill. But you will get better now you are here.'

The girl's chatter made Adam's head whirl, but there was no stopping her.

'You remember Eleanor? Yes, of course you do. I am Rosa. We are Philippe's cousins. Has he told you of me? No? It does not matter; he and Eleanor have told me much about you. Eleanor, go and tell Cook our guest is awake. Then send someone for Dr Ewing.'

As Eleanor Benavides hurried from the room, Adam called urgently: 'Wait!'

When the cry left his dry throat he began to cough painfully. Rosa Benavides hurried to the bedside. Pouring water in a glass, she put an arm beneath Adam's shoulders. Lifting him clear of the pillows with a frightening ease, she held the glass to his lips.

Adam thought he had never drunk anything that tasted better. When the last drop had gone, Rosa eased him gently back on the pillows and he sighed gratefully.

'How long have I been ill?'

'When he brought you here Dr Ewing said you had been ill for five days. That makes six altogether.'

Six days! It meant that more than a fortnight had passed since he left Nacogdoches. Struggling vainly to sit up, he croaked: 'I must speak to President Lamar before it's too late.'

'Too late for what, Señor Rashleigh?'

The question came from the doorway as a tall and distinguished Mexican entered the room. Advancing to the bedside, he added: 'You must not upset yourself. You have been very sick. Very sick indeed. If there is something I can do, you have only to ask. I am Victoriano Benavides. I have never had the opportunity to thank you personally for giving my daughter Eleanor back to me. I do so now, from the bottom of my heart. All I have is yours. Whatever it is you want . . . you have only to name it.'

'I must get a message to President Lamar. It's of vital importance.' Adam found that speaking was coming easier now. 'He must give Chief Bowles and his Cherokees more time. Driving them from Texas will only prove to the Comanche and other Indians that there is nothing to be gained by living in peace.'

'Drive out the Cherokee? Surely you are mistaken? Lamar's intention is to wage war on the *Comanche*. *They* are our enemies. The Cherokee have always lived in peace with both Mexico and Texas.'

'There is no mistake. I went with the Cherokees to meet Lamar's commission. Chief Bowles has been told to remove his people from Texas.'

Victoriano Benavides looked perplexed. 'This I do not understand. If only Dan Manuel were here. . . . He knows Lamar. He would know what to do.'

'Can you send someone to find out what is happening? It is very important to me.'

Victoriano Benavides was curious about Adam's great concern, but he asked no questions. 'I will send a horseman to Houston immediately.'

Some of the tension left Adam, and he realised just how weak he was. At that moment a servant came to the room with soup. Adam was raised to a sitting position and fed the soup by Rosa Benavides. While he was being fed, Dr Ewing came to the room and beamed his approval.

'You're looking fine, laddie. Another couple of weeks and we'll have you up and about again as good as new.'

Adam spluttered out a mouthful of soup. With matters in their present crucial state, two weeks might prove to be a lifetime for the Cherokee – but Dr Ewing was talking to Señor Benavides.

'The lad will improve now he's away from Mother Tobin's lodging-house. They'd murder a man there for one of Lamar's new redback dollars – and the Lord knows they're worth nothing at all. In the meantime, you mustn't fret about things, young man. You've got two of the prettiest nurses in Victoria looking after you. Just lie there and let them tend to your needs. We'll have you up and about when you're fit – and not before.'

Adam had his own ideas about that, but he deemed it wise to keep his intentions to himself.

The even tempo of life in the Benavides household was unexpectedly shattered on the third evening of Adam's stay.

He heard the carriage draw up outside the front door, immediately beneath his window. A moment later doors were thrown open all over the house and excited, Spanish-speaking voices began calling back and forth outside. Moments later the excitement spilled into the house. One woman's voice dominated the loud and animated conversation. Adam could not hear all that was being said, but he recognised the voice. So, too, did Rosa Benavides, who had been reading to Adam when the carriage arrived. Lowering the book to the bed, she cried: 'It's *Tia* Antonia!' Filled with excitement, she leaped to her feet. 'Excuse me, Adam. I must go to find out what is happening.'

Adam smiled at Rosa Benavides's attempt to depart from the room as though she were only casually interested in what was happening downstairs. Rosa Benavides reminded him of a warm, happy and rather overweight young puppy, eager to please and anxious to offend no one.

The arrival of Rosa downstairs brought about an immediate rise in the level of sound. Soon afterwards, Adam heard feet upon the stairs. Then the door was flung open and Dona Antonia stood in the doorway. Philippe was with her, and Rosa and Eleanor peered at him from behind their cousin. Beyond them stood Philippe's nanny, Maria.

Dona Antonia showed genuine concern as she came across the room towards him. 'Oh, my poor Adam. How pale and thin you are! What have you been doing to yourself?' Leaning over him, she kissed him warmly on both cheeks.

'Dona Antonia . . . Philippe! What a wonderful surprise. But where is Don Manuel? Isn't he with you?'

As suddenly as though he had snuffed out a candle, all the joy of the unexpected reunion fled from the room.

'Don Manuel is in prison, in Mexico City.'

Adam could not contain his astonishment. 'What for ...? What has he done?'

'If General Antonio Lopez de Santa Anna Perez de Lebron orders a man to prison, no one questions *why*. It is enough that such a great man has pointed a disapproving finger in his direction. Bustamante may be President of Mexico, but it is Santa Anna who once more wields the power.'

'I thought General Santa Anna and Don Manuel were related?'

'Only because my sister was foolish enough to marry Santa Anna. He is most dangerous to those who are closest to him, especially if they have breathed the air of rebellion.'

'What will happen to Don Manuel?'

Adam had always thought of Dona Antonia as a most formidable woman. Now, as she struggled to find an answer to his question, he saw her only as a deeply distressed wife, whose husband was in great danger. Señor Benavides had come into the room and he moved to Dona Antonia's side as she said shakily: 'He is at Santa Anna's mercy. Few men have survived that.'

With Señor Benavides's arm about her, Dona Antonia recovered some of her familiar composure.

'Don Manuel should never have agreed to go to Mexico on such a foolish mission. President Bustamante would never dare to make peace with Texas. The whole of Mexico sees the Texans as rebels. If it appeared that Bustamante was about to agree with the terms offered by Lamar, Santa Anna would take over the country and have Bustamante shot for a traitor. General Houston would never have sent a friend on such a dangerous and ill-conceived mission.'

Dona Antonia began showing signs of distress once more, and Victoriano Benavides led her from the room.

Turning to Rosa, Adam said: 'Will you have pen and paper brought to me. I am acquainted with the British ambassador to Mexico. I will write and ask him to take a personal interest in Don Manuel's welfare. It may not secure his release, but it should ensure that he is kept alive. Now, Philippe, come and sit here on the bed and tell me all you have done in Mexico. ...'

With the arrival of Philippe and his mother, Adam gained many more nurses. Dona Antonia spent as much time as her nieces in the sickroom. Occasionally Maria took her place, sometimes with Philippe, but more often she stayed with him while the family were eating. It was on these occasions that Adam found he was able to speak about Tiski as he could to none of the others. The good-natured nanny did her best to reassure Adam that all would be well, but Adam fretted that there had been no news from the messenger sent to Houston by Señor Benavides. He cursed the weakness of the body that frequently let him down on the few occasions when he left his bed and tried to walk about the room.

The Mexican servant returned to Victoria on the day Adam persuaded Dr Ewing that he was strong enough to leave his room and sit outside the house to enjoy the midsummer sunshine.

Adam watched the horseman arrive and knew, without being told, that it was the messenger who had been sent to Houston. The dusty rider came straight to the house, and Adam tackled him before he reached the door.

'What news have you brought from Houston? Is Lamar allowing the Cherokee to harvest their crops before making a final decision . . . ?'

'President Lamar allowed the Cherokee no time, Señor. There has been a great battle. Chief Bowles and most of his warriors have been killed. Their crops and houses burned. President Lamar has issued a proclamation. There are now no Cherokees left in Texas.'

CHAPTER TWELVE

PRESIDENT LAMAR'S COMMISSION returned to the Cherokee village only three days after Adam had left for Houston. This time the commission did not ask that a meeting of the council be called to discuss removal. The came with *orders*. Chief Bowles was to gather his people immediately and travel northwards until they crossed the Red River, leaving Texas behind them.

Still Chief Bowles tried to gain time. He *had* to. Time was his only ally. He told the commissioners that leaving the lands he and his people had tilled for so many years was not an undertaking to be considered lightly. Children had been born in the village and grown to manhood knowing no other home. Old men of the tribe had died and been buried here. There were many matters that needed to be discussed.

The commission refused to grant the Cherokee any more time. Lamar's latest directive was quite explicit. The Cherokee were to remove from Texas forthwith, peaceably if it could be achieved, forcibly if not. The time for talking had passed. The Cherokee must go.

The aged Cherokee leader made one more attempt to postpone the inevitable. The corn was almost ripe in the fields about the village. Without it his people would not survive the unknown rigours that lay ahead. They had nowhere to go, and it might be many months before they found a new home. For the sake of the women and the small children he begged that the Cherokee be allowed to gather their harvest.

The answer was a curt refusal. Lamar's orders called for *immediate* removal – and the commission was now in a position to demand that its orders be obeyed. Five hundred well-armed Texan troops had been hurriedly assembled and were at that very moment camped only six miles from the Cherokee village.

Chief Bowles looked into each of the faces before him. He saw no compassion or understanding, no sympathy for the plight of the Cherokee people. The men of the commission were indifferent to the suffering they were about to inflict upon innocent women and children. Chief Bowles knew white men well. He had fought them, killed them, befriended and helped them. The men standing impatiently before him were eager to carry out their appointed task. When it was done, each man

287

would return to his community and take his proud place in the history of his people as one of the men who had rid the land of 'those damned Indians'.

Chief Bowles had tried to put his people beyond the horizon of the white settlements. He had failed. Now time had run out for him. Texas had grown faster than any man could have anticipated. The white men had caught up with the Cherokee and realised Chief Bowles's worst fears.

He had failed his people. Now he had nothing, was no one.

Spurning the hands of the younger men of his council, Chief Bowles struggled to his feet and stood looking about him. He looked at the trees of the distant hills, at the river, at the sky, and at the fields and homes of his people.

'The Cherokee have had peace and happiness here. We have been happy to share that peace with others. When your people fought against the Mexicans, The Raven came to speak with us. He asked us to remain at peace and not join the Mexicans against you. This we did, even though the Mexicans promised that our land would always be ours if we helped *them*. The Raven promised that his people would prove no less generous than the Mexicans. He told us the land would belong to us and to our children, and to our children's children, for all time. This he said little more than three harvests ago.'

Chief Bowles looked sadly at the commission. 'When you fought the Mexicans, you were weak. Your women and children – yes, and many men, too – were fleeing to the north, seeking the safety of the White Man's land where you would send us now. My young warriors wanted to fight you then. We could have helped the Mexicans to drive *you* from Texas for ever. I would not allow them to fight. I had given my word to The Raven. I know now I was wrong. Once more my warriors say we should fight you. I cannot deny them again. It will not go well with us. You are strong now and your people are not running away. You will beat us in battle and many men will die, but my warriors will die as *men*. They will die looking in the faces of those who take what is rightly ours and who seek to destroy us. For me, it does not matter. I am an old man. I have seen foolishness before – and I have known wisdom, too. I am *ready* to die. If you see my tears, they are for my people who must die only because they were born as Indians. Go now and tell your soldiers that the Cherokee will fight.'

When the commission hurried away to give the news to the Texas army, Chief Bowles carried his dignity to the waiting warriors in the village.

288

It was war! The news brought a thrill to the younger warriors, but struck fear into the hearts of the women. Some of the grandmothers could remember earlier wars, when the band of Chief Bowles had broken away from their northern brothers and fought both white men and Indians in their search for a new home.

Tiski was totally confused. The baby was only weeks away and there was no one to tell her what she should do, where she should go. All about her women and children were hastily packing their clothes and a few valuables, so Tiski did the same. She wished Adam were here. Perhaps he would want her to go to the white men and stay with them until his return. But who should she approach . . . ? She decided she must remain with the Cherokee. Adam would find her.

Tiski knew Adam must have failed in his bid to delay the expulsion of the Cherokee, but neither she nor Chief Bowles's people would ever blame him for that. He was a white man, but he was not a Texan. Even if he were, it was doubtful whether anyone would have listened to his voice when he raised it on behalf of the Cherokee people. They had not listened to The Raven, and *he* had been their chief.

As she packed her belongings and thought her thoughts, the baby inside her belly kicked out. She rested a while, supporting the uncomfortable bulk of the unborn child with her hands. She hoped Adam might return quickly. The baby would not be long in coming.

When she heard a noise in the doorway, Tiski swung around quickly, hopeful that her unspoken prayer had been answered. It was Yellow Bear. He carried with him the gun that had been Adam's – the gun that had killed the Mexicans sent to stir up trouble against the Texans.

Yellow Bear told Tiski of the promise he had made to Adam that he would try to take Tiski to the white settlement in the Hill Country if trouble came. He displayed none of the excitement of the other young Cherokee warriors. Yellow Bear had killed men. Enemies had tried to kill him. He knew it was not a game.

'I cannot take you before the battle. I must fight with the others. Stay close to Quaty and I will find you. When the fighting is over we will go south. I will take you to your husband's people. Quaty and the children will come with me to Mexico. Some of our people are there. I will find them.'

'How will it go with our people – with the Cherokee?'

'I have been to see the camp of the white soldiers. They are many and they have good guns. We cannot beat them.'

'Then, why fight? Why not do as they tell us? We can make a new life somewhere else. Men don't have to die.'

'You speak as a mother already. It cannot be. If we do not fight, no Cherokee warrior will have the right to call himself a man again. When others talked of fighting for what is theirs, Cherokee warriors would need to bow their heads and look at the ground. This is not the way of a man. I must go now. Remember, stay with Quaty and look for me after the battle.'

'Go in safety, my brother,' Tiski hugged Yellow Bear briefly, and then he was gone.

In the Cherokee village that night, only the very young slept. The warriors prepared for battle, those with guns making musket-balls and preparing paper cartridges. Less affluent Indians and the older boys renewed bow strings and made new arrows. The women packed and repacked, now discarding clothing from their bundles, then adding something more for the children. Older women helped young girls and childless widows to prepare food to be eaten on the trail. There was not sufficient for a journey of any length. Stocks had been allowed to run low in anticipation of the new harvest.

While these preparations were going on, Chief Bowles and his council were in permanent session. There was much to discuss and resolve. There were war leaders to be chosen for a people who had lived in peace for many years, battle tactics to be discussed. It had to be decided in which direction the women and children should travel in order to stay clear of the fighting. There were so many questions – and all too few answers. Meanwhile, beyond the village, young untried warriors bearing arms for the first time squatted and shivered nervously in the darkness as they performed sentry-duty against a surprise night attack by the Texan army.

The women and children moved out of the village before dawn, laden with all those things they thought were the essentials of life. During the next few days most would be lost or abandoned in the desperate fight for survival. They headed westwards. It had been decided by the council that they should head for the Great Plains and throw themselves upon the mercy of the Comanche. It would mean changing the whole Cherokee way of life, but this had been agreed by them all. The way of the White Man had not succeeded for the Cherokee. They must learn to live as Indians once more.

The women had fewer horses than they would have liked to carry all their goods. The horses were needed for the warriors who would follow, keeping between the women and the white soldiers.

By mid-morning the women were crossing the Neches River, helped by a few warriors who had been sent ahead of the main body. Because of her condition, Tiski crossed on a horse. Before she reached the far bank, a wail went up from those already there. Turning, Tiski saw a pall of black smoke rising into the cloudless sky behind them. The Texans had set fire to the village. There were groans from the women, and a few tears, too. The smoke brought them face to face with their predicament. They were now a people with no homes and few possessions – and they had a powerful enemy behind them.

Once across the river, Tiski relinquished her horse to an aged and lame member of the council. Almost as old as Chief Bowles, he was numbed by what was happening and had given way to the crushing weight of his years.

Tiski was uncomfortable, but she made no complaint. She walked beside Quaty, a bundle slung over her shoulder, helping to shepherd Quaty's two young children along.

They were not yet out of sight of the river when the women heard the sound of desultory shooting behind them and they hurried the children along. Soon after noon, Chief Bowles and his warriors caught up with them. The Cherokee chief wore the sword that General Houston had once given to him, the wide sash slung across his shoulder.

The Texans were crossing the river in strength. If they were allowed to come on at the same speed, they would soon overtake the Cherokees. Chief Bowles ordered the escort to take the women to a position about five miles to the north. It was wooded, hilly country. Here the women and children would be able to hide if it became necessary. Chief Bowles and his warriors intended making a stand to delay the Texan soldiers for as long as possible.

The Cherokee women did as they were told without question, but the children were hungry and they sensed the fear that was in the air. Some began crying. Tiski lifted Quaty's three-year-old daughter and dried her tears before hurrying after the others.

The battle began before the women and children reached their temporary sanctuary. They could hear the crackle of musketry for a long time, but this was still no more than skirmishing. The main battle was not fought until an hour or so before sundown.

It ended in a predictable victory for the Texans, and many wounded warriors were carried to the hill where the women hid.

When the war leaders moved among them, calling the names of their warriors, more than twenty failed to reply.

But the battle succeeded in delaying the Texans, and they, too, had suffered casualties.

Next morning the women and children were on the move again before daybreak, working their way towards the thick cover of trees that followed the course of the Neches River. Behind them the warriors took up a defensive position in a long, shallow ravine, throwing out skirmishers to gauge the Texans' strength and direction of advance.

Chief Bowles, mounted on a 'paint' pony, rode to and fro behind his warriors, giving them words of encouragement to bolster them for the forthcoming battle. Inexplicably, the old Cherokee chief had decided to employ the white men's own tactics in a war that was of the Texans' choosing.

Chief Bowles's decision was a tragic error of judgement witnessed by the whole of his people. As the opposing skirmishers met and exchanged fire, the women and children halted their flight to watch the battle, the crackle being too far away to frighten the children.

The Texan soldiers fought on foot, their horses held in the rear of the action. Facing the Indians in a long line, they advanced time and again, only to be driven back by the Cherokees and their ancient muskets and bows and arrows.

As each Texan attack broke, the Cherokee women shrieked encouragement to their men, believing the warriors were performing a miracle and winning the unequal battle.

From where they were they could not see that each new attack added to the already heavy casualties sustained by the inexperienced warriors. Many of the Cherokee fighting men were lying dead in the shallow ravine and hardly a man among them remained unwounded.

Behind them, his voice almost gone as a result of his constant encouragement, Chief Bowles sat a dying horse that had been wounded so many times it was a miracle it still stood. Chief Bowles had himself been shot in the thigh, and blood coursed down his leg and into his moccasin.

For two hours the battle raged. Then the Texans launched a final, determined attack – and at last the Indian line was rolled back. Young warriors who had seen brothers, fathers and friends die about them broke and ran. Some, hardly more than boys, threw their bows from them as they went. A few, John and Yellow Bear among them, went after them in a futile attempt to bring them back to the line and cover the flight of the women and children.

Chief Bowles, still wearing his fringed sash and scabbard, waved his sword aloft, calling on the warriors who fled past him to halt and fight on. Panic had gripped the warriors and few heard his words. None heeded them.

Chief Bowles was the last Cherokee to attempt to leave the battlefield. When his horse collapsed beneath him, the aged chief dismounted and hobbled after his warriors, the wounded leg causing him great pain. One of the Texas soldiers ran after him and shot him in the back. The bullet passed through his lung, but still the tough old warrior would not die. Stumbling on for a few more paces, Chief Bowles fell. Pushing himself up from the ground, he sat facing the advancing Texan soldiers, blood dribbling from his mouth.

His incredible dignity remained with him to the end. He sat looking at the Texan army as one of the captains ran towards him, pistol in hand. He heard the cry: 'Cap'n Smith . . . don't shoot him.'

Then Chief Bowles saw the finger of the white-faced captain tighten on the trigger. . . .

The bullet entered Chief Bowles's brain and he fell backwards. He was dead before Houston's sword was prised from his hand and his body stripped of 'souvenirs' by those who came after.

When the women saw the warriors break and run, they took their children and fled towards the cover of the riverside woods, in blind panic. They had seen at the end how many warriors lay dead on the battlefield. There would be no Cherokee army to protect them from the white soldiers now.

Tiski was one of the last to reach the wooded shelter. She could not run as fast as the others. As it was, the muscles of her distended stomach hurt more with every step. Anida, Yellow Bear's young daughter, held her hand tightly, unsure of what was happening about her, but caught up in the fear that gripped the Cherokee women.

At the edge of the trees Tiski paused, partly to gather her strength, but also to see what was happening behind her.

There was still a small cluster of men gathered about the stripped body of Chief Bowles. A couple of soldiers who had not been in the forefront of the fight were checking the Indians lying on the battlefield. Any who lived were quickly dispatched. A few soldiers were pursuing Indians on foot, but the horses were being brought up now and mounted men were setting off in small groups of half a dozen or so to take up the chase.

'Tiski, we must go on before the white men reach us.' Quaty stood in the shade of the trees, her eight-year-old son by her side. She had little fear for herself, or for Tiski and Anida, but her son was a tall boy for his age. From a distance an excited soldier might mistake him for a warrior.

The two women and the children fled into the woods, following the sounds made by the others. Cherokee women were not so skilled in passing silently through the forest as were their men. They toiled through the dense undergrowth until Tiski gasped that she could go no farther. Her stomach hurt as though every strained muscle was on fire, and she felt sick.

'Tiski, we must go on. The soldiers are coming nearer. Listen, you can hear them.'

The noise of the fleeing Indian women had grown fainter, but for some time the sounds of pursuit had been moving closer, horses crashing through the undergrowth beneath the trees faster than those who fled on foot.

'You go on. Take Anida. I must rest.'

'No! We all go on together,' Quaty bullied Tiski; and, in spite of her protests, she began moving on again.

Soon they reached a wide clearing and the going became easier, but the soldiers were gaining rapidly now. As the two women and the children reached the far side, the soldiers broke from the woodland behind them. There was a shout of jubilation and a musket-ball cut through the undergrowth between Quaty and Tiski.

The two women separated, but Tiski had taken no more than a dozen steps before she stumbled and fell into a shallow hollow. The ground beneath her trembled with the sound of pounding hooves, and Tiski knew she could not outrun the soldiers. Holding Anida to her, she squirmed farther into the hollow, working dead, damp leaves up about their bodies. She just had time to pull a few twigs and rotting leaves about her head before hoofs were churning up the woodland floor, no more than an arm's length away.

Anida squealed in sudden protest and Tiski put a hand over the child's mouth, holding her close.

'Sh!' she whispered urgently in the child's ear. To her great relief, Anida stopped squirming. 'You must keep very quiet, do you understand?'

The child nodded and, cautiously, Tiski removed her hand.

Quaty also realised she could not outrun the horses and she

found a hiding-place in some bushes, not forty paces from where Tiski and Anida lay. But she had not been so fortunate in her choice of hiding-place.

There was a long silence – so long that it became almost painful. Then one of the Texans shouted and the boom of a buffalo rifle reverberated through the forest. Quaty screamed, and as the scream became a wail of grief Tiski knew the soldiers had shot Yellow Bear's son.

The wailing continued without abating, and once more Tiski had to clamp a hand over Anida's mouth.

'Jesus! Put a bullet through her head and stop that noise.'

The horses were milling about close enough for Tiski to hear most of what was said.

'There weren't no call to shoot. He was just a kid.'

'So was Sam Slade's boy. The Indians scalped *him*.'

'Shoot the squaw. . . .'

'Don't shoot her. . . . She ain't a bad-looker. I've got a *much* better idea. . . .'

'You can't do that, Jeff! Her kid's just been shot. . . .'

'She's a squaw. If you don't like it, you can ride off and see nothing. . . . Grab her! Get those clothes off. . . .'

There were the sounds of a horse crashing away from the scene as Quaty began screaming. Then she began hurling abuse at the men about her until Tiski heard the unmistakable sound of blows being struck and the screaming stopped abruptly. A man laughed, Quaty moaned as though in pain, and the laughter was repeated.

Tiski did not know how long she lay beneath the leaves listening as Quaty was raped by one man after another. Then a voice asked: 'Anyone else, before I send her off to her happy hunting-ground to boast of how much better it was with a white man?'

'Hell! We don't have to kill her, do we?'

'D'you want her to go off and teach a little bastard how to kill his own daddy?'

As the laughter died down, the same voice said: 'I'm damned if I'm going to waste a bullet on her. Give me your knife.'

There was a moment's silence, then Tiski heard Quaty choking and gurgling as the knife did its work and Quaty choked in her own blood.

Horrified, Tiski pulled Anida closer to her in a bid to keep the dying sounds of her mother from her.

'We going on after the rest of them Indians?'

'No, we've done enough for one day. We'll pick up the trail easy enough tomorrow. ...'

Tiski met up with Yellow Bear and some of the other Indians later that night by the river. All the Cherokees had headed for the river bank, but there were far fewer than there should have been, and women and warriors wandered from group to soft-talking group in the vain hope of finding the missing members of their families.

Tiski told Yellow Bear of the death of Quaty and his son, sparing him as many details as she could. Yellow Bear listened in silence. Only his taut body and bowed head gave a hint of the suffering he felt at the news.

When Tiski had finished talking, Yellow Bear turned and walked away into the darkness. He returned after an hour and picked up the sleeping Anida.

'Come, we go.'

'Where? Where *can* we go?'

'To your husband's people. I made him a promise. I will keep it.'

'What of the others?'

'They will go north. John will take them. He is their chief now.'

They walked all night, Yellow Bear choosing the ground carefully. He did not think there were any Indian trackers with the Texan soldiers, but he took no chances.

By the time dawn came Tiski was reeling from exhaustion. She felt she could not walk a step farther. They made a cheerless camp among trees and rocks on a hill well away from the Neches River. Yellow Bear stayed awake until almost noon before he, too, lay down and closed his eyes, a restless Anida held in his arms.

They travelled for three nights, resting during the day. Then, on the third night, Yellow Bear kept Tiski walking after the sun had come up.

When Tiski questioned the change in their routine, Yellow Bear explained: 'We need horses. It is almost time for your baby, and I want you to be with your husband's people when it comes.'

They walked until midday before Yellow Bear called a halt.

'You will stay here. I am going on, but I will be back tomorrow morning. Light no fires. Rest and eat anything you can find. Tomorrow we will need to ride hard.'

Yellow Bear reached his destination in an hour. It was a small valley cabin with a neat kitchen garden and a corral behind the house. Yellow Bear had hoped the occupants would be out in the fields with their oxen, thus giving him an opportunity to steal the horses and ride away, but the man was in the house, so Yellow Bear waited.

There were a number of callers during the day, among them a small troop of Rangers. They stayed to water their horses and enjoy a cup of coffee, then rode off northwards. They would not interfere with Yellow Bear's plans.

Shortly before dusk, the man locked his four horses away in the lean-to behind the house and Yellow Bear settled down to sleep. He knew the barn had bolts both inside and out. At night the man would bolt it from the inside, leaving via a smaller door that opened out on the long passageway separating barn from house. There were flimsy doors on both ends of the passageway, and the space between them was the sleeping-area for the family's large dog.

Yellow Bear was awake before dawn. He made his way silently down the hillside to the cabin. Squatting beside the barn door, he waited. Dawn came swiftly to the valley, but not until the sun had hauled itself clear of the low eastern horizon did Yellow Bear hear the family stir inside the house. He heard the house door open and the man came out cursing the noise of the dog. Then the man went inside the barn. A few minutes later the heavy wooden bolt on the inside of the lean-to was drawn back.

As the large door swung open, Yellow Bear was waiting. The dog came out first, frisky with early-morning foolishness, looking behind him at the horses.

Yellow Bear broke the animal's back with a single blow from the butt of his rifle; then, leaping over the body, he was inside the low-roofed barn.

Gustav Miesenbach saw him too late. He died with a bullet in his heart and an expression on his face that combined recognition and fear. The shot frightened the horses, but they all wore rope halters and it was the work of a moment to gather them together and get them outside. Riding one horse and leading three more, Yellow Bear was through the open corral gate before Henrietta Miesenbach ran from the house, a loaded musket in her hands. She fired at the fast-moving Indian but, crouching low over the neck of the horse, Yellow Bear rode as though he were a Comanche and the shot went wide.

CHAPTER THIRTEEN

WHEN ADAM RODE into Austin, he was reeling in the saddle, suffering from fatigue and the after-effects of his recent illness. Ignoring the combined protests of Dr Ewing and the Tolsa and Benavides families, Adam had set off from Victoria on the day he learned of the defeat of the Cherokees.

Dona Antonia and Philippe travelled with him part of the way; but, when the indifferent road swung towards San Antonio, Adam continued to follow the course of the Guadalupe River, north-eastward. He refused the offer of an escort, preferring to travel alone. One man could pass through the country unnoticed, if he were careful. A group of men could not. This was Comanche hunting country. Although he was confident the truce was holding in the settlement, Adam would not like to encounter a Comanche hunting party elsewhere.

Adam had come to Austin to find out what had happened to the survivors of Chief Bowles's Cherokees. The messenger sent to Houston by Victoriano Benavides had reported that rumour put President Lamar in Austin. The new capital was nearing completion, and the Texan president was taking a personal interest in his brainchild.

Unfortunately, Adam was too late yet again. Lamar had left Austin more than a week before, heading for Washington-on-the-Brazos, a town that had played a prominent part in the Texan revolt against Mexican rule.

Worried about Tiski, and still weak from his illness, Adam could have broken down and wept from sheer frustration. Instead, he took a room in the town's unfinished hotel. With work going on all about him, he slept undisturbed for fifteen hours.

When he woke he was able to think more clearly. There was a Ranger post in Austin, and here Adam received first-hand information of the fighting between Texans and Cherokees from a grey-haired Ranger who would have looked more at home sunning himself on the front porch of a comfortable town house. It came as a surprise to Adam to learn that the neatly dressed, quietly spoken Ranger had been a frontiersman and Indian fighter in places as far apart as Mexico, the Canadian border, and numerous places in between.

The Ranger told Adam of the two days of fighting, followed by a pursuit of the Cherokees that took the Rangers all the way to the Red River. When he told of the death of Chief Bowles, the Ranger looked up from the piece of wood he was whittling and caught the expression on Adam's face.

'I'm telling you what happened, boy. I'm not saying I'm proud of it. I'm no Indian-lover, but I wouldn't go around bragging that I was a hero because I'd shot an eighty-three-year-old man in the back – or because I'd blown his brains out with a hand-gun when he was lying defenceless. I reckon the Old Bowl deserved better than that.'

Adam thought of the proud old man as he had often seen him, the undisputed father of his people. But another picture haunted him: that of a young girl who loved Adam just as Chief Bowles had loved his people. The girl who carried Adam's child.

'Did *all* the Cherokees go north, across the Red River?'

'We thought so, but it seems some of 'em must have slipped around us. A small party was seen not very far away, heading towards the Hill Country. That's why I'm here on my own. Captain Dollar and most of the boys left three days ago to hunt them down.'

Adam knew that Tiski and Yellow Bear would be among the Cherokees heading for the Hill Country. His blood ran cold at the prospect of the red-bearded Captain Dollar and his Indian-hating Rangers finding them before he did.

Thanking the grey-haired Ranger for his information, Adam hurried away. Within an hour he was on his way. He took a spare horse with him, purchased with money he had borrowed from Victoriano Benavides. It was close to a hundred miles across country to Caleb's settlement, but Adam was determined to be there by nightfall.

It was a long, hard ride to the Hill Country, but Tiski bore it well. They had left the soldiers far behind them, and she was going to where she would be with Adam for always. It would mean a complete change of life-style, but that would not be so hard now. The old ways had gone forever. It would be good for Adam's son to begin life learning the ways of his father's people. She wanted the two always to be close to each other. Convinced that the child she carried was a boy, Tiski was determined he would have a bright future. Often on the long trail from the Cherokee lands she had looked at Yellow Bear's taut, unsmiling face. He was grieving for Quaty and the son she had given him. She did not want Adam ever to suffer such grief. Yellow Bear would find another wife, of

299

course – and Quaty would have wished it for him. It was not right for a man to live without a woman, especially when he had a young daughter to care for.

One morning when they broke camp, Yellow Bear told Tiski they would reach the valley where Adam and his friends had their cabins before nightfall. At the news, Tiski's nerve suddenly failed her. She wondered whether it might have been a mistake coming to Adam in this way. What if she found he already had a *white* wife living in his cabin? He might be embarrassed at having an Indian wife arriving at his house. If Adam were not there, would his friends know anything of her? Why had he not come back before the battle?

Yellow Bear was watching her closely, and her thoughts might have been pictures painted in her eyes. His smile was the first Tiski had seen since the battle at the Neches River.

'I have met many white men. They speak from one side of their mouth when in a Cherokee village, and from the other when they return to their own people. The Englishman is not like these. He stood before the man who talks with God and took you for his wife. Such talk is sacred, even to the White Man. Your husband will be happy to see you and relieved to know you are safe.'

The panic subsided and Tiski felt ashamed of her doubts. 'It is as you say. Adam will be happy to see me – and concerned for his son,' she patted her swollen stomach. 'It will soon be time. Come, we will go now.'

It was soon after noon when Yellow Bear saw the men riding fast on their trail. They were less than a mile away and must have spotted the Indians from a distance. Yellow Bear had been careless. He had been too concerned with looking for the landmarks Adam had mentioned and watching for signs of civilisation ahead. He had not expected anyone to come after them this far from the scene of the battle.

Anida had been riding one of the horses by herself, but now Yellow Bear scooped her from the animal's back. Seating her in front of him, he called on Tiski to hurry. When there was a copse of tall trees between them and the riders coming behind, Yellow Bear changed direction, putting the horses up a rise to a well-treed ridge.

Here he stopped. From the cover of the trees he watched the men sweep by below him. There were twelve of them, all well armed. He knew then they were Rangers, experienced fighting men, used to fighting Indians. They would not be fooled by his simple ruse for long.

Yellow Bear urged Tiski on. Travelling in the direction in which they needed to go, he tried to remain on high, treed ground for as long as possible, but he was eventually forced down, in order to cross a wide valley. It was here that the Rangers found them once more. Emerging from trees no more than half a mile away, the Rangers fanned out and charged towards the Indian trio.

'Go up there.' Yellow Bear pointed up a hillside slope to where there was a cluster of large rocks scattered about three or four stunted trees. They rode until the gradient became too steep. Clutching Anida and leading his horse, Yellow Bear made the safety of the rocks and turned just as the Rangers commenced firing. Tiski fell to the ground, and Yellow Bear thought she had been shot, but she scrambled to her feet and clawed her way up the slope to the rocks. Unfortunately, in the fall she had released her hold on her horse. It now slid down the hillside in a small avalanche and galloped after the two horses which had taken off when the first shots rang out.

The Rangers put their horses to the slope as Tiski scrambled awkwardly to the shelter of the rocks. Yellow Bear fired and one of the Rangers sagged in the saddle. As the Rangers' charge lost some of its momentum, Yellow Bear fired again. This shot wounded one of the horses. Supporting their wounded companion, the Rangers drew back.

Reloading his gun, Yellow Bear looked about him grimly. It was as good a defensive spot as he could have hoped for in the circumstances, but it was far from perfect. Before long the Rangers would work their way behind him to the crest of the bluff. Then the position among the rocks would become untenable. They might stand a chance if they could hold out until darkness fell – but there were at least another four hours of daylight left. He doubted if they would survive that long.

The Rangers had regrouped in the valley, just out of rifle range. They seemed to be having a disagreement. Yellow Bear watched as the men pointed first to the rocks, then to the bluff above them. As he feared, the Rangers intended sending men to get behind and above their quarry. If he were to attempt an escape with Tiski and Anida, it had to be now.

He turned to Tiski – and found her kneeling on the ground, her face contorted in pain.

'You have been hit? Where . . . ?'

'No . . . the baby . . . it comes.' Perspiration streamed down Tiski's face as she gasped out the words.

Yellow Bear gazed at Tiski in disbelief. Then she suffered a spasm that held her body in its grip for half a minute. Tiski gripped the thin trunk of one of the trees for support. In that moment, Yellow Bear knew he would not leave this place alive. The knowledge brought him unexpected peace of mind. He had never feared death. Now, with Quaty, his son, his father and most of his friends dead, Yellow Bear welcomed its coming.

Frightened more by the sight of Tiski in labour than by anything else, Anida clung to her father's leg. Reaching down, Yellow Bear stroked her hair. It would be hard for her to lose her mother and father within such a short time of each other, but she was very young. She could forget. He did not believe the white men would harm her or Tiski. Adam could decide whether he and Tiski would keep Anida. If not, Adam would find the surviving Cherokees and return the child to her people. John would take care of her.

Yellow Bear knew he needed to act now, before the Rangers made up their minds about who would go to the bluff. Once in position they would pour their fire into the rocks, shooting at anything that moved.

The remaining horse was tied to one of the stunted trees. Yellow Bear would not take it with him. The horse would make travelling easier for Tiski and Anida. On its back was the half-cured hide of a deer Yellow Bear had shot on the way to the Hill Country. Stripping it from the horse's back, Yellow Bear dropped it at Tiski's side.

'Here. It is not good for your child to be born on the ground.'

Gritting her teeth against the continuing pain, Tiski nodded acknowledgement of his thoughtfulness.

Yellow Bear placed the loaded rifle beside the hide. After resting his hand on Anida's head for the last time, he walked from the rocks towards the Rangers.

They saw him coming. Leaving the injured Ranger behind, they began cautiously walking their horses towards him. Yellow Bear walked slowly and had not covered quite half the distance between them when he heard a loud cry behind him.

'Do-da . . . ! Do-da . . . !'

He turned to see Anida running after him. Left alone with Tiski, the child had become frightened by her groans and strange cries. When she saw her father walking away from her, she ran after him.

'Go back! *Go back!*'

Twice Yellow Bear called to her. When she ignored his shouts he ran to pick her up and return her to safety.

Behind him, the mounted Rangers raised their rifles. Two of them fired simultaneously. They both aimed at Yellow Bear, but it was Anida who dropped to the ground when she was almost within her father's grasp. On his knees beside her, Yellow Bear saw that the heavy bullet had struck her just above the left eyebrow. It had killed her instantly.

Screaming his hatred for all white men, Yellow Bear drew his knife and ran towards his daughter's killers, shrieking as though he were a madman. He took the first two shots in his body without faltering. The third staggered him, and he fell to the fourth. But he was not yet dead. He tried to rise when the Rangers drew closer and was on all fours when Captain Dollar leaned from his horse to deliver the *coup de grâce* with a shot from his hand-gun.

The other Rangers steered their horses around the two bodies, some of the men keeping their eyes averted from the smaller of the two figures lying on the ground.

'There's a squaw up among the rocks. Go carefully; they can be as dangerous as their men.'

As they approached the rocks, Captain Dollar held up his hand. When the men stopped, Tiski's gasping could be clearly heard.

'She's hurt.'

'Sounds like it. Henry . . . Clem . . . you stay here and hold the horses. The rest of you come on foot with me – but take no chances.'

The nine Rangers spread out and advanced towards the rocks, holding their guns in readiness for whatever they might find. The gasps were louder now, but one or two of the men were looking puzzled. These were not the sounds of a dying woman.

When they reached the rocks, Captain Dollar signalled for two of his men to circle around them and approach from the far side.

Moments later, the waiting men heard one of their two companions exclaim: 'Well, I'm damned! Just come and look what's going on here. If this don't beat all. . . .'

Tiski was kneeling on the deerskin, legs wide apart, her hands grasping the thin trunk of the tree with all her strength. Her buckskin dress was pulled up and tucked into the belt she wore. The baby had almost fully entered the world.

'What's so special about this? Ain't you ever seen a cow giving birth . . . or a horse? It's just the same.'

'No, it ain't. This is an Indian. I say put a bullet in her head and have done with it right now.'

'Not yet. I'm a city boy, I've never seen *anything* being born.'

'Hell! Did you see *that*? It was almost out, then it just went right back in again!'

'You know, that squaw's mighty pretty. If she weren't working so hard at getting something out of there, I could think of better things to do with it. . . .'

Panting heavily, Tiski leaned forward and rested her head against the tree. She heard most of what was being said, but it did not matter to her. Nothing mattered now except the task of bringing her baby into the world. She was close to exhaustion, but that feeling would pass once it was all over.

The contractions began again, and this time nothing would prevent the baby from coming all the way. She felt it slide free of her body and sank down on her haunches in relief. But it was not yet time to rest. The baby's umbilical cord was circled about its tiny neck and she untwined it quickly. The baby was bloody, and Tiski wished she had some grease to rub over its body. When she picked it up, she saw to her joy that it was a boy.

Tiski's joy showed in her face. Suddenly, she and her baby – Adam's son – were the only two people in the world.

But something was wrong. The baby had not yet moved. It lay limp in her arms. Tiski put a finger inside the baby's mouth. It was clear. She did not smack the child; that was not the Indian way. Instead, she tickled the baby beneath the chin. Still it did not move. Tiski held the newly born child to her breast, but already it was growing cold.

'It seems we've been saved a job of work,' said Captain Dollar. 'The Indian brat's already dead.'

Tiski heard the words spoken by the red-bearded Ranger captain and she knew they were true. The baby she had carried inside her for so long was dead. Killed by the actions of men such as these. Tiski's hatred for them welled up inside her and she lunged for the gun Yellow Bear had left beside the deerskin.

Her move took the Rangers by surprise, but they were quick to react. Even as she picked up the rifle with the intention of killing Captain Sam Dollar, the Rangers shot her.

Tiski's finger never found the trigger and she slumped over the tiny figure of the baby, her body torn by nine bullets.

Another few minutes and the tragedy might never have occurred. As it was, Eli Varne arrived just in time to witness the manner of Tiski's death.

BOOK THREE

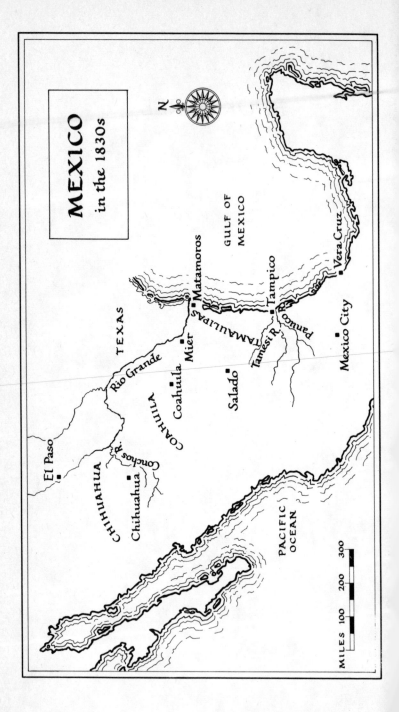

CHAPTER ONE

ELI HAD HEADED for the scene of the unequal battle when he heard the initial exchange of fire between Yellow Bear and his pursuers. With him was Caleb and Gilpin McCulloch, the young son of one of the Scots settlers, who had been visiting the Ryans with his mother.

Looking at the bodies lying on the hillside, Eli held on to his anger, but he could not hide the contempt he felt for Captain Dollar and his Rangers.

'Is this another of your great Ranger "victories", Sam? The son of a man who was the most peaceful Indian in Texas before he was stirred up. A three year-old girl – and a woman with her newborn son?'

'It was me or her, my men will tell you that.'

'I'd say she had good cause to want you dead. You better hope her husband doesn't feel the same way. He's not as slow with a gun as she was.'

'Husband? You know her?'

'She was married to my partner, Adam Rashleigh.'

'The Englishman? I had him figured for a squaw man the first time I set eyes on him.'

'She wasn't just his "squaw", Sam. They were married in a church, by a white preacher. I was along as a witness. That's his child lying dead with her.'

'Well, how was I to know? I wouldn't have killed her had there been any other way.' Captain Dollar had paled at Eli's words. Adam's skill with the weapons of the frontier had become a byword among the settlements. 'But what was his wife doing riding a horse that carries Gustav Miesenbach's brand?'

'I wouldn't come close enough to ask *him* that question if I were you, Sam Dollar. You and your men had better get mounted and ride out of here. Every time I look at that girl's body I feel myself filling up with more anger than I can rightly cope with. You stay here and I'm likely to do something only one of us is going to live to regret.'

Captain Dollar was about to make a reply when Eli held up a hand to silence him. It was Eli's left hand. In his right he held the long-barrelled rifle.

'Talking's finished. Shut up and go, or take me on – here and now.'

Sam Dollar was no fool. He knew he was as close to death as he would ever be. Striding to where a Ranger held his horse, he mounted and rode away without looking back. Eli searched the faces of the other Rangers, but not a man among them was prepared to take up the challenge on behalf of their captain.

As they rode away, Eli threw his gun to the ground in disgust.

'Damnation, why wouldn't he fight me? Now Adam will have to go after him – and Sam Dollar don't fight English-style.'

Stripping the saddle from his horse, Eli removed the blanket that lay folded beneath it and laid it carefully over Tiski and her dead baby.

'Caleb, go back to the cabin and fetch the wagon. Bring the women here with you, too. Getting Adam's wife ready for burial is women's work.'

Adam reached the valley two days later. Eli and Caleb were away hunting a bear that had played havoc in Caleb's hen-run the previous night. It was left to Nell Plunkett to break the news of Tiski's death, and to take Adam to where Eli had dug a single grave for Tiski and the baby, on Adam's own land. Yellow Bear and his daughter had been buried on the hillside, where they had fallen.

Before leaving Adam at the graveside, Nell, her voice choked with emotion, said: 'She looked beautiful when we'd got her dressed up. I wish I could have known her when she was alive. I'm sure I would have liked her a lot.'

Adam merely nodded, and Nell returned home hot-eyed, seeing nothing along the way.

Adam had not returned to Caleb's cabin when the men came back from the hunt and, when night fell, Eli set off to fetch his friend. He found Adam hunched on the ground at the side of Tiski's grave.

'Adam . . . come back to Caleb's place with me. Your friends are concerned for you.'

To Eli's surprise, Adam rose unsteadily to his feet and walked with him to where Adam's horse was long-reined to a tree.

'I don't have to tell you how sorry I am, Adam. If only I'd got there a few minutes earlier. . . .'

'Tell me about it. Everything.'

Eli told Adam the manner of Tiski's death, leaving out as much as he dared, trying to spare his friend more grief. When he began apologising again, Adam stopped him.

'You did all you could. Tiski didn't want to live. Not with the baby gone, and the tribe broken up. .... I'm to blame as much as anyone. I should have brought her here long before the battle. But I thought she'd want to be with people she knew when the baby came. That it would be easier for her. ....'

Adam's voice came close to breaking. He had spent too many hours on his own, thinking of what might have been. Eli understood. He was a man who had walked lonely paths for much of his life. But there were things that needed saying, even though they might hurt.

'I saw what happened at the end, Adam. Sam Dollar had no choice. She picked up the gun and would have killed him. There's no court in Texas – or in America, either – that would convict him. Not even if Tiski had been a white girl.'

'I'm not thinking of getting Captain Dollar into any courtroom. Oh, I don't blame Dollar, any more than I blame Lamar's men for killing Chief Bowles and his people.' Adam sounded bitter. He *was* bitter. 'It's a way of thinking. Texans hunt Indians the way Englishmen hunt gamebirds. You don't need me to tell you anything about this. You've been around Texans and Indians for long enough. No, I don't *hate* Dollar – but I'm going to kill him anyway.'

They had reached Adam's horse now and he unfastened the rein and swung up to the saddle.

'I won't come back to Caleb's. I don't feel much like company. Thanks for what you did for Tiski and ... the baby.'

There was something about Adam's words that alarmed Eli. They sounded too much like a final goodbye.

'Adam, you've made a lot of friends hereabouts. Good friends. Caleb and Eileen, Nell, Kathie – and Peggy Dooley, too. They're all of 'em grieving with you.'

'I know, and I'm grateful. But, *because* I know, I need to get away for a while. If I don't, everyone's going to be careful of what they say to me. They'll try so hard not to remind me of what's happened, I'll never be able to forget.'

'When you figure on leaving?'

'First thing in the morning. I'll stay in my own cabin tonight.'

There was a long pause while Eli thought out his next words. 'You remember when we left Velasco to come out here? You and me set out as partners. You've grown some since then, but I reckon you could still learn a thing or two from me.'

'I don't doubt it, but many things have changed. You've got land – and there's Kathie. It's me who needs to find somewhere new now.'

'Do you know which way you'll be heading?'

'Yes. I'll find Dollar and then go south – to Mexico. Don Manuel's in a Mexican gaol. I want the British ambassador to use his influence to have him released.'

The news of Don Manuel's imprisonment had shocked the settlers. Don Manuel Tolsa had been a good friend to them.

'You been to Mexico before?'

'No.'

'That settles it. I have. I'm coming with you. To get Don Manuel out of gaol you'll need to be able to bribe, cheat and lie better than a Mexican. You wouldn't know where to begin. I've done it all before.'

'What about Kathie – and your land? You're running cattle there now.'

Eli's grimace was lost in the darkness. 'I don't quite measure up to Kathie's standards – and it isn't right for a woman to set out to change a man. I reckon he's entitled to be what he wants to be. When Kathie comes round to that way of thinking I'll marry her and we'll have a happy life together. If she's going to spend married life trying to make me exactly like her first husband, we'll both wind up miserable. My going away will be good for her ... for both of us. If she still wants to marry me when we get back, well, I might give it a try. As for the cattle, Caleb will look after them.'

Eli laid a hand on the neck of Adam's horse. 'I'll see you right after sun-up – but you'd better come to Caleb's cabin. I'll explain things to Kathie now and spend the night in Caleb's barn. Most of my things are there anyway.'

When Adam reached the Ryan cabin, Eli had his horse saddled and laden with bulging saddlebags. As Adam rode up, Caleb came from his cabin, tucking a shirt inside corduroy trousers. There was no sign of any of the women. Caleb grasped Adam's hand and expressed his sympathy. Adam nodded without replying, and Caleb changed the subject hurriedly.

'We were all hoping you'd be staying for a while this time. But Eli's told us about Don Manuel. You'll have the good wishes and the prayers of the whole settlement riding with you. Don Manuel is much liked in this community. Without him we'd none of us be here, as well you know.'

From what Caleb was saying, Adam knew that Eli had said nothing about Sam Dollar. It was better that it remained unsaid. He also knew he was right to be going away. This was an unfamiliar, formal Caleb. The Irishman's natural free-and-easy manner was missing and, although Adam knew it was intended as a mark of respect for the loss of Tiski, he hoped that by the time he came back to the settlement – if he ever did – things would have returned to normal.

Turning to Eli, Caleb relaxed a little. 'I couldn't help overhearing what Kathie was saying to you last night, Eli. As a matter of fact, Eileen thought they probably heard as far off as San Antonio. She didn't seem keen on you going. Can I take it we'll not be having a wedding here this year after all?'

Scowling, Eli said: 'You'd better put that question to Kathie. She figures that marrying a man is the same as putting a ring through his nose and leading him about on the end of a piece of rope. That being so, I guess you're not likely to see me back here again.'

Eli spoke unnecessarily loudly, but then Adam saw that the door of Kathie Casey's cabin stood ajar, and he understood. As Eli secured a bedroll behind the saddle with a tug that startled his horse, a small figure ran from the Casey cabin. It was Dermot. He stopped a couple of paces from the Tennessee frontiersman and looked up at him pale-faced and dark-eyed. It looked as though he had been crying.

'Eli . . . you going away for good?'

Eli's face became a battleground for confused emotions, then he shook his head in resigned disgust. 'Goddamit, Dermot. What did you have to ask me that for? No, of course I'm not going away for good. I'll be home again long before you've learned to handle that gun I bought you. You make sure you practise good and hard – and look after your ma, you hear me?'

Dermot Casey's misery changed to undisguised relief. Rushing at Eli, his arms went about the frontiersman's waist and hugged him; then he turned and ran back to disappear inside the cabin.

'That boy's getting too old to go around hugging folk,' said Eli, not meeting the eyes of the other two men. 'I'll have to set him straight when I get back.' His voice was just a shade too gruff, and Adam realised that the Tennesseean was as proud of the boy as though he were already his father. The thought only served to accentuate Adam's own loss.

Nell Plunkett, Eileen Ryan and Peggy Dooley turned out to wave goodbye to the two men, but not until they were about to pass out of the unfinished stockade gate did Kathie Casey put in an appearance.

Calling to Eli, she hurried after him, carrying a cloth-wrapped parcel. When she reached the horses she said: 'Shame on you, Eli

Varne. Were you *really* going off without so much as a word of goodbye for me?'

Eli was nonplussed. 'After what was said last night I thought you didn't want to see me again.'

'I don't believe in carrying an argument forward to a new day, Eli Varne. You'll learn that when you return.' She looked up at him, and for a moment her self-assured pose broke. 'You *will* come back to us?'

'Is that what you want?'

Kathie Casey could only nod her head.

'Then I'll be back. I'll *always* come back to you and the boy.'

'May you travel with the Lord's protection – both of you. Now come down here and take these few things I've baked for you, Eli Varne. I can't lift them up there to you; they're far too heavy.'

Eli swung out of the saddle and took the bag of food from Kathie. A moment later he was being hugged by a member of the Casey family for the second time that morning.

Adam rode off a way and waited for Eli to catch up with him. Meanwhile, at the Ryan cabin, Eileen told her husband that she thought the settlers might have their wedding after all.

Adam's search for Captain Sam Dollar led him only as far as Austin. Here he learned that the Ranger captain had been sent to the United States of America. He was part of a delegation to Samuel Colt's arms factory, hoping to persuade the arms designer to make modifications to his revolvers, especially for the Texas Rangers.

The news came as a great relief to Eli. He did not doubt Adam's ability to outshoot Sam Dollar, but gunning down a Ranger captain would have resulted in Adam being lynched, especially once his reasons became known.

Now the two men were on their way to Mexico, and Eli knew that by the time they returned Sam Dollar would be safe, just so long as his path did not cross that of Adam.

Adam had decided that their best method of travel to Mexico was by sea. With this end in mind, they travelled to Matagorda, a busy little port serving the established settlers scattered along the Colorado River as far inland as the new capital of Austin. They arrived in the seaport after a heavy shower of rain and were depressed by the drabness of the adobe-and-timber buildings. On the waterlogged thoroughfares, horses picked their way carefully. The mounts of less cautious travellers were liable to sink hock-deep in the soft mud.

The accommodation in Matagorda's two-storey hotel was only

slightly less depressing than the town itself. The narrow window in the room was so dirty it could not have been cleaned since the hotel was built; but at least the room was dry, and there was good stabling for their horses.

When they had cleaned up, the two friends headed for the saloon. It was mid-afternoon, but the saloon-keeper was doing good business. The men crowding the long bar were noisy, mostly drunk, and inclined to be quarrelsome. Ignoring the sailor who objected to him squeezing in beside him to order a drink, Adam acquired a bottle of whisky and two glasses and made his way across the room with Eli. They were seeking a table when Adam suddenly recognised a bearded man sitting alone at a corner table.

'Captain Lelean! I never expected to meet up with you in Matagorda. I thought *Liberty* never came farther south than Velasco?'

'Well, well, if it isn't the Englishman. How are your settlers? They been eaten by Indians yet?'

'A few have been killed. The remainder will make out all right.' Adam introduced Eli and poured drinks into three glasses as the men shook hands.

After drinking a toast to Texas, Captain Lelean asked: 'What are you doing down this way? I thought all your interests lay inland. Somewhere near San Antonio, as I remember.'

'Your memory serves you well, but we're on our way to Mexico right now. Do you remember Don Manuel Tolsa, another of your passengers? He went to Mexico on a mission for President Lamar, and the Mexican government threw him into prison. We're on our way there to see if we can get him released. I don't suppose you're heading in that direction?'

One or two men at nearby tables were showing an interest in the conversation, and Captain Lelean said hurriedly: 'Me? No, I trade between Texas and New Orleans. If you boys want a comfortable trip up north any time, you just let me know. I'm freight-carrying these days, but I'll always find room for you.'

Tossing back his drink in one practised movement, Captain Lelean reached across the table towards his own bottle. When his head was close to Adam's, he said in a hoarse whisper: 'There are too many ears in this place. Come onboard *Liberty* in about half an hour's time – and bring a new bottle with you.' Clutching his bottle of whisky to him, Captain Lelean wished Adam and Eli 'Good day', and made his way from the saloon.

Less than thirty minutes later the three men were seated together around a table in Captain Lelean's cabin on board the paddle-steamer *Liberty*. The ship's captain had not been abstemious since leaving the saloon, and his blue-veined face had taken on a ruddy glow.

Accepting a drink from one of the two bottles Adam and Eli had brought with them, Captain Lelean beamed at them across the table. 'This is better. We can talk business without having everything we say passed to the Texan authorities. They've got a navy again now – a damned great side-wheeler bought from up north. It's got three times the speed of my boat and could run me down with as little fuss as ploughing through a decent-sized wave.'

'Does this mean you *are* trading with Mexico?'

'I go where the money is. Mexico wants cotton and hides. There's both right here in Texas. Texans are always crying out for good horses – they breed them in Mexico. I do my best to keep everyone happy – and that reminds me, how do you intend paying for this trip? I'm taking none of Lamar's dollars. A holdful would hardly pay my berthing fee in New Orleans.'

'I've got Mexican silver, or American gold, whichever you prefer.'

The money had come from Victoriano Benavides. Adam would repay him with money being held for him at the British embassy in Mexico City.

'I'll take American. You got much luggage?'

'No more than can be carried on a riding-horse.'

'Good. Go back and get everything. Have it on board before we get down to some serious drinking. Sell your horses to the livery man. He'll offer you as much as anyone else – but bring your saddles along.'

'We sailing tonight?'

Eli's question contained the fear felt by so many landsmen of the time when it was necessary to go to sea, and the sight of the captain of *Liberty* drinking heavily hardly inspired confidence.

'We leave tomorrow, but you'll find the beds on board better than any in Matagorda – and there'll be no one to overhear you when you're talking about where you're going and what you plan on doing when you get there.'

Captain Lelean timed his departure perfectly. By the time *Liberty* nosed out into the waters of the Gulf of Mexico it was too dark for anyone on shore to see whether the paddle-steamer headed north or south. When daylight came again, the little vessel was out of sight of land.

Four nights later, *Liberty* was chugging along within sight of a

314

low-lying shore that was painted grey by moonlight. In the early hours of the morning the engine was stopped and an anchor clattered over the side.

Liberty rode gently at anchor until dawn, then Captain Lelean took her into the wide estuary at the confluence of the Tamesi and Panuco Rivers. Early though it was, Adam and Eli were in the wheelhouse with Captain Lelean when he brought the paddle-steamer alongside a ramshackle jetty that was in complete harmony with the village from which it had grown. At the shoreward end of the jetty two Mexicans wearing ill-fitting, once white uniforms leaned on ancient muskets and watched with bored indifference as a Negro leaped ashore and secured *Liberty*.

Captain Lelean ordered the engine to be shut down, then turned to his two passengers. 'Here you are, this is *Madre* Mexico. The capital is roughly two hundred miles south-west. There are better roads from other ports, but I've learned from hard experience that the officials here ask fewer questions than elsewhere. The value of that shouldn't be underestimated in Mexico, believe me.'

'How are we supposed to travel those two hundred miles to Mexico City?' Eli was relieved to be within stepping distance of solid ground once more, but he would need convincing that their safe arrival was anything more than a very lucky accident. Captain Lelean was a heavy drinker when he was ashore. At sea he consumed twice as much.

'About half a mile back from the river you'll find a pen containing some of the finest horses in the whole of Mexico. Tell the man in charge that I sent you. Choose two of the best – but make sure you pay no more than a quarter of what you got for your own horses in Matagorda. I don't want you pushing the price up for me. Tell anyone who might ask that you've travelled here from New Orleans. Forget you've ever seen Texas. The Mexicans don't like Americans, but they let them live – usually. Mention you're from Texas and you'll be grinning from ear to ear, but below the chin. If you need me again, I'm here once a month about this time, depending on weather.'

Thanking Captain Lelean, Adam and Eli set off along the jetty carrying saddles and saddlebags. They exchanged nods with the two Mexican guards and, less than an hour later, were heading for Mexico City, riding two of the finest horses Adam had seen since leaving Europe.

The landing and the purchase of horses had been accomplished without anyone asking a single question.

CHAPTER TWO

ADAM KNEW their good luck could not possibly last for ever, but it did not desert the two men until he and Eli were in the mountains, no more than thirty miles from Mexico City. They were staying at a whitewashed inn that overlooked the square of a small town, when a large troop of cavalrymen rode in. The two men had met with many Mexican soldiers on their journey to the capital city. All had been ill-fed, underpaid and illiterate to a man. It had been a simple matter to overcome their suspicions with an outward display of arrogant authority, or, on rare occasions, with a couple of silver Spanish dollars.

The mounted men who rode into the square outside the room where Adam and Eli stood were very different. They wore smart blue uniforms and plumed hats. Each man was clean and smart and might have been hand-picked from a Spanish cavalry unit. In fact, the soldiers were cavalrymen of the Mexican Presidential Guard.

The two men stood back from the window after witnessing the arrival of the horsemen, but it came as no surprise when there was a heavy knocking on the door a few minutes later. Adam opened the door to see a captain of cavalrymen standing outside the door, flanked by two of his troopers.

It seemed that for one of the ragged soldiers along the route neither silver nor arrogance had been enough. He had reported the presence of two *gringos* in Mexico, travelling without documents issued on behalf of the central government.

The Presidential Guard was on its way back from Tampico, escorting a large fortune in long-overdue import tax, confiscated from an errant general who had intended using it to finance his own revolution. The Presidential Guard was the only regiment in a corrupt army trustworthy enough to execute the rich general and return his money to central government coffers. On the road, the colonel commanding the cavalry had been given word of two mysterious strangers. He had sent the captain ahead to find them and learn the purpose of their journey along a trail little used by foreign visitors to Mexico.

Adam answered the captain's questions with a confidence he did not feel. Mexican politics was no longer simply a conflict of ideals or personalities. The provinces were in an almost continuous state of revolution. Leaders of both sides switched allegiances with confusing frequency. It was expedient to execute suspected spies rather question them at great length. Quite often an executed man turned out to be a true supporter of the cause that ordered his execution, but it mattered little. The state of confusion in the country was such that today's friend might easily prove to be tomorrow's enemy. For the same reasons, it was not advisable to claim friendship with any of the country's leading figures.

Instead, Adam told the cavalry captain that he was on his way to Mexico City to visit Mr Pakenham, the British ambassador to Mexico. The visit was being made at the suggestion of Lord Palmerston, Foreign Secretary of Great Britain – a friend of Adam's late father. As for the journey along a little-known road, the ship bringing Adam and Eli to Mexico had disembarked them at its destination and enquiries made along the way had dictated their route.

The Mexican cavalry captain was extremely courteous. He knew of Mr Pakenham, and had heard of Lord Palmerston. However, both these men were British. The colonel of the President's cavalry was Mexican. He was also the captain's commanding officer. Adam and Eli would be lodged in prison in Mexico City – in a comfortable cell, of course – until the colonel arrived to check on their story personally.

Adam and Eli were taken under escort to Mexico City. Here, in prison, they found Don Manuel.

The meeting came as a complete surprise to all three men. Adam and Eli were being taken to the prison courtyard for an exercise period when they came face to face with Don Manuel. He was being escorted to the yard from the opposite end of the same corridor.

Adam was the first to recover from their surprise and he shook his head. Don Manuel bit back a shout of recognition, much to Adam's relief. To have it known that the three men knew each other would have been disastrous for all of them. Once in the courtyard, in the bright sunshine, they were able to clasp hands in greeting, in the manner of men introducing themselves to each other.

There were only about a dozen prisoners sharing the exercise period. While the guards took the opportunity to enjoy a smoke and a chat to their colleagues, it was possible for the three friends to walk and talk together without exciting undue interest.

Don Manuel's first concern was that Adam and Eli had been caught attempting a rescue. When they told him the story of their arrest, he agreed they would soon be free. No doubt there would also be a handsome apology. Next, Don Manuel asked anxiously about his wife and Philippe and was greatly relieved to learn they were safe in Texas.

Not until he had satisfied himself on these matters did Don Manuel discuss his own plight. His situation was serious. He had been arrested on Santa Anna's orders, for daring to bring peace overtures from a rebellious province. Normally this would have meant remaining in prison only until someone sufficiently high in Mexican government could be bribed to sign a release form, or until a change of government resulted in an amnesty for political prisoners. However, it seemed that General Santa Anna was determined to bring Don Manuel to trial, charged with 'treasonable activities'. The charge carried a mandatory death sentence.

'Why should Santa Anna want you executed? I thought family ties were stronger in Mexico than anywhere else in this part of the world.' Eli was puzzled.

Don Manuel shrugged. 'I am a reminder to Santa Anna of his defeat at the hands of General Houston. He can never forgive me for being on the winning side at San Jacinto. Perhaps he sees my presence in Mexico as a threat, no matter how remote, to his ambitions. Such considerations weigh heavier with Santa Anna than family loyalties. He intends to take the presidency again very soon.'

'Then we'd better make plans to get you out of here as soon as possible,' said Adam. 'Do you have any friends in Mexico who might help?'

'None who would risk incurring the wrath of Santa Anna. They send in small sums of money to buy a few luxuries, that is all.'

'Then I'll need to enlist the aid of the British ambassador.'

'No.' Don Manuel was adamant. 'Enlisting the aid of a foreign government – any government – on my behalf would strengthen Santa Anna's claims that I am guilty of treason. Securing my conviction and execution would then become a matter of Mexican pride.'

'Then what are we to do?' asked Adam. 'Do you have any ideas?'

'Yes, but it will require money. More than I can raise from my friends here, without exciting suspicion and revealing my intentions.'

'You mean resorting to bribery. Who?'

'Who better than a man who is paid very poorly to ensure I do *not* escape?'

'A prison guard? Do you have a particular one in mind?'

Don Manuel nodded. 'The gaoler in charge of the evening guard. He is a man of middle-age who has married a young and pretty girl, a *mustazzo* – a half-caste – from near the Texas border. She is not happy in Mexico City and would like to go home. He is agreeable, but it seems her family and friends think she has married a rich man, who will one day bring her home and buy a farm for her. He is always telling me such a thing is impossible. What little he earns is very quickly spent. It seems his wife needs constant material assurance that her husband is in love with her.'

'And you think he might help you to escape?'

Don Manuel spread his arms wide in front of him. 'It is possible. He is a great *talker*. If the money is enough ... who knows? In Mexico, guards with far less pressing reasons have helped men to escape.'

'How much do you think would be needed?'

'Not less than five hundred Mexican dollars, not more than a thousand. Too much money will frighten him. But it is impossible for me to get such money.'

'I can get it. *You* sound out the gaoler.'

Don Manuel's eyes showed new hope at the prospect of escaping from the prison that had already held him for more than three months. Suddenly, he gave them an amused smile. 'Do you not find it incongruous that we are planning *my* escape, when you, too, are prisoners?'

'Perhaps. But we hope to be released soon. Once we are free there will be no opportunity to discuss your escape. We need to make our plans while we are here.'

'That is so. The gaoler likes to come to my cell for a game of cards and a drink – bought with my money, of course – before going off duty. I will speak to him tonight.'

'Good. Now it looks as though our exercise period is over for today. We'll talk about it again tomorrow.'

The next day Don Manuel reported that, although the gaoler agreed that helping Don Manuel was the only way he would ever make enough money to fulfil his young wife's ambitions, he was too nervous to make any firm commitment to an escape bid.

'Keep working on him,' said Adam. 'We must have his agreement before Eli and I leave here.'

Adam's hopes were frustrated that same evening. Only minutes after the last meal of the day was distributed, there was

319

a commotion in the long corridor outside the cell shared by Adam and Eli. The door swung open to reveal a cavalry officer dressed in similar fashion to the soldier who had arrested them, but this one was older and had a profusion of gold braid adorning his shoulders. The prison governor was with him, together with a tall, distinguished, fair-haired man and about a dozen soldiers and prison guards.

The fair-haired man was the first to step inside the cell. Extending his hand, he said: 'Mr Rashleigh? Mr Varne? I am Robert Musgrove, vice-consul at the British embassy. His Excellency the ambassador sent me to sort out this ridiculous mistake as soon as we learned you were here.'

His nose wrinkled in distaste at the glutinous substance heaped upon the two tin plates. 'We appear to be not a moment too soon.'

The British vice-consul was immaculately dressed and groomed, and exuded cologne. Adam was very aware of the fact that he and Eli had neither bathed nor had a change of clothing for more than a week.

Behind Robert Musgrove, the Mexican colonel pushed his way inside the cell and bowed as low as the cramped conditions would allow.

'Gentlemen, my humblest apologies. I am Colonel Juan Lozano, Commander of the Presidential Guard. It was I who ordered my captain to investigate reports that two unidentified foreigners were in the country. Of course, your *arrest* was entirely unauthorised. The officer concerned will be punished, I assure you.'

'Are we free to go?'

'Of course, Señor Rashleigh. I have arranged for you to be escorted to the British embassy by my own guard.'

'That will not be necessary. I would much prefer letters from you legalising our stay in Mexico, thus preventing a similar occurrence.'

Colonel Lozano bowed again. 'I will sign them personally and send them to your embassy. I trust you will enjoy the remainder of your stay in our country, señors.'

Outside the yellow adobe walls of the prison, Robert Musgrove held open the door of a carriage for the two released prisoners, explaining that their horses had already been taken to the embassy stables. Then he climbed in beside them.

'Don't be fooled by Colonel Lozano's impeccable manners. He was with Santa Anna in Texas and personally supervised the

320

execution of some of the prisoners taken there. He is a ruthless man who seems to enjoy killing his fellow-men.'

Adam thought that fortune might have smiled on himself and Eli – and Don Manuel. Colonel Lozano had promised to sign the visas issued to the two men he had imprisoned. No Mexican soldier would risk falling foul of a man with such a reputation. Travel through Mexico would be considerably easier for them now; but, first, they had to engineer Don Manuel's escape.

Robert Musgrove took the two men straight to the British embassy, where Richard Pakenham, Great Britain's ambassador to Mexico awaited their arrival. Adam was greeted by the ambassador cordially, but Pakenham expressed keen disapproval for the manner in which Adam had entered the country, and for not informing the embassy he was coming.

Adam explained, without going into too much detail, the nature of their visit and the manner in which they had arrived.

Richard Pakenham frowned uneasily. 'I cannot approve of a British subject becoming involved in such matters. We have friendly relations with Mexico. Texas, on the other hand, is not yet recognised by Her Majesty's government. In the eyes of Great Britain, Texas is merely another of those tiresome provinces that are in a state of permanent rebellion against the government of Mexico.'

'Anybody who believes that is either a damn fool or a Mexican – and I don't think the Mexicans take it too seriously.' Eli expressed his contempt for the British ambassador's detached assessment of the Texan situation.

'H'm! I see.' Richard Pakenham looked carefully at Eli for the first time. He saw a tall, lean, unshaven man, tanned brown from a lifetime spent in the open air, and dressed in stained buckskin jacket and trousers.

Returning his attention to Adam, Pakenham said: 'You must be quite exhausted by your ordeal. Go off with Musgrove now. You'll both be staying at his house while you are in Mexico City. I would like to see you in my office in the morning, Adam. I think we should have a long chat. I expect Musgrove can arrange for Mr Varne to be shown something of the city sights in your absence.'

Robert Musgrove's home was a delightfully secluded house, surrounded by a high wall, only a short walk from the British embassy. The garden was a riot of colour from flowering bushes that filled every corner. Adam took a walk about the gardens before leaving for the embassy the following morning. He noted that the gardeners, in common with all the servants in the house, were all from the British West Indies. There did not appear to be a single Mexican employed in the house or grounds. It suited Adam well. He had already formulated a rough plan for rescuing Don Manuel.

Richard Pakenham was much more relaxed with Adam now there was no third party present to witness his remarks. Being Great Britain's ambassador to Mexico was not the most comfortable of appointments. Revolution and counter-revolution had followed each other in quick succession for as long as anyone could remember. In between, successive governments substituted bankrupt pride for good administration, their tactics based solely on a policy of survival. It made the task of a professional political observer well-nigh impossible. Lesser men than Richard Pakenham would have been recalled after the first revolution, or two. But Pakenham was himself a great survivor, and a diplomat of no mean talent.

When Adam told the ambassador of his hope that Great Britain might intercede on Don Manuel's behalf, Pakenham endorsed Don Manuel's own view that such an attempt would undoubtedly seal the Mexican landowner's fate. It might also undermine Great Britain's present delicate role as mediator between Mexico and the numerous countries currently in dispute with the troubled republic.

Pakenham had recently scored an impressive personal triumph by persuading Mexico to honour the claims of British holders of Mexican government bonds. It was a matter that had soured Mexican–British relations for many years. Pakenham did not want anything to go wrong before the agreement was ratified by all the parties involved.

He was also a realist. In spite of what he had said the previous evening, he agreed that each passing day made the likelihood of Mexico reclaiming Texas even more remote. What was more, Pakenham knew that French recognition of Texas was only a matter of weeks away, and it distressed him to see increasing French influence in a situation that the British government should be manipulating to its own advantage.

To support his views on the matter, he asked Adam if he were in a position to give him a detailed political and economic report on Texas, to be forwarded to the Foreign Office in London.

'I could try, but much of what I can give you is sheer guesswork. On the other hand, you have a man right here in Mexico who knows the land, the politics, and the men behind them. His assessment would be of the greatest value to you.'

322

'I know of whom you are speaking, Adam. Unfortunately, Don Manuel is in prison and I regret I am powerless to help him.'

'*I'm* not.' Adam stood up and began pacing the room. 'Don Manuel will be out of prison before another week has passed, but he'll need a place to hide for a while. Somewhere safe. . . .'

'My dear boy! You're surely not suggesting I offer him asylum in the embassy? That is *quite* out of the question.' Adam's words had shaken Pakenham to his diplomatic core. 'If I brought Don Manuel here, the Mexicans would storm the embassy! Oh, no – and if *you* intend violating Mexican law I would rather know nothing about it, nothing at all. Furthermore it is my duty to warn you against any such action – and I do, *most* emphatically.'

'Yet you agree that the information possessed by Don Manuel might well be crucial in determining Great Britain's future policy towards the whole of the Americas?'

'I don't underestimate the value of such information,' Pakenham began cautiously, 'but. . . .'

'That's all *I* want to hear,' Adam broke in upon the ambassador's guarded deliberations. 'You know why I am in Texas, Your Excellency. I feel it is my duty to obtain this information for Great Britain. How I go about it is entirely *my* business, of course. I will leave a note in your keeping, declaring that you have warned me against breaking Mexican law and have no knowledge of my activities in Mexico. However, I am going to need money – a great deal of money, and all in silver dollars.'

Richard Pakenham opened his mouth to ask a question, but quickly closed it again. The less he knew, the happier he would remain. 'How much do you need?'

'A thousand dollars, and I need it within the week.'

CHAPTER THREE

THE SMALL, nail-studded door set in the great gate of the ancient Spanish-built prison swung open noisily. Gaoler Gomez Bravo stepped through to the street outside and set off to walk home. It was eleven o'clock at night, but the streets were still busy. The saloons and *cantinas* were open, and the noise from within assailed Gomez as he passed by. Once or twice a girl standing in the shadows beside a doorway reached out and tried to detain him, only to be shrugged off none too gently. Gomez Bravo kept his head down and plodded on his way. A man wearing uniform expected to attract attention from such girls. Men in uniform were poorly paid, but they were more likely than anyone else to have at least a few pesetas in their pockets.

There had been a time when Gomez Bravo shared many of his off-duty hours with such girls. When he entered a *cantina* there would always be a girl to call his name and claim his favours. That was before he met Kiata.

Born in an Apache Indian village, Kiata was the daughter of a Mexican woman captive and an Apache war chief. For ten years she lived as an Apache, knowing no other way of life. Then Mexican soldiers raided the village, killing her father and 'rescuing' her mother. Four times Kiata had tried to run back to the Apaches, before finally accepting life in the tiny Mexican village from which her mother had been taken.

The village sprawled along the bank of the Conchos River, north of the town of Chihuahua. Slowly, Kiata learned to be happy here. She spent her days tilling the fields owned by her grandfather, and tending his many goats.

One day, her grandfather dropped dead as he winched up water from the deep well behind the house, and Kiata's brief happiness came to an abrupt end. Kiata's mother had many brothers, and it was hard to eke out a living for growing families on their parched inheritance. There was no room for an unmarriageable sister with a half-Apache bastard.

Kiata and her mother drifted southwards. For a while, Kiata's mother earned money enough for them both in the whorehouses of Chihuahua, but then the soldiers left the town to follow the revolutionary path of their general and Kiata and her mother headed south again.

By the time they reached Mexico City it was Kiata who earned money to keep them both. Kiata worked well at the only vocation for which nature had supplied her with the means. She now had a goal in mind. It was her burning ambition to return to her mother's village and buy more land than was owned by her many uncles. Her mother's early death was a spur to this ambition. So efficient did she become at her calling, it was claimed she once satisfied the needs of half a troop of cavalrymen in less time than it took four farriers to shoe their horses.

Then the army marched out of Mexico City to meet the threat posed by the French in the port of Vera Cruz. Business in the brothels was at its worst. The proprietors of those establishments still in business demanded an exorbitant percentage of the takings from their women. It was now that Kiata met Gomez Bravo. Convinced he was rescuing her from a newly embraced career of vice, Bravo married her.

It was the first wrong decision Kiata had made on the path to achieving her ambition. The uniform and Bravo's boasts had fooled her. She had believed him to be an important man in the Mexican prison service, a man with money enough to help her realise her ambition. When she learned the truth, it was too late.

Gomez Bravo took Kiata and her worldly possessions in marriage. She yielded one with an enthusiasm that never failed to awe him, but he never learned the extent of the other. Not that it mattered. Gomez Bravo was absolutely besotted with his young wife. Even though she kept them short of food and nagged him for not providing more money for her life's goal, he still loved her with a guileless and truly touching passion.

Gomez Bravo was thinking of his wife as he walked home. In his pocket he carried a small gold locket, payment from one of the prisoners for the letters Bravo had smuggled out to the man's wife. Such little 'gifts' always pleased Kiata. There would be no nagging tonight.

Opening the door to the windowless adobe shack on the edge of town that was the Bravo house, Gomez Bravo dangled the locket in front of him as he entered and was rewarded with the anticipated cry of delight.

As Kiata reached out to take the gift, there came a heavy knocking on the door at Gomez Bravo's back. He frowned. Visitors to the house were rare, and none came at such a late hour.

The knocking was repeated and it was more insistent this time. Kiata spoke sharply to her husband: 'Are you going to stand there like a fool while someone knocks down the door? Open it.'

325

Gomez Bravo lifted the latch and was brushed aside by a tall man in Mexican dress. Not until he was inside and had removed his wide-brimmed *sombrero* did the gaoler recognise him as one of the *gringo* prisoners released from prison a couple of days before.

'Good evening, Señor Bravo ... Señora.' Adam inclined his head to the Mexican gaoler and produced a deeper bow for his wife.

'What are you doing here? How did you learn where I live?' Gomez Bravo was frightened. There was a gun tucked in the *gringo*'s belt. Bravo could not remember behaving particularly badly towards this man while he was a prisoner, but after many years in the Mexican prison service there were many things it was convenient to forget. There were also prisoners who held totally unreasonable grudges against those who had kept them captive.

'I followed you home,' replied Adam easily. 'Don't worry, Señor Bravo, I am here to discuss a matter greatly to your advantage. The future of one of your prisoners. I believe Don Manuel Tolsa has already broached the matter of his freedom with you.'

Instead of being reassured, the fear of Gomez Bravo increased. Licking suddenly dry lips, he said: 'There is nothing I can do for Don Manuel Tolsa. I have told him this.'

Kiata Bravo had heard the stranger's words and seen her husband's reaction to them. She was astute enough to realise what was being discussed and felt it better for her to leave the room. There was a lean-to kitchen at the back of the shack and she was making her way there when the late-night visitor called her back.

'Señora, I would like you to remain here and listen to what I have to say.'

'This has nothing to do with my wife.' Gomez Bravo's reaction was a genuinely chivalrous one. He did not want Kiata involved in any talk of an escape, even though it would never progress beyond mere *talk*. Adam had other ideas.

'I think this has a great deal to do with your wife. Don Manuel tells me she is anxious to go home and buy land. Can you give her money enough for this, Señor Bravo? I can.'

Kiata returned. Standing before Adam she looked up at him with eyes that suddenly and painfully reminded him of Tiski.

'Tell me more, señor.'

'No! It cannot be done; it is too dangerous. Don Manuel Tolsa is Santa Anna's prisoner. If it is learned that I have even *discussed* such a matter, I will be immediately shot. You would not wish for this, Kiata?'

'I am offering a thousand silver dollars in exchange for Don Manuel's freedom. That should buy enough land to begin a new way of life.'

'No ...!' Gomez Bravo pleaded with his wife, but she was looking at Adam and seeing the realisation of her dream. A thousand dollars, added to what she already had, would be enough to buy the land, stock and plant it, and still leave plenty to live on during the early, uncertain years.

'Please sit down, señor. Gomez! Where are your manners? Bring some *mescal* from the kitchen. We will talk.'

Gomez Bravo would have continued the argument had not Kiata fixed her gaze on him. He went for the *mescal* and some cups.

Adam had drunk the heavy Mexican drink of *mescal* whilst in Texas, and again on the journey through Mexico with Eli. He had learned to treat it with considerable respect, but Kiata drank it as though it were tea while he explained that Don Manuel had been unjustly imprisoned and why his friends were willing to pay a thousand dollars to secure his escape.

All the time Adam talked, Gomez Bravo sat gazing into his cup, occasionally shaking his head and wishing he had never confided in Don Manuel Tolsa.

'Do you have a plan for the escape of your friend, señor?' The question came from Kiata.

Adam shook his head. 'No. I was hoping your husband might think of a way.'

'It cannot be done, I swear to you. It cannot be done.'

'Gomez, you are being offered a chance to answer all my prayers, to fulfil my life's dream, and you tell me it can't be done? I tell you it *will* be done! You have boasted to me how you smuggle girls inside the gaol for the prisoners, and then smuggle them out again. If you can do that for a prisoner in return for only a dollar or two, you will do *this* for me – for *us*. For our future together.' She hissed the words at him, and Gomez Bravo put his head in his hands and groaned.

Kiata Bravo suddenly stood up. 'You will go now, señor. Do not worry, Gomez will do as you wish. Your friend will be freed.'

She ushered Adam to the door and, once there, whispered: 'Come and see me tomorrow, as soon as it is dark. We will speak again then.'

Outside the house, his wide-brimmed hat pulled low on his head, Adam hoped he had not committed a grave error. He doubted whether Gomez Bravo could be trusted to say nothing of what was being planned. The thought was dismissed immediately. Kiata Bravo had an obsession about buying land in Chihuahua province. She would allow *nothing* to stop her now it lay almost within her grasp. Certainly not her fear-ridden husband.

When Adam returned the next evening, he passed the decrepit adobe shack twice, checking for a possible trap before opening the door quietly and slipping inside.

'You are early, señor.'

Quiet though he was, Kiata Bravo heard him. Her dress pulled down to her waist, she was bending over a bowl of water, rinsing soap from her long black hair. With no hint of embarrassment, she completed her ablutions and rubbed the water from her hair, watching him all the while. Not until she had put a band about her forehead to hold the hair back from her face did Kiata begin to pull the top of her dress up. Before covering her breasts, she stopped.

'You like what you see, señor? Gomez does. So should you, too, I think. When your friend is safely at home with his family you will tell him he owes his freedom to the beauty of Kiata's body.'

'Your husband has agreed to arrange the escape?'

'Of course.' Shrugging the dress over her shoulders, Kiata tied the cord at her bodice and said belligerently: 'You do not see anything beautiful in the body of a girl who is half-Indian?'

'I see too much beauty, Señora Bravo. My wife was Kiowa.'

Kiata's eyes opened wide in a rare expression of surprise. 'My father was called an Apache by my mother's people, but he was a *Kiowa*-Apache. You say your wife *was* Kiowa. She is your wife no longer?'

'She's dead. Shot by a Texan. . . .' He discovered it still hurt to talk about Tiski. 'It's a long story. Too long. Tell me about Don Manuel's escape.'

Kiata had seen the pain in Adam's eyes. 'I am deeply sorry about your wife, señor. I, too, know the pain of having a loved one killed by those who say they are my people. It was never possible to tell them how kind my father really was, or how much I loved him. . . .' Kiata bit back her tears. She had not cried since the day her father had been killed. She would not do so now, in front of a white man she had met only once before.

'The escape . . . ?' Adam urged her gently.

'It will be soon . . . tomorrow night. Gomez must not have too

328

much time to think about it. In the evening when he is on duty he will take me inside the prison to your friend. He will leave me there and bring out your friend, dressed in my clothes. Gomez says he is about my size and it will be necessary only for him to shave off his moustache and beard. Do not worry, señor. The lights in the prison are bad, and he will have a shawl to cover his head. This is the easiest part of all. I shall remain in his cell and make up the bed to look as though your friend is still there. Gomez will go off duty at about eleven o'clock. You will meet him and give him half the money. He will also need a horse.'

'What about you? You'll still be inside.'

'Ah, yes! This is the part that is *not* quite so easy. The night gaoler is a man who enjoys drink far too much. Gomez will have a bottle of good brandy and a few dollars – a present from Don Manuel for allowing him to have a "friend" in his cell, you understand? Do not worry, it happens all the time if a man is wealthy enough to pay for his pleasures. Gomez will stay long enough to see that the night gaoler drinks well from the bottle. When Gomez leaves the night gaoler will come to your friend's cell to see what is happening. It is always so, believe me. When he gets there I will be ready to leave. It will be dark in the cell and your friend will appear to be asleep in his bed. The night gaoler will escort me to the gate. You will be waiting there with the other half of the money, and a second horse. By the time it is discovered that your friend has escaped it will be morning. There will be much argument about who is responsible for the escape, but Gomez and I will be far away by then.'

Adam whistled almost noiselessly through his teeth. 'I don't like it, señora. The plan is too full of "ifs" and "buts", especially for you. Why can't your husband let you out of the prison before he goes off duty?'

'Because, if he did, the night gaoler would discover your friend had escaped as soon as he came on duty. He does his rounds, calls the name of each prisoner and demands an answer. You know this yourself. Our plan will only succeed if the escape is not discovered until morning.'

Adam remembered the nightly rounds by the gaoler, but he was still not convinced that the plan would work. 'It's too risky for you. What if the night gaoler insists on waking Don Manuel? He'll discover the dummy in his bed.'

'All men do not find my charms as easy to dismiss as do you. He will have eyes only for me. But why should you concern yourself of this? Your friend will be free – and you will have paid only half the money!'

329

'I'm concerned because you're doing this on my behalf. Besides, if you're caught, your husband will go to pieces and tell the authorities of my involvement. That would be very embarrassing.'

'You do not fear I might tell who is responsible, if I am caught?'

Adam looked at the half-Indian girl and found once again that she stirred painful memories. 'No. I don't think you would tell them anything.'

'Thank you, señor. Now let us talk about the details of the escape once more. . . .'

They ran over all the details again, discussing times, where Adam and Eli would be with the horses, and a number of other minor, but important, details. When they were both satisfied, Adam rose from his seat and said he would leave and begin preparations for the escape immediately.

'Señor Adam. . . .' He had almost reached the door before she called to him. As he turned, she undid the cord that laced the front of her dress. 'Do you have to leave so soon? There are many hours before Gomez returns. Stay for a while and when you leave you will no longer worry that the night gaoler might take more interest in your sleeping friend than in me.'

Adam felt the stirring of an animal desire rising in him, but such feelings had no place at such a time. 'Your charm is not in doubt, señora, but my memories would make me a poor lover. I will see you tomorrow. Please be careful.'

Kiata nodded and reluctantly retied the cord at her bodice. Given time she could have taught this *gringo* to forget. It would have been an enjoyable experience for both of them. But perhaps it was as well he had not stayed. She would need to direct all her wiles and energies towards Gomez if he was to do all that was required of him the next night.

Gomez Bravo was every bit as nervous as Kiata feared he would be. During the early evening of the escape, the prison governor put in an unexpected appearance at the gaol and announced that he wished to visit Don Manuel in the prisoner's cell.

Escorting the Governor along the gloomy corridors, the gaoler was so nervous he could hardly fit the keys in the locks of the corridor doors. Twice he dropped them, earning an ill-tempered rebuke from the impatient Governor.

Gomez Bravo was convinced the Governor must have heard something of the escape plans. Had he possessed sufficient nerve he would have made his escape from the corridor, leaving the Governor locked inside. Instead, he escorted the head of the prison to what he was quite convinced would turn out to be his own doom.

When the cell door swung open, Gomez Bravo began to back away, but the Governor halted him. 'Wait. My business will take only a few minutes.'

Don Manuel was as surprised as Gomez Bravo. He could also see that the gaoler was close to terror. Rising to his feet, he bowed to the Governor.

'Good evening, señor. I regret I cannot offer you my customary hospitality, but you are welcome to all I have here. Very welcome.'

'I do not doubt you had more comfort in Texas, Don Manuel, but you will not have to endure these miserable conditions for very much longer. I am here to inform you that President Bustamante has personally issued instructions for you to be brought to trial before the end of the month. The charges involve offences against the State. Treason, Don Manuel.'

'So! It has taken my brother-in-law longer than I expected. It is reassuring to know he still leads the President of Mexico by the nose. Texas has nothing to fear while Santa Anna dictates the policies of Mexico.'

The prison governor's manner was icy. 'I have discharged my duty towards you, Don Manuel. You will, of course, be given every opportunity to prepare your defence.'

'Of course. Good evening again, señor.' Don Manuel resumed his seat on the hard bed, and the Governor stalked from the cell, furiously aware that he had been summarily dismissed by his aristocratic prisoner.

Behind him, Don Manuel prayed silently that nothing would go wrong with the plans for his escape. There was not likely to be another opportunity, and a 'trial' would lead inevitably to his death.

Don Manuel was not the only prisoner to have company that evening. More than one man was taken by surprise when a woman was shown to his cell, but none refused the visit. Each prisoner assumed it had been arranged by his friends outside the prison. As a result, the irascible guard on gate duty spent much of the evening shift opening the small door in the prison gate to women as they entered or left the prison.

When Gomez Bravo brought one more along, 'her' face hidden by a dark shawl, the gatekeeper grumbled that the gaoler must be making a fortune satisfying the carnal lust of his charges. When the gate was opened, the shawl-draped figure passed through into the night – and Don Manuel was free!

Eli was waiting in the shadows, and Don Manuel was whisked away with no more than a silent clasp of hands to acknowledge his escape. There would be many more dangers to overcome before he reached the safety of Texas, but for now it was enough to get him to the house of Robert Musgrove.

In the cell vacated by Don Manuel, Kiata lay beneath a blanket on the hard bed listening to the muffled sounds of the prison. Twice Gomez came to see her. Once it was to tell her that Don Manuel was safely out of the prison, and the second time to inform her that the night gaoler would soon be arriving to take over his duties.

Gomez Bravo's nervousness was painful to see, but his concern was not entirely for his own part in the escape of Don Manuel Tolsa. Gomez urged his wife to leave the goal now, before the night guards arrived, thus ensuring her own safety.

Kiata refused. The arrangements could not be changed now, nor should they be. Gomez was well aware of his night-shift colleague's routine. Within minutes of Gomez going off duty, Don Manuel Tolsa's escape would be discovered and soldiers hurrying to arrest the man responsible. Their chances of escape would be slim indeed. This way, Don Manuel Tolsa would not be missed until the morning. By the time they brought back the night men and finally learned the truth, Gomez Bravo and his wife would be many miles away, heading for a remote part of the country where soldiers were seldom seen.

Kiata needed Gomez. Without him she could never hope to reach her old home with a thousand silver dollars. Kissing her husband, she assured him that all would be well. All he had to do was ensure that his colleague commenced his night duty with a bellyful of good brandy. She would do the rest.

Kiata heard the night guards arrive, calling along the dimly lit corridors to the men they were relieving. Rising from the bed she carefully arranged the spare bedding that Gomez had brought to the cell, covering it with a blanket. Viewing it from the doorway, she rearranged it twice before she was completely satisfied. It would fool anyone glancing casually through the grille in the door.

She waited at the doorway for so long that she began to worry that something had gone wrong. Perhaps her husband's nerve had failed him. She dismissed the fear immediately. Had anything gone seriously wrong, someone would have come to the cell by now.

Eventually, Kiata heard voices coming nearer along the

corridor outside the cell and she knew a brief moment of panic. She had not realised there would be *two* men.

The gaoler was accompanied by one of the guards, and she heard the same voice calling into the cells along the passageway, receiving a muffled reply from each one.

She tensed herself, and suddenly there was a flushed face staring at her from the other side of the grille.

'Sh! The señor sleeps. Let me out, I wish to go home now.'

'Oh! Has Don Manuel had enough of you?'

'No man ever has enough of *me*, señor. But he is an old man. I have exhausted him. He sleeps like a baby.'

The two men chuckled, and there was the sound of a key turning in the lock. Before the door swung open Kiata pulled the dress down off her shoulders and loosened the cord that held the front together. She was determined that neither man should look beyond Kiata Bravo.

When the door opened, the glances of both men went exactly where she intended. Swinging her hips provocatively, she walked through the doorway and stood against the corridor wall, looking up at the gaoler. 'Who is going to walk me to the gate and let me out of this stinking place?'

The gaoler hesitated and looked in through the open cell doorway. For one terrified moment Kiata thought he would try to rouse the dummy he thought was Don Manuel Tolsa. Sliding one of her breasts from the dress she began to massage it gently and found she had the full attention of the two men once more.

'Your beds are so hard, señor. I don't know how a man can sleep on them.' Still rubbing her breast, she moved to the middle of the corridor and the men's eyes followed. 'Please, will you take me to the gate?'

'I will take her if you wish to finish your rounds,' the young guard spoke eagerly.

'When you become a gaoler, *you* can make the decisions,' grunted the older man. 'Until then you'll do as you're told.'

To Kiata's relief the gaoler slammed the door of the cell shut and turned the key. 'I'll take her to the gate. You check the rest of the prisoners. Don't trouble me unless you discover something seriously wrong.'

He glared at the young guard, who quickly turned away and moved on to the cell beyond that recently vacated by Kiata.

'You are a man of much authority, señor.' Kiata looked up at the gaoler with feigned admiration.

'I am. During the night I am responsible for every man in the prison. Guards and prisoners. We have some important people here. Colonels – a general, even. They all do as I tell them, or life in here becomes very difficult for them, I can assure you.'

The gaoler opened a door and they began to walk along a corridor illuminated even more sparingly than the others. The cell doors stood open on either side, and Kiata saw two blankets folded neatly on the end of each plank bed.

'Some of the prisoners are from wealthy families. They're not afraid of spending money. A girl like you can make a fortune here . . . with my help.'

The goaler took hold of Kiata's arm and brought her to a halt. 'Of course, you'll need to be nice to *me*, too.' He brought his face down close to hers, and she could smell brandy fumes on his breath. Gomez had performed his task well. Perhaps *too* well.

Crushing her lips with his mouth, the gaoler put a big, rough hand down inside her dress. Kiata stood without moving a muscle, but the gaoler seemed not to notice. He stopped mouthing her eventually, but his hand pulled her left breast clear of the dress and he rolled the nipple between finger and thumb until she gasped with pain.

'Ah! I thought that would excite you. Come in here.' He put his free arm about her and began pulling her towards one of the open cell doorways.

Kiata tried to hold back. 'No . . . please. It's time I was home . . . my baby is waiting for me.'

'It'll wait a while longer. Come on.'

Kiata could have fought the gaoler. She had learned long ago how to deal with a man who was being too rough with her, but it would be foolish to anger him. The only way to freedom depended upon the keys at his belt.

She relaxed and went with him. She would need to draw on her experience to ensure it was all over before the brandy took effect and made him drowsy.

It took even less time than she had dared hope. Five minutes later the gaoler was fumbling clumsily to fasten his trousers, while Kiata pulled her creased dress down about her body, smoothing it with her hands.

The gaoler scowled. 'You'll need to learn some skills if you want to please the men we have in here. They'll expect more than a few minutes' pleasure for the money they are prepared to pay.'

'That will not be hard for me, señor.' Kiata moved closer to him and helped push his crumpled shirt inside the linen trousers. 'With you it has been different. I was not able to control the passion I feel for you. Let me come to you tomorrow night. Just

334

you ... not the prisoners. You can teach me how best to please you. We will make it last all night.'

Her words restored the gaoler's dented pride, and he reached for her again. Kiata slipped out of reach quickly. The last thing she wanted was to arouse him again. 'Not now, señor. I am concerned for my baby. Tomorrow night I will make arrangements, then my thoughts can be for you alone.'

A few minutes later Kiata stepped out into the street. As the door closed behind her Adam moved from the shadows across the street. He was leading a horse. Across the animal's back were slung two heavy bags.

'I was getting worried about you. I expected you long before this.'

'Time moved faster for you than for me, Señor Adam.' Kiata balanced the saddlebags more evenly upon the horse's back. 'Did Gomez leave safely?'

'He was so relieved that his part was over, he couldn't stop shaking. You both have good horses. Be far away by morning – and thank you for all you have done.'

'If you find yourself another Kiowa girl and need a place to settle, come to the river the Kiowa call "Onguapa", and the Mexicans the "Conchos". Gomez and I will be there. If you get lonely, come by yourself.'

Kiata sprang to the horse's back in the easy manner of a Plains Indian and pulled its head around to face away from the prison.

'Travel in peace, Señor Adam.'

'Walk with happiness, Kiata.'

There was a gleam of white teeth in the darkness, then Kiata was gone.

CHAPTER FOUR

RICHARD PAKENHAM wanted to know nothing of Don Manuel Tolsa's escape, and Adam did not discuss it with him. The British ambassador would have thrown up his hands in horror had he known that the man being sought by every soldier in Mexico City had found sanctuary in the house of his vice-consul.

It was an ideal refuge, with no Mexican servants to run to the Mexican authorities with news of Don Manuel's presence. The West Indians employed in the house owed their allegiance to Great Britain, and their contempt for Mexicans was almost equal to that felt by the Texans.

It was assumed by the excited Mexican authorities that Don Manuel was making for the coast. Soldiers galloped along every road that led to the east from the capital, in a vain bid to head him off. As an additional precaution, the houses of all his known friends were being searched.

Adam intended remaining at the house of Robert Musgrove for at least two weeks. By the end of this time the success of the escape would have been accepted by the Mexicans. Don Manuel, Eli and Adam would then slip quietly out of Mexico City and make for the village at the mouth of the river, where Captain Lelean was due to call with his little paddle-steamer.

Initially, Robert Musgrove was a reluctant host, even though Adam had convinced him of the importance of Don Manuel's unique knowledge of Texas. A personal friend of Presidents Houston and Lamar, as well as of most of Lamar's administration, Don Manuel could discuss with great authority the young republic's hopes and prospects, together with the ambitions and capabilities of its leaders. Under Don Manuel's guidance, the vice-consul began to compose a letter calculated to influence Great Britain's policy towards Texas, and so chart the course of history for the whole of the American continent for centuries to come.

Nevertheless, Robert Musgrove lived in a state of constant nervousness, and on the third day he returned to the house visibly shaken. The gaoler who had been on night duty at the time of Don Manuel's escape had been publicly shot for his alleged involvement.

The execution was a tacit admission by the Mexican authorities

336

that the escape had been successful. The night gaoler had been made the scapegoat. With his death the momentum of the pursuit dropped away. It was as though the Mexican government was anxious for the whole business to be forgotten as quickly as possible.

Once Robert Musgrove relaxed, he began to enjoy the company of his 'guest'. It did not take the astute young diplomat long to realise that Adam was right. The value to the British government of Don Manuel's knowledge was inestimable. The talks between the two men became longer, and Musgrove worked late into the night, adding further facts and observations to the lengthy report he was preparing for London.

It was timely. Word was received from Europe that France had recognised the independence of Texas. Instead of using the situation to increase her own power and influence in the area, Great Britain was being left behind.

Don Manuel informed Robert Musgrove that the Texas cotton plantations had the potential to produce high-quality cotton more efficiently than the traditional American cotton States. Indeed, such cotton was already being grown in large quantities, but the markets of Europe were being denied to the Texan plantation-owners. They were forced to sell to America. Sold in Texas for eight cents a pound, the cotton was immediately put upon the American market at three times this sum, and was much sought after. This was only one aspect of Texan trade that was operating to the great advantage of American merchants. Working on a 'take it or leave it' basis, they were able to buy Texan products at rock-bottom prices, at the same time selling the young republic much needed goods at highly inflated rates.

It was an opportune moment for Great Britain to step on to the scene and enjoy unfamiliar popularity, but Don Manuel warned that Great Britain needed to move quickly. If recognition were to be delayed for too long, a wave of resentment would build up *against* Great Britain. It might even cause the issue of annexation by America to be resurrected once more.

It was now that Don Manuel gave Robert Musgrove the startling news that General Houston had spent most of the summer in America as the guest of ex-United States President Andrew Jackson. This great politician's dream had always been to include Texas in a greatly expanded United States. The Mexican landowner warned that, whatever General Houston might say to the contrary, *this was Houston's wish also*. Don Manuel added that it was one of the few issues on which he and the hero of Texan Independence disagreed strongly. Don Manuel

337

had fought beside General Houston for the sake of Texas, not to further the aims of American expansion.

'But Houston is no longer the President of Texas. If he was unable to persuade America to annex Texas after independence, he certainly will not do it now.'

The argument was put forward by Robert Musgrove.

'*Never* underestimate General Sam Houston,' Don Manuel warned. 'In 1841 Houston will be eligible to take office again – and he assuredly will. By that time Lamar will have bankrupted Texas. Effective government, together with law and order, will be on the verge of collapse. The United States will feel obliged to annex Texas in order to protect the many thousands of its citizens resident there.'

Don Manuel disclosed a good knowledge of Great Britain's own problems and suggested that, by recognising Texas, Great Britain would provide herself with a very useful dumping-ground for the starving millions caught up in the famines of Ireland and Scotland. The shrewd Mexican ventured to suggest that access to such a vast force of cheap labour would provide a powerful argument for the anti-slavery lobby to use against Texan plantation-owners. It might even be that the slave-owners themselves would not be so hard to convince. The economic facts were there for them to see. The price of a slave was enormously high, and he had to be housed, clothed and fed. An immigrant worker would be happy with twenty dollars a month and would clothe and feed himself.

Robert Musgrove and Don Manuel discussed at great length the future of Texas, and with it the future of Mexico and the United States. It was becoming increasingly apparent to everyone that the policies of the Mexican central government were alienating many of its own provinces, especially those farthest from the capital. One of the most valuable, both commercially and strategically, was California, commanding, as it did, so much of the Pacific coastline. Lamar was already looking in this direction. If it could take in this western Mexican province, Texas would be a prize that the United States of America could not refuse.

Long before Don Manuel left his house, Robert Musgrove was totally convinced that Great Britain should recognise Texas and force Mexico to face the fact that Texas was gone from her for ever. Musgrove's report to London was a long and reasoned argument of these convictions.

Adam left Mexico City well satisfied. By bringing Don Manuel to the vice-consul's house he had made an important contribution to the mission given to him by Lord Palmerston, almost two years before.

The three men left Mexico City before dawn on a cool September morning. It was an ideal time to travel undetected. The lights of the capital had long been extinguished, but enough Mexicans were abroad to ensure that travellers caused no excitement. They skirted the high-walled gaol where Don Manuel had been imprisoned, and heard the drowsy murmurs of those guards in the watchtowers who had not succumbed to sleep. Soon afterwards they rode through the evil-smelling shanties of the suburbs. Here there were many more Mexicans awake, setting off to prepare houses and work-places for their later-rising masters.

By the time dawn streaked the mountain peaks around the city, the three men had left the Mexican capital behind and were urging their horses to greater speeds. The search for Don Manuel had been called off soon after the execution of the unfortunate gaoler, but Adam would not breathe easily until they were many miles from the capital.

Shorn of his beard and growing a moustache that drooped down on either side of his mouth, Don Manuel was dressed as a Mexican servant; but even an excessively large *sombrero* could not entirely disguise his aristocratic features.

Travelling the same little-used trails along which Adam and Eli had arrived in Mexico City, they bypassed the towns and larger villages, setting up a night camp in deserted countryside whenever possible.

They succeeded in avoiding any contact with Mexican officials until they were no more than fifty miles short of their destination.

Following a narrow track that wound through the hills, dropping steadily towards the coastal plain, Adam and his companions rounded a bend in a steep-sided valley and came upon an encampment of Mexican soldiers. They could not have turned back without arousing immediate suspicion. Slouching lower in the saddle, Don Manuel took the reins of the three spare horses and dropped back behind Adam and Eli.

The camp was filled with sick Mexican soldiers, part of the army of General José Ignacio Pavon. Making its way along the unhealthy coastal plain, the army was bound for Tamaulipas, the Mexican coastal province which shared its northern border with Texas. Encouraged, perhaps, by his neighbours, the army commander-in-chief in Tamaulipas had raised the well-worn banner of revolution against the central government. General

Pavon was on his way to bring his colleague into line. Unfortunately for the government cause, a great many of Pavon's troops had been brought down with fever and sent to the hills.

This information was given to Adam and Eli by the young lieutenant who was in charge of the camp. There was no doctor, the Mexican army rarely bothering with such supernumerary personnel. The Mexican fighting man lived only to serve his country and mattered little to anyone. If he died, there was no shortage of his fellows to take his place.

Suspicious of the *gringos* when they first arrived, the lieutenant's mind had been put at ease by Adam's command of Spanish and the visas signed personally by Colonel Juan Lozano.

While Adam spoke with the Mexican officer and Don Manuel stayed back with the horses, Eli wandered among the unsmiling soldiers. When he returned, his face registered disbelief. In English, he said to Adam: 'I don't believe it – these men have hardly a scrap of food between them.'

Looking accusingly at the lieutenant, Eli said: 'You've brought these men here to die!'

The lieutenant caught the gist of what Eli was saying and he shrugged indifferently. 'Food is scarce. It must be kept for the soldiers who will soon be fighting for Mexico.'

'There's no need for *anyone* to go hungry. There's all the meat you need back in the hills.'

The Mexican lieutenant shrugged. 'We are soldiers, not hunters.'

Eli was disgusted. Speaking to Adam, he said: 'We can't just leave men to die, no matter who they are. Ask this city boy to give me a couple of soldiers with horses. I'll take them back along the trail and shoot something to eat.'

Eli strode away to his horse, and the young lieutenant followed his progress angrily. 'Your friend does not like Mexicans.'

'He'd hardly want to save the lives of your soldiers if that were so,' Adam replied quickly. 'He doesn't like to see men dying unnecessarily, that's all. If you give us a couple of soldiers with spare horses for packing meat, we'll go off hunting.'

Much to Adam's relief, the lieutenant appeared to accept his explanation of Eli's behaviour and gave the orders to his men. Adam would need to have a word with Eli. He had to keep his opinion of Mexican soldiers well hidden until they were safely out of the country.

The mountains in the area had not been extensively hunted, and a sweep through the foothills using the long rifles of Adam and Eli was sufficient to shoot enough game to feed the sick soldiers and their small escort for some days.

That evening, the Mexicans huddled about the cooking-fires with a new mood of hope among them.

'I am most grateful to you, Señor Rashleigh.' The lieutenant carefully wiped grease from his moustache with a handkerchief as he spoke. 'I came here with dying men but will return with soldiers able once more to fight for the glory of Mexico.'

The Mexican officer was looking towards Eli as he spoke, and Adam prayed that the Tennesseean would not be goaded into making an unguarded anti-Mexican remark.

To Adam's relief, Eli did not take the bait. Instead, he said: 'What we've shot today will keep their bellies filled for only two, maybe three days. If you want your men to stay alive, for fighting or for anything else, you'll need to send hunting parties up into the hills every day. I doubt if there'll be any more Americans or Englishmen this way to help you out again.'

In order to fill the hostile silence that followed, Adam asked the lieutenant why his army had not journeyed northwards by sea, so avoiding the unhealthy coastal plain.

'It would be even more unhealthy than travelling by land. The rebels in Texas have bought warships from the United States. These pirates patrol our coasts, sinking unarmed merchant vessels and even fishing-boats. Our own navy is helpless, the ships having been seized or sunk by the French at Vera Cruz.'

Once again the lieutenant was looking hot-eyed at Eli, as though expecting to see some reaction at the news of Mexico's misfortunes. As soon as he was able, Adam drew Eli away, explaining to the officer that they needed sleep as they would be making an early start in the morning. There was no doubting that Eli's earlier scorn had angered the young officer. The sooner they left the camp the better it would be for all of them.

Adam was also concerned for Don Manuel. In keeping with his role as their servant, the aristocratic Mexican ate his meals with the soldiers, most of whom were from poor, ignorant, part-Indian peasant stock. Adam was worried that among such men Don Manuel would have great difficulty maintaining his pretence.

Adam need not have worried. Don Manuel had fought alongside both Mexican and Texan soldiers. He was familiar with both their ways and their manner of speech. Any sign of gentility that he unwittingly displayed was accepted by the soldiers as a result of living and working among rich Mexicans and *gringos*.

So well did Don Manuel play his part, the soldiers shared a

confidence with him that the lieutenant neglected to tell Adam. The Mexican army *was* on its way to the rebellious border province of Tamaulipas, but the soldiers did not expect to wage war against their countrymen. Instead, they hoped to join forces and march on Texas, heading for the rich town of San Antonio. The sick soldiers were anxious to regain their health, in order to collect their share of the loot they had been promised when they took the Texan town.

Don Manuel gave his information to the others as they rode on their way, leaving the lieutenant and his sick soldiers behind. It was another reason for returning to Texas as quickly as possible. Don Manuel's ranch lay in the path of an army advancing upon San Antonio from Mexico.

The following day the three men reached the village where Captain Lelean docked his paddle-steamer, but the quay was deserted. This was not all. They found the riverside village occupied by the army from which the sick soldiers had been detached.

When General José Ignacio Pavon heard that Adam and Eli had arrived, he sent for them to explain their movements. General Pavon was no less impressed than his lieutenant had been by the visa carrying the signature of the commanding officer of the Presidential Guard. He insisted that Adam and Eli dine with him. As they tucked into the sumptuous spread before them, the two men could not help comparing it with the lot of the sick soldiers, sent to the mountains to die, without food or medical assistance.

During the course of the evening, General Pavon made no secret of the fact that his primary objective in leading an army northwards was to attack Texas. He boasted that he expected the raid to bring the rebellious province to its senses.

Don Manuel had disappeared from view the moment they entered the Mexican camp, but Adam was not concerned about him. He had made out well enough among the soldiers in the mountain valley, he would do the same here.

Much later that evening, when Adam and Eli entered the spacious tent graciously supplied for them by the Mexican general, they found Don Manuel waiting for them. He had disturbing news. The suspicions of the lieutenant they had met in the hills had finally overcome his gratitude. He had sent a messenger to General Pavon suggesting that the two *gringos* were probably spies, sent to Mexico by the Texan government.

He hinted that the visas they carried were most probably forgeries.

'There is another problem,' added Don Manuel. 'One of the colonels on General Pavon's staff knows me well. We fought together many years ago. I have aged since then, but not so much that an old comrade will not recognise me. However, all is not lost. General Pavon is not a man given to instant decisions, especially when he has a full belly and has enjoyed too many glasses of wine. He told his aide he will decide what to do about you in the morning. We will need to be gone before he wakes.'

An hour before dawn, Adam, Eli and Don Manuel untied their horses from the picket line and saddled up, telling a drowsy sentry they were going hunting. By the time the camp awoke and General Pavon was told of their disappearance, they were many miles away.

They set up camp in an area of dense undergrowth, close to the river, about ten miles inland from the Mexican army camp. From a sandstone bluff behind the camp they were able to follow the progress of the search-parties sent out by the Mexican general to scour the country. The soldiers did not appear to be taking their task very seriously and they did not enter the undergrowth.

By early evening the soldiers had returned to their camp, and Eli volunteered to ride to the village to check whether Captain Lelean and *Liberty* had arrived. He returned late in the night to report that there was no boat alongside the ancient jetty.

It was the same story when Adam checked the following evening, but he was able to report that General Pavon's troops had begun to cross the wide confluence of the Panuco and Tamesi Rivers. He estimated it would take at least two days, possibly three, to ferry the soldiers and their equipment to the far bank. Once they had crossed, it should be possible for the three men to make a camp closer to the village.

Far more serious was the absence of Captain Lelean and *Liberty*. If something had happened to prevent *Liberty* from making the voyage to Mexico, they would need to make the 550-mile journey to San Antonio overland, risking capture by Mexicans and attack from Indians.

Leaving two thoroughly dispirited men behind him, Eli set off on the evening of the third day to check once more.

He failed to return, and Adam and Don Manuel sat up all night, keeping the fire burning, and risking discovery in the hope that it might guide the Tennesseean to them if he had missed his way in the darkness.

At dawn they packed up camp and were about to set off to search for Eli when he returned, looking relaxed and cheerful.

'*Liberty*'s arrived,' he said before they could put their questions to him. 'It came in yesterday and will be loading all today. Captain Lelean says to come on board tonight. He'll be setting off at first light tomorrow.'

'You've spoken to him?'

'Of course. Where do you think I've been all night? I waited until dark, stole a boat from along the river bank, and went aboard. This morning I rowed back to where I'd left my horse – and here I am. With any luck we'll be back in Texas before General Pavon has his army across the river. They've got no idea of crossing with wagons and equipment. Captain Lelean said they lost two cannon in the river yesterday. Took them both over on the same raft and it capsized. Now, how about some breakfast? I'm starving. . . .'

After the events of the past few weeks, boarding the steamer proved so easy that Adam could not believe they had succeeded until the mooring-ropes were cast off and *Liberty* chugged her slow way out to the open sea.

The three men had boarded the vessel in the same manner as had Eli the previous night. When they were safely on board, the small boat they had taken from the river bank was allowed to drift away down-river. The three men hid among the cargo until the boat left, just in case General Pavon ordered a shipboard search made for them. But the Mexican general was already across the river and a day's ride ahead of his divided army. There was a mission station seventy miles to the north. Here a Mexican general might expect good food, a comfortable room, and the company of men with a knowledge of the arts – and who did not smell of sweat, horses and woodsmoke.

When *Liberty* was two days out from the tiny riverside quay, the engines of the tiny paddle-steamer spluttered to a halt and the vessel was carried slowly but certainly back towards Mexico as it lifted and fell hopelessly with the swell.

While Captain Lelean swore through the open engine-room hatch, the engineer and two Negroes toiled in the heat below. Occasionally the irate engineer, stripped to the waist and streaked with black grease, emerged to offer the equally angry captain a spanner and invite him to do better. All the time the steamer drifted closer to the low-lying Mexican coast.

Once the engine grumbled into life and Captain Lelean was able to take the little paddle-steamer almost a mile from the coast before a cloud of steam escaped from the engine-room hatch and the paddle-wheels stopped turning once more.

Captain Lelean and his Negro crew managed to rig up a makeshift sail. It was not large enough to drive *Liberty* through the water, but it held the vessel clear of the shore.

Towards evening, with the engines seemingly no closer to repair, a plume of smoke was sighted on the northern horizon. As it drew nearer, those on board *Liberty* could see that it was a very large side-wheeled steamer. Then the men saw the single star of Texas on the flag at her masthead. It was the Texan warship *Zavala*.

Zavala hove-to close to *Liberty*, and a shouted conversation between the two captains quickly established the facts of the situation. The Texan captain agreed to take *Liberty* in tow; but, first, the two ships drew together and Don Manuel, Adam and Eli were transferred to the warship.

Don Manuel quickly convinced the captain of *Zavala* of the importance of the information he had. When Captain Lelean signalled some four hours later that his repairs were completed, *Zavala*'s captain cast off the other vessel and set off at speed, heading for the Texan port of Matagorda, two hundred miles away.

CHAPTER FIVE

THE SPEED of the Texan warship *Zavala* was such that sixteen hours after the two vessels parted company *Zavala* dropped anchor off the large town and seaport of Matagorda. This was the nearest port to the inland capital of Austin, and freight lines were already operating between the two towns. It was hoped eventually to run steamboats on the Colorado River between Austin and Matagorda. Flatboats were already being poled down-river to within fifteen miles of the sea, but from here to Matagorda there was a massive 'raft', a series of sunken timbers carried downstream by storms and floods, effectively barring navigation.

The three men were rowed ashore. Purchasing horses, they set off on the 180-mile ride to the Texan capital.

They arrived in Austin, weary and aching, three days later. When Don Manuel's name was conveyed to the presidential office, there was none of the delay Adam had experienced once before. Word of Don Manuel's arrest whilst on a mission to Mexico on behalf of the Texas Republic had aroused enormous sympathy for the Mexican landowner.

Mirabeau Buonaparte Lamar hurried ahead of the orderly in his haste to greet Texas's unofficial envoy. Compared to his predecessor, Texan voters found Lamar a 'dull' president. He headed a colourless administration. With Congressional elections only days away, Lamar's government desperately needed a national hero. Now, at the eleventh hour, Lamar thought he might have discovered one.

Don Manuel had no wish to become a hero – certainly not to bolster up the regime of a president whose policies were bankrupting the country. He wished only for action to be taken immediately to meet the threat posed by the advancing army of General Pavon. When this had been achieved, Don Manuel would brief Lamar on the talks he had held with the British vice-consul in Mexico City, then return to his family and their San Antonio ranch.

To Lamar's credit, he wasted no time in acting upon Don Manuel's information. The rebellion in Tamaulipas was being led by General Antonio Canales, and Canales had already asked for Lamar's help in his struggle against the Mexican central government. Until now Lamar had been reluctant to involve Texas in what was jokingly referred to as 'Mexico's national pastime' – revolution. However, assembled not far from San Antonio were a group of armed men, loosely classed as Texans – and still more loosely engaged in 'frontier protection'. Most were men who had fled from United States law and had earned a living in various dubious ways since reaching Texas. Spoiling for a fight, they were a danger to law and order in the area. Lamar dispatched an army commission for their leader, with orders for him to take his men across the Rio Grande and put his volunteer force at the disposal of General Canales.

By this move, Lamar hoped to defeat the Mexican army of General Pavon before it set foot on Texan soil. It had the additional advantage of keeping the fighting on Mexican soil, with both sides fighting under the same Mexican flag, thus causing Texas no embarrassment.

Having taken action to counter Pavon's threat to Texas, Lamar insisted upon showing off the three weary men at a hastily arranged public dinner that same evening.

Adam hated every moment of the politically inspired social gathering. The more he drank, the more he remembered that it was Lamar who had ordered the attack on Chief Bowles and his Cherokees, triggering off the series of events that had led to Tiski's death. Finally, when one of the assembled members of Congress gave a speech praising Lamar for the manner in which he had brought about the demise of the Cherokee, Adam rose abruptly to his feet and made his way unsteadily from the room.

Behind him, the exhausted Eli slumped in his seat and was ignored by the assembly until his snores began to disrupt the many toasts that were being proposed.

Don Manuel saved the occasion. When he rose to speak, the thunderous applause woke Eli and he was forced to listen while Don Manuel told of the part he and Adam had played in Don Manuel's escape from prison. Smiling at Eli, the Mexican landowner said it was hardly surprising that one of his rescuers had been forced to depart and seek his bed, while weariness had overcome the other, even while he was enjoying the splendid meal served up in his honour by the grateful country he had served so well.

Don Manuel led Eli from the room to a standing ovation from the assembly – but the voters of Texas refused to be moved by the occasion. When the new Congress was voted in, it contained only a handful of Lamar's supporters.

The following day, Don Manuel and Eli rode out of Austin

together. One was returning home to his ranch, the other heading for the Hill Country, and the widow who awaited his return. Adam remained in Austin. President Lamar had unexpectedly asked him to remain in the capital in order to advise the Lamar administration when the expected British move on recognition was made.

Adam was still in the capital when news reached Austin of a battle between the army of General Pavon and the rebel forces of General Canales and his Texan allies. The battle took place some fifteen miles south of the Texan border. It resulted in a crushing defeat for the Mexican government forces. They were routed, losing a third of their number. However, if Lamar thought that the victory would fill General Canales with overwhelming gratitude for Texan help, he was sadly disappointed. Although impressed by the fighting qualities of the Texans, Canales was so appalled by their lack of discipline he could never again make up his mind whether he preferred fighting *with* Texans or *against* them. For many years he was to do both, with varying degrees of success.

Adam was in Austin, too, when General Sam Houston returned to Texas to attend the end-of-year session of Congress. Houston was met outside the town by veterans of his victorious war with Mexico, and his entry into Austin became a triumphant procession.

General Houston greeted Adam as an old friend. As an old friend, he commiserated with him on the death of Tiski. In public, he demanded that President Lamar be brought to account for his callous treatment of the Cherokee and their violent expulsion from land that was theirs morally as well as by virtue of actual physical possession.

It was Houston who suggested to Adam that they ride to San Antonio to visit Don Manuel and the settlers of the Hill Country. Houston declared he wanted to get away from the 'sour taste of politics' and breathe the sweet air of the Texas frontier settlements. The anticipated diplomatic flurry between Great Britain and Texas had not materialised, and Adam agreed.

On the way to San Antonio, General Houston told Adam of his own intended wedding. It would take place sometime in mid-1840. The future bride of the forty-six-year-old ex-President was twenty-year-old Margaret Lea of Alabama. The daughter of a Baptist minister, and deeply religious, she and Houston had met only that year. In true Houston fashion, the ex-President had fallen passionately in love with her. He told Adam, in all sincerity, that once they were married he intended forsaking his

348

old, drunken ways to become a husband of whom Margaret would be proud. Adam smiled at the promise, made when they had opened the second bottle of whisky in their riverside camp, halfway between Austin and San Antonio; but he never for a moment doubted Houston's ability to do *anything* to which he set his mind.

From San Antonio, they sent word ahead to the Tolsa ranch that they were on their way. When they arrived, Don Manuel and Dona Antonia were waiting outside the house to greet the new arrivals. With them were Philippe and Victoriano Benavides, Rosa and Eleanor from Victoria.

They were all delighted to see the ex-President, who had long been a friend of both families, but their warmest welcome was reserved for Adam. He was the hero of the moment. Victoriano Benavides pumped his hand before embracing him. Rosa, still as plump as a young puppy kissed him, as did Eleanor. Dona Antonia, in a rare display of emotion, clung to him and wept her gratitude for the return of her husband. Philippe, looking more frail than Adam had ever seen him, gave Adam a warm, shy smile. He had not been well for many weeks, and his condition was giving everyone cause for concern.

Over dinner that evening, Adam was obliged to relate the story of the rescue of Don Manuel, from the time he and Eli set out to the moment the three men returned safely to Texan soil. He made much of Kiata's part in the rescue, emphasising both her personal role and the manner in which she bolstered the flagging courage of her husband.

Dona Antonia murmured that she would burn a candle for the half-breed Apache girl. Adam wondered whether she had reached her village in safety. He also wondered whether Kiata's future would go according to her plans. He decided that the answer on both counts was a firm 'Yes'. Kiata Bravo was a girl who *made* things go her way.

Don Manuel declared he would have liked to have shown his gratitude by giving Kiata and her husband a better parcel of land than they were likely to find in her homeland, but Adam knew it was more than a desire to own land that had driven Kiata on. It was a fierce pride and a need to prove herself to those who had driven out her mother and the young 'Apache bastard'.

Adam looked up to see everyone looking at him and he realised he had been asked an unheard question.

'I'm sorry, I was day-dreaming. Did someone speak to me?'

'It does not matter; it was nothing important. I expect you were thinking about your Indians. . . .' General Houston smiled.

'My Indians . . . ?' Adam began bitterly, then he looked across the table to where Eleanor Benavides sat wide-eyed, her face suddenly pale. He bit back the words he was about to utter. The young girl had experienced all the terror and degradation that was the lot of a prisoner of the Comanche. He could not defend Indians in her presence. Instead, he said: 'The Indians don't belong to anyone, or to any place.'

'I agree.' Victoriano Benavides had misunderstood Adam. 'The sooner the Commanche are all killed, the better it will be for Texas. While you were away they raided not more than five miles from Austin, killing three men and a woman, and carrying off two children.'

Across the table Eleanor Benavides shuddered. Adam tried to put a stop to the conversation, but General Houston had begun talking and it was very difficult to interrupt the ex-President.

'While Lamar pursues his present policy against the Indians you've got to *expect* trouble. He ought to be parleying with them, not sending out boys with guns. The whole business is treated as though it's a turkey shoot. You fight Indians and they'll fight right back – and keep on fighting. Make a treaty with them and they'll keep it. Yes, even the Comanche. You ask Adam. He made a treaty with them on behalf of those settlers in the Hill Country, and it hasn't been broken yet. The trouble with Lamar is he won't talk to Indians and can't tell one from the other. Cherokee, Apache, Comanche, Tonkawa, they're all the same to him. They're *Indians*. He has only one way of looking at them – along the barrel of a gun. Dammit, they are no more alike than, say, an American, a Chinese, a Mexican, a Negro or an Eskimo. We've each got our own ways. What's more, this country of ours belongs to the Indian, too. If we want peace, we need to include them in our plans for the future. If we don't, we'll carry on spending money we haven't got, fighting them – and continue to lose men, women and children who ought to be building Texas into a great country.'

'What would be your solution, General Houston?' The soft-voiced question came from Dona Antonia.

'I hope you mean what *will* my solution be, when I'm President of Texas again.' Sam Houston smiled at Dona Antonia. 'Why, I'll make Adam here responsible for Indian affairs and send him off to make treaties with every Indian chief in the country. Believe me, it would be a wise choice. Adam has already fought or parleyed with more Indian chiefs than most other men have heard of. He's known to them and respected by their people. What do you say, Adam? Will you take on the job for me?'

'I'd certainly like to discuss the matter with you, General – but right now I think we ought to change the subject.' He nodded towards the pale-faced Eleanor Benavides. 'Otherwise, someone I know is going to be troubled by nightmares tonight.'

One look at Eleanor was enough for the sharp-witted ex-President. He immediately launched into a hilarious story about a dozen piglets that had been released at a Governor's ball in Tennessee during his visit there. Minutes later the little girl was laughing as merrily as the other guests seated about Don Manuel's table.

Much later that night, when all the women had retired to bed and General Houston and Victoriano Benavides were having an alcoholic discussion about the future of the Republic, Don Manuel invited Adam to accompany him on a late-night check of the stock-pen and ranch outbuildings.

It was warm outside, despite the lateness of the year, and the moon was shining through a thin veil of high white cloud, providing enough light for the two men to see about them.

Don Manuel walked around the ranch, checking buildings in a somewhat desultory manner. When he reached the roughwood bars of the stock-corrals, he took a long, thin cheroot from his pocket and put a light to it, the sudden flame causing a number of half-broken horses to gallop to the far side of the corral in sudden panic.

'It is a beautiful night, Adam. There are many such nights, here in Texas.'

Adam agreed, but he knew Don Manuel had not brought him from the house to discuss the Texan climate.

'It is a good place to live, especially for a young man. Do you think you will remain here?'

'I don't know. There is nothing waiting for me in my own country, but . . . I just don't know.' Adam was being deliberately noncommittal.

'Adam, I do not know your real reason for coming to Texas, but I am aware it involves far more than you have said. I suspected it when we first met. I became certain when you sheltered me in the British vice-consul's house in Mexico City. There I saw the esteem in which you were held. Yes, I realise your father was himself a diplomat, but that does not explain a great many things. The ease with which you were able to obtain the money to secure my escape – and which I still have to repay to you; the chances the embassy staff took on my behalf. These things were done for *you*.'

Adam started to protest that the British embassy had not been involved in the escape, but Don Manuel waved him to silence.

'It does not matter. I will never mention this to anyone else. I am grateful – deeply grateful. I owe my life to them . . . and to you. Especially to you. Come, let us walk.'

As the two men walked farther from the house, Don Manuel said: 'I am still a Mexican, Adam, just as you are an Englishman. But I am also a Texan. I have fought for Texas. My home and all those I love are here.'

Don Manuel smiled. 'You probably do not realise it yet, but I believe your heart is here, too. One day you will be proud to declare, "I am a Texan". For now it is enough that you and I agree on what is good for Texas. It is the same thing Great Britain wants: an independent country, controlling its own future from within, and strong enough to overcome the ruthless ambition of the United States of America and the crippling corruption of Mexico.'

Don Manuel stopped walking again and for a minute or so he said nothing, the red glow of the cheroot keeping time with his breathing before he removed it from his mouth.

'General Houston is a good friend, but he does not think as we do, Adam. He is a great Texan, perhaps the best we have – *but he is a greater AMERICAN*! I believe his dearest wish is to see Texas become one of the States of America. Serve him well if he asks you – as a friend. But never forget what I have said; it is important for us all to remember.'

Before Adam could think of a suitable reply, Don Manuel was talking again. 'There is one other matter I would like you to think about. I have my life, thanks to you, but I am no longer a young man. I wish to hand over the burden of running this ranch to someone else. I would like you to make the Tolsa ranch your home and take on this task for me. Run the ranch and share its profits with the Tolsa family.'

The offer took Adam by surprise. 'But . . . such a task should fall to one of your own family . . . to Philippe, one day.'

Again Don Manuel was silent for a long time. When he spoke again, both men were glad of the darkness. 'I have always hoped this would be so, Adam. After Philippe's illness I *prayed* that one day he would be well enough to take over the ranch from me. Even when doctors told me Philippe would not survive to reach manhood, I refused to believe them. To contemplate death is hard enough when it comes to a man who has enjoyed many years. There have been few years and little great joy in Philippe's life. Much of the time he has had to battle with pain. Such bravery deserves reward. I try very hard to remind myself that Philippe will one day receive his reward, but I wish the Great God of ours would reward my son in *this* life.'

'Doctors have been known to be wrong, Don Manuel.'

'You have seen Philippe today. Would you say the doctors were wrong?'

Adam said nothing.

'Think of what I have said, Adam. I need help here. Having you here with us would make Dona Antonia and me very happy. It would make Philippe happy, too.'

The following afternoon, Adam was in the Tolsa stables checking his horse, while Don Manuel and the women and girls were resting in their rooms. General Houston and Victoriano Benavides had gone turkey-shooting. Adam decided his horse would need new shoes before he moved on.

He heard the tapping of Philippe's wooden crutch approaching and turned to meet the small, crippled boy.

'Have you seen this horse, Adam?' Philippe stopped at the next stall and put a thin arm through the wooden rails to pat the sleek black animal. The horse put its head over the rails and nuzzled Philippe's neck. For a moment, his expresion was that of the boy Adam remembered from the journey to Texas, when Philippe was stronger.

'It looks as though she comes from good Spanish stock.'

Adam was speaking about the horse, but Philippe suddenly smiled. 'Do you know, those are the exact words used by one of the women at a tea given by President Lamar before we went to Mexico. She was talking about Mamma.'

Giving the animal a final pat, Philippe said: 'You must come and see our latest foal. She'll be better than this one in a couple of years' time. Papa says she's probably the best-bred foal in the whole of Texas.'

'I'd like to find the stableman first. I want my horse shod.'

'You're not leaving us so soon? Aren't you going to stay with us after all?' Philippe could not hide his dismay.

'I haven't decided anything yet, Philippe. Your father has made me a very generous offer, but I want to go to the Hill Country to be alone and think about things for a while.'

'Do you not think it possible to be alone *here*, Adam?' Philippe spoke with a sudden bitterness that took Adam by surprise. 'I sometimes think this ranch must be the loneliest place in the whole world.'

'*You* lonely? There are always dozens of people around you – visitors, relations, your parents, the ranch-hands.'

'Yes, there are many people *around* me, but rarely anyone *with* me. Can't you see, I *want* you to accept Papa's offer, Adam. You are the only one who doesn't treat me as a helpless invalid the whole time. I know I can't do *all* the things other boys do, but one day I won't be able to do *anything*. All I'll be able to do is *remember* – but I need to *do* things if I'm to have anything to remember, and I need to do them soon.'

Turning away and heading for the house, Philippe said in a muffled voice: 'The foal's in the end stall. Go and see her if you want to. . . .'

Adam caught up with Philippe outside, in the bright sunshine. Scooping the boy up, he sat him on the lid of a huge rain-butt sited at the corner of the stables. He was shocked at the lack of weight in the young body, but was careful not to let his feelings show.

'Young man, how badly do you want me to stay and work for your father?'

Tremulously, Philippe replied: 'Now Papa is home with us, I want it more than anything in the world.'

'All right, I'll stay – but only on one *very* important condition.'

'What . . . ?' Philippe tried to contain his joy until he heard what Adam had to say.

'I never again want to hear you talk as though there's no future ahead of you. I'll help you to do all the things every other boy does. You'll ride, shoot, fish, go hunting, and do a hundred other things, but there will always be something more you are *going* to do, one day when you have the time. There has always got to be at least one thing you're looking forward to doing. You promise me this and I'll accept your father's offer.'

It hurt Adam deeply to see the sheer physical effort it took Philippe to draw back his shoulders and try to hold himself erect, but he did it, and held the pose long enough to say 'I promise'.

Adam clasped Philippe's hand solemnly and resisted the urge to hug the boy to him. 'Then we've got a deal. When I've tied up one or two other things I have to do, I'll come and work on the Tolsa ranch.'

CHAPTER SIX

ADAM AND GENERAL HOUSTON rode to the Hill Country with no escort, even though Don Manuel protested that such behaviour was foolhardy for a man of Houston's stature.

The ex-President's reply was typical of the man. 'Don Manuel, the day I can no longer go any place without having half a hundred men along to wet-nurse me is the day I'll head east and retire. Quit worrying; Adam's made peace with the Comanche. I have no worries about them keeping their word. I'm always telling other folks they can rely upon an Indian's promise; I can hardly have it said *I* don't trust them.'

General Houston's brave words were put to the test before the day was out. The two men were riding along a deepening valley that marked the south-eastern limits of Caleb's settlement, when a file of Indians emerged from the woods farther along the valley, following the path towards them.

Both men reined in their horses, and General Houston threw a one-word question at Adam.

'Comanches?'

Adam nodded; he had recognised the man who rode in the van of the Indians. 'They're Penateka Comanches. The warrior leading them is Hears-the-Wolf, a man to be reckoned with. He's a minor war chief now, but no one doubts that one day every Penateka warrior will follow him into battle.'

'Do you think this is a raiding party?' General Houston displayed no nervousness; it was a straightforward question.

'Not with so many women and children along.' The last pony had cleared the woods now. There were many women, some with children seated on their horses in front of them; others were leading heavily burdened pack-horses.

Hears-the-Wolf had seen the two white men. Accompanied by no more than half a dozen warriors, he rode towards them. When he recognised Adam, he appeared genuinely pleased to see him. He jumped from his horse and when Adam did the same the Comanche war chief embraced him. 'I hoped I might meet with you again, Englishman. How is it with you?'

'It is good – and with you?'

'We are not as many as we were, but we hunt, we eat and we

fight. It is much as it has always been. Your wife . . . she was not with the Cherokee when they were driven away by the Texans?'

'She was . . . killed.'

Suddenly, it all seemed to have happened a long time ago. The realisation made Adam feel unreasonably disloyal.

'I grieve for you, Englishman.' Resting both hands on Adam's shoulders, Hears-the-Wolf looked past him to where General Houston had dismounted and now stood by his horse.

When Adam introduced the two men, Hears-the-Wolf shook hands gravely. 'I remember you. My father was a chief. I was with him when he came to Houston to talk to you of peace. It was a good peace, but it did not last long enough. Now we have a peace only here. Too many Comanche warriors die.'

'When I lead my people again the grass shall not grow on the path between us, Hears-the-Wolf. We will have another *lasting* peace and there will be laughter in the tepees of the Comanche once more.'

'By then, perhaps, my people will have forgotten how to laugh. Your new chief sends many soldiers against us.'

'Too much blood is being shed by both sides,' said Adam. 'I spoke to the new chief of the Texans soon after I last saw you. He does not believe it possible for there to be peace between your people and his. It will be better to do as General Houston says. Keep clear of the Texans until he once more leads his people.'

'I will remember, but Muguera is an old man. He cannot wait so long. He wants to make a peace now.'

'Remind him that Chief Bowles was also an old man,' said General Houston. 'It saved neither his life nor his people. Stay away from the settlements. Avoid trouble and when I'm once more in power we'll make a peace that will last for ever.'

'Chief Muguera heeds only the voices that speak in his own head. He does not listen to other men. But I will tell him the words of The Raven. We go south now, to trade with the Mexicans.'

Hears-the-Wolf mounted his pony and waved to the remainder of his party, who had stopped a safe distance away when the warriors came ahead. Raising a hand to Adam, he said: 'Ride in peace, Englishman.'

Adam and General Houston each raised a hand in salute, and the Comanche trading party filed past, the black eyes of the serious Comanche children resting on the two white men until they passed from view.

When the two men resumed their ride, General Houston looked at Adam with undisguised admiration. 'I always dreamed of the day I would meet up with Indians on a frontier trail and have them greet me as a friend. Lamar's a fool for not taking you into his administration. There will be a place for you when I'm back in office. I hope you'll take it.'

'That time's still some way off, General. A lot could happen between now and then. Besides, I've no intention of softening up Indians just to make it easier for your successor to kill off the warriors and drive their women and children right out of Texas.'

'If I thought such a thing would happen again, Adam, I'd move right in with the Indians. It *won't* happen. Texas will never have the curse of another Lamar. The people's votes will make sure of that.'

Adam grunted and said nothing more. Minutes later, General Sam Houston was patting the heads of children belonging to the nearest of the Hill Country settlers.

It was dark when they reached Caleb's cabin. Houston was welcomed as though he were still the President. Two new rooms had been added to the cabin and one was immediately turned over to the unexpected guest.

Word had gone around the settlement that Houston was visiting, and Eli was among the first to come calling. He brought two corked jugs of whisky with him and they showed signs of having been newly dug up from his secret store. Houston had earlier expressed his intention of adopting the cause of abstention, but at the sight of the whisky he declared that such a decision should not be made in haste – and lost no time in sampling Eli's gift.

Irish and Scots settlers were still riding up to the cabin at midnight. Dressed in their best clothes, they self-consciously came up to the rocking-chair beside the fire where Houston sat and gravely shook his hand. Houston, for his part, expressed great pleasure at meeting them all and asked many questions about their progress and their families. He marvelled that it was safe enough for them to come visiting after dark without fear of Indian ambush, and this invariably drew Adam and Eli into the conversation.

Although many settlers arrived, few left. By morning the women and children were distributed about the various rooms of the cabin – eight of them on the sleeping-platform high in the eaves of the room where the impromptu party had almost run its course. The men sat about on the floor in various states of drunkenness. Two were singing softly, each pursuing a different song. Others sat staring before them, glassy-eyed. Most sat about Houston, listening to his stories of how Texas had been wrested from Mexico, and his views on the wonderful future the country held for all its people, whatever their background.

Through the single, unshuttered window, Adam saw the hills to the east of the valley outlined by the roseate shadows of dawn. He was on the edge of the crowd about Houston and it caused no stir when he stood up and headed for the door. Drinking men had been doing the same all night.

Closing the door behind him, Adam stood in the yard for a few seconds and shivered. There was a keen edge to the early-morning breeze. His bags were still in the stable, with his saddle and bedroll. Going there, Adam soothed the startled horses and found the fringed Cherokee coat that Tiski had made for him. Shrugging it on, he walked along the valley to where his own land began.

By the time he reached the grave of Tiski and his stillborn son, day had come. The sounds about him were similar to those he might have heard in the heart of the English countryside. At varying distances, at least three cockerels were vying with one another in a bid to wake the world. A cow, recently parted from her calf, complained loudly and instinctively at the callous separation. From Caleb's yard a dozen half-grown pigs squealed in bad-tempered impatience as they waited for the door in their overcrowded sty to be thrown open. Aromatic woodsmoke poured from the chimney of Caleb's kitchen and was distributed along the valley in the narrow ribbon of low-lying mist that followed the course of the river.

It all added up to a picture of tranquillity that was at odds with the manner of Tiski's violent death. Adam looked down at the narrow mound of earth. He knew it covered the bodies of the girl who had been his wife and the baby who had once squirmed in her belly beneath his touch. But that had been in the cabin of a Cherokee village that no longer existed. It was somehow unreal, belonging to another time, another place.

Adam felt he should make some gesture . . . say something . . . perhaps speak of the new life he was planning. Yet he knew there would be no meaning now in any words he spoke here. This was only the place where the *bodies* of Tiski and the child had been laid to rest. She lived on in the lands that had belonged to the Cherokee; in the wooded canyon where they had spent their honeymoon – and in the recesses of his memory. Here most of all. Adam dropped to his knees to say a goodbye prayer to the girl he had known for such a brief period of his life.

Far along the river, below Caleb's cabin, Nell Plunkett watched the distant figure bowed over the grave. She understood what he was feeling. She, too, had wept over the graves of her family, telling them of her troubles, as though they might still help her. Then, one day, she had kneeled at their gravesides and opened her eyes to see only grass-covered mounds of earth. The comfort she had always gained from them was gone. That was the day Nell knew there was nothing to keep her in Ireland any more. She knew, by the way Adam stood at the graveside of Tiski and his baby, that his own moment of truth had arrived. He had realised it was not Tiski who lay in the grave, but decaying bones that meant nothing. She wondered what he would do now.

She was standing in the doorway of the kitchen when Adam returned.

'There's coffee on the fire, if you'd like a cup.'

Adam nodded his thanks and came inside. General Houston and the men of the settlement were still discussing the future of Texas, but he did not feel like joining them in their drunken policy-making. Three young boys lay beneath a blanket in the corner of the kitchen. Unaccustomed to late nights, they would sleep soundly for another hour or two yet.

Nell poured out two coffees and handed one to Adam. Picking up the other, she stood cradling the mug in her hands.

'What are you going to do now? Will you stay here?'

'I've had a good offer to run Don Manuel's ranch for him.'

For some unknown reason, Adam felt a need to defend his decision. 'It's a wonderful opportunity. I'll enjoy spending more time with young Philippe, too. He's a very sick little boy.'

Nell looked down at her coffee for a long time. When she raised her head again it was not possible to read her thoughts. 'You'll earn more with Don Manuel than you're ever likely to make scratching dirt for a living here. What will you do with your land? You won't want to come here looking after it when you're dressed up in your fine Mexican clothes and hobnobbing with Don Manuel's rich friends.'

'I'll keep the land and buy a few head of Don Manuel's cattle to run there. If he'll let me, I'll put some of his cattle with the other settlers, too, letting them keep, say, every third calf. That way Don Manuel will get a good return on his cattle and have someone keeping an eye on them while the settlers build up their own herds. What with attending to that and visiting Eli, I'll be spending more time here than before.'

'It will be your cows and not Eli that will bring you here. Eli's no dirt farmer; he never will be. I think he knows this. Kathie certainly does. Had she not, she'd have wed him long since. No, he's a man like yourself, Adam Rashleigh. He's sure he'll find the fairies over the next hill. I'm not saying I blame either of you. If I were a man I'd be just the same, so I would. There's more to life than breaking your back scratching a living from the land, and dying the quicker because of it.'

Adam looked curiously at Nell. He had never stopped to think what she might want from life. There was certainly little of *anything* for her here, in Caleb's settlement.

When he asked her, she shrugged off the question. 'What does any girl want? I'd like to live the life I've never known, the sort of life the Tolsas take for granted. But enough of such foolishness. I'm sorry you're leaving the settlement again, Adam. It would have been nice to have you here.' Looking unexpectedly embarrassed, she added hurriedly: 'This valley needs someone like you. Someone with the learning to start a school, and get the people together to build a church. To turn this "settlement" into a "community".'

'Caleb can do all this.'

'No. He *could*, but Caleb is too happy turning this particular part of God's wilderness into the sort of farm he's always dreamed of owning. But I shouldn't be bothering you with such things. Haven't you done enough for us all, as it is? Will you help me carry this coffee to the other room? There's some in there who wouldn't be sobered if they bumped into the Devil himself, so we'd best be making an early start on them. Careful now, it's boiling hot. . . .'

Nell ran to open the door for him as he carried the heavy kettle of scalding coffee into the room where General Houston still talked. His glassy-eyed audience was smaller than before, two of the settlers having slumped to the ground where they had been seated.

Houston greeted the arrival of the coffee with a great roar of approval. 'Gentlemen, I think we are being politely informed that the party is over – and it's not before time. I've talked myself hoarse. It's been a delight meeting you all. Damn it, if I had my time over again, I'd probably be right here with you. . . .'

When the coffee was gone, each of the settlers stumbled from the cabin, helped on his way by a handshake and a slap on the back from ex-President Houston. Outside, they were met by sleepy, bad-tempered children, and sharp-tongued, thin-lipped wives who were aware they would be obliged to bear the burden of the day's chores.

General Sam Houston was still eulogising the qualities of settlers who were 'the backbone of Texas' when he retired to his room to sleep the day away.

Houston remained in the Hill Country for three days, spending the days hunting, and the nights carousing with the dwindling number of settlers who were able to keep up with the pace he set. He might have stayed longer had not a messenger arrived from his friends in the Texan capital. A number of matters were due to come before Congress. The oratory of Houston could turn them to the advantage of his supporters. It was essential that he return immediately.

Eli escorted Houston as far as San Antonio, and the ex-President's passage through the settlement was a triumphal procession. Whatever his presidential prospects elsewhere, General Houston need have no fear of losing the votes of the Hill Country settlers.

Adam remained at the settlement for a while. He wanted to see for himself how many cattle each family holding could comfortably support if Don Manuel agreed with his scheme. There were also one or two essential tasks to be carried out on his cabin if it were not to become a total ruin during his long absences. It had developed a serious leak in one corner of the roof. Caleb had undertaken a number of small improvements in the cabin, he had even made some sturdy furniture, but he had his own cabin and land to attend to. Adam admitted to himself that the cabin really needed to be occupied permanently, but it would have to wait a while yet. He lit a large fire in the hearth to dry things out and set to work.

He was working inside the cabin when he heard a sound outside. Lifting his rifle from where it stood against a nearby wall, he cautiously opened the door.

In front of the cabin, Nell Plunkett was tying her horse to a rail. A basket stood on the ground nearby.

'Are friends who drop in for a meal always greeted with a gun?'

Adam looked up at the sun. It was well past midday. 'You won't get much to eat here. I'd forgotten about food.'

'That's what I thought. So I've brought plenty for two.'

She picked up the basket and pushed past him into the cabin. Once inside she stopped and looked about her. 'It's no wonder you're always in such a hurry to leave the settlement. This cabin is a disgrace! I'll come over here and clean it up while you're away. You'll see a difference when you come back again, I promise you.'

'You stay close to Caleb's place. I trust Muguera's Comanches, but they're not the only Indians around. Come to that, there are many white men I wouldn't trust if they met up with a woman on her own.'

'And what makes you think you have the right to tell me where I should go, and what I should be doing? Who do you think went off and shot the turkey I've cooked for you?' Nell Plunkett gave him a sidelong glance as she brushed off a dusty and littered table to put the basket down. 'Don't tell me you've forgotten the knife I carry?'

Adam gave her a wry smile, and she thought he looked tired.

'I haven't forgotten, although I sometimes think the journey from Velasco must have happened to someone else.'

'We've all changed since then, Adam – become bigger, somehow. This country does that to a person.'

As she talked, Nell Plunkett took food from the basket. As well as a fair-sized turkey, there were potatoes that had been wrapped in mud and baked whole, sweetcorn, and a loaf of oven-baked bread.

The food tasted as good as it looked, and when Adam produced a jug of whisky that had been buried behind the cabin on one of his earlier visits the meal became a feast. Yet Adam could not help wondering why Nell had taken the trouble to bring the meal to him.

They were seated on crude benches set either side of a rough-hewn plank table when Adam put the question to her. Her grey eyes looked across the table steadily at him for a few moments, as though she were making up her mind whether to give him a reply.

'I brought it because I didn't think anyone else would bring you a meal. Do you realise that everyone else in this settlement has someone to think about and care for? Husbands, wives, children – mothers or fathers? Even poor Peggy has someone now. Only you and I have no one. That's not to say no one cares what happens to us, for they do. Yet if we stood back and said nothing it might be days before anyone even noticed. At least, that's how it seems to me sometimes.'

Nell's shrug and quick smile were meant to be nonchalant, but they did not quite succeed.

Adam suddenly realised that Nell, whom he had always regarded as probably the most confident and self-sufficient girl he had ever met, was desperately lonely. The realisation came as a shock.

Nell watched his expression change and she stood up abruptly. 'I'm just being foolish. You can keep the remainder of the food, but I'll take the basket back with me. It belongs to Eileen.'

She turned to go, but Adam was on his feet and he reached out and grasped her arm.

'Wait, Nell. You're right. We *are* alike, you and I, even though we come from opposite sides of the Irish Channel. We've both suffered the effects of violence and bigotry. Yet I never realised you felt lonely, too. You've always seemed so self-assured.' He smiled fleetingly. 'Carrying a knife probably does that for a girl.'

Without taking her eyes from his face, Nell stooped and hitched up her skirt. Taking the wicked-looking little knife from its sheath, she held it out to him, handle foremost, without saying a word.

As Adam struggled to grasp the full implications of her action, they both heard the drumming of hoofs on the ground outside, then a young voice was shouting Adam's name.

The knife was immediately returned to its hiding-place and Adam ran to the door, picking up his gun along the way.

Outside, a heavily perspiring young man pulled his pony to a halt. It was Gilpin McCulloch. His family lived on the edge of the settlement.

'It's Indians – Comanches. There's been a fight.'

'With settlers?'

To Adam's great relief, the boy shook his head vigorously. 'No, there was some shooting across the creek from our place and we saw the Indians crossing just afterwards. Some were hurt. Pa sent me to Mr Ryan's house with Ma and my sisters while he went to warn some of the others. Mr Ryan told me to come here and tell you.'

Adam was already unfastening the reins of Nell's horse. Calling to her, he said: 'You catch my horse. The two of you ride to Caleb's place – and stay there. Load all the guns you can find, just in case. . . .'

At the Ryan cabin, Adam saw confirmation that Caleb was looked upon as the natural leader of the settlement. Those families who did not feel secure within the walls of their own cabins had flocked here to the stockade, seeking safety.

From the father of Gilpin McCulloch, Adam learned more of what had happened. The Indians fleeing across the creek appeared to have been mostly women and children, some of them obviously hurt. There was some shooting still going on behind them, but because of the trees the Scots settler had not been able to see what was happening.

It sounded to Adam as though Hears-the-Wolf and his party had run into trouble. The last thing the settlers wanted was to have the fight spill over on to their lands. If Comanches were killed here, it would mean the end of the treaty.

There were eight men at the cabin now. Adam said he wanted six to come with him. The other two would remain behind. With the older boys and women it should be enough to beat off all but the largest war-party, but Adam did not believe the settlers would need to fight – unless he failed to reach the creek in time.

Caleb was one of the men Adam took with him. He might be needed to ensure that the other settlers followed Adam's lead.

The Indian women and children were waiting among the trees about a mile on the settlement side of the creek. When they saw the mounted men bearing down on them, they scattered. Without pausing, Adam led the armed settlers on to the creek.

He slowed down when he heard a burst of desultory shooting. At the crossing there were a number of Indians crouched among the bushes on the near bank. Another lay on his back, bleeding from a stomach wound. One of the crouching Indians was Hears-the-Wolf. Adam advanced slowly, his hand held up, palm forward. Even so, he would have been shot by the Indians had Hears-the-Wolf not spoken sharply to his warriors.

'What's happening?' Adam asked the question in Spanish as one of the Comanches fired across the river, although there was no one to be seen there.

'We had traded and were returning when we met some Texans.' Hears-the-Wolf held up ten fingers, then three more. 'They did not come close, but shot from afar. They killed three horses and two women. We made for the creek but they followed. We lost another woman, and three of my warriors have been wounded. One will die soon. We can hold them off here for a while, but we need powder and shot. We are not at war with you. You will give us what we need?'

Adam shook his head. 'I'll not give you powder and shot to kill Texans, but I will prevent the Texans from killing any more of your people. . . .' Even as Adam spoke two shots rang out and a bullet buried itself in the bark of a tree no more than four yards away. 'You and your warriors gather the women together. Get back to your village as fast as you can. I'll stop the Texans from crossing here, but they may ride off and find a crossing somewhere else.'

Hears-the-Wolf hesitated for a moment only. He ordered two of the warriors to pick up the wounded Comanche. Adam winced as the wounded man's companions picked him up and lifted him clumsily to the back of his horse. There was an agonised expression on the wounded Comanche's face, but he never uttered a sound as he rode away, sagging in the saddle, a Comanche warrior on either side of him.

Hears-the-Wolf mounted his own horse. He looked at Adam briefly, then kneed his horse and followed the others. The look was sufficient to tell Adam that the peace still held between Caleb's settlers and the Penateka Comanche.

Adam turned his attention towards the creek. He had the Texans to deal with and knew it was not going to be easy. Another shot from across the creek sliced through the bushes nearby, and Adam shouted: 'Hold your fire! The Comanches have gone.'

He urged his horse forward, at the same time signalling for the armed settlers to line up on either side of him and advance to the creek bank.

There was a shout from across the river, and men showed themselves.

'Have you killed all the sons-of-bitches?'

'I hope you saved some of them Indian girls for *us* to round up.'

The men from across the creek mounted their horses and were halfway across when a shot from Adam's revolver brought them splashing to a startled halt.

'That's as far as you and your men come, Dollar.'

The Ranger captain had been one of the last of the men to ride from the cover of the bushes on the far side of the creek and enter the water. At sight of him Adam had been seized by a blind rage. For a moment he actually had Dollar in the sights of his gun. He had shifted aim only a split second before pulling the trigger.

'What the hell you talking about? We're chasing Indians – Comanches. While we're gabbing here they're probably getting away!'

'You come beyond the middle of that river and you'll have chased your last Indian. I've got reason enough of my own to kill you, Dollar – I'm in two minds about doing it anyway, but right now there's more than a hundred lives at stake. The settlers have made a peace with the Comanche, and it's holding. You start killing Indians here, in the settlement, and you'll be signing a death warrant for every man, woman and child.'

Captain Dollar had recognised Adam and he was well aware of the danger he was in. But he had twelve well-armed Rangers with him and he did not believe Adam would shoot him in front of them.

'We're chasing a Comanche war party. They take no notice of any treaties and have killed their share of settlers already. Get out of the way, Rashleigh. Better still, come with us and make sure your settlers sleep easily tonight.'

Captain Dollar urged his horse forward, and Adam shot the animal from under him, using his short-range rifle.

As the horse dropped dead, Dollar disappeared beneath the surface of the creek. Before he rose above the water again, Adam had swung his rifle along the line of mounted men, threatening each of the confused Rangers in turn. Alongside him, Caleb brought his musket to his shoulder. The other settlers, although as confused as the Rangers, did the same. Pale-faced, Caleb hoped he would not be called upon to fire. He was not certain he would be able to kill any one of the men who sat their horses in the creek.

Sam Dollar came up coughing and spluttering, one of his feet still entangled in the stirrup of his dead horse. He went under twice more before it was extricated. He grabbed for the revolver he kept in his belt, but it had disappeared in the creek.

'Goddam you, Rashleigh! I'll kill you for this. You had no call to shoot my horse. I know you're an Indian-lover, but you've gone too far this time.'

As Dollar splashed his way towards the near bank, he stumbled and fell. When he rose again, Adam warned: 'The moment you touch ground this side of the creek, you're a dead man, Dollar, and at least six of your men will die with you. As far as I'm concerned it's a small price to pay for the lives of the settlers I helped bring here. That's no raiding party you've been shooting up, and you know it well. It's a small trading party, and so far you've succeeded in killing three of their women. The Comanche don't like that any more than we do. Whichever way you look at it, you've won no great victory, even by Lamar's standards – and I'll be explaining my actions directly to *him*.'

Waist deep in the waters of the creek, Captain Dollar came to a halt. He knew Adam had direct access to the President, and he did not doubt he would do exactly as he promised.

Sensing the Ranger captain's indecision, Adam pressed home his advantage. 'If you want to come over here and settle our personal differences, I'll be more than glad to give you satisfaction – but your men stay exactly where they are.'

Adam had turned the confrontation into a personal matter, and Dollar could expect no backing from his Rangers now. He was no gunman, and Adam's skill with a gun was well known. The Ranger captain knew he would lose his life if he accepted Adam's challenge – and Sam Dollar was not ready to die just yet.

366

'I'm paid to come out here and kill Indians, not to settle personal differences with a squaw man. You going to let us get after those Comanches?'

'You've already got the answer to that question.'

'Then, to hell with you and your settlers. Don't come squealing to the Texan government when Comanches come screaming through these hills killing your kids and raping your women. You deserve all you've got coming to you.'

Captain Dollar turned and splashed his way back to where his men waited. One of the Rangers, a big, black-bearded man who sported the same model Colt revolver as Adam, looked at Dollar in disgust. 'You can't leave it there, Cap'n. You get on the bank. I'll go across there and take on the Englishman. . . .'

'Damn you! You'll do as I tell you. We're paid to fight Indians, not settlers.'

It seemed for a moment that the bearded Texan would argue the point. Instead, after a last, malevolent look at Adam, he turned his horse and followed his captain to the far bank. The remainder of the Rangers did the same.

Caleb lowered his musket and breathed a deep sigh of relief. 'You had me worried for a while, Adam. Had there been any fighting we'd have all been killed, for sure.'

Adam said nothing. Reloading his rifle, his gaze was on Sam Dollar as he squelched away from the creek.

Following Adam's eyes, Caleb asked quietly: 'Would you really have shot him, Adam?'

Ramming the loaded rifle into its saddle holster, Adam replied: 'Ask Captain Dollar that question. *He* knows the answer.'

CHAPTER SEVEN

ADAM LEFT the settlement the following day. Eli had returned during the night, having met Don Manuel in San Antonio. The Mexican landowner had told him there was a letter at the ranch for Adam – from the British government.

It was Adam's hope that the letter would give him some news of Great Britain's recognition of Texan independence at last. He was disappointed. The letter was from a minor government official. Adam was requested to look into the matter of land grants sold by an American judge, currently travelling in Great Britain. It was believed they were fraudulent.

The enquiries would necessitate a journey to the capital, but Don Manuel reminded Adam that Christmas was only a few days away. He would learn nothing until the festivities were over.

It was the Mexican custom to give presents at Christmas. Fortunately, Adam had been forewarned and he rode to San Antonio to buy presents for the Tolsa family. Here, he discovered he was a wealthy man by Texan standards. Don Manuel had repaid him the money borrowed from the British ambassador in Mexico. It had already been agreed with the ambassador that Adam should keep the money to cover the expenses he had incurred in the service of his country.

Don Manuel paid his debt with gold coins, American 'gold eagles', and the San Antonio storekeepers offered Adam incredible discounts on their wares in order to gain possession of a few gold coins. The Lamar government had recently made a new issue of paper money, known throughout Texas as 'redbacks'. Already their value had fallen to a quarter of their face value. 'Real' money was at a premium, and the man who possessed gold was a welcome customer anywhere.

For Dona Antonia, Adam bought a pair of delicately worked drop-earrings. They were purchased from a Mexican storekeeper who produced the jewellery on a velvet tray from the stout safe at the back of his store. Also on the tray was a small crucifix on a fine gold chain. Acting on a sudden impulse, Adam bought this also. He tried to tell himself he would probably never give it to anyone, but he knew different. He had bought it for Nell Plunkett. The Irish girl wore no jewellery at all, but he remembered that the first time he had spoken to her, in a Velasco store, she and Peggy

Dooley had been admiring some cheap wooden crucifixes. She was a girl with few material possessions, and Adam smiled in anticipation of her reaction when he offered her the gift.

Adam had already consulted Don Manuel and Dona Antonia on the subject of the present he intended buying for Philippe. There had been initial resistance from Dona Antonia, but when Adam had repeated part of the conversation he had held with Philippe outside the stables she reluctantly agreed to Adam's choice.

He bought Philippe a small-bore hunting-rifle.

Over the Christmas period, Adam would be living in the house with the Tolsas, but when he took up his duties as their ranch manager he would live in a small but very comfortable stone cabin sited in its own garden, only a short walk from the main house. It had originally been built to accommodate the many guests who came to the Tolsa ranch, but over the years new rooms had been added to the main house and it was found more convenient to accommodate them there.

Adam had been invited to furnish the house to suit himself, the furniture being made by the many craftsmen employed on the ranch. Responsibility for making curtains and soft furnishings was shared between Dona Antonia and Maria, Philippe's nanny. Both took their duties seriously. On Christmas Eve, when everyone else on the ranch was preparing for the religious and secular festivities of the next few days, Maria insisted on taking Adam to his new home and showing him the Hopi Indian carpets she had acquired only that day.

Her enthusiasm was infectious and Adam found himself smiling easily for the first time in many weeks as he followed her from room to room, examining her purchases, while she described in great detail what was going to be put on this wall or placed in that corner.

When she turned and caught his smile, she tried to assume the Spanish haughtiness that came so naturally to Dona Antonia.

'Why do you laugh? Is it funny that I should want you to be comfortable here?' Suddenly, she relaxed again. 'It has made Philippe so happy that you are coming to stay here, Señor Adam. For doing this I would work day and night for you. I was beginning to believe I would not have him for very much longer. Now I have hope again.'

'You love him very much, Maria.'

'I first held Philippe in my arms a few minutes after he was born. I was fifteen years old then. It is almost as though he is my own.'

Although Maria had devoted the whole of her life to the Tolsas' crippled son, she was not unattractive. Adam asked: 'You have put Philippe before marriage, Maria?'

'I have put him before *everything*, Señor Adam. It is not because no one has asked me. There is someone . . . but he, too, works for Don Manuel. He understands.'

'Philippe is fortunate to have you to care for him. He needs you. Why, you even manage to make *me* feel happy just looking at you, and it's quite a while since I knew such a feeling.'

'And it was for this I became angry? Please forgive me, Señor Adam.'

'Forgive you for what?' Feeling ·so much older than the Mexican girl, Adam resisted the urge to hug her to him. 'We both care for Philippe. We will be good friends.'

'I would like that, Señor Adam. Knowing about . . . what will happen to Philippe is sometimes a great responsibility. It will help to be able sometimes to share my concern with you.'

At that moment two carpenters entered the house to carry out some last-minute work, and Adam returned with Maria to the main house.

Christmas Day at the Tolsa house began early. The ranch was astir at dawn and the essential chores hurriedly completed. Then everyone changed into their best clothes and a long procession of horses and horse-drawn wagons carried them to the ancient and decaying mission church of San José de San Miguel de Aguayo, for a Christmas service. Adam did not go with the family, preferring to remain behind with those few men left to guard the ranch.

The churchgoers returned in the early afternoon. Maria had been left in San Antonio. It was the one day in the year that she spent with her own family. The men at the ranch could hear the singing and shouting when the convoy of wagons was still a mile away. During their absence, Adam had helped the Mexican guards to set out tables and benches on a cleared patch of ground to the rear of the Tolsa house, in preparation for the meal that would follow.

When the wagons came to a halt, women and children spilled from them and the quiet of the ranch came to an end. Women of all ages began scurrying back and forth from kitchen to tables, while more children than Adam had ever seen on the ranch were underfoot everywhere. Excited Mexican voices were raised in happy anticipation of the feast to come, and music, singing and dancing soon added to the din.

Before long, drinks were passing among the men. There was fiery tequila, the cruder *mescal*, and whisky, too – the last especially for Adam. Whenever he put down his glass, even if only a mouthful had been taken, it was refilled immediately.

Gradually, a semblance of order came to the festivities as the Mexicans took their places at the tables which now sagged beneath the food heaped upon them. Don Manuel was by nature a generous man and he had not stinted today.

The Tolsa family and Adam remained with the employees until there were more scraps than untouched food upon the tables and the drink had begun to take hold of the volatile Mexican ranch-hands. Adam would have stayed with the employees, but Don Manuel would not hear of such a thing. He explained that not all the Mexicans on his ranch had supported the Texan cause in the recent war between Texas and Mexico. An Anglo-Saxon presence at their celebrations, especially by one in authority over them, might spark off an unfortunate incident. Besides, Adam was required in the house.

It was time for the family to exchange presents – and Adam was included in their circle. The Tolsa family had taken this opportunity to express their gratitude to Adam.

From Dona Antonia, Adam received a beautifully engraved gold watch. Inside the case were inscribed the words 'In gratitude, Antonia Tolsa. Christmas 1839'. It was a very valuable watch, probably a family heirloom, but Dona Antonia cut short Adam's thanks.

'Compared with your gift to me – the return of my husband – it is as nothing. I would happily give you all my possessions, and still remain in your debt, Adam.' With this, she stood on tiptoe and kissed Adam affectionately. Such a display of her feelings revealed the depth of her gratitude even more clearly than her words.

Next it was the turn of Don Manuel, and he, too, had something special for Adam. It was a flat box of polished mahogany. Inside, on a backing of dark-red satin, were a matched pair of .44 calibre, six-shot Walker Colts, the very latest design from Samuel Colt's workshops. They were superb weapons, heavier than the Colt revolver Adam already owned, and specifically designed with the horseman in mind. Armed with a pair of these each, ten mounted men would have superiority over more than a hundred cavalrymen – or hostile Indians. Adam balanced each gun carefully in his hand, and Don Manuel was gratified by Adam's obvious pleasure at the present.

In order to receive Philippe's Christmas gift, Adam was

required to walk to the stables, accompanied by the Tolsa family, Philippe excitedly hopping and swinging his way ahead of them. Here Adam was presented with a magnificent Mexican saddle, with silver trappings and Adam's initials worked in the leather with tiny silver studs.

Then, even as Adam was expressing his delight at such a beautiful example of Mexican craftsmanship, one of the grooms led a magnificent black stallion into the stable. Don Manuel said this was a gift from the whole Tolsa family. Bred on the ranch, it was a superb animal. Don Manuel put forward a suggestion that Adam use the stallion to build the finest herd of horses in Texas.

Adam declared that only such an animal could do justice to the saddle Philippe had given to him.

Back inside the house, Adam presented the family with their presents. Philippe was bitterly disappointed that Dona Antonia would not allow him outside to shoot his rifle on Christmas Day. He had to be content with Adam's promise to teach him to use the gun well.

Later that evening, the family were entertained to an evening of song and dance by the ranch-hands and their families. Everyone on the ranch was present, from the oldest grey-haired grandfather to the youngest, squealing, fist-sucking infant, hanging from a tree inside an Indian-style cradleboard, out of harm's way.

The entertainment ranged from classic fiery flamenco to much cruder songs and dances that had much ancient Indian culture in their make-up. The glasses of spectators and dancers were kept well filled and, in the darkness, Philippe clutched his empty gun. He had not parted with it since Adam had given it to him, and he was determined that it would also accompany him to bed.

That night, as Adam made his somewhat unsteady way back to the house, he echoed the general appraisal of the day. It had been the most enjoyable Christmas he had ever spent.

CHAPTER EIGHT

BETWEEN CHRISTMAS and the arrival of 1840, Adam remained at the Tolsa ranch, learning the daily routine. It soon became apparent he would have little actual work to do in running the ranch. There was a perfectly competent foreman who could be relied upon to keep the ranch-hands hard at work and ensure that things ran smoothly.

When Adam put this to Dan Manuel, the ranch-owner shrugged off the observation. 'It was never my intention that you should work yourself into the ground. Yes, the ranch is worked well. It always has been. But what is needed is a young man, like yourself, with young ideas. Someone who is aware of how much this country is changing and who can lay plans for the future. You do not even have to be *here* to carry out such work. You can think of it while you are riding along somewhere . . . anywhere. While you are away you might see something new, something to improve what we have. Why, I feel a new man already, just knowing you are in charge!'

In between his far from onerous duties, Adam taught Philippe to handle his new gun. The small boy mastered it quickly and even managed to use his disability to good advantage. By resting much of his weight on the crutch tucked beneath his arm, he was steadier than most standing riflemen.

Philippe's enthusiasm quickly dispersed all his mother's doubts, and when he hit the centre of a target, with all the family watching, his excitement and delight were shared by everyone.

On the first day of 1840, Adam set out for Austin, to investigate the land purchases made in Britain by would-be Texan settlers. He found the Texas capital in a state of administrative chaos. Part of the documentation in respect of land grants had been brought here, but much was still in Houston, awaiting transportation. The staff of the Land Office was likewise divided between the two towns. As a result, it took much longer than it should have done to discover what the British government wanted to know. Nevertheless, Adam's findings left no room for doubt. The sales of land were fraudulent. The land being sold *had* once been on offer – by the Mexican government – but the offer had not been taken up and the land was withdrawn long before Texan independence.

It had been Adam's intention to complete his enquiries and return to the Tolsa ranch at the earliest opportunity, but word that he was in Austin reached the ears of President Lamar, and he sent for Adam.

When he entered Lamar's office, Adam found the volatile President in a state of high excitement. On the desk in front of him were letters from General James Hamilton, the Texan representative in Europe, and James Treat, who did his best to take care of Texan interests in Mexico.

'Things are finally moving, Mr Rashleigh,' Lamar declared, shaking Adam warmly by the hand. 'Your letters *and* your actions in Mexico seem finally to have awakened Great Britain's interest in Texas. Lord Palmerston has instructed your ambassador in Mexico to seek that country's recognition of our independence. He has also asked General Hamilton to submit a draft treaty for his consideration!' Ushering Adam to a chair, the jubilant President declared: 'Young man, I believe you have rendered Texas a great service – a *very* great service indeed.'

'Good.' Adam wished he liked the man who sat across the desk from him. 'Perhaps you will do me a favour in return?'

'Of course.' Lamar lost some of his enthusiasm, and his face assumed the expression of a man in high public office who had been asked a great many favours. 'What is it you want?'

'Keep your Rangers out of Caleb Ryan's settlement in the Hill Country.'

'Ah, yes!' Lamar brushed an imaginary speck of dust from the desk in front of him and looked impassively at Adam. 'It seems you have little regard for our Ranger companies.'

'I have none at all for Captain Dollar,' retorted Adam bluntly. 'He blunders about the country stirring up as much trouble as the Comanches he's supposed to be hunting. I've made a peace with the Comanche on behalf of Ryan's settlement, and it's holding. But it won't if Captain Dollar starts fighting Indians there.'

'Most settlements welcome the presence of Rangers. Indeed, the presence of Captain Dollar and his Rangers has been instrumental in saving many lives.'

'Change your government's policy and make peace with the Comanche and you'll save many, many more.'

'Unfortunately, neither I nor my administration shares your confidence, Mr Rashleigh, especially when dealing with the Comanche.' Lamar leaned forward and wagged an admonishing finger at Adam. 'This country is expanding ... pushing its borders westward at a pace undreamed of in the United States of

America. We *must* keep the Indians beyond those borders if we are to build a strong and enduring Republic.'

President Lamar smiled winningly. 'You are a man of learning, Mr Rashleigh. Can you tell me of one successful general in history who has advanced and left a well-armed enemy behind him? And let us make no mistake, that is what these savages are, our *enemies*.'

'President Houston seemed to have Indian affairs in hand. He had little trouble—'

'Don't talk of Houston in this office, Mr Rashleigh. Not to *me*. Houston is a blow-hard – a man whose drunken boasts do not accord with the facts. He made treaties, yes, but how many of them were kept? Can you answer me that? I can. I will provide you with documentary evidence, right here in this office, of men brutally murdered, women raped and degraded, children tortured and brutally misused – all this during Houston's so-called "peace". No, Mr Rashleigh, I want to hear nothing of that man's "accomplishments" here. Houston is not looking to build a great nation, one that is well able to take its place among the nations of the world. He wants things to remain quiet, with no breath of trouble in the air. Then he will be able to carry his gift northwards to the United States, and say: "Here is a huge and prosperous territory, a rich land . . . a *mighty* land. Take it as my gift – to my own true country."'

Uneasily, Adam recalled that Don Manuel had more than once issued a similar warning – but Lamar was still talking.

'Texas deserves a better fate. The souls of those heroes who died for Texas *demand* a fitting and enduring memorial: a proud and independent country, stretching from coast to coast, washed by the Atlantic Ocean on one shore and the Pacific on the other. It was with this dream in mind that I had my capital built here. Men complain that Austin is a frontier town. Some of my own Congressmen refuse to come here because they fear Indian attack. They may well be right . . . *now*. But Austin is an expression of my faith in the future of Texas. One day it will be the hub of a great nation. Texans will look westwards from Austin, not with fear but with hope and pride. In order to achieve this *the Indian must go*. Peaceably, if he will – driven before sword and gun, if he will not.'

Adam looked at the Texan president, who had pushed back his chair and now stood before him, flushed by the vision conjured up by his own oratory. Adam did not see him as a great Texan visionary. He saw only the man who had hounded Tiski and Chief Bowles to their deaths.

'You'll also need someone who can make gold from rocks. You won't be able to pay for all this by printing more redbacks – and you're certainly going to need money. Your present policies will require a dozen Rangers to protect every settler who leaves his cabin to till the land. The Indians to the west of here are Comanche, Kiowa and Apache – not peaceable Cherokees. They won't run away, they'll fight back.'

'If it takes a *hundred* Rangers for every settler to build my nation, I'll find them. Texas is expanding westwards – and soon.'

Adam realised it was futile to argue with Lamar. He was a man with a heady dream. The practicalities of his ambitions were for lesser men.

However, the visit to Lamar was not a total failure. When he left the office, Adam carried with him Lamar's promise that any immigrant from Europe who had bought land from the fraudulent agent would be granted an equivalent amount of land in the Hill Country, adjoining Caleb Ryan's settlers. In order to facilitate future settlement here, Lamar asked Adam to guide a government survey team to the area.

When Adam set off with the survey team a week later there were at least four times the number of men needed to carry out survey work, but Adam raised no objections. The surveyors would be in the hills for six months, surveying and pegging the lands to be allocated to future settlers. They would be outside the protection of Caleb's settlement and so would present a target for Comanche raiding parties. It needed to be a strong force if it were to survive.

Adam first took the surveyors to meet Caleb. The faces of the young surveyors brightened considerably when they saw the number of women about the place. President Lamar may have decreed that Austin was the country's capital, but he had not been able to attract any women of marriageable age to the town. It was a rare treat for a man to converse with a woman in the frontier regions of Texas.

The introductions over, Adam rode off to his own cabin, pausing on the way beside Tiski's grave. He no longer felt the closeness of her here, but there was something of the peace he had always found with her. He had also come to realise in recent weeks that Tiski had influenced his way of thinking more than any other single factor in this raw, young country.

That evening, Eli came to the cabin to find him. He had some unexpected news for his friend and partner. The Tennesseean frontiersman and Kathie Casey had confounded Nell's confident prediction by deciding to marry after all.

Adam was delighted, and in response to his congratulations Eli self-consciously explained his decision.

'She knows I ain't the kind of man who'll stay about the cabin, fixing things. I'll have a try at breaking ground and planting, but I reckon she'll end up doing most of the work while I'm out looking at something new or hunting. Kathie knows this. We had a long talk about it, but she says I suit her ways, so we've decided to marry anyway.'

Eli scratched his chin and gave Adam a lopsided grin. 'Besides . . . it didn't seem right, a handsome, strong man like me and a healthy woman like Kathie going to waste. Then there's Dermot. . . . He's at an age when he needs someone about to teach him to hunt, and track, and fight, and do all the things expected of a grown man.'

Adam smiled at Eli's view of the qualities that went to make up a man. He doubted whether he had discussed *this* with his future wife.

The arrangements for the wedding had not yet been made. They had been waiting for Adam's return to the settlement. Eli wanted him for his best man. The wedding would take place at one of the missions in San Antonio. They were run by Mexican priests, few of whom would venture into the Hill Country. Eli intended riding to San Antonio to make all the necessary arrangements and he fell in with Adam's suggestion that they leave together in a day or two, and that Eli should come to the Tolsa ranch first. The post of *Alcalde*, which Don Manuel had held, had been abolished, but the landowner was still the most important man in the area. His support would ensure that the Mexican-conducted wedding went without a hitch.

The next morning, Adam went to Caleb's cabin. Nell was there, helping the other women to cook for the surveyors. She gave Adam a fleeting smile of welcome across the width of the kitchen, but there was no opportunity to speak. The present Adam had bought for her in San Antonio was in his pocket, but he did not want to give it to her in front of the others. It needed the right moment – but it never came.

The survey party displayed little urgency in going about their business. One of their number in particular was taking a more than casual interest in Nell. He was never far from her, no matter where she went, and the settlers watched his attentions with much amusement, referring to him as Nell's 'lovelorn swain'.

The description was never used when Henry Stillwell was around. 'Lovelorn swain' he might have been, but the bearded man was no starry-eyed, callow youth. Originally from the same

Tennessee hills as Eli, Stillwell possessed a similar toughness and quiet confidence in himself. In charge of the surveyors' escort, Stillwell was not a man one mocked to his face.

The morning Adam set off for San Antonio with Eli, he rose early. Saddling his horse, he set out for Caleb's cabin to await Eli's arrival. He rode along the river bank and it was here he surprised Nell. She had been bathing in the river but, hearing the jingling of horse harness, she hurriedly pulled her dress on before horse and rider came into view.

When Adam saw her she was fastening the button at her throat, long dark-red hair lying wet about her shoulders.

They looked at each other in silence for a few moments before Adam said: 'You're up early, Nell.'

She snorted. 'Early, you say? And what time do *you* start the day on your fancy Mexican ranch? I've already cleaned out the ashes from the kitchen fire and lit it afresh. I was just having a bath when you came along; it's the only time when there's no one else about.'

Adam raised an eyebrow. 'I thought you enjoyed being followed everywhere.'

Nell tilted her head to one side and wrung out her hair as though it were a dark, wet cloth. 'You never have understood what I enjoy, Adam.'

'I hope that isn't true. I bought this for you in San Antonio.' Reaching in his pocket, he pulled out the small package containing the crucifix and held it out to her, smiling at her expression of disbelief as she held the package in her hand.

'You've bought something . . . for *me*?'

'It's a Christmas present. I'm sorry it's a bit late.'

Nell held the tiny parcel as though it might blow away at any moment.

'Well, aren't you going to open it?'

Her fingers fumbled with the paper, making hard work of opening the package. When it was eventually achieved, she lifted the crucifix and chain in the air, gazing at it awestruck.

'I haven't seen you wearing one. I thought you might like it.'

His voice sounded unexpectedly gruff, even to him. Nell seemed not to notice. Her gaze was fixed on the crucifix, which mirrored the golden rays of the early-morning sun.

'Put it on.'

'I . . . I don't think I can. You put it on for me.' She looked up at him, her expression unreadable. 'Please, Adam.'

Dismounting from his horse, he took the crucifix and chain from her hands and walked behind her. When he put the chain about her neck, her hand flew up to the crucifix. With her long, wet hair against his hands, he found it difficult to hook the two ends of the chain together. When it was eventually fastened, Nell turned towards him, holding the crucifix out in front of her as far as the chain would allow, going cross-eyed as she tried to look down at the golden cross.

Embarrassed by the obvious delight his gift had given to her, Adam said awkwardly: 'It's nothing special, really.'

She rounded on him immediately. 'Don't you *dare* to say such a thing, Adam. I'll let *no one* say that. It's beautiful. Very, very beautiful.'

Had it been anyone else, he would have sworn there were tears in her eyes when she added: 'It's the first present anyone's ever given me. I'll treasure it always. . . . I promise.'

Suddenly she clenched her fists at her side and her face twisted in anguish. 'Damn you, Adam Rashleigh! Why didn't you give this to me *before* . . . ?'

Having hurled this astonishing remark at him, Nell lifted her skirt and fled to the sanctuary of Caleb Ryan's cabin.

Adam was both puzzled and hurt by her strange outburst, but Eli was ready and waiting for him at the cabin and Adam did not see Nell again before leaving the settlement.

Approaching San Antonio, Adam and the Tennesseean were talking about the forthcoming wedding. Indeed, Eli had spoken of little else since setting out. Suddenly he said: 'Perhaps we ought to tell this Mexican preacher that it might well turn out to be a double wedding.'

'Double wedding?'

'Yes, you know, two brides and two bridegrooms. They used to have them back in the hills, in Tennessee. A preacher might visit only once every year or so, and they saved the weddings up for him. Sometimes there would be more than two couples. I've known as many as five, father and son and mother and daughter among 'em. There was my Uncle Gideon. His wife died the same year as his son was fixing to marry a widow from Sugar Hill. Damned if my uncle didn't up and marry the widow's sixteen-year-old daughter. It caused some confusion when folks were talking about their relationship to each other, I can tell you. As it happened, it weren't worth all the fuss. Before the year was out my Uncle Gideon was a widower again. His wife got took off in childbirth.'

Adam listened to the story with impatient amusement. Eli was a fund of such stories; it was impossible to distinguish truth from fiction.

'I *know* what a double wedding is, but who else is planning to marry?'

Eli cast a surprised glance at Adam. 'You mean you don't know? It's the talk of the settlement. Seems this Henry Stillwell has quite a way with women – with one of 'em, at any rate. Last night he asked Nell to marry him, and she agreed. Funny, really. I always figured she'd set her bonnet in your direction. . . .'

CHAPTER NINE

THE WEDDING of Eli Varne and Kathie Casey was fixed for March 1840, and Don Manuel took charge of all arrangements in his customary generous manner. The wedding and subsequent party would both be held at the Tolsa ranch. The Mexican landowner was even providing them with a honeymoon home. A cabin used by the ranch-hands, half a day's ride from the main house, was being rebuilt and furnished in a suitable fashion for two newlyweds. Despite his protests, Dermot had been told he would not be accompanying his mother and Eli to the honeymoon cabin. Instead, he would be returning to the settlement to be looked after by Nell and the Ryans.

In the weeks preceding the wedding, Adam remained at the ranch. He sent a number of cattle to the Hill Country, leaving the drive to the experienced Mexican ranch-hands.

Don Manuel suggested that Adam also send a horse herd to the settlers on the same terms, but Adam did not deem this wise. The cattle would be reasonably safe from Indians because other meat was readily available, not too far away. A herd of well-bred horses was a temptation that might prove too strong for some of the young Comanche warriors – and Adam was determined to maintain peace in the Hill Country. He wanted to prove to President Lamar that a treaty with the Comanche *would* work.

Adam continued instructing Philippe in the use of his rifle and one day took him hunting. It was more in the nature of a pleasant excursion than a serious hunting expedition, but when Philippe surprised and shot a wild turkey all the hours Adam had spent in tuition were amply repaid. The Mexican escort showered congratulations on the young boy, and he returned home in triumph.

For Adam, the occasion was tinged with sadness. The brief excursion had shown up the deterioration in Philippe's general condition. It would be the only hunting trip he was ever likely to make.

A month before the wedding, word reached the Tolsa ranch from San Antonio that a small party of Penateka Comanches had ridden openly into the town and requested peace talks with the Texan administration. The Indians were met by a Ranger colonel.

Acting on behalf of the Texan government, he agreed to a meeting with Muguera and some of the minor chiefs. The Comanches were to come to San Antonio, bringing with them all the white captives they had in their villages. It was estimated at this time that the Comanches held no fewer than two hundred white women and children as a result of years of frontier warfare.

What was not realised, except by a few men like Eli and Adam, was that these captives were spread among the many divisions of the whole Comanche nation, and Chief Muguera represented only a few bands of the Penateka Comanche. He could not possibly fulfil the hopes of all those who had lost kin to the Indians.

Adam was concerned about the sincerity of the Texans who were to meet Muguera, especially in view of Lamar's declared policy towards them. He would have liked to attend the talks himself, but it was doubtful whether he would have been allowed to take part, and the date fixed for the first meeting with the chiefs was the day of Eli's wedding.

His concern was increased when he paid a visit to San Antonio a few days before the proposed meeting and saw that at least three companies of ill-disciplined Texan soldiers had been brought to San Antonio to strengthen the regular Ranger garrison. He tried to reassure himself with the knowledge that the Comanches would be entering San Antonio under a flag of truce, but it did little to dispel his unease. However, the talks were likely to last some days. Adam determined to ride to San Antonio when the wedding was over to learn what was happening.

The settlers arrived at the Tolsa ranch the day before the wedding. Most came in wagons, but a few rode wiry little ponies, traded from the Comanche. Almost everyone Adam remembered from the wagon train was there, some of the women carrying Texan-born babies in their arms. Nell was with Caleb and his family. So, too, was Henry Stillwell.

The marriage ceremony took place in a long feed-barn, the only building on the ranch large enough to hold all those attending. The walls had been whitewashed for the occasion, and the mud-and-dung floor had been pounded hard and washed until it shone like marble.

There were Indians here, too. A few scattered families of Tonkawa Indians were allowed to live on Tolsa lands. No more than thirty in all, they helped with the less savoury tasks about the ranch, receiving household scraps in lieu of payment. They took a great interest in all the activities of the ranch and were almost as excited about the wedding as everyone else. Those who could, dressed in European clothing, mostly tattered but invariably clean. They crowded about the barn doors, paying so much attention to the ceremony it was difficult to believe they did not understand a single word of what was being said.

At the height of the ceremony, just before the bride and groom exchanged vows, a small Tonkawa boy provided an unexpected diversion. An Indian mother, tired of holding the chubby and apparently naked child in her arms, set him on the ground in a doorway, halfway along the makeshift church building. There was an immediate ripple of mirth among the congregation which rapidly grew until it threatened to disrupt the service.

Looking about him for the cause of the disturbance, Adam looked towards the doorway. There, oblivious to the laughter of the congregation, stood the little Tonkawa boy, not quite as naked as he had at first appeared. A neat bow of blue ribbon adorned the tiny portion of his anatomy that older Indians hid with a breech-cloth. Only when the child's mother was ordered to pick up her young son again was the service able to continue.

The wedding was held in the morning, in order that the newly married couple could join their guests for lunch and still arrive at their honeymoon cabin before nightfall.

They were sent off in style, driving in a buggy belonging to Don Manuel, horse and buggy decorated with flowers and ribbons.

Once the buggy passed from sight, the remainder of the day was given over to singing and dancing. Nell's own husband-to-be remained in close attendance. Once during the afternoon Nell appeared to be heading in Adam's direction, but Rosa Benavides claimed him for a dance and when he next saw her she was dancing with the tall, bearded Henry Stillwell.

About an hour before dusk, the celebrations were in full swing when a Mexican rider on a lathered horse came pounding along the road from San Antonio towards the ranch. He began shouting his news long before he reached the house. As he spoke in Spanish, none of the settlers realised anything was wrong until the music of the Mexican band came to a ragged and discordant end.

'What is it? What's happened?' Caleb put the questions to the ashen-faced and visibly shaken Adam.

'Those damn fool soldiers tried to arrest the Comanches who came to San Antonio for peace talks. Muguera and the other chiefs have been killed. God Almighty! No one will be safe in the settlements now. Get your people together. Ask Don Manuel for an escort – a *strong* escort – and travel home overnight. As soon as you get back, start strengthening the stockade about your place – and build another somewhere else. Get every settler inside, *and make them stay inside*. The Comanche will go all out to avenge Muguera's death. No white family will be safe anywhere. There will be ten dead Texans for every finger on Muguera's hands before this year is out. Lamar wanted a fight to the death with the Comanche; now he's got it. I hope to God the people of Texas remember who is to blame for the slaughter he's brought down upon them.'

Chief Muguera, painted and dressed for council, rode proudly into the ancient town of San Antonio at the head of twelve similarly attired chieftains. All were dressed to impress the white men, with headdresses of buffalo horns and feathers, and the side-braids of their hair liberally adorned with strips of fur. Even the horses were especially decorated for the occasion, with coloured ribbons attached to their manes and tails. Behind the chiefs rode their women and children, bedecked in beaded and painted buckskin finery. There were sixty-five Indians in all. With them they had brought two captives, one a fifteen-year-old white girl, the other a Mexican boy.

It was not the first time Muguera had visited San Antonio. In the days of Spanish rule, the town had been a busy and important trading post for the Indians. They had been welcome here – by the trading community at least.

The citizens of San Antonio took to the streets to witness the arrival of the Comanche delegation. The gasps as the Indians rode by were enough to satisfy the vanity of the most conceited of Indians, and Muguera rode at the head of the chiefs looking neither to left nor to right.

The gasps were not for Muguera. Nor did they signify admiration for the dress of his chiefs, or for the women. They were gasps of anger as the people of San Antonio gazed upon the white captive the Comanches were returning to her people.

Matilda Lockhart had been thirteen years old when the Comanche raiders swooped down from the Guadalupe Mountains and carried her off, together with the four young children of a neighbouring settler. For eighteen months the young white captive had endured rape and torture while forced to serve her Indian captors. When she fell asleep from sheer exhaustion, the Indians adopted the habit of waking her by holding a lighted stick to her flesh, the end of her nose being a particularly amusing target for her tormentors. When she cried from the pain they beat her and threatened her with even more extreme variations of the torture. In the long hours of darkness the Comanche men did things to her that made her come to loathe her body because of the pleasure they took from it.

She rode into San Antonio among the Indians, her dirty and ragged appearance accentuated by the finery of the Indians about her. Matilda's face and body were covered in sores and bruises, the flesh completely burned from the end of her nose.

As soon as the Indians pulled their horses to a halt outside the courthouse where the meeting was to be held, some of the San Antonio mothers darted in among them. Ignoring the Indians, they lifted Matilda Lockhart from her horse and led the weeping girl away. Behind them the young Mexican boy looked in vain for succour from the white men and women standing in an angry crowd about the Indians. They had been expecting the Indians to bring all their *white* captives to the meeting. Mexicans did not count.

As the Comanche chiefs and some of the women filed inside the courthouse, Matilda Lockhart was taken to a nearby house by the women. The Indian clothes were stripped from her and burned and the young girl immersed in a bath of hot water, in order that the shocked and sympathetic women could clean and delouse her. What they saw on her body appalled even the most hardened of the frontier women.

Few young girls would have survived the treatment meted out to Matilda Lockhart by her Comanche captors. The girl herself admitted she had often prayed for death. Her torture was not yet over. She would never again be able to hold her head high among civilised people.

Details of the girl's condition and the ordeal she had survived were passed from the women in the house to the men outside; and, as the crowd grew in size, so, too, did its anger.

Inside the building, the commissioners appointed by Lamar to treat with the Indians caught the mood of the San Antonio citizens. Their faces set in grim lines as an interpreter passed on the price demanded by the Comanche chiefs for the return of the remaining white captives. It was high. There were to be guns and ammunition, blankets, beads. ... As the list grew, the patience of the Texan peace commissioners wore increasingly thin.

Messengers were scurrying into the courthouse now, passing on the information given to the women by Matilda Lockhart. It seemed that Chief Muguera's Comanches had many more white captives – thirteen in the camp from which Matilda Lockhart had come. She said it was Muguera's intention to bring them in one at a time in a bid to secure the highest possible price for each.

The lips of the peace commissioners drew tighter as the crowd

385

outside became noisier. They began to hurl questions at Muguera. Why had he not brought in all his white prisoners as he had promised? Where were the four Putnam children, taken by the Comanches at the same time as they had taken Matilda Lockhart?

Muguera shrugged his indifference. He did not know captives by their white names, only by those given them by his people. No doubt the children were with another band. They could be bought. *All* white captives could be bought – but only if the price were right.

By now the senior army officer present in the courthouse was beside himself with rage. He was a lieutenant-colonel in the army of the Texas Republic, unused to holding council with arrogant Comanche chieftains. His home also happened to be in the settlement from which Matilda Lockhart had been abducted. He knew her family. He decided the charade had gone on long enough.

As his soldiers marched into the courthouse, the lieutenant-colonel told the interpreter to inform Chief Muguera that he and his fellow-chieftains were being arrested. They would remain in custody until all white captives had been released.

The interpreter looked at the lieutenant-colonel in disbelief. The Indians had come in under a flag of truce, fully confident that the truce would be strictly observed. One did not break a promise made to a Comanche. . . .

The officer cut the argument of the interpreter short. The Comanches had been told to bring in their white captives. They had not done so. The interpreter was *ordered* to inform them they were now under arrest.

Hesitantly at first, but with increasing speed, the interpreter fulfilled his duties – and promptly bolted from the courthouse.

Behind him the reaction of the Comanche chiefs was exactly what the interpreter had anticipated. Screaming their anger, they made a rush for the guarded door. The Texan soldier on duty there died with a knife in his chest. The soldiers who had been brought inside the courthouse opened fire. Blinding black smoke filled the room and the crack of musket-fire mingled with the screams of dying men. As the chiefs spilled from the building, the waiting Texans joined in the battle. So, too, did the young Comanche boys who had been amusing themselves playing in the street outside.

The 'battle' was brief, but brutally bloody. When it was over Muguera and every one of the Comanche chiefs were dead, as were all the men in his party. Some of the women and children died, too – thirty-five Indians in all. Eight more were wounded and the remainder taken prisoner. Seven Texans had died, and they, too, had eight wounded.

Excited Texans outside the courthouse walked from body to body, some with guns still in their hands in order that latecomers might know they had killed an Indian. It had been a notable victory. Dead Indians outnumbered Texans by five to one.

The ratio in favour of the Texans was a purely temporary equation. The killing of Chief Muguera would be directly responsible for the slaughter of almost every white captive in Comanche hands and lead to the deaths of hundreds of settlers who would fall before avenging Comanche raiding parties. As a result of the treachery at the San Antonio courthouse the Comanche would never again place their full trust in the word of the White Man.

But the mood of the Texans was still one of euphoria when Adam rode into San Antonio that evening. Those who had been involved in the fight at the courthouse were firmly ensconced in the town's many saloons, relating their part in the fight to men who had ridden in from outlying ranches and cabins, eager to buy drinks for the 'heroes' of the courthouse battle.

Captain Sam Dollar was one of the men receiving his share of adulation. Adam came up against him in a saloon where he had stopped for a drink before making the return ride to the Tolsa ranch. Adam had been to the courthouse and learned the details of the fight. Afterwards he had gone to a stable-yard at the rear of the courthouse and identified a couple of the Indian chiefs he remembered from his visit to the Penateka village of Chief Muguera.

Adam's first instinct when he saw the Ranger captain was to turn around and find another saloon. Instead, a perversity, influenced by his smouldering anger at the events of the day, made him push his way to the bar and stand close enough to the Ranger captain to ensure he would be recognised.

Sam Dollar saw him and faltered in mid-sentence, but he recovered quickly and spoke more loudly than before, in order that Adam might hear every word.

The Ranger captain had drunk enough to drown discretion. When Adam turned his back on him, he stopped the story he had already told a dozen times and said: 'You boys don't want to listen to me any more. Let's hear what an *expert* on Indians has to say about the day's work.'

Adam downed his drink without turning and ordered another.

'I'm talking to you, Adam Rashleigh. Aren't *you* pleased to hear we've killed ourselves a whole bagful of stinking Comanches?'

Adam turned casually to look at Sam Dollar, and men who stood between them backed away uneasily. They were not certain what was going to happen, but they *did* realise this was not a meeting between two old friends.

'It doesn't much matter what I think, Dollar. The damage has been done. The fact that you've killed a few Indians might make you a big man – but that's only here, in San Antonio. You go out to the settlements in a week or two's time and brag of what you've done. I doubt if anyone will give you a drink of water, never mind free whisky.'

There was some angry muttering among the men in the saloon, and Captain Dollar said: 'You think we should have let them go, do you? So they could go back home and carry on treating the white children they're holding captive in the same way as that poor girl they brought in today? Hell, no! We've sent one of Muguera's squaws back home to tell them they'd better release all their white captives pretty damn quick if they don't want us to string up the rest of the Indians we're holding.'

The shouts of approval that greeted Sam Dollar's words left Adam in no doubt of where the crowd surrounding the two men stood.

When the noise died down, Adam said quietly: 'Then you might as well string those Indians up right now. Muguera came in with his chiefs because he'd been promised a safe conduct. Now he's dead, and so are those who came in with him. I know something of the way Muguera did things. He'd have come in with the chiefs, leaving a large body of warriors not far away. They probably brought their captives with them, just in case agreement on the price for their release was reached. Within an hour of that Comanche woman arriving in their camp there won't be one white captive left alive. They'll be hung upside down over a fire and roasted. When they're dead the Comanche warriors will mount up and go out looking for new victims. If any man in this saloon has left a family alone in a cabin somewhere, I advise him to get home quickly and bring them in to San Antonio. Better still, get Captain Dollar and his Rangers to ride out with you and stay put. It's out *there* he'll learn the cost of what's happened today, not in a San Antonio saloon.'

Putting his empty glass down heavily upon the wooden-topped bar, Adam said: 'I'll see you in the settlements sometime, Captain Dollar. We'll all be fighting Comanches now.'

388

CHAPTER TEN

THIRTY SETTLERS DIED in Comanche raids during the three days following the death of Muguera and the Comanche chiefs. Among the first was the newly wed Mrs Eli Varne, killed within twenty-four hours of the San Antonio courthouse battle.

Kathie never stood a chance. Adam had been right: Chief Muguera had a large party of warriors waiting only a few miles from San Antonio. Leading them was the war chief Hears-the-Wolf.

It was Hears-the-Wolf who rode at the head of his Comanche warriors when they swept through the thinly manned outer defences of Don Manuel's ranchland, on the remote distant range.

Eli was an experienced frontiersman, but on honeymoon in an area hitherto safe from Indian attack he was taken completely by surprise in the dark hours before dawn.

Eli's life was inexplicably spared by Hears-the-Wolf, but the price he paid was high. Tied to a tree, he was forced to watch in the light from the burning cabin as warrior after warrior raped Kathie. When they had done with her they hung her over a fire and rode away, leaving Eli to listen helplessly as her screaming faded to a mumbled plea for death.

The fire was still warm when Adam and sixty of Don Manuel's men reached the charred ruins of the cabin. Sagging in the ropes that held him, Eli was babbling incoherently. He would have stumbled to where the Mexicans were cutting down the remains of Kathie, had not Adam knocked him mercifully unconscious with the barrel of his long rifle. Then, sick at heart, Adam supervised Kathie's burial, thankful when loose earth hid her disfigured remains.

Leaving the Mexicans to take Eli back to the Tolsa ranch, Adam rode to the Hill Country to break the news of Kathie's death, and to reiterate his earlier warning to the settlers. He found that the surveyors had fallen back upon the settlement and was grateful that Nell had someone to comfort her over the loss of her sister.

With the help of the surveyors a second stockade was quickly built. Inside both stockades, women and children practised loading the wide variety of weapons owned by the settlers. Eventually they could pack the barrel of a muzzle-loader with an

Indian-killing charge in a matter of seconds – in total darkness if need be.

Dermot Casey carried out the same task with a numb but terrible determination. He had lost his father and his mother to Comanches. He lived for the day when he would be old enough to run away from the settlement, join the Rangers, and dedicate his life to killing Indians.

He would be following in the footsteps of the man who was now his stepfather. Don Manuel sent one of the ranch-hands to tell Adam that Eli had remained at the Tolsa ranch for only one night. Then he rode off to offer his services to the Rangers, as a scout. His duty would be to seek out Comanche villages for the Rangers to destroy.

As the days became weeks and no Indian attack came, the settlers grew restless. Adam urged them not to relax their vigilance, but it was difficult to maintain fear of an unseen enemy when the land they had worked so hard to win was being reclaimed by the wild.

The uncomfortable confinement was becoming irksome, too. Children squabbled and fought, and their mothers longed for their own cooking-fire in the familiar surroundings of the family cabin.

Soon the settlers began to leave the stockades, ostensibly to fetch items from their homes to make life easier inside the stockades. Meeting no Indians, they saw nothing but the beauty of early summer and the lure of their own cabins and land. Many decided not to return.

When these families came to no harm, the remainder, still inside the stockades, were made to feel foolish. They, too, returned home. Adam could hardly blame them. Few had experienced the savagery of a Comanche attack. They had not seen the dangling corpse of Kathie Varne.

Adam never doubted that the Comanche *would* attack the settlement. It was possible they had been waiting for the settlers to abandon the stockades and return to their lonely cabins. He decided to go out on a scouting trip, taking the trail to the west of the settlement, along which the Comanche would come.

Henry Stillwell, the man who was to marry Nell, offered to accompany him. After some hesitation, Adam declined his offer. Stillwell was a reliable and steady man, but he had little experience with Indians – and there had been loss enough in Nell Plunkett's life.

Instead, Adam took Gilpin McCulloch with him. Gilpin had

been just one of many settler youngsters on the boat and wagon train that brought them to their new homes, but in the last two years he had grown into early manhood. Eli had taken Gilpin with him on a number of occasions and been impressed with his natural talent for hunting and tracking. Gilpin was also keenly interested in all things to do with Indians and never tired of questioning Adam about their ways. He was a young man with a cool head, a keen eye and an instinct for survival. He was also young enough to obey Adam's orders without question – and this could make the difference between life and death to everyone in the settlement.

The two men rode westwards until they reached the high grassland plains that lay beyond the Hill Country. Here they proceeded with great caution, lighting no fires and spending most of the daylight hours hidden among the sparse trees, watching the ancient Comanche trading trail.

The very fact that the Comanche had not yet made a move suggested to Adam that they were planning something on a larger scale than the usual series of raids. He was equally certain that when it came the Comanche would come this way, towards San Antonio. They would want the residents of the town to know what was happening – and why.

Adam and Gilpin McCulloch were on the High Plain for a full week before they saw their first Comanches. There were a dozen of them, dressed for war and riding boldly along the trail towards the Hill Country.

In a hoarse whisper, Gilpin McCulloch asked Adam whether they should now ride back the way they had come and warn Caleb and the others.

Adam shook his head. 'Not yet. There's something not quite right about this. They're riding along just a little *too* cocksure of themselves. Stay down – and don't let that horse of yours make a noise.'

Adam was quickly proved right. The clump of trees in which they were hiding was on a hillside that sloped down to the trail. A few minutes later a second band of Indians rode along the low ridge behind them. A third could be seen the same distance on the other side of the trail.

'These are just *scouting* parties,' said Adam when the Indians passed by. 'Stay quiet. I've an idea we're in for quite a surprise.'

It was almost half an hour before Adam's 'surprise' came into sight. It was something neither men would ever forget. There were three columns of Indians, each led by a chief in full war regalia. They rode along and beside the trail, the column stretching back as far as the two white men could see. In an awed whisper, Adam commented that there must be more than a thousand Indians. Hears-the-Wolf was here – but it was not only Penateka Comanches. Metete was here, too, with a greatly increased band of Kiowa Indians. There were also Quahadi Comanches, Wichitas and many more Indians from lesser tribes of the Plains. The San Antonio battle had incensed the Plains Indians, uniting them as never before. Now they were setting out to avenge the death of Muguera and his fellow-chieftains.

'Jesus!' Only when the word came out in a whispered rush did Gilpin McCulloch realise he had been holding his breath. In his excitement, his Scots accent was more pronounced than usual. 'I didna' realise the Comanche could muster so many warriors.'

'Before Muguera was killed in San Antonio, they probably couldn't,' replied Adam grimly. 'What you're seeing now is every fighting Indian from within a hundred miles of Muguera's village. Sam Dollar and those who were with him have done more to unite the Plains Indians than any council held by the Indians' own chiefs.'

'What do we do now?' Gilpin McCulloch saved the question until the columns, stretching for a mile and a half, had passed their hiding-place.

'I'm going to stay with this lot. As soon as it's dark I want you to get back to the settlement and warn everyone. Get them back inside the stockades as quickly as you can. Ride a wide arc around the Indians, but waste no time. This will be the most important ride you're ever likely to make.'

Gilpin McCulloch set off as soon as the moon began to show through a wispy veil of clouds. Adam settled down for the night in a cedar brake within sight and sound of the great war-party. They were holding a council. Adam would dearly have loved to be able to hear what was being said. It might save a great many white lives. By tomorrow they would be in the Hill Country. Hopefully all the settlers would have reached safety by then, but Adam wanted to know which direction the Indians would take after this and, if possible, warn all those in their path.

When the Comanche army reached the Hill Country the next day, it divided into three, each column heading in a different direction. Adam had to make a choice. Any one of the columns could swoop upon San Antonio. He decided to follow the Indians who were heading towards Caleb Ryan's stockaded cabins.

To his great relief, he saw that the stockade was fully manned and the gates securely closed. The settlers were also alert. A long shot from one of the hunting-rifles brought down an Indian pony while the Comanches were discussing their next move. The single shot decided the issue. Giving Caleb's stockade a wide berth, the Indians headed towards the second stockade.

Here they had more luck. The gate stood open. But even as Hears-the-Wolf's warriors swooped down from the hills a number of men fled from the woods nearby, running towards the stockade. It was a wood-gathering party, sent to gather fuel for the cooking-fires in anticipation of a lengthy siege.

All but two of the men made it to safety. The others were shot down and forfeited their scalps, but the Comanches paid dearly for their small success. Adam counted eight Indians downed by the guns of the settlers. The Scots and Irish immigrants had learned to handle their guns well since reaching the Hill Country.

The two scalps were enough to satisfy the war-party, and they stayed only long enough to drive a couple of dozen captured cattle to within a hundred yards of the stockade and slaughter them brutally, within full view of the occupants.

A couple of miles farther on, the column Adam was following met up with one of the others and they turned eastward, as though intending to pass by San Antonio.

Of the remaining three hundred or more warriors there was no sign, and Adam decided it was time the citizens of San Antonio got wind of what was happening not so many miles from them.

In San Antonio he learned that the alarm had already been raised. Someone had seen the missing third column of Indians passing well to the west of San Antonio – heading towards the home of Don Manuel.

Adam tried to persuade the officer in charge of the San Antonio Ranger post to send some of his men to accompany Adam to the Tolsa ranch, but he bluntly refused to move any of his men from the town. With a thousand hostile Indians on the war trail he needed every able-bodied man he could find to defend San Antonio. He had already sent riders to the outlying communities, to muster as many militiamen as could be found, for the same purpose.

Eventually, Adam set out alone for the Tolsa ranch. His hope was that the Indians had given it a wide berth. It was not stockaded, but Don Manuel had a great many armed men. They were capable of inflicting heavy casualties upon even such a large army as the Comanche had.

Adam did not begin to doubt Don Manuel's ability to fight off the Indians until he picked up the trail of many unshod horses merging as they headed towards the main ranch-house. Horrified, Adam realised that the two columns he had been following had circled around San Antonio to meet up with the third column. More than a thousand warriors had converged on the Tolsa ranch!

Then, when he was still three miles away, he saw the smoke from the burned-out buildings and put his horse to a gallop. As he drew closer to the house, his eyes searched for signs of movement about the house. There was none, neither Indian nor Mexican. There were only bodies. A great many bodies. He could see them long before he turned off the trail and rode up to the house.

Adam prayed hard he would not find any of the Tolsa family among the dead. He prayed as he never had before. One of the first bodies he found close to the front door was that of Rosa Benavides, stripped and mutilated.

Moving on he began to pray aloud, a hoarse, desperate plea.

Inside the lounge Adam found Victoriano Benavides and his second daughter, Eleanor, the girl Adam had rescued from the Comanche chief, Ten Trees. She had been shot by her own father. Victoriano had not let the Comanches have her again. His duty done, he had turned the gun upon himself.

Don Manuel was dead in a back bedroom. For some reason known only to the Comanches, the Mexican landowner had been neither scalped nor mutilated. Perhaps the Indian who killed him had been one of the very many people to benefit from Don Manuel's catholic generosity. But the body had been stripped of all its clothing. Lying in naked death, Don Manuel looked frail and vaguely indecent. Adam used a torn curtain as a shroud for the man who had been his friend and benefactor.

There was no sign of either Philippe, his mother, or Maria inside the house, and Adam's hopes began to rise that they had not been at home when the Indians attacked. His hopes were dashed in the wide yard that stretched from the house to the smouldering stables, and his eyes burned with hatred for the merciless savages whose cause he had so often championed against men who felt exactly as he did at this moment.

Dona Antonia lay as though she had been crawling along the ground when death came. She was naked, and the proud Dona had suffered the same fate as the half-dozen women servants who lay lifeless about her.

Maria lay on her back, no more than an arm's length away from Dona Antonia. She, too, was naked and lay with legs wide apart, pinned to the ground by a Comanche lance. Anger fought with grief and pity as Adam thought of what she must have suffered.

Finally, Adam found Philippe. He lay with his back to the

corral, two arrows through him, the crutch that had been so much a part of his life lying beside him in death. Like his father, Philippe had been left unmutilated. It was unnecessary; fortune had mutilated him as successfully as any Comanche.

Looking down at the frail, wasted body, Adam felt a lump rise in his throat. Suddenly, the sheer horror of the carnage all about him overwhelmed Adam. Falling to his knees in the courtyard, he wept over the body of the small boy.

He wept for Philippe, for Dona Antonia, for Maria, and for the generous and kindly Don Manuel. He wept for Kathie, for Yellow Bear and Quaty and their two children. He wept for Rosa Benavides and Eleanor, and he wept for Tiski and his unnamed son. Kneeling in the yard of the Tolsa ranch, he wept until there were no tears left to fall. Then he went in search of a spade and began digging graves.

He was still digging when a company of militiamen came from San Antonio, now no longer under threat of attack from the Comanche army.

Adam remained only long enough to see the Tolsa and Benavides families properly buried; then he turned his back on the ranch and rode away.

CHAPTER ELEVEN

WHEN ADAM JOINED UP with Eli and the Rangers, they followed the wide path of the Comanches and their allies as they plundered the settlements along the length of the Guadalupe River. Along the way the Rangers were joined by militiamen and settlers who had managed to escape the wrath of the avenging Indians. They harried the flanks of the Comanche horde, occasionally killing a warrior who had been foolish enough to detach himself from the main army, but they were never strong enough to launch a full-scale attack against the determined and fast-moving Comanches.

Adam, with some of the others, fought a fierce skirmish with the Indians when they took the town of Victoria and ran off a huge herd of horses. Then they followed all the way to the sea, watching helplessly as the Indians destroyed the small town of Linnville and forced the inhabitants to flee out to sea in their boats.

By now the Indian allies had cut a vengeful swathe through Texas from the High Plains to the coast. They had killed four white men for every Comanche massacred at the San Antonio courthouse. Muguera had been avenged. It was time to go home.

Laden with loot, the Comanches drove three thousand horses ahead of them, and they travelled more slowly now.

Hears-the-Wolf wanted the Indians to head westwards from the coast, reaching the High Plains through the no man's land between San Antonio and the Mexican border. But Hears-the-Wolf led only one of the three Indian bands. The overall war chief was an older and more experienced Comanche chief, Buffalo Hump.

The many victories that had been his since leaving the High Plains had made Buffalo Hump arrogant. He chose the more direct route, passing between San Antonio and Austin, not more than twenty-five miles from the Texan capital.

This piece of bravado proved the undoing of the Comanches and their allies. At one of the creeks flowing into the sluggish San Marcos River, the Texans had finally managed to gather together an army. Adam was with them. So, too, was Eli – and Captain Sam Dollar, together with many more Ranger captains and their men. They were joined by militiamen, farmers, and some regular soldiers led by army general Felix Huston, who assumed overall command of the motley white army.

The Indians were aware of the presence of the Texans, and when they came within sight of the men at the creek they had formed a long battle line, driving the stolen horses before them.

The Texans waited until the horse herd passed by; then, with a great shout and with Eli well to the fore, the Texans charged the Comanches. The horse herd stampeded, many of the Indian mounts went with them and a running battle began that would extend over many miles of countryside, in every direction.

Adam tried to keep up with Eli, but soon found himself fighting Comanches in a soft creek bottom, half-in, half-out of the water. He was shooting at an Indian on his right when his horse began prancing crablike through the water. Adam turned and found himself face to face with Hears-the-Wolf. The Penateka Comanche's face showed no recognition, only a savage hatred as he tried to bring his lance into play.

Adam's first shot knocked Hears-the-Wolf from his horse, the second took him in the head as the Comanche fell face down in the shallow water.

The next few minutes were absolute pandemonium. A large party of Comanches chose this spot at which to cross the creek and here they clashed with a small party of Rangers led by Captain Sam Dollar. Eli was with him.

Sheer weight of numbers drove the Rangers before the Comanches, and many of the Texans were dislodged from their saddles. Adam had dodged one lance and was meeting another Comanche head-on, when a wet and bloody figure rose from the water before him.

It was Captain Dollar.

Afterwards, Adam wondered whether there had been time to remember the part Dollar had played in the death of Tiski. It was doubtful. He was faced with two simple choices. The first was to check his horse and risk being run through by the lance of the Indian bearing down on him. The second was to ride on and trample the Ranger captain beneath the hoofs of his horse. Adam rode on and, as he fired at the Comanche, Captain Sam Dollar disappeared beneath the iron-clad hoofs of Adam's stallion.

The body of Sam Dollar was recovered later. Miraculously, his was the only death among the Texans, although a great many suffered wounds.

Eighty Comanches were killed, and much of their loot recovered. Their victorious sortie through the Texas settlements had turned sour. Never again would they raid deep into settled territory on such a grand scale, although their attacks on the frontier settlements would continue with a terrible ferocity.

Adam rode with Eli to Austin. He felt empty, as though Texas held nothing for him anymore. Perhaps there was nothing for him anywhere. Then, in Austin, he and Eli discovered the Rangers were recruiting a long-range force to seek out Comanches in their homeland. He and Eli were asked to act as guides and they both accepted.

The Rangers, together with Adam, Eli and some Lipan Apache Indian scouts, spent many months deep in Comanche country, riding farther west than any of the white men in the party had been before. With familiar country far behind them, they rode for mile after mile across plains rich with tall grass. It was a vast, rolling landscape such as none of them had ever known before. They destroyed small Comanche villages wherever they found them, leaving no Indians alive. And then one day Adam and the Lipan Apache scouts located a very large Penateka Comanche village in a valley, close beside a river.

The Ranger captain had his men in position well before dawn, with picked riflemen covering the escape route to the river. When the first rays of the sun touched on the tepees of the sleeping Comanche village, the Rangers launched their attack. Eli went with them, but Adam stayed with the men who guarded the Rangers' horses. Many an otherwise successful attack had been turned to defeat by the Comanche trick of striking for the horses during a battle, and this fight was no exception.

At the height of the slaughter that was taking place in the Indian village, the Comanches launched a counter-attack against the horses in a vain bid to draw the main Ranger force away. About twenty Comanches fought Adam and the Rangers who were with him. More than half the warriors died before the attack faltered and fell away.

The one-sided battle lasted for less than an hour. When it ended, more than a hundred Indians lay dead in the remains of their village. The Rangers had lost one man dead, another wounded.

Adam could not share the jubilation of his companions. Many of the dead were women and children, and he remembered watching Cherokee children at play on too many happier occasions. It gave him no pleasure to see them in death. When the flames from the burning tepees began to die down and the task of counting the Indian dead had been completed, Eli threw a small, screwed-up bundle of blood-stained clothing at Adam's feet.

'Here, look at this. It might ease that conscience of yours. I took it off one of the dead warriors.'

When Adam opened out the bundle, he saw a fancy Mexican vest with the Tolsa emblem embroidered on it in silver thread. Adam had seen it many times before, worn by Don Manuel when he went riding.

It made no difference. Don Manuel and the Tolsa family were dead. Killing one or a thousand Indians would not bring any of them back to life. There had been far too much killing.

The battle at the Comanche village was the culmination of the successful Texan foray to the High Plains. The Ranger captain decided it was time to return home.

The Lipan Apaches had performed their duties well and they, too, were going home. The Ranger captain rewarded them with many of the captured horses and as much booty as they could pack on their ponies. Highly delighted, the Apaches took leave of the Rangers and rode off to the south-west, heading for their homeland among the mountains that bordered the Rio Grande, beyond the Pecos River.

Adam went with them.

The country through which he now travelled was unlike any Adam had ever seen before. There were vast deserts, breathtaking mountain ranges, and deep, high-walled canyons where it felt as though the real world had been left far behind.

In such a vast, awesome country a man felt very small and insignificant. The Apaches understood this feeling. They told Adam it was necessary for a man to pass through such country before he was able to appreciate the might and power of the great spirits who made him and the lands in which he dwelled.

Eventually they crossed a wide river, just above a gorge where the river narrowed dramatically and disappeared into the dark, roaring shadows. To Adam's surprise, the Apaches informed him that this was the Rio Grande. They were now in undisputed Mexican territory.

When he questioned them about their eventual destination, he was told they were heading for the winter camp of the Lipan Apache, close to the Onguapa River. The name struck a chord in Adam's memory, but it was a little while before he remembered where he had heard the name before. It was where Kiata, the half-Apache wife of the Mexico City gaoler, had said she would buy her farm.

When Adam asked the Lipan Apaches whether they knew Kiata it was as though he had made a joke.

'There are few men within two days' ride of her village who do not know Kiata,' said the Apache who had been senior scout for the Rangers. 'Now it seems her fame has spread to Texas. You have met her?'

'Yes. She helped me once, when I was in Mexico.'

The Indian's grin widened. 'Kiata has helped many men.'

Adam would have liked to question the Apache further but they began to ascend the steep side of a crumbling bluff, along a narrow trail barely the width of a horse. At the top was a long, shallow canyon, fed with water from a stream that gushed from a sheer rock-face. Here the Lipan Apache had their winter camp.

Their approach had been observed long before Adam and his companions toiled to the top of the trail. Later, Adam learned that the Apache, unlike any other Plains Indians, made a habit of setting sentries when they were in their permanent winter quarters. He never discovered whether this was general practice, but it *was* in the band led by Chief Conche.

Conche and a number of armed Apaches met them at the top of the steep trail. He greeted the senior scout warmly, and Adam later learned the two men were brothers. There was a greeting, too, for each of the returning scouts, but Adam's presence brought only a frown and Chief Conche upbraided his brother in no uncertain terms for bringing a stranger – a *white* man – to the winter camp. The one-sided argument continued until Adam offered to ride away without entering the Apache camp. He spoke in Spanish, and Conche replied in the same language.

'That will not be necessary. You have been brought here as a friend by my brother. But the Apache have many enemies and few friends among your people. He says *you* are one of our friends. He says this is said of you even among your own people.'

'It is said. I was married to a Kiowa girl, a captive of the Cherokee.'

'One of my wives is a Mexican girl. I captured her when I raided her father's village. It does not mean I am a friend of her people. You say you *were* married? Where is this wife now?'

'Dead. Killed by one of the men who drove the Cherokee from Texas.'

Conche's face gave no hint of his feelings. 'I have heard of this. The Cherokee obeyed the white men and lived as women. They had forgotten how to be warriors.' For half a minute Chief Conche stared silently at Adam. Then he said: 'You may stay.'

When Conche rode back among his warriors, they moved their horses aside respectfully, to allow him to pass. He had a rare authority and a dignity that would have set him apart from his fellows in any gathering.

Adam remained in the canyon village for five days. Long before he left he had developed a great respect for the Lipan Apache and their chief. They were a people with a highly organised way of life, and a strict code of conduct. Adam knew his presence in the village was resented, yet he was never threatened in any way, and any questions he asked of Conche's people were always met with a polite response.

Adam left the camp regretting he had not been able to spend more time with the Apache chief, but it seemed that Conche was organising a raid against the Mexicans. As in everything else he did, Conche left nothing to chance. Every man in the raiding party knew what was expected of him before leaving the camp. This same caution ensured that Adam was given no inkling of when or where the raid would take place.

When Adam left the mountains behind he came upon the settlements of the Mexican 'farmers'. The land here was hot and arid, and the people more than usually indolent. Adam saw only half-hearted attempts at cultivation. Even the cattle seemed lethargic and they had little flesh clinging to their bones. There were many goats everywhere, but these, too, were skinny, listless creatures.

At the first cluster of yellowing mud huts, Adam made enquiries for Señora Bravo from a barefooted Mexican who was seated on the ground, his back against the flaking adobe wall of his home. Lacking the energy to shrug, the Mexican declared he had no knowledge of either a Señor or Señora Bravo.

Adam received the same reply from three ragged Mexicans he found resting in the shade of a solitary tree on the river bank – and again in a tiny village a mile farther on. Contrary to the words of the Lipan Apache scout, it seemed *nobody* knew the girl he had met in Mexico City. Then Adam mentioned the name Kiata, and for the first time he had the attention of the Mexicans to whom he was directing his question. Sure they knew Kiata. *Everyone* knew Kiata. Her place was in the village of Fresima, four miles upstream. He would find it nestling in the big bend of the Onguapa River.

The *aldea* of Fresima hardly merited the appellation of 'village'. It was no more than an untidy and haphazard sprawl of adobe buildings. Patches of white on the walls of some of the dry-mud buildings hinted that they had once been painted. Most had not.

Hardly more imposing than any of the other buildings, but certainly very much larger, was a *cantina*. Serving the purpose of café, hotel, inn and bordello, the *cantina* was a peculiarly Mexican institution. It was the social centre for the men of a very wide area, satisfying all their needs except for those few that were the declared province of the Roman Catholic Church.

The Fresima *cantina* was no different from many others in Mexico, and it was here that Adam went to enquire after Kiata. He entered the long, dark, low-roofed bar-room, pausing inside the door until his eyes adjusted to the change of light. He was surprised at the number of men inside. They sat at tables drinking, or playing cards – or just talking. A few stood at the long wooden bar. Most were Mexicans, the remainder Indian. Among them were a number of girls.

There was little doubt that Adam's entry stirred their interest, but for some moments his presence was studiously ignored. If the men looked at him at all, it was from beneath lowered eyelids, as though no man wished to be the first to attract his attention. Their apparent indifference was the result of hard experience. This was a remote border area, where men came to seek refuge from the law. It was not wise to take too much interest in a stranger, especially one who carried two matched revolvers tucked in his belt.

The same rules did not apply to the women. Soon one left her place at the bar and came to link her arm through Adam's. Long past her prime, she now relied on initiative to supplement her faded charms. Speaking in poor English, she said: 'Hello, señor. You looking for a good time, eh? Come, buy me a drink.'

Adam allowed himself to be led to the long counter, and the atmosphere in the *cantina* immediately relaxed. Men began to talk naturally once more and eyes were raised from the tables.

He bought a beer for himself and a drink for the woman who had spoken to him. Hers would be no more than highly priced coloured water, for which she would receive a percentage of the price. It was a game played in every tavern, saloon and *cantina* in the world.

'You here to stay, or you just passing through Fresima?' The question was not prompted by mere inquisitiveness or idle curiosity. It was a business query. If Adam were merely passing through the village, she would work hard to make him part with the maximum amount of money in the shortest possible time. If he were staying, she would play the game differently. By keeping him happy and not costing him too much money today, she could make more money over a longer period.

'I don't know yet.' Adam was thirsty. He downed his beer and pushed the glass across the counter for another. Not one to miss such an opportunity, the girl did the same. 'I'll decide what to do when I've spoken to Kiata.'

'You a friend of Kiata?'

Adam was aware of a sudden upsurge of interest on both sides of the bar.

'I think you could say that. Do you know where she is?'

The woman shrugged, but Adam had not missed the almost imperceptible nod to the second barman, who promptly slipped away through a bead-curtained doorway beside the bar.

'Who knows? She is . . . Kiata.'

For a few minutes the Mexican woman questioned Adam to no avail about his plans. Then a voice he remembered asked: 'Who is looking for Kiata?'

Adam turned and saw her. No more than a pace behind the half-Apache girl were two huge, well-armed Mexicans. Eyeing Adam suspiciously, they left him in no doubts about their function.

They were not needed today. Kiata's slightly bored expression became one of sheer delight. 'Señor Adam! You have come to find me?'

Kiata flung herself at Adam, and he just had time to register the astonishment on the faces of her escort before she pulled his head down to her and kissed him soundly.

When Kiata released him every head in the *cantina* was turned towards them. Placing her hands on her hips, Kiata glared about the large room. 'What's the matter with you? This is an old friend. Haven't I always told you Kiata has important friends?' She called to the barman: '*Camarero*, give them all a drink on the house, then they will *know* I speak the truth.'

Followed by the cheers of the *cantina* customers, Kiata led Adam through the bead-curtained doorway and along a narrow passageway to a room at the far end of the *cantina*. A large, unmade bed stood in one corner and women's clothing was strewn around the room in profusion. As Kata went about picking up the clothes, she apologised to Adam for the untidiness, explaining that her maid had got pregnant by one of the smooth-talking Mexican *rurales* who had passed through Fresima nine months before, in pursuit of Apache raiders. The girl was now cursing his name as she sweated in unwedded childbirth in an adobe hut in the village.

'Where is your husband?' The total absence of any item of masculine clothing among the chaos prompted Adam's question.

'Ah! Poor Gomez. He never lost his guilt for having helped your friend to escape from the gaol. I think it came as a relief when the soldiers came and took him away.'

'Soldiers found him . . . here?'

'I have some whisky. Very few men in Fresima choose to drink it.' Kiata poured some in a tumbler and passed it to Adam. 'I think someone must have whispered in the ear of an army officer. It was most sad, but Gomez died bravely and was loyal to the end. He admitted it was he who had arranged your friend's escape, but did not say a word about the help I gave him. Poor Gomez. I miss him . . . sometimes.'

'What happened to the farm you were going to buy? I thought that was your reason for returning here.'

Kiata shrugged. 'I bought a farm. Three labors of land,' Adam made a rapid calculation and was impressed. A labor of land was 177 acres. 'At least, they told me it was land. We never dug far enough through the dust to find out. When we planted seeds the gophers would eat half and the wind would blow the remainder all the way to Texas. When Gomez was taken away I bought this place. It was going cheap. The owner had been killed in a fight with Comancheros. He left behind a grieving "widow". The union had been blessed with many children, but not by the Church. She was happy to take what I offered her. It is a living.'

Adam sat back in his chair and looked at Kiata as she spoke. She was a striking girl who went to no great lengths to hide her charms inside the clothes she wore. There was also a vibrancy in her similar to that he had seen in Tiski.

'Didn't you have enough of this sort of life before you met Gomez?'

Adam knew immediately he had made a grave error. Putting her drink down so suddenly that the contents leaped from the glass, Kiata cried angrily: 'You think I am the same as the women out there in my *cantina*? You think this of me? No! I own this *cantina*. I own *them*. When a man wants a woman he must first pay the money to me. But no man can buy *my* body. No, not for all the money in Mexico. I do not sell myself, Señor Adam.'

'I'm sorry, Kiata. I shouldn't have said that.'

The anger died in her, and she refilled his glass before attending to her own. 'It does not matter. I am glad you have come to see me.' Suddenly she smiled. 'But why *are* you here? Have you married another Indian wife and come seeking a place where you can live with her, away from the disapproval of your own people? I can sell you a dust-farm. Very cheap. . . .'

'No, Kiata. I haven't married again.'

'Then you must be in trouble with the authorities. You have come to the right place. We are used to men who look over their shoulders when they ride. Few stay long. Some are afraid to settle anywhere for fear of what they run from. Others are quarrelsome and pick fights with the wrong people. Then there are those who come with too much money to spend, and too much to say. One day they do not return to my *cantina* and are never seen again. The Comancheros also come here. They say little. They drink, they use my girls, and then they ride on. Everyone knows they trade with the Indians and that they sometimes fight on the side of the Indians. Sometimes a stranger will come here to speak to them; to offer them great sums of money for the Comancheros to buy back a son or a daughter who has been taken by the Indians. But most men keep away from them. They are the most dangerous of all those who come here.'

The whisky was warning Adam that he had not eaten since sun-up, but he chose to ignore the warning.

'You have some rough customers, but I'm not running from anyone – unless it's myself. I had nothing better to do so I came this way with some Lipans I'd been scouting with. I spent a few days with Chief Conche's people in the mountains and then came on here.'

Kiata's eyes widened. 'You have ridden with Apaches – and met Chief Conche?'

'I was fighting Comanches with the Lipans.' He would have liked to leave the explanation there, but found the whisky had loosened his tongue. 'Comanches killed my friend – the man we released from prison. They also killed his wife . . . and his small son . . . he was crippled and didn't have long to live anyway. There was no need to kill him. . . .'

Refilling Adam's glass, Kiata said nothing. There was a time for talking and a time to listen. Life had made her a good listener.

For Adam it was a rare unburdening of his soul. He told Kiata of Tiski and of the brutal removal of the Cherokee, of Don Manuel and Philippe, and of the settlement. He told her of the Comanches he had killed and seen killed. And he told her of Sam Dollar.

It was dark by the time he finally talked himself out and sat staring drunkenly into his never-empty whisky-glass.

After Kiata helped him to the bed he lay, unmoving, while she first removed his boots and then the remainder of his clothes. By the time she tucked him in he was fast asleep.

It was a noisy night in the *cantina*, but whenever Kiata came to check on Adam he was sleeping as soundly as though he were in a quiet English country house.

He did not stir until Kiata returned to the room for the last time at three o'clock the next morning. Only a couple of drunken

Indians remained in the *cantina*. The barman would eject them and lock up.

Undressing, Kiata slid beneath the bedclothes, aware of the warmth of his body, but doing her best not to waken him. Not until he reached across for her did she realise he was no longer asleep. She came to him then and it was the joining of two hungry bodies, expunging the loneliness that had lain heavily within each of them for so long.

CHAPTER TWELVE

ADAM HAD BEEN at Fresima for a full year when he heard of the disastrous Santa Fe expedition. It had been sent off from Texas by President Lamar, five months before, in an incredibly naïve bid to persuade the Mexican inhabitants of New Mexico to throw in their lot with the Texans.

The people of New Mexico suffered under the governorship of the despotic Don Manuel Armijo and groaned loudly at the misdeeds of their governor – but they were not ready to rise in rebellion in favour of an alien government.

Ostensibly on a trading mission, the Texans set off from a point just outside Austin and headed out across the virtually unknown prairies of western Texas. They travelled, hopefully, in the direction of Santa Fe, more than six hundred miles away. Five companies of Texan infantry and one of artillery accompanied the merchants and their twenty-one ox-drawn wagons – 321 men in all.

They stumbled from one disaster to another on their long, ill-advised and badly organised journey. Never certain of their true direction, they had no accurate maps, misidentified rivers and landmarks, and were finally deserted by their totally unreliable Mexican guide.

An advance party was sent on in a desperate bid to find help, only to learn that Governor Manuel Armijo knew of their approach and was waiting for them with his soldiers. They promptly surrendered to the Mexicans.

Broken in health and spirit, the main body followed the example of their countrymen when they, too, encountered Armijo's men. Lamar's conquering merchant army had fallen into Mexican hands without a shot being fired, five months after setting out to create a Texan empire.

Adam learned the news when the prisoners, chained and shackled, crossed the Rio Grande at El Paso, on the long march to Mexico City. They were thankful to be passing from the jurisdiction of Governor Armijo. Many of their number had failed to reach the Rio Grande. Beaten, ill and exhausted, those unable to maintain the pace set by Armijo's soldiers were shot, their bodies abandoned at the side of the trail.

The months spent at Fresima had healed many of the hidden

wounds Adam had carried with him from Texas. Out of bed, Kiata made few demands on him. He was free to hunt and fish, or occasionally visit the Lipan Apache in their mountain stronghold.

When he was at the *cantina*, Adam mixed freely with the bandits who terrorised the border settlements, men who were wanted in both north and south America. He passed the time of day with the uncommunicative Comancheros, whose coming and going was as unpredictable as the wind. He knew by name all the Indians who spent their days sitting on the earth outside the walls of the *cantina* and bought them a drink on occasions.

In spite of this carefree way of life, Adam had become restless in recent weeks. He knew that his skill with a hand-gun and rifle was respected by those men who frequented the Fresima *cantina*. He also knew that the only reason it had not been put to the test was because of the power Kiata wielded in the Onguapa River valley. She used her influence with great skill. If bandits caused her trouble, it seemed to them that wherever they turned in the area they came up against the Mexican government *rurales*.

If local Mexicans fell out of line, there was a series of Indian raids on the homes of the ringleaders. If the authorities became too greedy in their demands upon the establishment, bandit activity increased so sharply that a change of local officials invariably followed. Then, if all other means failed her, there were always the Comancheros.

Adam knew in his heart it was time he became his own man again. The disaster that had befallen the Santa Fe expedition provided him with all the incentive he needed. When the column was reported on the main trail from El Paso, no more than ten miles from Fresima, Adam rode off to witness the passing of the Texan prisoners.

The Texans were a sorry sight. Adam sat his horse watching the gaunt and tired men shuffle by, heavily shackled. A few faces looked familiar to him, but not all the men raised their heads until an excited voice called: 'Adam . . . Adam Rashleigh!'

The owner of the voice tried to hobble from the ranks of the Texan prisoners. He was promptly clubbed back in line by the Mexican escorts, but not before Adam recognised the bearded features of Henry Stillwell, the tall man from Tennessee who had been Nell Plunkett's intended husband at the time Adam left the Hill Country.

Stillwell's outburst brought Adam to the attention of the young Mexican guard commander, and four men were sent to bring Adam to him. They came at him eagerly, intending to treat him with the same contempt in which they held their Texan prisoners. However, his expensive saddle and horse, and his fluent command of Spanish gave them pause. Here was a rich man. In Mexico, wealth spelled power, and power meant life or death to ordinary people.

They walked respectfully beside Adam as he accompanied them to their commander. In the meantime, the Texan prisoners, grateful for the break the incident gave them, dropped down to rest in the dust of the trail.

In answer to the young Mexican officer's questions, Adam produced the tattered letter given to him by Colonel Juan Lozano, Commander of the Presidential Guard. With it was the letter of identity provided by the British ambassador.

Somewhat apprehensively, Adam asked after the health of Colonel Lozano. Military officers, especially those of high rank, tended to have a short life in trouble-torn Mexico.

'*General* Lozano is in excellent health, Señor Rashleigh. He is leading an army to put down a rebellion in Yucatan. A rebellion supported by the province from whence these prisoners came.'

The captain handed back the letters to Adam, but he did not relax yet. 'One of my prisoners called to you by name, Señor Rashleigh. Would you explain this to me, please?'

'Of course. The man is an American, from Tennessee. I knew him there. With your permission, I would like to speak with him.'

'I regret that cannot be permitted, señor.'

Adam knew better than to argue with a young officer in front of his men, but he was not ready to give up just yet.

'I feel his presence among your prisoners is the result of a mistake – on his part, of course. Perhaps you will allow me to purchase his freedom. I am quite certain his government, the American government, would appreciate your understanding. I have money. . . .'

'I am sorry, Señor Rashleigh. These men are prisoners of the Mexican government. Only an official order can secure the release of any one of them.'

Adam cursed the fact that the escort commander was a young and zealous soldier. An older man would have been happy to negotiate the release of a prisoner – for a good price, of course. He bowed to the inevitable.

'You will be so kind as to tell me what you are doing in such a remote area of my country, Señor Rashleigh.'

'Of course. I am here to study the ways of the Indians.'

'Why? They are dirty, untrustworthy and dangerous. What more is there to learn of them?'

Adam smiled. 'They are a little-known race. People in Great Britain are fascinated by them.'

'Your government is too indulgent, señor. It should give the British people more worthwhile matters with which to concern themselves.'

Adam rode away from the tragic column of men aware that the young officer would report his presence in the area to the Regional Governor in Chihuahua. It was definitely time he moved on. But he had some unfinished business to settle first.

That night the Texan prisoners were lodged in a corral, part of a small farm, seven miles along the road to Chihuahua. Adam sent a half-breed ahead of him to bribe the guards. As he had expected, the poorly paid men lacked the high principles of their commanding officer and a few silver dollars ensured that they patrolled only three sides of the corral for an hour.

Approaching the corral in the darkness, from the side farthest away from the camp-fires of the Mexican escort, Adam whispered his message through the widely spaced rails. Moments later the clanking of shackles on the inside of the corral heralded the arrival of Henry Stillwell.

In a hoarse whisper the Tennesseean told Adam the full story of the expedition's failure and capture. He also told of the cruelty of Governor Manuel Armijo, and of the murder of a number of Texan prisoners.

'Things are better now,' Stillwell whispered. 'The young Mexican captain's a stickler for discipline, but he's human.'

'Where are you headed now, Mexico City?'

'Yes – first off, anyway.'

'I'll get a message to the British ambassador there and ask him to inform the United States ambassador. We'll see what can be done to get you released. In the meantime I'll go back to Texas and let them know what's happened to you.'

Adam hesitated. 'Do you have any message for Nell?'

'Nell? Hell, no! I haven't seen her in more than a year.'

'I thought you were to be married . . .?'

'You mean you haven't seen her since then? She told me right after Eli's wedding that she couldn't go through with no marriage.'

Henry Stillwell's news jolted Adam. He thought that the last year might have been very different had he known of Nell's decision. Adam passed all the money he had on him through the corral bars to Henry Stillwell. He had not been able to secure his release, but the money would help buy a few extras for the Texan prisoners on the long trail to Mexico City.

Kiata took the news that Adam was leaving Fresima with no outward signs of emotion. He told her that the young escort commander had questioned him and was certain to pass the news of his presence on to the army authorities in Chihuahua.

'I will be informed that the army is coming when they are still ten miles away – and they will not stay long. You can hide in the hills until they go. . . .'

'That isn't my only reason for leaving. More than two hundred Texans have been taken prisoner. Some have been treated brutally. The Texan government should know, so it can begin moves to have them freed.'

'You have already sent a man with letters to your ambassador in Mexico City. There is no need for you to do more.'

'I'm going, Kiata.'

Adam wished Kiata would become angry with him. Anything would be better than the cold, matter-of-fact manner she had adopted.

'I know – and you know it, too – so why do you have to search for a reason? I have always known you would leave me one day. I knew it would be soon, even before news came of the Texan prisoners.'

He did not ask *how* she knew. There were many things about Kiata that were beyond his understanding.

There was a moment as he kissed her farewell when she clung to him and he thought her apparent indifference was about to desert her. Instead, she pushed him from her and said simply: 'Go. Walk in peace, Englishman.'

He looked back twice as he rode away. Although he waved, there was no response. He wondered whether Kiata really would miss him, or whether life at the Fresima *cantina* would go on as though he had never been there.

He would never know that Kiata stood outside the *cantina* all that day, awaiting his return. When the sun sank below the rim of the tall bluffs to the west of the village, she threw a small bag to the dusty earth and ground it in with her bare foot. It was a powerful charm, obtained from a well-known Apache 'holy man' to ensure that Adam would never leave her. Then Kiata went to her room and no one saw her face for a full week.

CHAPTER THIRTEEN

ADAM REACHED AUSTIN in time to witness the inauguration of General Sam Houston for his second term in the office of President of the Republic of Texas.

Houston was a changed man. Gone for ever was the jovial drunkard who caroused the nights away with his many friends. He was now married to the former Margaret Lea. At forty-eight years of age, he was twenty-six years older than his wife.

The combination of a young, sensitive and inexperienced woman married to a hard-drinking, hard-living, hard-fighting man of the world should have been a certain recipe for disaster. Instead, a miracle had occurred. Margaret had completely captured the heart of the hero of Texan Independence. In return, she gave him all the love and understanding that his warm and affectionate nature demanded.

Sam Houston was now a sober and upright man, a promising member of the Baptist Church. He was also the President of a bankrupt Republic, and Texas had little prospect of becoming solvent during his term of office. However, there were many improvements on the diplomatic front.

Great Britain had finally agreed to grant recognition to the Republic. Three treaties had been drawn up between the two countries. The first was a detailed document covering all aspects of commerce. The second dealt with monetary matters. Both these treaties had been ratified by Texas and returned to Great Britain. The third treaty was still awaiting ratification by the Texan Congress – and it was this that was the only barrier to full recognition. This third treaty, while not going so far as to demand the emancipation of Texan slaves, called for Texan help in barring the shipborne trade from Africa. This was an emotive issue on both sides of the Atlantic Ocean.

General Houston assured Adam that, now he was once more President of Texas, this final treaty would be signed and returned, early in 1842.

Houston also gave Adam news of some important changes in the British political scene. There had been an election and, after years of directing his country's overseas policies, Lord Palmerston was no longer in office. Great Britain now had a Tory government, headed by Sir Robert Peel. The responsibility for foreign affairs rested with Lord Aberdeen.

A number of letters awaited Adam in Austin. Most were from the former Foreign Secretary. They repeatedly called for information on the Texan political scene and urged Adam to apply pressure to President Lamar to have the third treaty ratified as quickly as possible.

One letter was from the new British Foreign Secretary. He noted the lack of dispatches from Adam during the preceding year, but accepted that this was probably due to the indifferent postal service operating in Texas. Couched in cautious terms, the letter noted that Adam had enjoyed the confidence of Lord Aberdeen's predecessor and assured him that his own government would ensure Adam received every assistance while he worked to further the interests of Great Britain.

Lord Aberdeen informed Adam that Her Majesty's government had appointed Captain Charles Elliot, RN, to be consul-general to the Republic of Texas. When the third treaty was ratified, Elliot would be accredited as Her Majesty's chargé d'affaires. Adam was asked to give Elliot every assistance upon his arrival in Texas.

Adam showed this letter to Houston, and the new President was delighted. He asked Adam to reply to Lord Aberdeen immediately. The treaty would be ratified at the earliest opportunity and arrangements made to accommodate Elliot upon his arrival in Texas.

When Adam told Houston of the fate of the survivors of the Santa Fe expedition, the Texas president exploded with a bitter tirade against his predecessor. Adam learned that Lamar had not been given the approval of Congress for the expedition. Instead, he had raised money from private sources to finance the ill-conceived project.

Houston thanked Adam for his efforts on behalf of the Texans and urged him to press for British involvement to secure the release of the survivors.

Finally, President Houston told Adam there was a wagon train of British immigrants stranded in Austin, bound for the new settlements beyond Caleb Ryan's lands. Their guide had been killed in a saloon brawl and no one else could be found to take them on. He asked Adam to accept the task.

Adam left the President's office with an assurance that the friendship between the two men was as strong as ever, but Adam knew different. The days of Houston's buckskin presidency were over. Sam Houston had changed during his years out of office.

He had gained in political strength and had the determination of a man with a purpose in life. Adam wondered whether the change had been brought about by marriage, or by the many months he had spent with America's wily old ex-President Jackson.

For the sake of British interests in the area, Adam hoped it was the former.

When Adam reached the place where the wagon-train immigrants were encamped it was as though the clock had been put back almost four years, to the time of Caleb Ryan's arrival in Texas. There was the same tired look on the faces of the women, the apprehensive hopes of the men, and a lamentable unpreparedness for the raw frontier life ahead of them.

Adam called the men together and told them exactly what they could expect when they reached the Hill Country and listed the tools they would need to build a cabin and break their ground. He also ensured that they had guns and ammunition to hunt food and ward off Comanche raiders.

Comanches were still the scourge of the frontier, but they would never again raid in such numbers as they had when they swept eastwards as far as the sea. They were now hit-and-run raiders, their tactics dictated by the success of the Texas Rangers under such captains as John Coffee Hays, helped by wily scouts like Eli Varne.

Still only in his twenties, Captain Hays had introduced a standard into the Texas Rangers that was transforming the force from a drunken, undisciplined rabble to an extremely mobile mounted army, rapidly shooting its way into legend.

But the Rangers were few in number and operated far from the settlements, seeking and destroying Comanche villages on the High Plains. The new settlers would need to learn to look after themselves – and learn quickly.

Adam decided that the best way for the settlers to see what needed to be done was to take them through Caleb Ryan's settlement.

The ox-drawn wagons of the new arrivals moved slowly, and it was five days before they creaked from the Hill Country woodlands to the cleared bottom-land meadows of Caleb's land.

Word of their approach travelled ahead of them, and Caleb and some of his neighbours were waiting to welcome the newcomers. There was a fair sprinkling of immigrants from the 'old country' on the wagons, ensuring that the news and information would not be all one way.

But Caleb first welcomed Adam, delighted to see him again after his long absence. 'We've all been worried about you, Adam. I doubt if a day has gone by when we haven't spoken of you. Eli came through a month or so ago and we chatted about you – as much as any man can talk to Eli these days. He's possessed of a bloodlust that will last until he is killed, or until there are no more Comanches left alive in Texas. But where have you been? What have you been doing all this time?' Caleb retained his grip on Adam's hand as though he might suddenly make off again at any moment.

'It's a long story, Caleb. One for telling by the fireside on a wet night. How are things here?'

'Oh, we're all a little older, perhaps a little wiser. Two families have gone. One was killed by Comanches, and their neighbours moved to San Antonio. We all miss Eli – none more than young Dermot. The lad's sprung up as tall as a corn plant. I hoped Eli would stay here for a while, for the boy's sake, but Eli treated him almost as though he were a stranger. Dermot took it very badly.'

Dermot had always idolised Eli, since the days when he had returned from his brief captivity in Comanche hands. Adam knew how Eli's behaviour must have hurt him.

'Have you taken Dermot into your family?'

'No, Nell took him on. She's done a job that Kathie would have been proud of.'

Adam felt a quickening of interest at the mention of Nell's name. He looked to where some of the settlement women were talking to the new immigrants. He saw Eileen Ryan and Peggy Dooley and waved a greeting to them, but he could not see Nell or Dermot.

'Where's Nell now?'

Caleb cast his eyes over the women. 'She must be up at your place. We've built a small cabin for her and Dermot inside the stockade, but she spends most of her time growing vegetables on land behind your cabin. She tends the livestock, too. You've got a nice-sized little herd running up there now.'

'If there are any milking-cows among them, I'll give them to the new settlers. They'll need all the help they can get. They have no Don Manuel around to give them a start.'

Caleb's pleasure at seeing Adam deserted him for a few minutes. 'That was a sad business. He was a great man. A wonderful man. It would have hit you harder than any of us, Adam. We all grieved with you when we heard.'

415

'A lot has happened since then, and mourning is a luxury few can afford in Texas.'

With this observation, Adam closed the conversation about Don Manuel. 'Come and meet the people who are to be your new neighbours. They've got a lot to learn, and they'll not meet a man more qualified than yourself to teach them.'

Soon the men from the settlement were taking the newcomers to see the land they had cleared and stock they were rearing. While the women prepared a welcoming meal, those from the wagons marvelled at the numerous innovations adopted by the settlers to make frontier life more comfortable.

After a brief conversation with Peggy Dooley, expressing amazement at the way young Ardilla had grown, Adam found himself unexpectedly on his own. Taking his horse, he set off for his own cabin. Along the way he paused to look down upon Tiski's grave. The mound of earth was lower now, almost level with the chalk-white soil of the surrounding ground. Someone had marked the grave with an oval of stones. Adam did not stay here long.

Nell and Dermot did not see Adam arrive. They were behind the cabin, feeding milk from a wooden bucket to a splay-legged calf. Nell held the bucket while Dermot tried to prevent the bewildered calf knocking it from her hands.

The Irish girl had not changed at all, unless she had lost a little weight. Dermot, on the other hand, had grown inches taller. He was now approaching fifteen years of age and, in common with all boys of his age on the frontier, was expected to put in a full day's work.

Adam sat his horse for a while, happy to observe the easy relationship Nell obviously enjoyed with her nephew. When she said something to him, Dermot flashed her a smile that held no hint of the tragedies he had experienced in his young life.

Suddenly, Dermot caught sight of Adam. For a second he froze. Then he let out a yell of recognition that so startled Nell and the calf that she dropped the bucket and the calf bolted past her.

'Adam! It really *is* you!' As Adam swung down from the horse Dermot ran to him, then stopped, an arm's length away, suddenly overcome with self-consciousness.

'You've grown too big to hug, young man – but it's good to see you.' Adam ruffled Dermot's hair affectionately, and it seemed the grin would split the boy's face in two. 'All the same, you should have seen me coming. I could have been a Comanche.'

'If you were, you'd have got both barrels of this.' Nell snatched up a double-barrelled hunting-gun that had been leaning against the fencing beside her. 'And there's another beside Dermot. Oh! We've heard all about your Indian-fighting, but we've done some, too, you know. You'll not need to come back here and tell us how we should be living our lives. Save that for your soldiers, or whoever it is you and Eli go chasing Indians with. Come on, Dermot. Mr Rashleigh's home again. He can look after his affairs for himself now.'

Dermot was bemused by the sudden, unexpected turn events had taken. He could not understand why Nell had taken such exception to Adam's innocent remark. In truth, she was not clear herself, but she had no intention of backing down.

She caught and mounted her horse, left saddled as an additional precaution against a Comanche attack, but before she could ride away Adam took hold of the animal's bridle.

'Nell, I wasn't trying to prove anything, or to impress you. I just want you and Dermot to stay alive. He *should* have seen me coming. Both of you should.'

'And *you* should have been around to tend your own animals, then Dermot and I would both be safe inside Caleb's stockade.'

Nell pulled the horse's head around and kicked back with her heels, causing the animal to set off at a canter. With an apologetic backward look at Adam, Dermot set off after her.

Behind them, Adam felt miserable and confused, wondering why Nell had been so quick to take offence. The last thing he had wanted was to quarrel with her. Not until now had he realised how much he had been looking forward to seeing her again.

CHAPTER FOURTEEN

In October 1841, General Santa Anna was once more given presidential power in Mexico. One of his first acts was ceremonially to bury the leg which had been shot away by the French at Vera Cruz in December 1838. Escorted by two regiments of infantry, plus cavalry and artillery, the whole procession accompanied by two bands, the leg passed in solemn ceremony to Santa Paula cemetery. Here, witnessed by the Mexican government and the army general staff, the disembodied limb was placed in a stone urn, atop a stone column that had been decorated with the flag of Mexico. The service over, the artillery fired a respectful salute and Santa Anna went away well satisfied.

Next, Santa Anna turned his attention to avenging the disastrous Texan intrusion into New Mexico. In a move that took Houston and his government by surprise, General Rafael Vasquez and seven hundred Mexican troops advanced unnoticed through the sparsely populated lands lying between the Rio Grande and Nueces River and fell upon San Antonio.

There were no more than a hundred Texan troops garrisoned in the town that in 1836 had witnessed the heroic defence of the Alamo by the small Texan force led by Jim Bowie and William Travis. Judiciously deciding that one legend was enough for any town, the Texan troops withdrew without giving battle, leaving San Antonio to the mercy of the Mexican army.

Adam was in Austin when news of the raid reached the capital, and he witnessed the ensuing panic. The Texan administration was convinced this was a full-scale invasion by the Mexicans, and Houston ordered the seat of government removed to the earlier capital that bore his name.

Concerned for the settlers, Adam rode fast to San Antonio. Here he learned that the Mexican army had slipped away as quietly as it had arrived, the ill-paid Mexican soldiers heavily laden with booty. It had merely been a raid, not a bid to reoccupy Texas.

Riding on to the settlements in the Hill Country, Adam found that here, too, there was panic, although they had seen no Mexican troops. A number of families were already heading northwards with their possessions. The remainder were in the course of loading up their wagons and following suit.

Adam's news was received with relief – and some embarrassment – but things quickly returned to normal. Meanwhile, Adam heard that Eli was with the small Ranger force harrying General Vasquez on his retreat from the country.

Adam remained in the Hill Country for a while, clearing his land and branding the cattle he was running there. Adam and Nell were friends once more, and she and Dermot helped him. Dermot had celebrated his fifteenth birthday and was a strapping, strong lad, looking older than he was. He could ride, shoot and hunt as well as anyone in the settlement – with the exception of Gilpin McCulloch – and Adam was grateful for his help with the work that needed to be done.

One day a week, Adam and Dermot went along the valley to help in the construction of a school on Caleb's land. Many babies had been born since the arrival of the settlers, and a schoolhouse would be needed for the future.

One day a letter arrived by messenger for Adam. It was from President Houston. He wanted Adam to try to arrange peace talks with the Indians. He was particularly keen to re-establish good relations with the Comanche.

Nell was horrified by Houston's request. 'The Comanche know you've fought them. They'd delight in getting you into their hands.'

'I don't think so, Nell. I believe they are as eager for peace as we are. That's why Muguera went into San Antonio.'

'Yes, and look what happened. They'll never trust Texans again. You've said so yourself.'

'I believe they'll trust *me*.'

'Adam! You're not seriously thinking of doing what Houston asks?'

'Someone's got to make a start. I think I stand more chance of succeeding than most.'

With hands on her hips, Nell snapped at him: 'If you're determined to commit suicide, it's a pity you didn't tell Dermot and me before now. We wouldn't have worked ourselves to a standstill doing things that won't be needed!' With this parting observation, Nell stormed from the cabin.

An hour later she was back. There was no apology, but she laid out the clothes she thought Adam would need, and packed a few things in his saddlebags.

Dermot's reaction to the proposed trip was very different. He begged Adam to take him along. Adam did not make the mistake of telling Dermot he was too young for the dangers of Indian country. Instead, he impressed upon the young man that he was being relied upon to keep things running smoothly on Adam's holding.

Adam rode off that same day and for the first time felt a real reluctance to be leaving the Hill Country. The reason was the small and lonely figure who waved from his cabin doorway until he was out of sight.

Adam would have liked to have Eli with him on such a delicate mission, but it was doubtful whether Eli would have accompanied Adam in search of peace, even had anyone known where he was. Instead, Adam took Gilpin McCulloch.

He proved a good choice. They needed to talk with the Comanche, but Adam knew better than to make a direct approach to them. With the present state of relations between Comanche and Texans, he would have been killed without the opportunity of saying a word. Gilpin suggested that Adam speak to Red Otter, chief of a small band of Wichita Indians whose home was well to the north, close to the United States border.

Adam did not ask how Gilpin McCulloch knew of the Wichita village. He had learned the young Scotsman was in the habit of disappearing from the settlement for weeks at a time. It was believed he spent much of the time with the Indians. Gilpin himself was close-mouthed about his travels.

They found the Wichita village exactly where Gilpin had said it would be, and it was immediately apparent that the quiet Scot was well known. When they dismounted, a young Wichita girl came forward to take their horses. Gilpin's hand closed on her shoulder for a second, and when the girl looked up at him Gilpin's secret was out. The girl was deeply in love with him, and he with her.

Adam's heart went out to them both. It was accompanied by a deep sense of sorrow. Even if a treaty could be made between the Texans and the Indians, there would be little permanency in the future of Gilpin McCulloch and the Wichita Indian girl.

Adam stayed in the Wichita village for a month while Chief Red Otter went off to speak to the Plains Indians. When Red Otter returned, he brought news that most of the *smaller* Indian bands were in favour of a peace treaty. The Comanche and their Kiowa allies were not. However, Red Otter believed the anger they still felt over the massacre of the chiefs in San Antonio was beginning to fade. He felt they would be ready to talk to Texans of peace before another year passed.

Those tribes in favour of peace talks were to meet at Red Otter's village in two moons' time to agree when, and where, they would meet Houston's representatives. Gilpin would convey their decision to Houston.

Thanking the Wichita chief for his assistance, and presenting him with a rifle on behalf of the Texan president, Adam set out for the capital to report on his progress. Gilpin remained behind in the village.

General Houston was well pleased with what Adam had managed to achieve, but at present he had other things on his mind. He had pushed Great Britain's third, 'anti-slavery' treaty through the Texan Congress and now eagerly awaited the arrival of the British chargé d'affaires.

There were letters for Adam from the British Foreign Secretary. One contained the news for which President Houston was waiting. Captain Charles Elliot, RN, was on his way and due to arrive in the Texan port of Galveston from New Orleans during the next few days. Adam was asked to meet him and give him a first-hand account of Texan affairs, before escorting him to Houston to take up his duties.

Adam barely reached Galveston in time. The ship in which Elliot was travelling was actually berthing when Adam rode into the port.

His first meeting with Great Britain's diplomatic representative was far from propitious. Adam was still dressed in the buckskins he had worn to carry out General Houston's mission among the Indians. The dapper Captain Elliot berated him for his dress, declaring it showed disrespect not only towards him personally, but also towards the country he represented.

Adam's inclination was to suggest that Captain Elliot try travelling through Indian country dressed in top hat and London city shoes. However, the chargé d'affaires was accompanied by his wife and son, and Adam held his tongue.

After scouring the town, Adam managed to hire a suitable carriage for Elliot and rode inside with him to Houston, briefing him along the way. Elliot spent most of the time leaning back against the seat, eyes closed, mopping his brow and complaining about the August heat and the bad state of the Texas roads.

Adam was not sorry when they reached Houston and he was able to settle Elliot and his family in temporary accommodation in one of the town's hotels. It was not the most salubrious of establishments, but Elliot could hardly lay the blame for this at Adam's feet. Owing to the sudden evacuation of the government from Austin, the hotels were overfull. Some recent arrivals were forced to live in tents at the side of Houston's notoriously muddy streets!

In one of the stores, Adam purchased a fairly presentable suit. Attired to the satisfaction of the chargé d'affaires, Adam conveyed Elliot to the Texan present's office.

It did not take Houston long to realise that Elliot did not approve of Adam, and the President was quick to show his own regard for the younger man.

Draping an arm affectionately over Adam's shoulders, Houston said: 'Adam and I remember the old days, when we rode some muddy trails together. I'm desk-bound now, but Adam is still going to faraway corners of Texas. He's just returned from a trip to the Wichita Indians. Hopefully, it will have laid the foundation for peace talks with the Wichita Indians and their neighbours.'

Frostily, Captain Elliot declared that he was certain the British government would be interested to hear of Adam's efforts on behalf of the Texas Republic. However, despite Elliot's antagonism towards Adam, he and Houston got on extremely well together.

It was the beginning of a friendship that was to cause great diplomatic concern within Texas – and consternation in the United States. The Americans feared that Texas was falling under the influence of Great Britain, but those close to Houston smiled knowingly, pointing out how Elliot hung on Houston's every word.

Meanwhile, Great Britain worked hard to bring about a truce between Texas and Mexico. Elliot sent letter after glowing letter praising Texas – and Houston in particular. He went so far as to say he was on the brink of persuading Houston to free all slaves in the Republic of Texas. He suggested that, if such a happy state of affairs came to pass, Great Britain might compensate Texan slave-owners for the loss of their human assets.

Adam was more sceptical. He believed Houston was playing a deep game in a bid to take Texas into the United States. Elliot's enthusiasm was playing into the Texas president's hands and pushing annexation by the United States closer. Elliot's conviction that slavery was about to end delighted the northern American States. If the slave issue were to be resolved, they would welcome Texas into the Union. On the other hand, the southern States felt they should annex Texas *before* the Texan administration did anything foolish.

Adam put his views in a letter to Lord Aberdeen. He suggested Great Britain should insist on written assurances that, in return

422

for Great Britain's mediation with Mexico, Texas would repudiate any suggestion of annexation by the United States.

The urgency that Adam felt the British government should give to the matter was lost in the deluge of correspondence flowing from Elliot's pen. The British chargé d'affaires was busily expanding his theory that Texas was about to abolish slavery. When it came, he assured Lord Aberdeen, the northern Mexican provinces would unite with Texas to form a great new nation. Elliot had no doubt that, when this day came, Texas would acknowledge its great debt to Britain and, by its very strength, nullify the growing might of the United States.

In November 1842, President Houston, piqued with the Houston town authorities, was in the process of moving his capital to Washington-on-the-Brazos, when the Mexican army swooped on San Antonio yet again. This time the surprise was total. The whole Anglo-Saxon male population was taken prisoner. Among their number were the judge and officials of the district court, sitting when the Mexicans took the town.

Adam was with Captain Elliot when news of the latest raid reached him.

Relations between Elliot and Adam had reached a new low. Adam had told the chargé d'affairs that he thought General Houston was using him as a lever to force the Americans to offer annexation to Texas.

Elliot's furious reply was to accuse Adam of trying to undermine his authority and destroy the friendship and trust that had been built up between the President of Texas and himself.

With such mutual dislike and mistrust, Adam had no feelings of disloyalty when he turned his back on overcrowded Washington-on-the-Brazos and returned to the settlement.

Adam felt a great sense of relief and joy when he saw smoke rising from cabin chimneys, and men and women working in the Hill Country fields. All was normal here. The Mexicans had once more ignored the settlement.

Adam's relief suffered a jolt when he reached Caleb's cabin where a number of settlers were gathered. Nell was among them. When she saw Adam riding towards her, she lifted her skirts and ran to him – but this was no warm, homecoming welcome.

'Adam. . . . Thank God you're here.' She was out of breath from the dash to meet him. 'It's Dermot. He's gone . . . to join the Texas army.'

'That's ridiculous! He's only fifteen. They'll never take him.'

'They already have.' Nell looked at him in desperation. 'Caleb went to San Antonio to bring him back. He was too late. Dermot has gone with the army to march into Mexico. They're going to pay the Mexicans back for raiding San Antonio.'

CHAPTER FIFTEEN

ADAM FOLLOWED the clear trail the Texan army made on its way southwards. It was not difficult. Unlike Indians, the soldiers made no attempt to travel with caution, discarding all manner of rubbish as they went.

Two days out from San Antonio he met the army commander with some of his men, returning to be disbanded. Dermot was not with them. The commanding officer told a story that was typical of the manner in which the ill-disciplined Texan troops operated. They had crossed the Mexican border and taken an undefended and surprisingly friendly Mexican town, before moving on to encounter rather more resistance in a small Mexican village. The Mexicans were made to pay for their folly. The Texans looted the village and committed a number of outrages against the Mexican women. As a result, the commanding officer had ordered the army back to Texas.

In a heated difference of opinion, the majority decision was that the men had not come all this distance to mess up a couple of piddling little Mexican *aldeas* and go home. They were spoiling for a crack at the regular Mexican army and did not intend going back until they had taught Santa Anna it did not pay to attack defenceless Texan towns.

More than three hundred Texans broke away from the commanding officer and those few men who remained loyal to him. They set off to attack the sizeable Mexican town of Mier, some miles from the border. Dermot had gone with these rebellious soldiers. So, too, had Eli Varne.

Adam knew he had cause to worry now. While the army had been commanded by a responsible officer, there had always been a good chance that Dermot would come to no harm. General Houston wanted no serious trouble with Mexico right now. He was committed to backing the peace overtures being made to Mexico on his behalf by Great Britain. The Texas army had made its point. It, too, could cross the border and occupy towns and villages belonging to the other. Honour had been satisfied.

However, things were now out of Houston's hands. Dermot was travelling with men who wanted to fight. Adam wished he could believe that Eli would keep his stepson out of trouble, but it was a forlorn hope.

Adam rode harder, hoping to find the now unofficial army and extricate Dermot before he was involved in any more fighting. He was not to know that even before he crossed the border into Mexico the irregular Texans had fought the battle of Mier – and lost.

Dermot Casey was scared. So scared he did not remember until he saw the wreaths laid at the foot of a crucifix, inside a small mission building, that it was Christmas night.

The Texans were closing in on Mier in the darkness. There was no question of taking the town by surprise. Camped within sight of the town for three days, the Texans had foolishly allowed the Mexicans to bring in reinforcements for the already sizeable garrison.

Dermot was in the second wave of Texans to enter the town. He heard the shooting begin before he and his companions reached the cover of the first house.

He knew what had to be done. The town was made up of square-built terraced adobe houses. Taking those on the outskirts, the Texans would batter their way through the wall into the next, and the next, and so on, thus staying clear of the bullets of the Mexican troops.

The first couple of houses fell without too many casualties, but when the Mexicans discovered what was happening they lay in wait for the attackers. As Dermot and those men with him broke through a mud wall, using the tongue of a wagon as a battering-ram, the Mexicans on the other side opened a withering fire on them.

In the darkness men screamed in pain. Suddenly afraid, Dermot dropped to the ground. More Texan soldiers came in behind him and returned the Mexicans' fire. One tripped over Dermot and his hand explored Dermot's body in the darkness for the feel of blood. When he found none he put the toe of his boot into Dermot's ribs. 'Get on your feet, you bloody coward. Where's your gun? Here. . . . Now get through that hole and start shooting.'

Dermot crawled through the hole in the broken wall and suddenly men were shooting and being shot all about him. Dermot staggered forward through the choking smoke until he found himself outside in the fresh air with other men. Whether they were Mexican or Texan he did not know, and he no longer cared. He had fired his rifle and should be reloading, but he was too frightened to stand still. He imagined he was surrounded by Mexicans, all waiting to shoot *him*.

Dermot began to run. Behind him someone let out a Texan yell and bullets began to fly past, scoring the mud walls of the houses only inches from his head. At the corner of the street he tripped and fell, the empty rifle falling from his hand. He did not stop to look for it but scrambled to his feet and carried on running. Once, he found himself in a small group of refugees, also fleeing from the fighting. Then he was in a vegatable-plot, tripping time after time over thin rope hung with cloth, no doubt put out to scare off the birds. Inside the adobe house beyond the garden he heard a woman's shrill voice and imagined she was calling to the Mexican soldiers. The gardens seemed to be surrounded by houses, and in the darkness Dermot could find no way out.

He began backing along a wall until he found a door. When it moved beneath his weight he pushed harder. The door opened just as firing began at the far end of the alleyway along which he had just run. Flinging it open as wide as it would go, Dermot plunged inside. It was totally dark inside here, but as he felt his way cautiously across the floor Dermot realised he must be in a storeroom. There were crates and sacks and boxes of all sizes stacked up against the walls.

Dermot sat on the floor, his back against a sack that felt as though it might contain grain. Only occasionally could a sound be heard that might have been shooting. Suddenly, Dermot began to shake uncontrollably and silent tears rolled down his gunpowder-blackened cheeks.

Dermot had no way of knowing how long he was in the storeroom. He must have dozed for a while. Suddenly, the door opened and early morning sunlight streamed in, startling him. Standing in the doorway was a small, dark-skinned Mexican girl carrying a flour-pan. Leaving the door open behind her she advanced to the centre of the store before she saw Dermot. Her eyes opened wide with fear and she stood quite still, just looking at him.

She reminded Dermot of Ardilla, Peggy Dooley's adopted Tonkawa daughter. 'It's all right; I won't hurt you. . . .'

Dermot's voice was thick and hoarse and it broke the spell that had been holding the girl. Slowly backing away from him, she suddenly broke and ran, flinging the flour-pan from her.

Dermot could hear her shrill young voice spreading the news of his presence in the storeroom, but he felt only a weary relief that the decision about his next move had been taken from him.

He was on his feet when the Mexican men crowded in at the storeroom doorway, armed with a variety of improvised weapons.

'You won't need them. I've not got a gun.'

His legs stiff from the long hours of squatting on the floor, Dermot limped towards them, empty hands held up to shoulder height. His tear-stained face was that of a young boy, but the Mexicans saw only a tall, heavily built *gringo*, one of the men who had inflicted staggering casualties on the Mexican troops guarding the town.

As Dermot reached the doorway, the Mexicans stood back to allow him to pass through. Outside, he was blinded by the sunshine and suddenly the Mexicans could see he was no more than a boy – and unarmed. One of them slammed the end of a long wooden stave in his face and screamed an oath at him.

Immediately, all the other Mexicans joined in, and Dermot was beaten to his knees, throwing his arms above his head in a vain attempt to ward off their blows.

He was crouching on the ground, only semi-conscious, when a woman, the mother of the child who had found him, threw herself into the crowd of howling men. Screaming at them to stop, she eventually reached Dermot. Not until then did the excited, perspiring Mexicans cease their beating.

An hour later, bloody and confused, Dermot was heaved through an iron gate to land in the dust of a compound where the surviving Texans were being held by the victorious Mexican troops.

Adam splashed his horse across the wide, shoal-littered Rio Grande only a few miles from Mier, and was promptly arrested by a troop of Mexican cavalrymen, out searching for any Texans who might have escaped from the battle in the Mexican town.

Adam presented his well-worn credentials to the officer in charge of the cavalry and was courteously requested to accompany him to the headquarters of General Pedro Ampudia, commander of the victorious Mexican forces.

The General and his staff were resting in the largest villa in Mier, and Adam was kept waiting for three hours before being shown into a room where the General and some of his senior staff were seated.

Ampudia had Adam's two letters in front of him. Frowning up at Adam, he waved one of the letters at him. 'This says you are English. What are you doing in Mexico?'

'I came looking for a fifteen-year-old boy who ran away from his home to join the Texan army.'

'Texas is a Mexican province. It does not have its own army – only rebels.'

'I am not arguing with your interpretation of the situation in

Texas, General Ampudia. I wish only to find the boy and return him to his home.'

'In Texas?'

'Yes.'

'A bullet from a fifteen-year-old's gun can kill my soldiers as effectively as one from a full-grown rebel, Señor Rashleigh.'

Once again Adam conceded the General's point, adding that he trusted Ampudia's magnanimity was equal to the situation.

General Ampudia suddenly flared into anger. 'Señor Rashleigh, this fifteen-year-old boy and his Texan friends have killed *six hundred* of my soldiers and wounded two hundred more. Yet you ask me to be magnanimous? If the boy fought with the others, he will *die* with them.'

'The boy is a British subject. I will ride to Mexico City and ask the British ambassador to make representation to your president on his behalf. . . .'

'I regret you will ride nowhere, Señor Rashleigh.'

Slowly and deliberately, General Ampudia tore in half the letters Adam had handed to him, then he folded the pieces and tore them again.

When Adam protested, General Ampudia cut his protest short. 'I do not believe your story, Señor Rashleigh – if that *is* your name. You ride into Mexico from *Texas* the day after a fierce battle has been fought, and demand the release of a Texan rebel. By way of identification your present me with two aged letters. One purports to be from a British ambassador who is no longer in Mexico. The other is from a general who was executed three months ago for plotting the overthrow of President Santa Anna.'

Dropping the torn pieces of paper to the floor, General Ampudia leaned back in his chair and scowled up at Adam. 'I think you, *too*, are an enemy of Mexico, señor. I believe you came here as a spy to learn what happened to the rebel soldiers and report back to the revolutionary government in Texas. You will not *be* returning to Texas, señor. Instead, you will suffer the fate of your companions.'

Waving his hand, the Mexican general said to Adam's soldier escort: 'Take him away and put him with the other prisoners.'

Angrily, Adam began to protest, only to receive a blow in the back from a musket-butt that knocked him to his knees. Struggling angrily, Adam was dragged from the room. Minutes later he was hurled bodily through the same gate that had opened to admit Dermot Casey a short time before.

'Pardon me if I don't say it's good to see you, Adam. Instead, I'll just ask you what the hell you're doing here.'

Eli Varne was the first man to greet Adam, gripping his hand in a firm expression of friendship.

'I came looking for Dermot,' explained Adam, adding ruefully: 'I thought I might persuade General Ampudia to release him.'

'Well. . . . I can't recommend your tactics, but Dermot's here.' Eli's heavily bearded face became suddenly serious. 'He wasn't captured with the rest of us. They brought him in later and he'd taken a bad beating.'

Men moved aside as Eli led Adam to the far side of the compound. Here, the overhanging roof of an adjacent building provided some shade for the Texan casualties.

Dermot was propped against the wall. His face was bloody and bruised, the nose certainly broken. The area around both eyes was so badly swollen he could not see.

Dropping to one knee beside him, Eli shook Dermot's arm. 'You got yourself a visitor, boy. Damned if Adam hasn't rode all the way from the Hill Country just to see you.'

Dermot raised his head painfully. 'Adam . . . ?' He reached out a hand uncertainly. 'Is Ma with you?'

'No, but don't worry. We'll soon have you home.' Adam took the hand that reached out for him. 'How are you feeling?'

'I wish Ma would come.'

'She'll be here soon enough. Just you rest yourself, Dermot.'

Adam disengaged his hand and followed Eli when he walked away.

'It's shock,' explained the frontiersman. 'I've seen it in grown men. He'll be all right in a day or two. As soon as he can see what's happening about him. Right now, though, I'd say he's better off where he *thinks* he is.'

'Can't we get a doctor to look at his face and that nose?'

Eli grunted. 'You're forgetting where we are. This is Mexico. There ain't a doctor to treat the wounded Mexicans – and, God knows, there's enough of them. Now, let's find somewhere to talk for a while and see if we can't think of a way out of this mess.'

CHAPTER SIXTEEN

THAT AFTERNOON, a Mexican colonel entered the compound escorted by a heavy guard and read out a proclamation. The Texans were deemed to be rebels who had taken part in armed insurrection against the lawful government of Mexico. Their actions had resulted in the deaths of many Mexican soldiers. It was ordered that the Texans be taken from their place of imprisonment and shot.

The Texans heard the proclamation in stunned silence. Then they erupted in noisy anger, and the colonel and his escort retreated from the compound hurriedly.

The anger of the prisoners increased throughout the remainder of that day. Shortly before dusk an escort arrived to take the senior Texan 'officer' to General Ampudia. When he returned, his words removed all hope that the Texan government would try to save two hundred of its men who were under sentence of death only a few miles from its own borders.

General Houston had disowned the Mier expedition, declaring that the men had acted without the authority of his government. Houston's statement was understandable – in Washington-on-the-Brazos. Talks between Great Britain and Mexico had reached a delicate stage. It was believed a negotiated settlement between Mexico and Texas was near. Houston did not want the actions of a few hundred hotheads to jeopardise the future of Texas. Nevertheless, his denunciation of the expedition was both ill-timed and thoughtlessly worded. By disowning the expedition General Houston branded the men as brigands and abandoned them to the dubious mercy of the Mexican authorities.

A new mood entered the compound. The anger of the men hardened. If they were going to die, there was no sense in going quietly to their execution. They would fight – and some of their captors would die with them.

The mood communicated itself to the Mexican guards, and they became nervous. By noon the next day they were refusing to enter the compound.

That afternoon, General Ampudia cancelled his execution order. All able-bodied Texans would be taken to Matamoros. From here they would be taken to prison in Mexico City.

The Texans set off on the hundred-mile march to Matamoros

431

in an almost jaunty mood. Dermot Casey still could not see through the swelling about his eyes, but Adam and Eli had no intention of leaving him behind. Dermot marched between them and they held his arms to guide and support him on the frequent occasions when he stumbled on the uneven road.

The prisoners had expected to be taken down the coast by sea, but this was not to be. The Texan navy was to blame. Aware that when they returned to harbour the impoverished Texas administration intended disbanding its navy and selling off the ships, the determined naval captains simply remained at sea and kept clear of their home ports. The Texan navy became virtually a pirate fleet, the ships of Mexico providing food and wages for the Texan sailors. As a result, not a ship could be found to take the prisoners southwards along the Mexican coast.

Adam and the Texans remained at Matamoros for some weeks, during which time Dermot Casey regained both sight and senses, much to Adam's relief. By the time they were ordered to make the long march to Mexico City, he was as fit as any of his fellow-prisoners.

The weeks spent at Matamoros were not wasted. The Texans constantly plotted escape, and as they were marched ever deeper into Mexico they awaited their opportunity. It did not come until they had covered more than two hundred miles and reached the small Mexican town of Salado.

When the majority of the Mexican soldiers went off to sample the basic pleasures of the town, the Texan adventurers, acting for once in concert, overpowered the remaining escort.

Fanning out in the mountains above the small town, some of the survivors had horses, seized from the guards. The remainder were on foot, but all pursued one course – northwards, towards the Texas border. Some felt happiest travelling in large groups, others tried to make it alone. Adam travelled with Eli, Dermot and four Texans who hoped to take advantage of the frontier skills of Adam and Eli.

For seven days they pursued a tortuous course through the mountains and were compelled to kill the one horse they had, to provide themselves with food. Then two of the accompanying Texans slipped in the loose shale of a mountain slope, injuring their legs. The others were faced with an agonising choice. They could either desert the two injured men and press onward towards the border, or take them along and risk capture. In the end they decided to travel on, together.

Two days later they were surrounded by a Mexican cavalry patrol of forty men. Herded back towards Salado, the two injured

Texans found it impossible to maintain the pace set by the Mexican horsemen. In spite of all their friends did to help them, they were shot by the Mexican soldiers.

One hundred and seventy-six Texans were returned to the scene of their escape. Others were murdered by their Mexican pursuers. A few died of starvation in the confusing Mexican mountains and only three reached the safety of Texas to tell their story.

When Santa Anna heard of the escape, he ordered that all those who had been recaptured should be executed.

The Mexican governor of the province, at great personal risk, refused to endorse the order, and intense diplomatic pressure was brought to bear on the autocratic Mexican president. Reluctantly, he bowed to the indignation of the civilised world. His order was amended. The prisoners were to be decimated. One in ten would be executed as an example to the others.

In Salado, the Texan prisoners were made to form a long line and an earthenware jar was filled with beans. One hundred and fifty-nine were white, seventeen were black. Those who drew a black bean would be shot.

Shackled together in a belated measure to prevent their escape, the prisoners shuffled up to the jar. When it came to Adam's turn, he prayed, and thrust his hand inside. The bean he pulled out was white. Eli was next. He kept his hand closed about the bean for what seemed an age. When he opened it, his bean, too, was white.

Dermot Casey was chained behind Eli. He put in his hand, pulled out a bean, and stared down at it in disbelief. The watching Texans did not need to be told the colour. The Mexican officer, inspecting the beans, reached Adam and asked to see the life-giving bean he grasped in his hand. Suddenly, a scuffle broke out behind him. Eli and Dermot were struggling on the ground. Mexican soldiers pulled them apart roughly, and as both men were pulled to their feet a single bean lay upon the ground. It was white.

Silently, Eli held out the black bean in the palm of his hand. He was unshackled and thrust towards the small group of condemned men. The white bean was picked up from the ground and thrust into Dermot's hand and he was shackled to Adam and pushed away from the table holding the jar.

Neither Adam nor Dermot saw Eli again. With his unfortunate companions he was placed in a separate courtyard and at dusk on 25 March 1843 the seventeen men were lined up and shot to death by soldiers of the Mexican army.

For fifteen months Adam languished in a gaol in southern Mexico, with the survivors of the Mier expedition, his health badly affected by his ordeal. He was given an opportunity to gain his release when he had been gaoled for slightly less than a year but he refused unless Dermot Casey were released with him.

On 14 August 1844, Nell Plunkett was working in the vegetable-garden of Adam's cabin in the Hill Country. Standing up, she put a hand to her aching back and saw two horsemen approaching along the river bank, one sagging wearily in his saddle.

For perhaps a full minute she watched them, not daring to believe. Then she dropped the hoe she was holding and began to run.

Dermot Casey slipped easily to the ground. Adam was slower but it was to him Nell ran first. He looked older and very, very tired, but some of his strength returned when he held Nell in his arms.

Looking up at him, tears sprang to Nell's eyes at the suffering she saw in his face, but now he was home, she would make up for all that had happened to him. It was a promise she had given in prayer, every day since he went away.

That night, when the last of the settlers had gone from the cabin, Adam made his way from the cabin to the river. Here he sat on the bank, his back against a tree, and thought of how far he had moved away from the duties set out for him by Lord Palmerston in Whitehall, on a cold London day all those years before.

Caleb had brought with him a letter he had been keeping for Adam for many months. It was from Lord Aberdeen, Lord Palmerston's successor. The Tory Foreign Secretary had thrown all his weight behind Great Britain's chargé d'affaires in Texas. Aberdeen accepted that Adam and Captain Charles Elliot had been unable to find common ground on which to agree, but regretted that Adam had felt it necessary to suggest Elliot was being misled by Houston.

In view of the fact that Elliot would continue to enjoy the full confidence of Her Majesty's government, it only remained to inform Adam that he was no longer an agent of the British government. If he wished to return to Great Britain, Charles Elliot was authorised to provide Adam with his fare. Once in England, Adam should report to the Foreign Office where a small pension would be arranged for services rendered. In the meantime, Adam was ordered to make it clear to President

Houston that any views he might express were his own, and in no way represented those of the British government.

There had been a time when Adam would have relished this moment, knowing he could remain and make his future here. Now he was not so certain. His views on Indians were out of step with the thinking of the vast majority of Texans, including most of those he had helped to bring to the Hill Country. . . .

Hearing a noise behind him, Adam drew a revolver quickly and turned to face the sound, crouching low behind the tree.

'Who's there?' It had been a light footstep, but not quite soft enough for the tread of an Indian.

'It's me. Nell. Were you expecting someone else? Do you mind if I come and sit awhile, or are you wanting to be on your own?'

'I don't think I'm the best of company. For me, or for anyone else.'

'I'll take that as an invitation.'

He knew she was mocking him gently, but it did not matter.

She, too, sat on the ground, and as she leaned back against the tree only the width of a man's hand separated them. A new moon hung over the hills across the river, a bright star in close attendance.

Adam remembered that Cherokee girls called this the 'loving star'.

'You've been away a long time, Adam. There were days when I doubted whether either you or Dermot would ever return. With Don Manuel and Eli both dead I thought there was little to bring you back.'

Suddenly, for no good reason he could think of, Adam asked: 'Why did you never marry Henry Stillwell?'

The question took Nell by surprise. 'Henry? I don't know. It all seems to have happened such a long time ago. Poor Henry. He died in a Mexican prison, did you know?' Without waiting for an answer, she went on: 'It was like having a little dog around, just waiting to be patted on the head occasionally. That isn't what I want from a man.'

'Was that your only reason?'

Nell was silent for a long time, then she said softly: 'No, not entirely. It also had something to do with a man who brought me a Christmas present a month late. Why *did* you buy this lovely crucifix for me, Adam?'

When Adam looked sideways at Nell, he saw the crucifix shining in the moonlight at her throat.

'I remembered seeing you and Peggy admiring a crucifix in the store in Velasco, when we first arrived in Texas. As soon as I saw this one I knew I wanted it for you.'

Nell said nothing, and Adam sensed she was somehow disappointed, as though she had been expecting something more. It was time to air all the thoughts that had come to him in the long months in prison.

'No, Nell, that isn't entirely honest. It was more than that. Do you remember coming to my cabin with a meal for me? Before Gilpin McCulloch came along to tell us about the battle between the Comanches and Captain Dollar? Afterwards, I thought we'd come closer to each other than we'd ever been before. I wanted to build on that. . . .'

He shrugged. 'Then I learned of Henry Stillwell.'

There was the rustle of skirts, Nell took his hand and his fingers closed about the warm, wooden handle of a small knife.

'Does this help, Adam? Is it too late to go back to where we were that day? We've lost so much time. . . .'

Adam reached for Nell, and when she came to him they kissed for the first time, the kiss spanning the lost years.

Adam and Nell were married on 29 December 1844, three weeks after General Sam Houston had been superseded as the President of the Republic of Texas by his friend and protégé, Anson Jones. Exactly one year later, United States President James Polk signed the Act that accepted Texas into the United States of America as a slave-owning State. The action provoked a war with Mexico that won for America all those Mexican provinces that Mirabeau Buonaparte Lamar had dreamed of bringing to Texas.

One of the two Senators elected to represent Texas in the United States Senate was General Sam Houston. It was an office he held for thirteen years, retiring only to become Governor of the State over which he had twice presided.

Charles Elliot, RN, Great Britain's chargé d'affaires, left Texas to become, in turn, Governor of Bermuda, Governor of Trinidad, Governor of St Helena, an admiral of Her Majesty's navy, and a Knight Commander of the Most Honourable Order of the Bath.

Adam purchased the lands that had once been owned by Eli Varne and, during a long and very happy life with Nell, went on to become the most successful and prosperous rancher in what was later named 'The Varne Valley'.